LIES OF OMISSION

LIES OF OMISSION

ELENA GRAF

PURPLE HAND PRESS

Purple Hand Press
www.purplehandpress.com

This is a work of fiction. Names, characters, places and incidents are the product of
the author's imagination or used fictitiously, and any resemblance to actual persons,
living or dead, businesses, institutions, companies, events, or locales is entirely coincidental.

Trade Paperback Edition
ISBN-10 0-9836960-3-2
ISBN-13 978-0-9836960-3-2
Kindle Edition
ISBN-10 0-9836960-4-9
ISBN-13 978-0-9836960-4-9
ePub Edition
ISBN-10 0-9836960-5-6
ISBN-13 978-0-9836960-5-6

10 9 8 7 6 5
08.08.2020

*To my father, who was an eye witness to
the rise and fall of the Third Reich.*

Part I
KONRAD

Chapter 1

A hot wind smacked my face as I emerged from the Anhalter Bahnhof. Gone now was the *Berliner Luft*, once so famous, it had inspired popular songs. The September air was dense with the smoke of coal-fired furnaces, the fumes of thousands of automobiles, the aromas of restaurants cooking the foods of many nations. As I inhaled the familiar scents, I knew without doubt that I was in Berlin.

My pleasure in returning to that vibrant metropolis was blunted by the purpose of my mission. The telegram in my breast pocket pressed against me like a thorn. I had dodged the previous requests from Schacht's office: first a pleasant note, then a formal letter, several telephone calls, until finally, this tersely worded telegram. Only the week before, the assets of a competitor had been seized by the state. The owners were remotely Jewish, which probably had something to do with it, but clearly, the action was meant to be a warning to us all. Comply or be nationalized.

An increase in the steel allotment was not something I could order on my own. My cousin rarely questioned my decisions, but such an important matter could only be decided by the head of the House of Langenberg-Edelheim herself. Allocating more steel for government contracts would not sit well with Margarethe. She preferred to think our steel would be used to make surgical instruments, tailor's scissors, and petroleum drilling equipment. Swords or plowshares? We all knew how that question would be decided. Our shattered economy was gradually improving, but the gains were built on the faint rumble of war. Faint now but growing ever louder.

I dreaded another bloody conflict; I opposed it with all my being. I had been spared from the battlefield, but many of my friends had died or returned blind, limbs shattered, their minds gone—an entire generation of young men sacrificed. Twenty years have passed since the Great War. Things are worse now, not better.

While the taxi negotiated the traffic around Potsdamer Platz, I mentally prepared myself to match wits with Margarethe. She'd once told me that she had hired me for my "silver tongue." Unfortunately, now I needed to turn it on her. Although the windows were open, the anticipation made me perspire. I've always hated sweating into a new suit, most especially that gorgeous pleasure of British tailoring chosen just for the occasion. A polished presentation is essential when dealing with Margarethe. Everything must be perfect down to the last detail.

As we entered the Grunewald district, I began to feel vaguely nostalgic. The Stahle villa on Winklerstraße with its imposing facade and walled gardens was still my official address, although I was rarely there. After my cousin's companion moved into the house in 1931, I felt like an intruder. Gone now were the intimate, late-night parties when Margarethe and I would lounge in our pajamas and drink brandy while we viciously dissected our friends. We no longer haunted the cabarets disguised as one another, both seeking our own sex. Katherine had put an end to all that. She had been raised strictly Catholic in her native Ireland and found our most ordinary practices too unconventional.

Despite this inconvenience, I am rather fond of Katherine. And really, I must always make an effort to be cordial because, according to official government records, Katherine is my wife.

The taxi let me off at the front door and I ascended the stairs. Krauss, the majordomo, showed not the least surprise at my unexpected arrival as he took my briefcase and hat. "Welcome home, *Herr Baron*," he said with an old-fashioned bow. He ushered me into the library so that I might greet my wife.

"Dear Konrad," said Katherine, rising to kiss me. "What a delightful surprise!" She looked even more lovely than I remembered. She is a delicate Celtic beauty in the style of the Pre-Raphaelites with hair the color of burnished copper, clear, blue eyes, a delicate mouth, and pale skin. That evening, she cut the very figure of a professional woman, entirely appropriate now that she had joined the practice of Berlin's pre-eminent gynecologist. Her afternoon frock was flowing and feminine, yet businesslike. Her makeup subtly enhanced her considerable natural gifts. She even painted her fingernails and looked quite the sophisticate. Needless to say, I approved.

"Here, sit beside me, Konrad," said Katherine, speaking in English, her native tongue and the preferred language in Margarethe's house. "How lovely to have you home again." She gave my arm a little squeeze for emphasis. "What brings you to Berlin?"

"A desire to see my family isn't enough?" I asked with a wink, trying to charm her away from questioning my mission. Margarethe forbade any talk of politics in her house. The less said the better, she believed, and safer too, despite the absolute loyalty of her servants.

These were strange times.

Krauss delivered an icy pitcher of his famous martinis. Katherine declined—she rarely drank spirits—but after some cajoling from me, she finally agreed to have a glass of wine.

I glanced at my watch and realized it was odd for Katherine to be home so early. "No consulting hours today?"

"I try to keep Thursday afternoons free."

"Of course." I chastised myself for not remembering and picked up the book she had set aside to greet me. It was not the latest novel, of course, but a dense medical text.

"Hardly pleasure reading, Katherine. You work too hard. You must take time to enjoy life."

"Follow your own advice. How long have you been away on business?"

"Nearly a month," I admitted with a sigh. "Our mistress thinks industrious enterprise will keep me out of mischief."

"Oh, I rather doubt that's possible," Katherine replied with a wry smile. Her sudden flashes of perception always took me aback, especially given her innocent looks and convent background.

"Dear me, I've been away for ages!" I said, striving for a diversion. "You must tell me all the news."

"Well, let's see," said Katherine, striking a pensive pose. "Margarethe says she will sing in Gürtner's new *Rosenkavalier* this season," she said casually, although she was well aware this information had the potential to shock me. Among Margarethe's many talents was a world-class singing voice. She had never sung professionally, of course. For someone of our class, such a thing would be unthinkable. Or at least, it was.

"Oh, Margarethe's only toying with Gürtner," I replied.

Katherine shrugged, but I detected more than a lack of interest in my opinion. Her coolness on the subject of my cousin suggested something more, but at that moment, the door to the library opened, distracting me from further speculation.

My daughter shot into the room. The nurse, chasing behind her, looked alarmed to have lost control of her charge, even more so when the girl catapulted herself into my arms. "Papa!" exclaimed Fiona, "Krauss told me you were home!"

Fiona's hair, like Katherine's, was red. She was tall for a girl of six. Her mother was rather petite, so she had undoubtedly come by her height from my family. The child climbed into my lap with a little laugh.

"Papa, I learned French today. Miss Carter taught me to say 'hello, how are you?"

"Let me hear, my darling."

"*Bonjour, Papa. Comment ça vas?*"

"*Très bien, merci, ma fille. Et comment ça vas?*"

"*Très bien, aussi.*"

"Heavens, child. Your accent is quite good. You must speak French with *Tante* Margarethe. She's far more fluent than I."

"*Tante* has been teaching me Italian," my daughter announced proudly.

"Italian, you say? How very odd." I glanced at Katherine for an explanation, but she only shrugged.

The nurse looked anxious, so I eased Fiona off my lap and gave her a little nudge in the nurse's direction.

"She's become quite the young lady," I said to Katherine as the nurse escorted our daughter away. "You must be so proud."

Katherine sighed. "No credit to me. I'm so busy, I barely see the poor thing." She frowned and added, "Margarethe intends to send her to school in England soon."

I needed a moment to absorb this news. Of course, no one had thought to consult me about the decision. We had agreed from the first that Katherine and Margarethe would direct Fiona's upbringing, but the little doll had stolen my heart, and I hated the idea of her going away. She was especially dear to me because I had never expected to be a father.

A moment later, my cousin strode through the door. Margarethe is an extraordinarily tall woman, standing only a few hairs shorter than I. Yet she is graceful in her movements, having the imperturbable poise that comes of being completely at home in one's skin. She embraced me as a man would, with a great clap on the back. Then she held me at arm's length and looked me over. As always, it was like gazing in a mirror. We looked so much alike, people often thought us twins. We were both towheads as children and still quite blond. After we turned forty, a few white hairs had begun to creep in—white, mind you, not gray.

"You devil, you might have told me to expect you," said Margarethe with a feigned scowl. She rang for Krauss and asked him to refresh the martini pitcher.

After we finished our drinks, Margarethe declared it was time for exercise. Since she'd given up cigarettes at Katherine's insistence, Margarethe had struggled for the first time in her life to maintain her slender figure. She saw a thickening figure as a sign of age. Nothing could be more distressing to a person of her vigor. Her response to this change was characteristically efficient and practical—renewed enthusiasm for athletics and an attempt to restrain her appetite. She even gave up chocolate, which she adored—a sure sign of her resolve.

I saw an opportunity for conversation, so I offered to join her in the basement gymnasium. While she labored on the motorized treadmill, I sat on the sidelines and went on about a Bette Davis film I'd seen. Although Margarethe grunted from time to time, I could tell she wasn't listening. During the serious part of the exercise regimen—the weight-lifting—I was forbidden to speak because Margarethe needed to concentrate, so I went upstairs to seek company.

I found Katherine listening to the wireless in the drawing room. Her forehead was furrowed and her auburn brows knit in consternation. When I heard the agitated words emanating from the wireless, I perceived the reason for the frown—Goebbels was ranting in condemnation of so-called "degenerate" art. Now really, how could a few abstract paintings be so dangerous? Katherine glanced in my direction with a questioning look. She often tried to elicit my opinion of the political situation, but I would honor Margarethe's prohibition of political discussion despite having much to say on the subject.

How I missed those glorious days of the Weimar Republic, when I was in the Reichstag and Brüning's right hand. The Great War and the revolution had bred chaos, and the inflation had nearly finished our economy, but our Center Party had been able to steady the nation for a time. Then we too were swept away in favor of the National Socialists and their *Führer*. What a vile man! His pale eyes were hypnotic, and that voice, that stunning voice, so convincing, it could summon the dead from their graves.

I shuddered at the thought of him and reached into my coat for my cigarette case. Katherine frowned in disapproval, so I moved to a respectful distance. The Goebbels speech had so unsettled me that I couldn't immediately return to ordinary sociability. Instead, I picked up *The Times* and scanned the financial pages. Katherine, intuiting that I was in no mood for conversation, went back to her wretched medical book.

From the music room next door came the sound of Margarethe's voice. After some scales and arpeggios, she began to sing the aria from Act II of *Der Rosenkavalier*, when Octavian, splendidly shining in a white-and-silver coat, announces that he has come to present the silver rose.

"Do you mind if I bring up the matter of the opera?" I asked.

Katherine shrugged. "I'm surprised she hasn't mentioned it to you."

"She doesn't tell me everything, you know," I replied with an unnecessarily catty smirk.

"I never thought so."

"But, Katherine, her mother would be scandalized!"

"Not if Margarethe uses a stage name," said Katherine, innocently revealing Margarethe's strategy.

"Then Gürtner will lose the advantage of Margarethe's following."

My cousin sang publicly only for charity benefits and occasionally in amateur opera, but she had acquired some admirers—young women who found more than her voice irresistible. I wondered why Katherine was never jealous.

"Evidently, he is so set on having her sing on his stage that he will allow her to appear incognito," said Katherine.

"And what photograph will they use in the program?"

"Margarethe is very good at disguises, as you know."

Not long after, Margarethe appeared in one of her disguises, dressed for dinner in a green Schiaparelli gown. She looked so utterly radiant that I decided to exchange my English suit for a dinner jacket.

The meal was preceded by a feast of oysters. Margarethe's devotion to this shellfish borders on obscene. It was not unusual for her to moan appreciatively as the delicately fluted creatures reached her tongue or to wax eloquent on their reputed qualities as an aphrodisiac. That night, however, there was no mention of aphrodisiacs. During the entire meal, the ladies barely exchanged a glance. Margarethe tried to occupy me with discussion of the stock market, while silent Katherine behaved as modestly as a nun.

How odd, I thought, although a part of me rejoiced. Before Katherine came between us, Margarethe was game for any adventure, even an occasional aside. After Katherine, all mischief was banished from Margarethe's life. Her watchword was fidelity. Her compass was stuck on true north. How utterly boring!

But now it seemed that something had gone awry. I tried to guess. It is said that men of my persuasion can be more sensitive than women to social cues. In fact, we share with all of our sex, the stupidity that comes of only noticing the surface. It's the reason we are so good at appearing to be women when we dress in their clothes. All the details are impeccably executed, but we completely miss the complexity of females, which includes a toughness that burly men can only imagine. That's why, when Katherine finally apprised me of the situation, she had to spell out the solution in great detail.

But I am getting ahead of myself.

After a dessert of chocolate torte, which my cousin virtuously declined, we repaired to the music room. Margarethe sang *Lieder* to Katherine's accompaniment, but my cousin was irritable and impatient. She complained about the tempo, chased Katherine off the piano bench and took over. She abruptly stopped in the middle of a piece that she herself had chosen and declared with a scowl, "I don't really feel like singing tonight."

I exchanged a worried glance with Katherine. She rose and offered Margarethe the barest peck of a good night kiss before she excused herself to see Fiona off to bed. This affectionless display heightened my anxiety. Something was amiss. No doubt of it.

Margarethe remained at the piano and began to play a Beethoven sonata. The familiar music soothed me, especially after being an unwilling witness to the tension in that house. Afterwards, I poured Margarethe a brandy hoping to induce her to relax. "Come, darling," I said, nudging her towards the sofa, "sit with me and tell me all your news."

One of the reasons Margarethe tolerates my presence is that I can amuse her. I cast about for a topic of light conversation. I had spent most of my adult life as a politician, so it is rather natural for me to slide into glib ease. First a little small talk, and then on to weightier matters. I politely asked after the children. Margarethe's son, Wilhelm, now twenty-two, was a medical student in Munich. He had chosen his mother's alma mater over being her pupil in Berlin. Margarethe's daughter had gone up to Oxford's Lady Margaret Hall, not Somerville, her mother's college.

"And can you believe it? Liesel wants to study medicine as well," said Margarethe. "I promise you. I've done nothing to encourage either of them to join the profession."

"Nothing except set a spectacular example. It must make you very proud." As their "uncle" and godfather, I was proud as well. I'd tried to fill in whenever I could for their dear dead father. He had perished in a boating accident when the children were very young. "Liesel intends to study medicine? A whole family of doctors. Whatever will I talk about when I visit?"

"You always find words, darling. You shall manage," said Margarethe, patting my shoulder. She reached into my dinner jacket for my cigarette case. Although I found the search deliciously intimate, I restrained myself from a response, knowing it was Margarethe's way to take rather than ask. She is the only woman whom I have ever truly desired, but her feelings for me were quite simple. She only gave in to me out of indulgence or in times of boredom or loneliness—never since Katherine had arrived on the scene. Margarethe located the case, extracted two cigarettes, and lit them.

"What would Katherine say?" I asked as she passed a cigarette to me.

"Oh, she knows," she said with a sigh, "but I refrain in her presence."

"You smoke in secret?"

"Katherine needn't know everything I do."

Her perfectly arched brows came together in a pained frown. I began to realize that she was genuinely troubled.

"Grethe, my darling, what *is* wrong?"

"What's not wrong?" she replied testily. "Every morning I wake up and find that the government has insinuated itself more deeply into my medical practice. Were you aware that I am an affiliate member of the NSDAP solely because I am a panel-certified surgeon?"

"No," I said, genuinely surprised.

"Neither was I until a week ago. Today I received curriculum instructions from the Chamber of Medicine ordering me to integrate the concept of racial hygiene into my surgical lectures."

"I cannot imagine how much this disturbs you," I remarked impassively, although I was surprised to hear her say so much about the political situation.

"Oh, yes, just a bit." She sat up and stubbed out her cigarette. "Disgusting," she muttered. It was difficult to know whether she was referring to the cigarette or the Nazis. She got up to refill her glass. "I hate politics, but when the government attempts to rewrite science and dictate the practice of medicine, something must be done!" I sat up, interested to hear what she had to say next. "The racial theories of the National Socialists are utter nonsense," she continued. "How can any physician with the least knowledge of genetics give them any credence?"

"Grethe, you believe so fervently in the superiority of the nobility, I would have supposed you to be the most ardent Social Darwinist."

She gave me a withering look. "What do you know about science? And how can you possibly understand the ways in which science is being corrupted by ideologues and politicians, being one yourself?"

This accusation stunned me. How unlike her to be so personal. However much she liked to win an argument, she unfailingly honored the rules of engagement.

"Forgive me, Konrad. That was uncalled for. I'm tired."

From the pinched look on her face, I realized that fatigue was the least of it, and that she had revealed only the periphery of her anxiety. "Thank you for the apology, but it's unnecessary. You do look tired. Perhaps you should get some rest."

"Rest," she repeated with a sigh, "What a very good idea." She rose and kissed me. "Good night, my dear. How delightful to have you home."

Once I was certain she had retired for the night, I called her chauffeur and directed him to drive me to the stevedores' district in Spandau. We parked across the street from a brightly lit tavern and waited.

Watching the patrons come and go, I imagined being an alligator. Margarethe had recently sent me to Louisiana to look after her business interests there. A rough man I'd befriended in a Creole pub told me about the fearsome beasts and offered to take me into the bayou at night. Navigating by the light of a kerosene lantern hung on a hook at the prow, he poled his boat through the water. Lightning flashes overhead provided moments of illumination when I could see the sleek reptiles, their large, stony backs gliding through the dark water. My heart pounded at the thought of falling overboard and being at the mercy of those stealthy, silent killing machines. I imagined being one of them, as I sat in Margarethe's large, black Mercedes, its twelve cylinders waiting to stir into powerful wakefulness.

A young man with a great shock of black hair and chiseled features came out and lit a cigarette. I opened the window and called to him. As he turned, my eyes delighted in the prominent bulge in his tight trousers.

Chapter 2

Once I had liberated myself from my overnight guest, I remembered my mission in coming to Berlin and felt instantly depressed. Our government contact required a response within forty-eight hours, which meant I was obliged to confront Margarethe before the end of the day. While I dressed, I made a plan. I decided to ambush Margarethe at her office, reasoning that the professional setting might discourage her from discharging the full force of her temper.

Margarethe, as most prominent physicians at the Charité, kept a consulting office on Luisenstraße. I showed my papers to the guard, who stared at my documents so long that I began to wonder if he could read. Finally, he looked up and studied me with narrowed eyes. He coughed bronchially before he spoke. "What is your business here today?"

"I wish to see Dr. von Stahle."

"Are you a patient?"

"It's personal."

He cocked a brow.

"I am her cousin," I added grudgingly.

He nodded. "One moment." As he sat down, a smoky odor arose from his woolen jacket. He dialed the telephone with a yellowed fingertip and murmured a few words into the mouth piece. "Someone will come for you directly," he said. "Sit there." He pointed with a crooked finger to a bench in the foyer, then ignored me as I moved to it.

As I watched him stare sullenly at those who came and went through the door, I reflected that the Third Reich had produced a ridiculous number of such useless, uniformed functionaries. There were just too many people in uniform. The Prussian affection for brass buttons and shiny black boots had infected the entire nation.

A young woman in a prim navy dress approached me. "Herr von Holdenberg?" I took off my hat and she stared at me, no doubt struck, as many people are, by my resemblance to my cousin. Once she got over her surprise, she ushered me to an ancient lift and instructed the operator to head to the third floor.

The domain of the senior doctors was well-appointed. An oriental carpet ran down the corridor. There were vases of fresh flowers along the way. Floor to ceiling mahogany doors stood guard at the entrance of each office suite. My escort opened a door at the end of the hall. The senior secretary rose from her desk as we entered. Unlike the young woman who had fetched me from the lobby, she knew me from past visits to Margarethe's office. She smiled as she took my hat. "*Frau Doktor* is leading Grand Rounds this morning. You may have quite a wait."

"I don't mind waiting."

"You may sit in the consulting room until she returns." She offered me the newspaper, the *Allgemeine Zeitung*. I accepted it, although I considered it an affront to honest journalism. It would help pass the time and, if nothing else, provide some amusement.

More than an hour passed before Margarethe arrived. She wore a white clinical coat with a stethoscope dangling out of the pocket. Of all her costumes, I find this one most evocative because it suits her so very well.

"You ought to have telephoned ahead," she said as she exchanged her white coat for her suit coat. "I could have been occupied for the entire day."

"No matter. I'm rather good at entertaining myself."

"Indeed? Grauer told me he took you to Spandau last night."

I clucked my tongue. "Naughty Grauer, betraying me in that manner. I could never trust him."

She gave me a scolding look. "Konrad, venereal disease is rampant in that district."

"I won't take anyone who's not clean."

"Unfortunately, that means nothing." She put down her stack of papers and gave me a careful inspection. "Come. Let's take a blood sample to be sure." She headed to the small laboratory off her consulting room. Like an obedient puppy, I followed. I took off my coat and rolled up my sleeve while Margarethe prepared a syringe. I tried not to wince as the needle pierced my skin. Margarethe loathes cowards. Fortunately, the process was quick and efficient.

Margarethe pressed a wad of gauze over the tiny wound. "Hold that for a moment." She labeled the vial and put it into the ice box for later inspection. "These are dangerous times, Konrad. You must be careful!"

"Don't preach. It's tiresome."

"Drop your pants."

"Really, Grethe!"

She rolled her eyes. "Konrad, let's dispense with your prissy, little modesty, if you please. I'm short on patience today."

Unfortunately, my body betrayed me as soon as she touched me. She made no comment but went quickly about her examination. "No obvious infection. You appear to be healthy."

"Just as I told you."

"If it's not your health, then what brings you?"

"I have business to discuss."

"*Here*?" she asked, looking shocked.

"Well, why not? It *is* your office."

"We have barely an hour. I am performing a demonstration surgery this afternoon, and I need to eat something beforehand. Can you bear eating in the doctor's dining room?"

We couldn't possibly discuss such sensitive business in a public setting, but I dared not refuse outright. Instead, I gave her a sheepish look.

"Never mind. I'll order sandwiches."

While she was giving her secretary instructions, I gazed at the painting behind her desk. It was a Dix and a rather fine one at that. Margarethe's taste in art has always been eclectic. She had more than a few expressionist paintings hanging about, even though that sort of art was now considered "degenerate" and probably should have been hidden away long ago.

Margarethe returned to the room and shut the door. "So, my dear, what's on your mind?"

Despite my rehearsals for this important moment, when it came, I was unaccountably speechless.

"Well? Out with it!" demanded Margarethe.

I took a deep breath and affected a casual pose while bracing myself for her response. "There has been another request to increase our first-grade steel quota for government contracts."

"But we stepped up our allotment only two months ago. One thousand, three-hundred forty-eight kilotons, if I recall."

I'd known since childhood that Margarethe had a photographic memory, but it never failed to astonish me how precisely she remembered details.

"Yes, but they want more, and we have no excuse now that the mill's been refurbished and the capacity much increased."

She sat back in her chair, turning it a bit in order to gaze out the window. "I should have known," she said. "I'd hoped the steel would go to new construction or retooling factories, now that the economy is recovering."

I knew the rationale, having been privy to the conversations surrounding the decision to upgrade the plant. However, one of my chief duties as Margarethe's lieutenant is to listen while she thinks aloud. Then I rearrange the main points and explain them back to her. But this time, she surprised me by asking, "What is your opinion?"

I shrugged. "You know my feelings about the military build-up. It's a flagrant disregard of our treaties, and it will make a war inevitable."

"Is it the matériel or the unjust treaty that will cause this new war?"

"That is a complicated subject."

"It is. But this is business, and it's rather simple. We have steel. They want to buy it. Sell it to them."

"Margarethe..."

"Don't argue with me, Konrad. Give them exactly what they want, and let's hope that's the end of it."

"You know it won't be."

"Of course, I do. But I won't tempt their displeasure by refusing. Neither will I cooperate with enthusiasm. Just give them what they ask. Not a gram more." I noted that we had gone from kilotons to grams in the space of a breath.

"There are other options," I said, removing my cigarette case from my coat. She declined my offer at first, but I knew if I left my case open on the desk, she would help herself. I lit her cigarette with my spirit lighter. "We could disable one of the blast furnaces."

She stared at me for a extended moment before saying, "I'll forget you ever said that."

"It could be done discreetly. No one need ever know."

"And accomplish what? Delay the inevitable at best. Perhaps I should refuse to sell them coal as well? Fool! They'll nationalize any firm that refuses to cooperate."

A knock at the door announced that our lunch had arrived. The secretary attempted to distribute the sandwiches, but Margarethe curtly dismissed her and dispensed the contents of the tray herself.

"We must attempt to deal with this situation with some grace," she said as we ate. "No tricks. Do you understand?"

"Quite clearly."

"And I have another assignment for you," she said. I dreaded what might come next. Margarethe often gave me the dirty work to do. When a layoff was necessary, I made up the list. In the lean years before the economy improved, I'd needed to break a dozen strikes.

"I want to sell our plants and factories. I especially want to be rid of the chemical plants. Retain the Bochum steel plant and the mine in Silesia. Can you find buyers for the rest?"

"I think so," I managed to say, despite my surprise. "But what will we do with the cash?"

"Swiss accounts for now. Establish a holding company based in Zurich and another in New York. Then inquire in the English-speaking world for interesting properties." It was a clever plan—liquidate the assets so they could be carefully and legally hidden. "Can you see to it, my fine *Advocat*?"

I nodded, my mind already working on how her scheme might be accomplished.

"Out of the proceeds from the chemical plants, invest in pharmaceutical firms and companies manufacturing prosthetic devices." When I gave her a puzzled look, she said, "There's going to be a war. Such things will be rather useful." The exploitation of those who might use such things was too blatant for my taste, so I steered the conversation towards a less controversial topic.

"Have you seen the financial pages this morning?" I asked.

"Good of you to mention it. There are a few things I would like you to investigate," she said, whipping out an annotated newspaper page. It was covered with her cramped, angular handwriting. I hoped she didn't expect me to read these notes, a practical impossibility. Instead, I reached into my pocket for my note pad and began scribbling her instructions. I was grateful when she switched from her brokerage requests to another topic, if only because it gave me relief from writer's cramp.

"Has Katherine told you we plan to send Fiona to school in England?"

"Yes, but don't you think she's a bit young?"

"We were the same age when we were sent off to school. We're no worse for it." One could debate this point, but I didn't dare. She was still a bit surly from our earlier conversation.

"England is so far away. Couldn't we send her to your grandaunt at Obberoth instead?"

Margarethe feigned a shudder. "An innocent like Fiona should never be exposed to that Catholic propaganda. It permanently deforms the mind."

"Have you considered a tutor?"

"Of course, I have. But the real problem is the girl has only her nurse for company. Katherine has no time for the child."

I detected a note of acrimony which surprised me, but it served as a clue to the nature of the discord between them. "I understand Katherine is overwhelmed by her professional life at the moment."

"Unfortunately, that's rather usual when one is establishing a medical career. If Katherine is to be successful, especially after beginning so late, she must put everything she has into it. I don't envy her. Her schedule is grueling. I was much younger at that stage in my career and had the energy."

"But my darling, you have boundless energy. You are indomitable."

She raised a brow to indicate she hadn't been taken in by the flattery.

"How long will this effort on Katherine's part need to continue?" I asked, both curious and genuinely concerned.

"Years," replied Margarethe. "We'll be lucky to have much opportunity to see her. I warned her that obstetrics is a demanding specialty. Sleep is a luxury."

"There were many years when you got little sleep."

"Yes, but I was a surgeon and could more or less decide my own schedule." When she frowned, I could practically read her thoughts.

"You still wish Katherine had become a surgeon like you."

"Of course, I do. And she would have been a damned good one."

"That would not surprise me. But do you think she has the mettle for it? She's not as…" I found myself searching for a word that wouldn't offend her. "…assertive as you are."

"You have a point. It takes a certain personality to make a surgeon, especially if one is a woman. I have such a woman among my surgical fellows. An American."

"I like Americans," I remarked. "They are so cheeky, but it's completely artless."

"Quite so." She glanced at her watch, not so subtly letting me know that I had taken up enough of her time.

***

My first stop was the post office to send a telegram to MEFO headquarters confirming that the request for steel had been approved. Next, I wandered down to the stock exchange. Our broker came down personally to wait with me while Margarethe's orders were listed. He knew better than to ask any questions because the draft for the purchases had been drawn on her personal account. As steward of the family fortune, Margarethe managed its wealth prudently and listened to sensible advice. With her own money, inherited from her grandmother, she traded with the abandon of a drunken gambler in Monte Carlo. Her brokers were driven to distraction by her stakes in highly questionable ventures. Yet in time, they nearly always paid handsomely. The broker was a good-looking man, and I chatted with him until the confirmations came through. That bit dispatched, I had the rest of the day free. I decided to pay a call on Nigel Calder.

The receptionist in the lobby of the British embassy knew me because

I called so often. She was always especially respectful, despite the fact that I no longer held a Reichstag seat and was now merely another German citizen.

Nigel received me in his office with all the warmth one would expect from a long-time friend. He clapped me on the back like an old school mate. Once the secretary closed the door behind her, he kissed me as well.

"You old bugger, where have you been keeping yourself?"

"Ah, doing the bidding of my mistress, of course. I've been away from Berlin for ages."

"And I thought you'd forgotten me."

"Never!"

Nigel was a very decent looking fellow, with bright-blue eyes and a shock of dark hair. I envied him its dark color, not a trace of gray, although he was nearly my age.

"What brings you?" he asked.

"A free afternoon."

"That's all?" He made a face of mock disapproval.

"That and the need to have the company of a good friend." Once we had been more to one another, but now we came together only when we needed the comfort of someone who was willing to turn a blind eye to all the flaws.

Nigel flipped open his diary. "Good timing, old boy. I happen to be free. Everyone's down at Berchtesgaden with Chamberlain."

"How's that going?"

He shrugged. "They haven't met yet, but the odds are old Neville will give it all away."

"What a depressing thought. Someone needs to stand up to Hitler."

"Don't hold your breath, my dear. Chamberlain hasn't got the bollocks," said Nigel with a sour look. "Listen, you old sod. I'm in the mood for a drink, if you're game."

I nodded my agreement. Nigel organized his desk in a flash and told the secretary he would be gone for the day. We took a taxi to the Adlon, where we established ourselves in one of the lounges.

"Why didn't you go to Berchtesgaden with the others?" I asked.

"Oh, they don't need me there. I'm the expert on industrial capacity, and they don't really want to know what I have to say."

"Which is what?" I asked, offering him a cigarette from my case.

He narrowed his eyes and lowered his voice. "You know exactly what, Konrad. Everything is ready. There needs only to be a pretext."

I nodded. "You're certain there will be a war?"

"Isn't it obvious? Hitler is clearly spoiling for it." He gave me a quick, anxious glance. "You ought to know. You're selling all that steel for government contracts."

I forced my face to assume a neutral expression. "How do you know about that?"

"It's my job to know."

"Perhaps then we shouldn't be talking," I replied in a cool voice. "We're likely to be enemies soon."

"Perhaps not. Hitler would like us to be allies instead."

"Is that a real possibility?" I asked hopefully.

He shook his head.

"Stupid question. We are cousins under the skin, and everyone knows the bloodiest feuds always begin in families."

"They'll be sending me home soon. I've accomplished my mission. Rumor has it that only vital embassy personnel will be allowed to remain. The others will be sent back to England."

"That should please you, I imagine, but I'll miss you."

"As I you. But I also won't mind going home. Father hasn't been well. And we're all worried about my sister."

"Do tell." I opened my ears. Margarethe would surely want to hear any news about Alexandra. Although the affair ended an eternity ago, Margarethe always remains unfailingly loyal to her friends.

"Poor Alex is odder than ever. She's always distracted. Her husband is posted to Singapore now and she refused to join him. She's quite a handful for my parents. Fortunately, Charles still lives at home and looks after her, but there's only so much he can do."

"A shame. I understand she's brilliant."

"Yes, she is. Small compensation for losing one's mind."

"Is it really that serious?"

He shrugged. "Hard to say. Alex has always gone her own way. But now it seems quite beyond eccentricity. She disappears for hours at a time and sometimes can't recall where she's been."

I tried to affect a sympathetic look, although I felt nothing but horror. "That's tragic, dear boy. Can nothing be done for her?"

"I suppose, if we can only determine the nature of the problem. One could say the only thing wrong is that she is a brilliant woman who can't find anything useful to do with her mind. It's not easy for women, not even in this modern age."

"Unless you're my cousin."

"Oh," he said with a snort. "That's not even up for discussion! Meg Stahle is a force of nature!"

We spent the next four hours catching up on politics. How I missed those days in the Reichstag, when our party had controlled the destiny of the nation. But no matter how pleasant it was to be caught up in the fervor of politics again or how much I loved Nigel, I needed to be circumspect. He was the under-consul responsible for industrial intelligence and very interested in Stahle factories and mines.

After our marathon orgy of political talk, we decided to dine at the Adlon. I should have informed Krauss of my plan to be absent, but Nigel and I got on to another interesting topic and I simply forgot.

I tried to enter the house discreetly around half past nine, but Grauer caught me coming up from the garage. He reported it to Krauss and soon the whole household knew I had returned.

And we had company. There was a large Mercedes in the circular drive in front of the house. I only needed to enter the hall leading to the music room for a clue to the identity of our visitors. Someone was playing the piano and female voices were singing the great trio from the third act of *Der Rosenkavalier*. Of course, I recognized Margarethe's voice but the powerful soprano that responded was superb, as was the lighter voice that joined in.

"What's this?" I asked Krauss.

"Herr Gürtner is here and two of his singers—Madame Lehmann and Fräulein Schwartzkopf."

The plot could not be more transparent. Gürtner knew that Lehmann was one of Margarethe's heroes, and he was shamelessly using his prize diva to persuade my cousin to sing in his opera. God love Gürtner. He was the most persistent, stubborn man I knew. He continued to allow Madame Lehmann to sing at his theater, despite Nazi disapproval, although there were now rumors that Lehmann would soon leave Europe once and for all to join the Metropolitan Opera in New York.

Krauss opened the door for me. Before me was an amazing sight—one of the greatest sopranos of our time singing with my own cousin. The performance raised the hairs on my arms because it was for themselves, not an audience, and was therefore deliciously intimate. The trio continued. I barely breathed as I listened. This was perfection, I realized, and it was an enormous privilege to witness it. I also saw that Gürtner had been entirely correct. My cousin made a perfect third voice in this role. She lacked nothing juxtaposed against two professional singers, having had superb training herself. I sighed as the trio moved on to its orgasmic close, and it was only because Gürtner stopped playing that they did not continue the act to its end. I felt cheated but was in no position to protest.

Margarethe finally noticed me standing there. "So, Konrad, you've decided to grace us with your presence. How very kind," she said, allowing her words, rather than her voice, to convey the sarcasm.

I saw my cue to get up and do something. Margarethe introduced her guests. I shivered a little as I kissed Madame Lehmann's hand, honored to finally meet her in the flesh after enjoying so many of her performances from the audience. The high soprano Gürtner had brought along to sing the role of Sophie was charming and a perfect Aryan beauty. I glanced at Margarethe to see if there was any erotic interest. She had a weakness for gifted singers.

"So, Lady Margarethe, *now* you see why you must agree to sing," said Gürtner, "and Madame Lehmann agrees. Yes?"

"Most certainly!" declared Madame Lehmann dramatically.

Margarethe glanced at each of her singing companions, allowing her eyes to linger on Fräulein Schwartzkopf. "Ladies, I'm flattered, but I'm too old to be singing Octavian."

Madame Lehmann laughed a perfectly operatic laugh. "Nonsense, Countess. You have the voice and you make a perfect boy. Such slim hips!" She gently patted Margarethe's behind. My cousin's quick blush made me realize how much she needed sexual attention, which brought another thought to mind. Where was Katherine? How could she bear to miss such a unique occasion? Madame Lehmann caressed Margarethe's face. "*Liebling*, you were born to sing Octavian. And you simply *must* sing it *with me*." She took Margarethe's face in her hands and kissed her full on the lips.

Margarethe blushed crimson. How easily she slipped into the role of the awkward young Count Rofrano. Or maybe it wasn't an act at all.

"How can I refuse such an invitation?" replied Margarethe. She made a courtly bow and kissed Madame Lehmann's hand.

"Quick, Gürtner!" exclaimed Madame Lehmann. "The contract! The countess will sign it."

Gürtner whipped the papers out of his coat and offered Margarethe his pen. "Three performances. That's all I ask."

Madame Lehmann, smiling with satisfaction, snatched her fox stole from the sofa. "Unfortunately, we must go now, but I look forward to our next meeting, my dearest Quinquin."

After they departed, my curiosity finally got the best of me. "Where's Katherine?"

"She said she was exhausted and went to bed."

"And miss this splendid recital. Is she deaf?"

Margarethe chuckled. "Sometimes she seems so. She claims she never hears me on her side of the house."

This was nonsense. My room was also on that side of the house, and Margarethe's powerful voice could be heard everywhere.

I put my hand on Margarethe's arm so I could be sure I had her attention. "My darling, has there been a rift between you and Katherine?"

"Ridiculous," she replied tersely, shrugging off my hand. "You're imagining things."

Chapter 3

The accountants were due for an early morning meeting so instead of repairing to my Tiergartenstraße flat, I stayed the night in Grunewald. The house was uneasily quiet. I could feel the tension as I lay in my bed in the room next to Katherine's. It was as if the very walls moved, pressing in on me as I lay awake, aching for no apparent reason. Finally, I got up and found a bottle of aspirin in the medicine cabinet. The pills upset my stomach, but after a while, I drifted off. I fell into such a stupor that the next morning, Krauss needed to shake me by the shoulder to rouse me. He left a tray with coffee on the bedside table and turned to leave.

"Stay a moment, Krauss."

"As you wish, *Herr Baron*," he replied, looking mildly surprised. He stood at military-correct attention. With the exception of being in service to Margarethe, he had spent his entire adult life in the army. He had served as quartermaster under my uncle, a field marshal during the Great War.

"Please relax," I urged. Of course, his idea of relaxing was to assume parade rest. "Really, Krauss. You look very uncomfortable. There's no need for such formality with me, and if you haven't noticed, times have changed."

"Yes," he replied. "Times have changed."

"Sit down," I urged, and the dear man took it as an order. He sat down in a nearby chair.

"How are you, Krauss?"

"I am well, *Herr Baron*, thank you very much."

I wondered what I could possibly say to get him to open up. "What do you think of the Nazis, Krauss?"

This finally garnered a reaction. Krauss scowled. "What can I say? They are here now," he said. He nodded, as if he had just understood something important. "It was so different under the Kaiser. Now, there's no honor."

I waited for him to say more, but he merely frowned and looked away.

"It's rather dismal," I agreed with a sigh and took a sip of coffee. It was very strong and boiling hot, exactly what I needed. "Everything's so serious now. Despite all the travails since the Great War, we used to enjoy life. Do you remember those times, Krauss? When Lady Margarethe and I were young?"

"Oh, yes. I remember." He smiled a little. How could he forget the many times he'd hauled me off to bed after one of our debaucherous parties? Or the time in the garden when drunk and completely naked, I began howling at the moon like a hound? Fortunately, he'd dragged me into the house before the neighbors called the police. He never raised an eyebrow when I returned home in Margarethe's clothes, nor she in mine. Ah, those were the days....

"There were always wonderful, interesting people in the house. Artists, musicians, writers. Now so many of them are gone." What I did not say was they were gone either because they were Jews or their art was now considered "degenerate." I drank more coffee and my head began to clear. I glanced at Krauss, who was gazing into the distance, evidently lost in his own memories. "Is everything all right here?" I asked.

He gave me a sharp look. "Of course, sir. Never better."

"But everyone looks so unhappy. Especially my cousin."

He shook his head. "Lady Margarethe is content. She has more time now and spends it on her music and Lady Fiona."

I had often wondered how my daughter's high energy affected Margarethe's orderly household. "How is it to have a little girl underfoot?"

"She is very well behaved," he replied. "It makes no difference."

I sighed. "I was afraid of that."

He gave me puzzled look, but I was not about to reveal my worries concerning my daughter. Most aristocratic children are conspicuously neglected by their parents. At least, Fiona had a proper nanny who appeared to take her job seriously.

As I drank my coffee, Krauss remained silent and looked increasingly uncomfortable. "Forgive me, my lord, but my duties..." he finally said.

I nodded my permission to leave.

❖❖❖

The meeting with the accountants was painfully tedious. They argued over *Pfennig*s until I wanted to writhe out of my skin. I made every attempt to pay attention because it was my duty, but I simply lack my cousin's endless capacity for inspecting ledgers.

After those wretched men left, I needed a change of wallpaper, so I headed to the cinema. I could sit for hours in those smoky theaters and lose myself completely in the pictures. It was a double feature of Hepburn and Grant—*Bringing Up Baby*, which made me laugh, and then *Holiday*, which was simply delightful. After that, I was nearly my old self. I had missed lunch, so I went to Kranzler's for ice cream. As the icy smoothness melted on my tongue, I felt wonderfully decadent. In those tense days, it took so little. I passed some time in a book shop and bought Graham Greene's latest novel. By then, I had run out of amusements and decided to take myself back to Grunewald. It behooved me to make an appearance at dinner, especially after my absence the previous night.

I discovered on my arrival that Margarethe had been detained at the hospital. Katherine was there, and I was pleased to see her. She looked absolutely gorgeous in a burgundy dinner dress that perfectly suited her pale complexion and red hair. Her hair was not as coppery as it used to be. A few strands of gray had insinuated themselves. How ungentlemanly of me to notice! But looking past these signs of age, I could remember why her beauty and vulnerability had once compelled me to take her to my bed.

"Let me get you a drink, Konrad," she said, playing the attentive wife. "What would you like?"

"Whiskey, please. No ice."

"Yes, I remember." Katherine went to the liquor stand and poured me some Scotch.

"Was your day at the hospital as busy as usual?"

"No, actually it was quite peaceful for a change," she said, handing me the glass. "Perhaps all the expectant ladies are on holiday."

I chuckled. "I'm sure you can do with a spell of leisure." I patted a space beside me on the sofa. "Sit here, my dear. It's been ages since we've caught up." I described my dreary meeting with the accountants and my visit to the cinema. Katherine, however, seemed unable to relax. She sat perched at the edge of her seat, as if to spring up at any moment. "Let me get you something to drink," I said.

She shook her head. "No, thank you. I'm tired and I'll nod off at once."

"But my dear, you seem so keyed up. Do let me get you something." I inspected the drinks table for inspiration. It wasn't difficult to decide. Krauss had thoughtfully left a bottle of Lillet chilling in the ice bucket.

When I returned with the drink, I sat a bit closer, hoping that a more intimate space would incline her to talk. I was tempted to put my arm around her to encourage an atmosphere of confidence but dared not lest it suggest some impropriety. Instead, I put my arm across the back of the sofa.

I remembered that discussion of her profession was always a safe topic. "Tell me about your work, Katherine. Does Becher treat you well?"

She nodded. "Yes, although I feel that he leaves the least interesting and most troublesome cases to me. That's to be expected. It's a junior doctor's role to clean up after the senior men."

"But it must rankle, particularly as your career would have been much further along, had it not been interrupted."

"Yes," she said softly, lowering her eyes. Occasionally, she relapsed into this convent custom, intended to convey an attitude of modesty. Of course, it also served to hide one's thoughts. But I didn't need to look into Katherine's eyes to know how much this topic distressed her. The cause of the delay was the unfounded accusation that she had killed her own mother by euthanasia. That had been cleared up ages ago, but the bad memories evidently persisted.

"I'm sorry I brought it up. I know you don't like to talk about it."

"No, it's all right. It's all in the past. Margarethe persuaded me to come back to medicine, and it's all turned out for the best. I'm grateful."

"Are you sure? Your medical career is so demanding."

"It's important that I succeed because Margarethe wants it so much."

I simply couldn't hold back from offering unsolicited advice: "You mustn't allow her to drive your life. Given the opportunity, she would drive all of our lives."

"As you well know," she said with a meaning look.

"But I have no choice. My brother is the heir, so I have no money of my own. I was a failure as an attorney. There's no room for my kind in politics in the Thousand Year Reich. Frankly, I need the income."

"Oh, Konrad, don't plead poverty. Margarethe has set you up very nicely."

"Yes, but I would miss the grand life to which I've become accustomed as her lieutenant."

"However, you could survive and so could I."

"You're right. We don't stay for her money," I admitted.

"No, we stay because we love her." Katherine finished the contents of her glass. I got up to refill it. "Thank you," she said with a sigh. She rubbed her eyes. "I'm sorry. I don't mean to be rude. I'm always so tired. I can never get enough sleep."

"It's all right, my dear," I replied and kissed the top of her head. As I drew near, I saw she was quite gray at the crown.

The telephone rang in Margarethe's study next door. In a moment, we heard Krauss's decisive rap on the door. "Pardon, the interruption," he said with a bow. "Lady Margarethe will be unable to join you for dinner."

"It appears we have the evening to ourselves," I said brightly. "Time for a party! Let's have dinner on the terrace."

We ate an excellent meal of scallops with gorgeous corals, followed by poached capon stuffed with rice and delicate greens. The food and drink in Margarethe's house would be reason alone to stay on her good side.

How had I failed to notice that Katherine had matched my alcohol intake, glass for glass? Fortunately, she is an elegant drunk except for little flights of silliness during which she is inclined to giggle, something she rarely does otherwise. She was deeply enough in her cups that when Krauss brought us *Eiswein*, I cut her off. Suffice it to say, I have never quite forgiven myself for our drunkenness on the night our daughter was conceived. I had no wish *ever* to repeat that experience.

As we moved inside for sweets and coffee, Katherine was a bit unsteady on her feet. I allowed her to lean on my arm. It looked proper enough. I was her husband, after all. I urged her to take coffee, thinking it might mitigate the effects of the alcohol. I was anxious that Margarethe would arrive at any moment and find us both in a state of inebriation. The associations with the past would do no one any favors.

Katherine drank another cup of coffee and yes, it seemed to have a steadying effect on her. The giddiness disappeared, replaced by a look of despair.

"Katherine, what's the matter?"

Without further warning, she burst into tears. Fortunately, I am not one of those men who is helpless when a woman begins to cry. I whipped out my handkerchief, which fortunately was still clean and offered it to her. I rubbed her back in an attempt to soothe her.

"Dear Katherine, please tell me what's troubling you," I urged, whereupon she sat up and buried her face in my shoulder. I had no choice but to put my arms around her, although I confess to worrying that her tears might stain my Italian dinner jacket, one of my favorites. She continued to cry, and I continued in my anxiety about stains.

Finally, the tears stopped. She sat up and took a deep breath. I saw that the worst of the storm had passed.

"Now will you tell me what's wrong?"

"Yes," she said after a long pause.

"Go on." I sighed for I feared I was in for siege.

"I'm overwhelmed. I just can't keep up with everything—my practice, Fiona, Margarethe. She practically begs me, and it breaks my heart to turn her away." She didn't have to spell it out. I could easily surmise that Katherine, exhausted by her work, was unable to give Margarethe the attention she needed. "Oh, Konrad," she said, squeezing my arm. "Don't get the wrong idea. It's not that I lack interest. I don't even have time to think about being interested."

"Well," I said, coughing behind my hand, if only as a ploy to rescue my arm from her grip. "Interest in Eros does require leisure, if only for the idea to occur."

"And it's not only Margarethe. Fiona would like to have more of my attention. I'm tired of telling the poor thing, 'I'm sorry, my little lamb, but mummy's too tired to read to you tonight.' She is such a dear child, and she's growing up so fast. I'm missing all the wonderful moments of her girlhood. When Margarethe suggested it might be time to send her away, I was quite beside myself!"

"I'm not completely in agreement with the idea, myself. I've spoken to Margarethe about it. I'll speak to her again."

"Don't say anything," she cautioned. "You know how she hates for anyone to interfere."

"Yes, but I am Fiona's father, for better or worse. I have a right to interfere."

"Please don't say a word, Konrad," she urged, sounding nearly desperate. "I can persuade her to keep Fiona here a few more years. I'm sure I can. She enjoys having Fiona about, and she's surprisingly good with the girl, perhaps better than I am."

I chuckled. "That's because the burden is on you, the girl's mother. I'm sure Margarethe is a very indulgent auntie, just as she'll be an indulgent grandmother." Katherine looked shocked, so I added: "You must realize that Margarethe's children are grown. In a few years, they'll be having children of their own."

"Margarethe, a grandmother?" she repeated with amazement. "I'm only a few years younger. I'm certainly not ready to be a grandmother."

"Oh, you needn't worry. Fiona is only six."

"But you don't understand," she said, looking directly into my eyes. "I want to be a mother again!"

"What!" I exclaimed. It took several moments to recover myself before I could even say, "You can't be serious!"

"Oh, but I am. Time is running out. I'm thirty-seven. I can't wait much longer."

"You can't be serious!" I repeated stupidly.

"Yes, yes, I am. Margarethe and I have been arguing about it for months."

"I'm sure this disagreement has done nothing for your intimate life," I observed, giving her a penetrating look.

She shook her head. "No, it hasn't." She cast down her eyes, suddenly reverting to convent modesty. I took it as a warning not to probe this subject too deeply.

"So how did you leave it?"

"Margarethe refuses to discuss it further." She looked up and gazed at me intently. "But I don't give up that easily."

Finally, I understood. "No, Katherine. Don't look at me like that. You remember what happened the last time. We were lucky to escape with our lives."

"Oh, Konrad, you exaggerate so. Besides, what can she do? Force us to marry? She's already done that."

My mind was racing. Then all the bits came together and ignited in a great conflagration. Suddenly I couldn't see any of it for the flames. I jumped up from my seat and scissored the air with my hands. "No! Absolutely not! Find another man for the job."

"But you are my *husband*."

"It is all for show…so that you wouldn't be disgraced, and Fiona would have a father. You know that! I'm sure any one of your doctor friends would be willing to oblige. And you needn't even suffer the attentions of a man. I understand there have been attempts at conception without intercourse."

"Oh, yes, it's really quite simple," she said casually, and I now saw the professional detachment I had earlier missed. "The male deposits his semen in a sterile container and it is inserted by means of a syringe into the vagina." Her description was so clinical. I felt repulsed and faintly nauseous. And given the potential for Margarethe's ire, I wouldn't even consider this less offensive option.

"No, Katherine. I'm sorry. I can't help you." She stared at me. I now saw that she was completely sober and had been for some time. Her plan had been revealed not out of a drunken need to confess, but with great deliberation. I began to perceive how skillfully I'd been played.

"Please think about it. You needn't give me your answer now," she said. "Just consider it. Please. If you have any affection for me. Any at all."

"Of course, I have affection for you," I admitted. "I've always been very fond of you, if for no other reason than Margarethe loves you."

"Ah, she loves you as well," she said touching my face.

"That's been over for years," I protested, pulling her hand away.

"But she still loves you. Her loyalty to you is unshakable."

"Katherine, not even for you would I dare test it!"

She gazed at me with no discernible expression. It was impossible to know what she was thinking. "I really must go to bed," she said, rising. "Please, just say you'll think about it."

"Very well, I'll think about it. But no promises!"

She reached up and caressed my cheek. "You look so like her," she said with a sigh before she left.

After that conversation, I needed something strong to drink. I threw down a whiskey. Even more than alcohol, I needed to get out of the house before Margarethe came home. I simply couldn't look her in the eye with this plot afoot.

Now that I knew Grauer couldn't be trusted, I called for a taxi before going up to change. My Italian dinner jacket simply wouldn't do for the destination I had in mind. I put on a tweed sport coat, moleskin trousers, and brogues. For this outing, I fancied myself a slightly rumpled academic.

I would have to make some effort to find the right venue. Gone were the fashionable clubs of an earlier time, all driven underground. One had to know someone to gain access to the closed-door clubs. I'd been out of circulation for so long, I'd lost contact with Berlin's smart crowd. Besides I preferred a different sort of man now—large, heavily muscled, and hirsute.

The taverns at the docks were mixed, but if one paid proper attention and watched carefully through the smoky haze, it was not difficult to perceive who was who and what was what. And there he was. A blond man, whom I guessed to be a Swede or a Dane, or perhaps one of our own. He was far taller than I. With massive shoulders, a great blond beard, and drooping moustaches, he cut the very image of a Viking warrior. I waited until the man beside him vacated his stool and then appropriated his place.

Part II
MARGARETHE

Chapter 4

A glance at the clock in the scrub room finally jolted my memory. The dinner party! Swearing aloud, I flung off my scrub gown and wondered if there were any evening dresses in my office closet. My Charité office was much smaller than the generous suite I had enjoyed as chief of surgery at St. Hilde's, but with luck, there might be something that would do. Amongst the clean blouses and suits, I discovered a Gerson in violet silk that had not been trotted out more times than I could bear. After a rapid shower, I dressed, but despite my haste, I took particular care with my hair and makeup for my hostess put great stock in appearances.

The early-evening congestion around Alexanderplatz blocked the shortest route to my destination. Rather than fret, I sat back and considered the prospect of a dreary evening among diplomats. I was no stranger to such circles. In fact, my encounters with the species went back to when my father was a military attaché to the foreign service. My mother hated to attend official functions, so I was often called to stand in her stead. Father found my ease in learning foreign tongues particularly useful.

Finally, the path forward cleared. I proceeded with all speed, but when I stopped my motorcar at a traffic light not far from my destination, I wondered how I had arrived at that point without any memory of the intervening route. Thoughts of Eva always affected me in this way, nearly from the very first.

It began, as these things often do, in complete innocence and in the service of the best intentions. The x-ray equipment at St. Hilde's hospital had been breaking down with alarming frequency. Everyone from the head radiologist to the chief of staff grumbled about it, even Katherine, who never complains. They all expected me to remedy the problem, which was entirely understandable as my role on the board was director of capital funding. Thus, I found myself charged with finding the means to replace the aging, cantankerous machinery.

Ordinarily, I would have simply reached into my own pockets for the money, but Raithshau's coffers had been depleted by my recent purchase of a very large tract of land. Edelheim's funds were also short because we'd refurbished the steel plant in Bochum. There was my personal money, but it was mostly invested in long positions, and the money squirreled away in Switzerland must remain untouched. Political conditions were uncertain and pilfering my hoard, even for that relatively modest sum, was dangerous.

Instead, I offered to sell my house in London, but my grandaunt, superior general of the nuns who operated the hospital, would not hear of it. It is a long-standing principle in our family—*never* sell real property. I knew without needing to be told that she expected me to give another benefit recital. I had something of a following in Berlin among musical sophisticates, and these amateur events were always successful in bringing in buckets of cash.

I called Gürtner, the director of the Deutsche Oper, and asked him to make the arrangements. Despite the fact that the concert had been my suggestion, my heart wasn't in it. Gürtner asked me what I would like to sing. I waved my hand dismissively and said, "I have no idea. Suggest something." And so he did. He proposed a program of German operatic selections to suit the nationalistic mood of the public. Although I have many favorites in the German repertoire, I dislike being constrained, and I disliked even more to admit that the constraint had been my own doing. Undaunted by my sullen attitude, Gürtner displayed an impresario's enthusiasm for the program, and eventually, I began to warm to it. We settled on an eclectic mix: Strauss, because I knew the maestro and adored his music, Weber, and Wagner, of course. Fortunately, Mahler and Mendelssohn had nothing significant in the operatic repertoire, for although I loved to sing their music, they were Jews and their works were banned.

On the day of the concert, I had been dashing about like a madwoman. Unfortunately, this was far from unusual. My duties at the Charité comprised overseeing the young surgeons in training. They were mostly brilliant but undisciplined, and their unending capacity for generating disasters never ceased to amaze me. That afternoon, I had been required to snatch one of their patients from the very jaws of death within hours of appearing on the stage. The inconvenience put me out of sorts. My irritability increased when Katherine called to say she would be unable to attend. One of her patients had unexpectedly gone into labor. So many times of late, she had disappointed me in exactly this way.

"Find a replacement," I hissed.

"I'm sorry, Margarethe. It's impossible at this late hour."

When we rang off, the anger was still hanging between us. The telephone call further delayed my departure. I raced through the streets of Berlin, narrowly avoiding an accident after deciding to ignore a red light. It was miraculous that I was on stage at the appointed hour.

As Gürtner had predicted, the house was full. Lately, he had been using my ability to turn out an audience as an inducement to take a role in the repertoire. As tempting as the idea of singing Octavian might be, I remained unconvinced.

I sang well enough that night, although I had a few moments of questionable voice in the early numbers, not surprising as twenty minutes of warm up is scarcely sufficient, especially for someone who sings as an amateur. As I took my curtain calls, my collapse from the waist was motivated by more than stage modesty. I was very near the edge of my stamina. My mind rebelled at the idea that I would need to sing a few encores, if only to oblige the good people who had opened their pockets for the benefit of the hospital.

I had already planned what I would sing, but as I headed for the refuge of the wings for the briefest respite, Gürtner approached. He handed me a note folded so many times that it made a tiny packet. I unfurled the paper and inspected its contents. The handwriting was very small and quite bad, although I should talk. I am told that mine is as illegible as any physician's. Penmanship aside, I cursed the fact that I had passed forty and could no longer read the minute script without the aid of my glasses. Eventually, I succeeded in extending my arm sufficiently so I could make out the words:

> "I want to hear that silvery voice raised in passion!
> Sing something in Italian."

What a cheeky request! I was about to toss the note aside, when I noticed the distinct aroma of expensive perfume emanating from the paper. I resisted the temptation to raise it to my nose to inhale it.

"Something in Italian..." I mused. This presented a dilemma. Many of the characters in my vocal range were young men before their voices had broken, and the best bel canto roles had been written for castrati. Given the scent that wafted up from the little note, I doubted my admirer had a boy or a neuter in mind.

"So?" asked Gürtner, craning his neck to see the message.

"Quick, Dieter," I said, snapping my fingers. "Help me think of an Italian aria. Something dramatic."

He blinked, startled. Yes, it was a great departure from the program, but one could do that with encores. "What can you manage at this late hour?" he asked. I rapidly scanned my mental catalog of the mezzo arias I could sing. Sister Elfriede, my voice teacher, insisted that I learn a wide variety so that she could determine my *Fach*. Whatever I chose had to be in the standard repertoire of the Deutsche Oper or I would be singing *a capella*. The Deutsche was almost as well known for Verdi as Wagner. In the end, I chose the most dramatic aria I knew: "O don Fatale" from *Don Carlo*. At this suggestion, Gürtner's eyes widened. "Are you quite certain you are able?" he asked doubtfully.

No, I was not certain, not in the least, but if I thought about it too much, my nerve would certainly fail. "Yes, yes. Go tell the conductor." As he walked away shaking his head, I felt invigorated by the challenge.

Behind the curtain, trying to muster the change of attitude necessary for this abrupt departure from the evening's fare, I mentally sang the aria, including the high notes. Yes, I could achieve them, though I might be a bit hoarse in the morning. I heard Gürtner on the other side of the curtain announce the selection. The audience murmured in surprise.

The curtain opened and the orchestra played the dramatic and rather loud opening to the aria. On cue, I launched in, singing on the energy generated by my admirer's impertinent dare. Silvery voice, indeed! I'll show you my *fire*!

I sang rather well and was relieved to execute the final splendid note with precision. I held it, forcing the conductor to adjust his tempo. This never fails to move the audience. Whereas their earlier applause had been enthusiastic, they were now in a frenzy. They began clapping in unison to indicate they wanted more. Did I dare? As I cleared my throat, I realized that I needed something with a lower tessitura, or I would never sustain the aria to the end. Madly ignoring my own good sense, I chose "La luce langue" from *Macbeth*. Although Lady Macbeth is technically considered to be a soprano role, it is sometimes sung by a mezzo. Even the conductor looked alarmed at this choice. Furtwängler came to the back of the pit to speak to me. "Countess Stahle, that is very ambitious."

"Maestro, please indulge me."

Furtwängler nodded but still looked doubtful. Although he had conducted me before, he did not know me in my other guise—the buccaneer surgeon. The greater the risk, the more delicious the triumph.

Somehow, I had forgotten the high notes at the end of the aria. Through sheer audacity I was able to hit them. This time the audience went mad and rose to their feet. Their cries demanded still more, but I had no more to give them. I bowed one last time before making a hasty retreat to my dressing room.

I shut the door and leaned against it for support. The bouquets of flowers from well-wishers oppressed me with their colorful profusion and their overwhelming scent. I hid my face in my hands to block out the scene. I would have dearly loved to change into street clothes and disappear into the Berlin night, but I had promised Gürtner that I would attend his reception at the Continental. The gathering was meant to thank the most generous donors, and as the guest of honor, I certainly needed to make an appearance.

There was a knock at the door. I opened it a crack and saw Gürtner standing there, looking sheepish. "Grethe, you have a visitor." I gave him a fish-eyed stare. "Yes, yes, I know," he said responding to my unspoken admonition. "You never receive visitors. But she has made a *very* large grant to your hospital fund, and I think you ought to see her." I opened the door little, and he squeezed his way into the dressing room.

"Who is she?" I asked irritably, shutting the door.

"Countess d'Allessandro, wife of the Italian under-consul."

"Is she waiting out there?"

"Yes. Please, see her." I raised my left brow and gave him a meaning look. "*Please,* Grethe, do it for me."

For friendship's sake alone, I decided to humor him. I contrived a gracious expression as my visitor was shown into the room. She was not what I expected, although, I cannot say what I imagined at only the mention of her name and the fact that she had been generous to our cause. She was diminutive, barely coming to my shoulder. She had dark hair, nearly black and dark, almond-shaped eyes, carefully made-up for dramatic effect. Her skin was pale and made paler still by the intense red of the lipstick she wore. Her figure, if one might call it such, for she was nearly gaunt, showed no hint of womanly curves. I prefer women with the usual female appointments, that is, discernible breasts and hips. But I could not deny that her thinness and pallor gave her an air of elegance, and despite her short stature, she had presence. One's eyes were drawn to her long, pale throat as to a flag. I instantly recognized the perfume from the note.

She smiled slightly and extended her long-fingered, elegant hand. When I took it in mine, I felt the bones so prominently that I dared not give my usual firm handshake.

"I am Eva d'Allessandro, a great admirer of your singing. I have been following your work."

I suppressed a cynical smile, but I fear my voice conveyed my skepticism. "That must be difficult," I replied in Italian. "I haven't been singing much of late."

She gave me the barest of smiles, although her eyes seemed to glow. "You speak Italian very well, Countess."

I shrugged. "If possible, I prefer speaking in the language of my listener. Our tongue is so difficult to master." I wondered why I was being so mean to this woman, even to the point of insinuating that her German was abominable, which it was.

She gazed around the room. "What lovely flowers. Have you received mine?"

"I arrived late and haven't had time to read the cards."

"It must be those," she said, gesturing to a noble display of white roses. "I sent them in honor of your silvery voice." Once again, those dark eyes glowed.

I remembered that she had donated a large amount to our fund, so I attempted to muster some grace. "I must thank you. Gürtner tells me you have been generous to the hospital. We shall make very good use of the new x-ray equipment. Of that, you can be sure."

"I understand you are a physician. How wonderful that one of our class takes such an interest in the public good."

I listened carefully but detected no note of insincerity in this remark, nor idle flattery. I decided to take it at face value, and certainly, given her generosity to our cause, it behooved me to be courteous. "Will you sit, Countess, while I make myself presentable for the reception?" I turned to the mirror to wipe away my stage make-up.

"Oh, I am looking forward to it. Herr Gürtner was good enough to invite me. However, I must find a means to get there. My husband has already gone home. He had a very difficult day at the consulate. So many Jews want to come into Italy on their way to Palestine or Spain."

I put down the sponge to look at her. "I hadn't considered that," I admitted candidly.

"Yes, it makes for many complications," she said with a solemn look, but then she brightened. "Herr Gürtner thought you might allow me to accompany you to the Continental."

"Really?" I asked, betraying both my surprise and indignation. I was in no mood for company or passengers. Gürtner had already departed in order to greet his guests as they arrived, so I had little choice but to agree. "You may come with me. I have my motorcar," I said, barely concealing my annoyance.

"You drive yourself?" she asked with astonishment, as if such things were not commonplace.

"Naturally. As a physician, I am called away at all hours."

"I don't drive," she confided. "But I would like to learn."

"Perhaps you can find someone to teach you," I said, padding on fresh powder and refreshing my mascara. All the while, I could smell her perfume, not so much overbearing as distinctive. Had any other woman worn the scent, it would probably not have smelled the same.

"Perhaps someone like you. I think it would be easier to learn from a woman. Men are always so impatient with such things."

I mumbled half-hearted agreement over the impatience of men, not the driving lessons.

"I am delighted you speak Italian so well," she said to my image in the mirror. "I still struggle with German. It's such a frustrating language."

"How long have you been in Berlin, Countess d'Allessandro?" I asked gathering up my things.

"Two years, since my husband was assigned to this post. Actually, we have a friend in common, Countess Treppen."

"Ah, yes, Mitzi. I haven't seen her in ages."

"She said she would introduce us. But the occasion never arose."

So, Countess d'Allessandro had made her own opportunity. I hardly knew what to make of this. Yes, I had my share of female admirers after a concert, but none so prominent, nor bold.

The clock chimed, announcing the hour. I tossed my personal cosmetics into my bag. The rest could be left for the dresser to look after. We needed to hurry to arrive at the reception on time. "We must be off," I said.

"A pity. I was so enjoying our little chat. When we arrive at the reception, I must share you with the others." She smiled to indicate this had been a casual remark, but I was not so sure.

I led her through the maze of corridors terminating at a stage entrance few knew. The Mercedes was in the automobile park behind the opera house. I opened the door for my passenger, surprised that I was suddenly so mannerly until I realized that I'd palpably felt her expectation.

I drove to the reception at my usual rapid pace. A glance at my companion revealed that she was unconcerned about the speed. "If I learned to drive," the countess said as I raced down Bismarckstraße, "then I could go anywhere I wished, without my chauffeur."

"Is there a problem with your chauffeur?"

"No, actually not. Except that he is very loyal to my husband."

"Ah, that could be inconvenient," I said, finally understanding. "Have you considered a taxi?"

"Yes, and I have resorted to such means on occasion."

"If your transportation is so constrained, how did you manage to get away tonight?"

"Herr Gürtner promised my husband he would make sure I got home safely." Privately, I wondered what Gürtner's plan might be. He couldn't simply leave his guests to escort her home, but that was his worry, not mine and I thought no more of it.

We shortly arrived at the Hotel Continental and went directly to the private room where Gürtner's party was underway. The champagne was flowing freely. There were mountains of canapés and a deep well of caviar. I was delighted to see the food. Having missed supper and expended so much energy singing, I was positively ravenous. While I gorged on canapés, Countess d'Allessandro ate nothing at all.

I succeeded in losing my charge while I mingled with the guests. Furtwängler was there and several of the principals of the orchestra, but mostly the crowd consisted of the glittering patrons who had given so generously to our campaign. Although I lack Konrad's political charms, I can muster a certain ease in such gatherings, especially after a glass of champagne. Within the space of an hour, I succeeded in making the rounds. I was just about to relax with another glass of champagne, when Eva d'Allessandro appeared at my elbow.

"I must leave shortly," she announced.

"The party's just begun."

"Yes, but I really must go. It's already quite late."

"I'll ask someone to call you a taxi," I offered, poised to summon a waiter.

She put her hand on my arm. "I really hate to impose, but..."

After staring at her for a long moment, I finally understood that she expected me to drive her home—a rather bold presumption.

Actually, I was glad for the excuse to leave. It was getting on to midnight, and between the extensive afternoon surgery and the concert, I'd had a full day. "Yes, of course," I muttered. "I'll drive you home, if you wish."

Our wraps were located, and we went out to wait for my motorcar. It was a lovely night for early-September, a bit cool, but not chilly. The sky was perfectly clear, and despite the bright lights from the city, one could see the stars twinkling overhead.

The countess took my arm. "I love the night," she said, squeezing my arm to her body. "It's my favorite time." I had no idea how to respond to this remark, so I remained silent. "Tomorrow is your birthday," she added.

"How did you know?"

"I read it in that big genealogical book you Germans have."

"The *Almanach de Gotha*?"

"Yes, that's the one. How noble you are, so many titles!"

This shameless flattery made me uncomfortable, as did her taking the trouble to look me up. The valet delivered my motorcar. I slid into the driver's seat, deliberately allowing the boy to do the honors for my companion.

Upon arriving in the embassy district, I parked across the street from the consulate. My passenger made no effort to leave, so it appeared that I would be obliged to get out and open the door for her. As I engaged the latch to exit, she put a hand on my arm. "Please, may I have a moment?"

"You must excuse me, Countess. I have an early lecture tomorrow."

"Just a moment. That's all I ask." She moved closer and her perfume tickled my nostrils. The light from the street lamp danced in her dark eyes. "I've been waiting so long to tell you this. I cannot let this opportunity escape." I allowed a pause to elapse to indicate my willingness to hear what she had to say. "Your voice so moves me that after I have heard you sing I can think of nothing else for days. I know you sing from your very soul. You may speak many languages, but music is the only language you truly speak." I was taken aback. She had spoken a truth that few understood.

"Are you a musician, Countess?"

"Eva," she said, "You must call me Eva." She squeezed my arm. "I'm a listener, a very good listener, and I know you are wasting your talent by avoiding the stage. You must sing." She reached out and gently caressed my throat, then my lips. Her touch electrified me. "You must sing for everyone. Promise me."

Her dark eyes glistened. Then she closed them, and her lips parted. She was inviting me to kiss her! The seconds seemed eternal as I stared at her in amazement. This could not be happening, but it was. She tugged at my arm slightly. I was barely aware of moving forward. Then I touched my lips to hers. Her eyes flew open and searched mine. Momentarily, I panicked, fearing I'd mistaken her intentions, and she would flee the motorcar in terror, screaming for her husband and the consulate guards.

But she did not. Her eyes closed once more, and she waited for me to kiss her again. I was unable to stop myself. Soon, I was filling her mouth with my tongue, and she moved closer, pressing her thigh against me. Shortly, my hand found its way under her dress, into the wide leg of her undergarment, and I touched her.

Her abundant moisture shocked me. I nearly withdrew, but her hand came over mine to guide it. She gave a little gasp and began to kiss me so hard that my lips ached. I moved in her for only a few brief moments before she broke the kiss and released a little cry. I tried to muffle it with my free hand, despite the fact that the windows were closed and the street, empty. She clung to me while I recovered from my shock.

Since I had given myself to Katherine, I had never touched another woman.

"Thank you," murmured the woman in my arms. She drew back a little and took my face in her hands. "I must see you again. Tomorrow. It's your birthday. Let me take you to lunch to celebrate."

"I don't know," I mumbled. "I have no idea what may be on my calendar."

"Never mind that. Say you'll come."

"Café Berlin at noon?"

She kissed me until my head began to spin. Then she opened the door and got out. "By the way, your Princess Eboli was brilliant," she said, "full of fire!" She blew me a kiss.

I watched her cross the street to the building. The doorman opened the door for her.

✻✻✻

I now sat gazing at the same door through which she had vanished that night. I had never visited her in the consulate before. All of our meetings had taken place in public places: restaurants, hotel lobbies, the cinema. One night, I boldly made love to her while we were watching the picture. I could only tell that she had reached a climax by the squeeze of her hand. I longed to take her in a proper bed, to see her undressed. She had promised the time was near, that she was making arrangements.

I handed off my motorcar to the parking valet and entered the building. The doorman instructed me to take the lift to the third floor, which was entirely occupied by the under-consul's apartment. The butler met me at the door, relieved me of my coat, and led me into the grand room where cocktails were being served.

Because of my height, there is little I need do to "make an entrance." Although I drew the eyes of the guests, their hostess conspicuously ignored me. I was, however, very much aware of her presence. As soon as I entered the apartment, the unique scent of her perfume insinuated itself into my nostrils. When I tried to get Eva's attention with a wave, she turned her back. Her servant approached and asked what I would like to drink. I ordered a martini, which arrived shortly in a silvery, iced glass. I rapidly drank it down in the hope of numbing my irritation.

Fortunately, I know how to amuse myself at ridiculous social events, being often enough in situations where I know no one. But it seemed I was not unknown. "Why, it's Countess Stahle," said a gentleman suddenly appearing at my side. His face was familiar, although he was much changed from my memory of the dashing, young lieutenant who had served on my father's personal staff during the Great War. "Lieutenant Kleber, how nice to see you again," I said, extending my hand.

"It's Captain Kleber now," he said. "I'm amazed you remember me. It must be well over twenty years since we last met." He took my hand and made the formal Prussian bow. "What brings you to our gathering this evening?" he asked.

"I am an acquaintance of the wife."

"Ah, Lady Eva. Lovely woman, she."

I glanced in the direction of my ice goddess. Feeling particularly ungenerous after being ignored, I found little reason to agree.

"And you?" I asked.

"Oh, I have a minor role in the diplomatic corps. I was assigned to the Italians, for whatever reason I can't fathom. But I've learned the language, so I get on." His expression softened. "I was so sorry to hear of your father's death," he said, looking genuinely sympathetic. The event had occurred almost seven years earlier, so I was long past active grief. I appreciated the thought, nonetheless. "How are your children?" he asked, smiling fondly.

"My children are well. Both off at university."

"You can't be old enough to have grown children."

"Oh, but I am. I was nearly twenty when we last met." He kindly continued to smile as he did the mental arithmetic and realized I was past forty.

We compared notes on some of the people we knew in common. Then he switched the topic to Hitler's economic policies. In response to his glowing assessment of *Der Führer*, my mind promptly began to doze.

The butler came out to announce dinner. Kleber arranged with my nearest neighbor at the table to exchange places. We were two dozen at dinner, so there was no general conversation, one had to make do with one's nearest companions. Fortunately, the gentleman on my right really knew something about finance. We discussed the recent recovery in the stock markets. Even the American economy seemed to be looking up since Roosevelt had been able to implement some of his programs.

After supper, we all gathered in the music room for coffee, the strong Italian variety with a strip of lemon peel. Eva sat down at the piano, and a hush instantly fell on the room. She began to play Liszt's "La Campanella," and I realized she was a far better pianist than any amateur I have ever known. She was truly gifted. The applause from the gathering was more than the courteous response of a sympathetic audience and rightly so.

She rose from the piano bench and headed in my direction. I tried to make myself small, but of course, that is impossible. She said not, 'hello, my dear, how are you?' but "You *will* sing for my guests." It was not a invitation, or even a request. It was a command.

"I haven't prepared anything," I protested.

"You are always prepared." She turned and announced for all to hear, "Countess Stahle will now sing for us."

This was met with polite applause. Having endured the after-dinner recitals of amateur singers, I knew what torture they could be for the hapless guests.

"What do you think you're doing?" I demanded in a harsh whisper.

"Showing you off. Why not?"

My refusal would only embarrass us, so I followed her to the piano. "You said you weren't a musician," I muttered on the way.

"I said that I'm a listener. And now I want to listen to you sing." She sat down on the bench. "What would like to sing?" she asked brightly.

The crowd was growing restless while we squabbled, which made me anxious.

"What do you suggest?"

She glanced at the assembled guests. "Perhaps you know Schubert's *Italian Songs*?"

"Yes, but it's been ages, and…" She began to play before I could even finish my protest. I'd intended to say that I had never committed the Schubert songs to memory because I'd found them unmemorable. Moreover, it had been decades since I'd last sung them. I was more or less sight reading the score over Eva's shoulder. Fortunately, I could easily see it at that distance without my glasses.

The applause was more than polite.

"Another," said Eva.

"No," I replied firmly. "Enough." I turned to go back to my seat, but she caught my hand.

"Please," she asked with an imploring look, "just one more. In fact, I'll allow you to sing something in German." She opened the score for a Strauss song, one of my favorites. Until I began to sing it, I gave no thought to the text: "*Wie sollten wir geheim sie halten*" or "How could we keep it secret?"

The audience's applause was more generous this time. Before Eva could ask for more, I hurried to my seat. Kleber leaned over and whispered: "How could I have forgotten how beautifully you sing? Exquisite, my dear." Until that moment, I'd nearly forgotten that I'd sung for my father's troops when I'd visited him on the front during the war. The impromptu recital had been punctuated by the sound of distant mortar fire. There is nothing so plaintive as music played against the sounds of war.

Out of the corner of my eye, I saw Eva approaching and steeled myself against further requests, but she had a request of a different kind. "Would you like to refresh your lipstick, *cara*?" The idea that the need might be obvious caused me some anxiety until I realized it was a ploy.

She led me through the halls of the large apartment to what were evidently her chambers. In the dressing room, she closed the door behind us and turned the key in the lock. Her hands slid up my bare arms and around the back of my neck. She pulled me down into a kiss, which instantly grew so profound that I found my hand lifting her gown. My goal was easily reached. I was startled to discover that she was wearing no undergarments. Her abundant moisture was always astonishing, but I forgot the thought. I forgot all thoughts as I made love to her.

That's not entirely true. I was troubled by the idea that, during the time we had been lovers, she had never once touched me.

❊❊❊

When I arrived home, I went directly to my bathroom where I bathed thoroughly, hoping to wash away every hint of Eva's scent. It always seemed to cling to me no matter how diligently I washed. Even after shampooing my hair and scrubbing myself with strong soap, her smell seemed to linger. It was only bad conscience, of course, and no one else could smell it, but the frantic hygiene had become a ritual—a way to separate my guilty moments with Eva from my otherwise orderly life.

Actually, the person I never wanted to know my secret wasn't even there. I was greatly relieved when Krauss told me that Katherine was attending a difficult birth. Her late arrival would allow me an opportunity to make a transition between my worlds.

As a young woman, and even during my marriage to Lytton, I enjoyed anyone who suited my fancy. But one must always exercise discretion or life can become untidy. Despite my caution, there had been a few mishaps.

One calamitous occasion was the concert of Zemlinsky songs I sang in London in 1928. Alexandra Calder, my lover at the time, decided to attempt suicide because one of the songs alluded, albeit so subtly, to a Sapphic connection between the characters. She was pursuing her soon-to-be husband and had gotten it into her head that I was jealous. Fortunately, for all of us, Alexandra opened her wrists with a dull penknife, cutting, as so many without a knowledge of anatomy do, in the wrong direction. She succeeded in releasing a stream of blood but missed the artery by a long shot. Her brother, Charles, also a surgeon, managed to suture and bandage her wrists before the police arrived. Even so, the inspectors demanded a careful explanation before turning the matter over to us as a medical case.

The harrowing event was an embarrassment never to be repeated. Perhaps I should have learned my lesson but tempting fate and narrowly avoiding danger is like a drug. Usually, I indulged my addiction in less social ways—driving fast cars or dangling from mountains. It had been ages since I had used the bedchamber as a means to tempt fate, and I wondered why I had suddenly abandoned my good sense.

I had taken every precaution to keep the affair contained. Eva was forbidden to call me at home or visit me at the hospital. We ate in restaurants I seldom frequented so I wouldn't be recognized. Even so, there was always the possibility of discovery. The evening at the consulate with its odd surprises and very public association with my lover had been very risky.

My mind raced with these thoughts as I sat in the steaming bath water. I knew I must try to calm myself before Katherine arrived or risk hinting at my secrets through overt anxiety. To distract myself, I got into bed with Baroness Blixen's book, *Out of Africa*. Secretly, I envied those of our class who were able to abscond to exotic locales while I was boringly stationed at home.

After an hour of vicarious adventure, I heard the scuff of Katherine's high-heeled shoes on the floor boards. She looked exhausted when she came into the bedroom, but as always, succeeded in offering me a smile. I smiled in return. Despite our being at odds, Katherine's honest devotion never failed to touch me.

"You're home. I'm surprised to see you so early," she said, slipping off her shoes and getting into bed beside me. She kissed me and gave me a little squeeze about the waist. "How was the dinner party?"

I shrugged. I hadn't enjoyed the evening, nor its furtive conclusion in Eva's dressing room.

Evidently, Katherine felt the need to explain her late arrival. "My elderly *prima para* finally gave birth after fifteen hours of labor."

"Why didn't you hurry it along?" I asked mildly. She hated my giving her advice, especially in her specialty, but this time she allowed any resentment to roll off. As was our habit at the end of the day, we exchanged a summary of our cases, as quick as the précis in the weekly morbidity-and-mortality conferences.

"I must get ready for bed," she announced. "I'm frightfully tired and desperately need sleep." This was the usual message, so I returned my attention to my book.

After a difficult day, Katherine often slept in her own room so that I wouldn't disturb her when I rose in the morning. To my surprise, she returned after attending to her evening tasks and got into bed beside me. I understood after a few moments that she wanted to talk, so I closed my book and switched off the bedside lamp.

"Dr. Becher examined me today…" she began.

"Are you ill?"

"No, in fact, Becher pronounced me perfectly healthy." Although it was dark, and I couldn't see her face, I could feel her hesitation and sense it in her breathing. I knew I probably wouldn't like what she was about to say. "He thinks I can still conceive and have a healthy child, despite my age."

"Must we have this conversation again?" I asked with forced patience.

"No," she said, rolling over on her side and giving me her back. "You've said all you have to say."

"Indeed, I have," I replied, ready to turn my back on her as well. Then

I saw that I was being unnecessarily harsh. I moved closer and put my arm around her waist. "Katherine, dear. I simply don't understand this great need of yours. It makes no sense to me."

"Nothing makes sense to you, Margarethe, unless it's *your* idea."

The prospect of an argument immediately before sleep was unwelcome. I tried to use affection to soothe her. I pushed aside the large braid she usually wound of her hair before bed and kissed the back of her neck. "Actually, I do have an idea…one you might like." I reached into her nightgown to caress her breast. What a lovely warm weight it was in my hand.

"Don't," she said gently shrugging off my hand. "I need to sleep."

"We can be quick. I promise you."

"I don't enjoy it when it's quick. We need to take time. Perhaps this Sunday when we're both free…"

I hated making appointments for sex, but it had come to that.

"Very well," I said wearily and rolled over to sleep. Although I was tired and quite drowsy, sleep would not come. For one thing I wanted Katherine. Paradoxically, my hurried encounters with Eva made me want Katherine all the more. Perhaps it was simply the need for release after all those one-sided joinings. Even more, it was the seemingly endless arousal I experienced in Eva's presence. It made me think of only one thing—sex. Even as I lay beside Katherine, I burned for Eva.

Katherine sighed. She reached over and patted my hip. "I love you, Margarethe."

Guilt over the idea that she might have been able to hear my thoughts overwhelmed me. After that, I lay awake for hours.

Chapter 5

My work became a refuge from the lunacy of my personal life—one of the many reasons why I am grateful to have a career. Since girlhood, I knew that I must do something beyond being decorative. There is a long tradition in my family of public service in the military and the foreign service. Obviously, I couldn't become a soldier, and who in those days before the Great War had ever heard of a female ambassador?

Fortunately, there were other possibilities. It had become fashionable for young people of my class to study for a profession. My grandaunt, the mother general of the Sisters of Obberoth, then headmistress of the convent school, steered me towards a medical career. She reasoned that with my head for science, medicine would be the exactly right thing for me, and she was correct. Medicine proved to be intellectually engaging, and I was surprisingly adept with my hands, despite the fact that I had never been trained to do anything useful. When I announced my intention to become a surgeon, my parents were deeply disturbed, especially my mother who cannot distinguish between the practice of surgery and other kinds of manual labor. In her mind, any labor, no matter how exalted, is beneath the station of a lady of the *Uradel*. We still have this argument from time to time, but in the main, she seems to have come around to my point of view.

After family obligations forced me to resign my position as chief of surgery of St. Hilde's in 1931, Sauerbruch recruited me to oversee the training of the junior surgical staff at the Charité. My charges were all young Turks and kept me hopping. However, I found the company of such talented and inquisitive young men very stimulating. They were all men, of course, save one—the amazing Sarah Weber. As a technical surgeon, I am certainly competent, but Dr. Weber had no peer.

One morning, she asked me to observe during a pneumonectomy, which meant she was nervous about the procedure and wanted reinforcements close at hand should something go awry. To be fair, the excision of part of a lung is messy work at best, and with all those vessels and the heart itself in the vicinity, anything can go wrong. I took my role seriously, scrubbing in so that I could be available to her at a moment's notice.

The beginning of the surgery went extremely well with Sarah working at her usual economical pace. I glanced up at the wall clock and speculated that we might wind down the operation well ahead of the allotted time. Sarah ran into a little trouble when she encountered some adhesions. The diseased lung, completely scarred from tuberculosis, had attached itself to the chest wall. This did not bode well for the prognosis but, in any case, the adhesions needed to be addressed. I was about to step in, when Sarah got control of the situation. The remainder of the procedure went smoothly, so I left before the close.

After her scheduled surgeries, Sarah came looking for me in my hospital office. She had the sort of expectant look on her face that could only mean she wanted to hear my opinion, whether praise or criticism. Surely, she could judge for herself that all had gone well, yet she often looked to me for confirmation of her abilities. This would not do. The training of surgeons past the technical aspects is mostly teaching them mental and emotional discipline, including unflinching faith in oneself. A failure of nerve can kill a patient...or end a career.

"Sit down, Dr. Weber," I suggested as she hovered in my doorway. In private, we always spoke English. She was fluent in German, having learned it from her German father, but her accent was not the best. I much preferred her honest, American English.

She took a chair on the other side of my desk and continued to gaze at me with an expectant look. She was not a conventionally beautiful woman. Her features were distinctive—an exceptionally high forehead, a long, patrician nose, and a generous mouth. Nonetheless, I thought her attractive and liked to look at her. When she was in a fervor about some medical topic, her gray eyes shone with intelligence and passion.

She spoke all in a rush: "Those adhesions, I should have guessed they would be there. I should have anticipated...."

Was she apologizing to me? "Yes, I saw," I said in a mild, friendly voice. "But you handled the situation splendidly." She stared at me, evidently waiting for me to say more. "I have no criticism," I assured her. "You do excellent work."

"Thanks," she replied with sincere modesty. She sighed in relief and sat back in her chair.

"Dr. Weber, why is my opinion so important to you?"

"Because you're my mentor," she replied with some impatience, as if the answer to this question were obvious.

"Doctor, you are at a point in your career when senior advice is rarely of the technical kind. I can find no fault with your technique. In fact, in this regard you outshine me."

"That can't be true!"

I endeavored to be patient, not my strongest suit. "Once one becomes adept at a skill, repetition does not necessarily improve it. Yes, of course, experience is useful. It allows us to anticipate what can go wrong and to be alert to that which isn't obvious." Sarah regarded me with the little puzzled frown I often saw on her face, as if I spoke a language she couldn't understand. Yes, I speak English with a British accent, but it is *English.* "You must learn to believe in your abilities and trust your instincts."

"But I do," she protested indignantly. "How do you think I got here?"

"Sometimes you believe. But why did you invite me this morning? It's clear that you had the situation entirely under control."

"I wanted you to see I had taken your lecture on adhesions to heart."

"Dr. Weber, you are a fellow here, not a student. You are not being graded on your performance. Why are you so concerned about what I think?"

Our conversation was interrupted by Sauerbruch's arrival. My door was open, so he merely breezed in, disregarding Sarah sitting in the chair. We both rose. The professor patted the air to indicate that we should sit and appropriated the chair next to Sarah's. "And how are my favorite lady surgeons this morning?" he asked, attempting to charm us. We were the only female surgeons in the hospital, so how could we be anything but his favorites?

Being the senior, it was my role to respond. "Dr. Weber just completed an exceptionally well-executed partial pneumonectomy."

"Ah," he said, glancing at her and giving her a brief, curious look. Technically, Sarah was his fellow, but he had shown little interest in her or her progress. I was disappointed on her behalf, especially because his role in my own career cannot be overestimated. I wrote off his disregard of Sarah to his increasing government responsibilities.

He turned to me. The sunlight through the window reflecting on his bald pate distracted me. "And so, Dr. von Stahle, *when* can I read your paper?"

Paper? Which paper? I scanned my mind for a clue but came up blank. Sauerbruch gave me a very impatient look. He glanced at Sarah. "Will you excuse us, *Frau Doktor*?" Clever Sarah exited at once and carefully shut the door behind her. Now that we were alone, Sauerbruch addressed me by my given name. "Margarethe, don't tell me you've forgotten. The conference in Rome is only three weeks away and the précis must be filed by tomorrow. As it is, you must send it by wire." The pipeline to my memory opened and through it the blocked information rapidly flooded. The unpleasant image of a culvert blocked with debris suddenly came to mind. Berlin is full of canals, and there were such scenes everywhere.

Indeed, the Charité's report on our breast cancer trials had once occupied a premiere place in my mind, especially because I had initiated the project and led the Charité research team since 1931. I'd offered to write the summary paper in Italian to the great delight of the conference officials in Rome. How could I have forgotten? I noted that the memory lapse coincided exactly with Eva's arrival on the scene.

Sauerbruch gazed at me with a worried look. The mental review of my distraction had perhaps taken seconds, but it was long enough to seem an unnatural pause. I quickly said, before he had too much time to think about it: "I'll have the précis to you by this afternoon as well as the outline. I'm afraid the paper itself will not be ready for a few days. I'm not as fluent in Italian as English or French. It will take a little longer."

"Show me what you have completed so far. Surely, you wrote it in German first," he replied, looking incredulous.

Not so surely, but I dared not lie to him. "No, I've been writing even the draft in Italian."

"I want to see the précis by the end of the day. *In German!*"

That part I could assure with confidence. It would be nothing to dash off a précis by the end of the day. "As you wish, *Herr Professor*," I replied with military briskness.

He did not look pleased, but he began to speak of one of our resident doctors, who had lately gotten himself into trouble that had required our mutual intervention. While this was also my responsibility, I did not take it as personally as the late paper, so I was happy for the change of subject.

After Sauerbruch left, I spent a few moments berating myself for allowing the fabric of my life to unravel so publicly. I resolved that I should put aside personal affairs, especially Eva, and concentrate on my work. That having been decided, my hand, seemingly of its own volition, began to creep towards the telephone. Once there, it dialed Eva's number without so much as a moment's hesitation. Eva's servant informed me that she was unavailable. I dared not leave a message, even as "Dr. von Stahle."

Instead, I refocused my attention on the paper. I called the head clerk of the hospital and inquired whether we had any secretaries who could take dictation in Italian. Wishful thinking, of course. I could have dictated it in German but translating the transcript would take so much time. Writing in long-hand seemed to be the best option, although I pitied the poor typist who must read my terrible penmanship. In a great act of procrastination, I cleaned and refilled my fountain pen. Then I went down the hall to the supply closet for a fresh pad of grid-lined paper. Finally, I sat down to write.

A short time later, the telephone on my desk rang. Absently, I picked it up. "Stahle, here," I said into the receiver.

"Oh, my darling," said the female voice on the other end.

Eva.

I swallowed hard and covered my eyes against the light.

"I needed to hear your voice. I've been playing the piano and thinking of you," she said.

I closed my eyes, unable to reply. It was as if she had reached through the telephone and touched my throat.

"I called earlier."

"I know."

"But I left no message."

"I knew it was you, but my servants are forbidden to interrupt me in the music room." How fortunate to have such a luxury, but as a physician, my time is not always my own. My moment of envy lured me back into the real world of medicine and my duties.

"I am going to Rome to attend a medical conference."

"When?" asked Eva in an excited voice.

"Three weeks from tomorrow."

"See? I told you there would be a solution." She laughed. "And it's perfect. My brother and his family will be on holiday in Tuscany. We shall have the villa to ourselves."

"Can you really get away?"

"Of course. Pietro always lets me go home for a visit around this time of the year." I could practically hear her smiling. "Oh, my dearest, you will come to me and I'll take care of you."

"I'm coming to Rome for professional reasons," I pointed out, trying to wrest away some control of the situation.

"Of course," she agreed. "I would never interfere in your work. But you could come a few days early. Yes?"

I said I would consider it. She asked me to provide the dates of the conference. Then she informed me exactly when I should arrive, ensuring that I would devote at least two days solely to her.

"I'll see what I can arrange."

"That is the wrong answer, *cara*. Say, 'Yes, Eva.'"

So I did. As I replaced the handset, I wondered if I had completely taken leave of my senses.

I resolved once more to force Eva and the visit to Rome from my thoughts. Now that there was a plan in place, I succeeded. For the next two hours, I wrote feverishly, completing a draft of the entire manuscript. I gave the German text of both the précis and the outline to my secretary to type and deliver to Sauerbruch.

❋❋❋

When I arrived home that afternoon, Fiona bounded away from her nurse and flung herself into my arms. "*Tante*, Miss Carter taught me to play the piano!" she declared. Fiona often sat in rapt attention while I played. Even an indifferent mother such as I knew that an animated child sitting so quietly indicated deep interest.

"Indeed, my sweet. That's wonderful," I replied, holding Fiona on my hip. She adored being carried as if she were still an infant, but Katherine thought she was too old for such behavior. In Katherine's absence, I happily ignored her opinions.

"Let me show you," Fiona said, squirming to be let down. Once on her own feet, she took my hand and led me to the music room. Miss Carter, following in pursuit, gave me an apologetic look.

Fiona played a little English ditty for me without a single error. "And I can sing it too," she told me. She played and sang the little song perfectly. This was not the moronic reproduction of something mindlessly learned by repetition. Moreover, she succeeded in getting both the phrasing right and staying flawlessly on key. Clearly, the girl had some native talent.

I looked up at Miss Carter and wondered why the woman never informed us of her intention to introduce music to the girl, but then she was not always forthcoming regarding her plans—if she actually had any.

"She must have music lessons," I said.

"I'll see to it, my lady."

"Never mind. I shall see to it myself." Miss Carter's distressed look indicated that she had understood this was a criticism. The sight of her suddenly annoyed me, so I dismissed her.

Fiona now played another tune, one of her own invention. It was quite good. But despite her delight in her new-found skill, the child was harboring a concern she wished to share. "Will *Mutti* be coming home tonight?"

"Yes, my little mouse," I said, putting my arm around her and pulling her close. "Your mother will be home soon."

Fortunately, Katherine did not make a liar of me. She arrived home in time for supper. After seeing Fiona to bed, Katherine came into my sitting room to offer the obligatory good-night kiss. I caught her hand and asked her to sit. I felt insensitive for detaining her, especially when she looked so bone weary, but I needed to tell her about my impending trip to Rome.

"Why haven't you told me before?" she asked with a frown after I recited the details.

Despite my anxiety over arousing suspicion, I endeavored to answer her questions with candor. "The truth is, it simply went out of my head. There's so much activity at the moment." Fortunately, this was a true statement.

"You should at least tell Krauss, so he can keep your calendar straight," she scolded.

"Yes, I should have told him. But he has only half the equation, namely our social engagements. Our professional calendars are managed by our secretaries." It was no excuse, but it made sense. "I'll probably leave a few days early," I said, attempting to sound casual.

"Really? Why?" asked Katherine. I could hear a slight edge in her voice, which unnerved me until I realized its cause was fatigue.

"I could use a little holiday. The Countess d'Allessandro has asked me to her villa."

Katherine narrowed her eyes. "Is that your musical friend who gave so much to the hospital fund?"

"Exactly."

"You could do with a holiday," said Katherine, picking up a magazine from the bedside table. She scanned the cover briefly. "You've been very testy with me." In fact, it seemed that I had barely seen enough of her to behave in any particular way.

"You could probably do with a holiday yourself," I observed. "Perhaps we should plan a visit to Edelheim."

"Oh, that's no holiday, with you bickering with your mother. I'm sure you would prefer something else. A little mountain climbing perhaps?" Now the edge in her voice was sarcasm. I decided to ignore it.

"Ah, the Alps might be nice. I hadn't thought of that." It was a foolish fantasy. Neither of us could afford to get away for that length of time.

"The last time I had a real holiday was during my pregnancy with Fiona."

"Pregnancy isn't exactly a holiday."

"Because you disliked your pregnancies doesn't mean I found mine unpleasant."

How could she possibly say such a thing? She had spent the final trimester of her pregnancy confined to bed out of concern that any physical exertion would precipitate labor.

"Katherine, let's not discuss this again. Please," I said in as tolerant a tone as I could muster. The direction of the conversation was progressively irritating me, and I was losing patience.

"No, let's discuss it," she said, raising her voice, which was very unlike her. She was normally so soft spoken. "Why is it so incomprehensible that I might want another child?" she demanded in the raised tone.

"You are thirty-seven. A little old to be having more children. You have a demanding career."

"My career? My career is going very well, thank you. I could take some time."

"Some time?" I repeated with astonishment. "You have no time for the child you have!" As soon as these words were out of my mouth, I instantly regretted them. Quick tears formed in Katherine's eyes and she fled the room.

What had possessed me to say something so obviously hurtful? I knew that guilt over lack of time to spend with Fiona tortured Katherine, yet I never hesitated to stab her with this knowledge, and this time, it went far beyond my need to win an argument at any cost.

I attempted to calm myself by sipping some brandy. At the very least, I owed Katherine an apology for my insensitive remark. I knocked gently on the door that connected our dressing rooms. No answer. I tried to open the door. It was locked! By this simple act, Katherine had revealed the depth of her injury and anger. Despite our many disagreements over the years, she had *never* locked the door against me.

Chapter 6

As I settled myself in the aeroplane at Templehof, I had a sudden, painful moment of clarity. What am I doing? I asked myself. I did not love Eva. To be sure, there were moments when I truly hated her. At such times, I hated her as deeply as I desired her. I began to understand Catullus' famous sentiment, which I had so often scanned and translated as a student: *"Odi et amo..."* Yes, I hated and I loved, and truly, I was crucified by my own naked desire.

I distracted myself by watching the airfield mechanic start the propeller. There is a certain beauty in how the individual blades suddenly cease to be visible and become one shining mist. Flying has always fascinated me. I moved to the other side of the cabin so that I could watch the mechanic engage the other propeller. Evidently, the pilot had been observing my childlike enthusiasm for the workings of his plane.

"Countess, would you like to sit in the cockpit?"

What a question! In a flash, I moved into the snug little seat beside his. Surrounded by instruments, levers, and dials, I was momentarily in paradise.

He extended his hand and introduced himself as Hans Baumert. The poor man patiently answered every one of my questions about the plane, the instruments and their purpose. Finally, he said, "I think we must take off soon or we'll be late." Of course, I agreed. I was paying for his time. "You can remain here for the flight," he said, "or go back to your seat. Your choice." I gave my decision not a winks' thought. Once we were airborne, and he had made the proper turns to set us in the right direction, he asked, "Would you like to fly the plane?"

"Could I? I mean, really?"

He smiled at my childlike delight. He explained what I needed to do, how to hold the helm to steer the plane. His hands rested lightly on mine until he was sure I knew what to do. "What a pleasure," he said, sitting back. "You do the work and even pay me for it." He told me the route and how to read the altimeter and the direction from the dials. He seemed very pleased when I was able to make a turn on my own.

"You're quite good at this. Have you ever thought of taking up flying?"

"Not until today," I answered candidly, although now, the idea of joining the ranks of such distinguished female aviators as Earhart and Markham was very exciting. It occurred to me that the business ought to have an aeroplane. It would be more efficient for Konrad to fly to his business destinations, especially now that he was traveling so much as we finalized the sale of the factories. It would allow me to come and go as I pleased, to England or France, all over the continent. We could build an airstrip at Edelheim and at Raithschau. It was so obvious a solution, I wondered why I had never thought of it before. With great excitement, I described my idea to the pilot.

"I'd be happy to help with your project," he said. "I'm tired of charter work. The last thing I want to do is work for the military."

We exchanged a sympathetic look. Evidently, he didn't like the Nazis either. Together we spun out a plan. It was ludicrous, in a way, because I was so short of cash. But that was a temporary problem. If I really wished to have an aeroplane or two, the money could be found.

The animated discussion passed the time, but even more, it allowed me to forget where I was going and why, but when we crossed the Alps into Italy, I began to remember. Instead of feeling joy at the prospect of joining my lover, I was anguished. "*Odi et amo...*"

Before we parted, I gave Baumert my card and asked him to call after my return to Berlin. I also gave him a generous tip. He helped the hired car agent load my luggage. Perhaps he would have done it without the tip.

I'd asked for a German motorcar, but the lease agent had reserved an Alfa. No matter. I had driven one of those snappy, little roadsters for years, and it was no hardship to put this one through its paces. The weather was warm enough to drive with the top down. As I headed towards the city, I enjoyed the wind in my hair and the delicious scent of vegetation. Every home along the road had its own enclosed garden. The vines were heavy with grapes and the citrus trees laden with fruit. I could almost taste the blood oranges, their deliciously bitter-sweet flesh the color of a bruise.

Presently, I arrived at the Allessandro family villa. It was set high on one of Rome's famous hills and enclosed all around by a wall. Within the wall was a profusion of colorful plants and flowers. In Berlin, at that time of year, we were grateful for chrysanthemums and a few late blooming perennials. Here, summer had not yet even thought of ending.

I parked in the circle near the fountain. Instantly, two footmen came to open the door and take my luggage from the boot. Eva appeared on the landing at the top of the stairs. She looked lovely in a simple white dress. She made no move to descend. She waited until I reached the top step to greet me. We touched cheeks, as women of our class do on meeting.

"Welcome to Villa Rosa," she said, hooking her arm in mine to lead me into the house. The interior was as ornate as one might expect from an Italian house, multi-colored marble and gilded rococo furniture everywhere. Floor-length mirrors adorned the entrance hall. I caught sight of my reflection. How large I looked beside my diminutive companion—Gargantuan!

"Would you like something to eat, *cara*?" asked Eva. "You must be hungry after your travels."

Actually, my stomach had begun to make its needs known by becoming musical. "I could do with a bite to eat, thank you."

We went out on to the terrace, where a table was set for one. There, I was served a veritable feast of toasted bread covered with chopped tomatoes and fresh basil. I envied Eva these beautiful gifts of the garden. The basil in my herb plot had already been blackened by the cold. Next came steamed mussels in white wine and garlic on fine, hand-made pasta. I found myself soaking my bread in the fragrant sauce. Eva watched me eat with a small smile of satisfaction, although she herself ate nothing.

"Aren't you eating?" I asked.

"I ate before you arrived," she said and took a sip of wine.

Whenever we met for a meal, she rarely ate more than a few morsels, although I had taken her to the very best restaurants in Berlin. I found it curious and disappointing because I passionately enjoy good food.

After coffee, Eva said, "Perhaps you wish to bathe. Traveling is such a dusty affair."

The idea of a hot bath sounded appealing, and I agreed. With her beautiful eyes, Eva signaled to a waiting maid, who left to do her mistress's bidding. We were finally alone. I covered Eva's hand with mine.

"I am surprised to see you," she said.

This took me aback. I pride myself in always doing as I say I will do. "Why surprised?"

"You are so devoted to your work and your little family in Berlin. I half expected you to cancel your trip at the last minute."

"But I am here."

"So you are," she said, giving me a warm look, "and I'm so happy to see you."

The maid returned, and I reluctantly released Eva's hand. "Your bath is ready, *Contessa*. This way, please."

The bathroom was one of those luxurious places that one finds in Italian palaces and the best Roman hotels—a large marble pool into which one descends. The water was very hot, exactly as I like it. The muscles in my shoulders simply ached. The journey had left me tense. Spending the better part of the previous evening in surgery had probably not helped either. I made quick work of washing and then lay back to enjoy the soothing effect of the heat on my stiff muscles. After a few minutes in the delicious water, which was scented with a lovely perfume, though certainly not Eva's, I felt completely relaxed. I nearly fell asleep, but the sound of the door opening roused me to wakefulness. I assumed it was the maid returning, and I slid deeper into the water for modesty's sake. But it was Eva, carrying two glasses of red wine.

"Enjoying your bath?" she asked.

"Of course. Few pleasures compare."

"Oh, I can think of a few," she said with a sly look. She handed a glass of wine to me. "This is just a foretaste," she said, bending to whisper in my ear, "For you, I have wine…between my legs."

I nearly dropped my glass into the bath water.

"I was just about to get out and dress," I said—a blatant lie. I could have happily lain in that hot water for hours.

"No hurry, my dear. Enjoy your bath." She settled herself in a nearby chair and studied me as she sipped her wine. It was the first time she had seen me undressed. I became suddenly uncomfortable under her scrutiny, which was very odd, because I am never self-conscious about being nude. "I thought you'd be a Rubens," she said, which rankled. The suggestion that she expected me to be not merely large, but obese was especially offensive because I took such pains to remain slender. Fortunately, she amended her statement. "However, I see you are a Botticelli, and quite lovely."

While she finished her wine, Eva continued to observe me as if I were a museum piece wanting study. Finally, she rose and said, "When you have finished your bath, meet me in your room."

I waited until she had left the room to exit the bath. I toweled myself and put on my dressing gown. When I ran a brush though my hair, I discovered that I was trembling. I had waited for this moment for weeks, yet I was inexplicably fearful.

Eva was sitting in a chair beside the bed. She rose to accept a kiss, but when I reached out to touch her, she grasped my hand and held it with surprising strength. I raised my head, confused and curious. She offered no explanation. Instead, she proceeded to untie the belt of my dressing gown and let it fall away. Slowly, she ran her hands up my body, grazing my breasts, and finally, resting on my shoulders. "You are as finely made as I imagined. Only more so. What a lovely strong body. Modern. Not classical." She pulled me close for another kiss. When it ended, she whispered, "This is our time, my love. It is finally our time."

She turned down the bed and motioned for me to get in. I lay, supporting myself on my arm while I watched her undress. Surprisingly, she was shy about it, giving me a sidelong, almost demure glance. Perhaps it was only a pretense to entice me and heighten my pleasure. With her back turned, she pulled her dress and slip over her head. This time, I was not surprised to see she was wearing no undergarments. Undressed, her extreme slenderness was more shocking still, but she was beautiful, as pale and formless as a girl on the edge of womanhood. Only her slightly widened hips gave away the fact that she was a fully adult woman. She had no breasts to speak of, just dark nipples on the barest rise above her chest.

She lay down beside me, and for a long time we lay side by side gazing into one another's eyes. Finally, I attempted to take her into my arms, but she stopped me with a gentle hand against my shoulder. "No, my darling. Let me take care of you."

She eased me on to my back and began to stroke my hair. "Your hair is so pale, silvery like your voice. You are the perfect image of the Aryan woman that your Hitler talks so much about. Eyes as blue as mountain pools and this lovely golden skin." She ran her hand down my length and I shivered at her touch. She cupped my breast in her hand. "So womanly, and yet it fits you." This remark made me suddenly shy. I turned my face into the pillow, but she turned it back and began to kiss me so deeply and sensuously that my head began to spin.

"What do you like, my darling?" she asked. She gently caressed my lips with her tongue. When I tried to answer, she said, "Never mind. I know exactly. I know you as you can never imagine." I wondered how she could dare to say this. Then, as if she had heard my thoughts, she added, "You reveal yourself when you sing. Everything in your soul is in your voice. All of your fears, your hopes, your desires. I have listened very carefully."

"I sing the words of others."

"But you feel them as if they are your own. And what you choose to sing says much. What an interesting program you sang that night we met. It wasn't your idea."

"How could you know?" I asked, fascinated.

"I simply knew," she said with a shrug. "But you chose the selections, and I knew that too. When you sang Brangaene's warning from *Tristan*, I saw you all alone with your horrible duties and your fears for the future. You sense the storm ahead."

I was amazed. Never had I met anyone so musically literate and sensitive to the nuance I try to invest in my performances. Nor had anyone so completely understood the secret connection between me and the music.

No one, except Katherine.

But this thought vanished as Eva began to kiss me again. She teased my ear with her warm tongue, and then whispered. "I am about to show you who you are. Have no fear. You will enjoy it."

The sweetness of her kisses, down my neck to my throat, was driving me nearly mad. Usually, it is difficult for me to lie still and receive pleasure. I want to be active, to make the pleasure happen, but I was nearly in a stupor as she continued to bathe me with her tongue. When she reached my breasts, I was quite sure no one had ever shown them such appreciation. Her kisses, sensual at first, became more insistent, until the pressure of her lips on my nipple began to hurt.

She raised her head and smiled. "There, my darling, now you know why they were made. Not for children, but for love." Her tongue found its way along the line of fine hair that ran down my belly. Finally, she parted my legs with her small shoulders. She blew a warm breath on my sex and I trembled. The warmth of her mouth was astonishing, and the way in which she anticipated the rise and fall of my excitement even more so. Just as I reached the edge of a climax, she would change, leaving me hanging in unrealized ecstasy. She began the dance again until I was nearly writhing, and finally, after seemingly endless invitations, she let me complete the pleasure. I was still in the grip of the spasms, when her elegant fingers found a place within, I hadn't even known existed. She touched it delicately until I was once more completely at her mercy and came to her again. This was repeated several times until I was so exhausted, I begged her to stop. But she ignored my pleas and touched me with knowing fingers until she coaxed yet another climax from me. Then I had to put an end to it. "Stop," I said, "You'll kill me, if you don't."

She lifted her head and smiled. "Enough for now." She reached up and stroked my hair. "How pale it is. Silver not gold."

I was tired and perfectly relaxed. I could have slept, but to leave her unsatisfied would have been plainly rude. I allowed myself a few moments of recovery before saying, "I mean to claim the wine that was offered."

"It's yours," she said. "You may have it whenever you wish."

My arm shook as I tried to raise myself on it. "Good heavens, Eva, what have you done to me?"

She smiled cannily. "What I said I would do."

I wobbled about on my elbow for a moment and then helplessly fell back on the pillows. "I hate you," I said in jest.

"I know you do," she replied in all seriousness, "but I wish you wouldn't."

I pulled her face towards mine so that I could reassure her with a kiss. Her response revealed her need for attention. Never let it be said that I left a woman wanting, so I attempted again to rise. She put her hands on my shoulders to push me back. "My darling, there are other ways."

Once more her lips came on mine, but she had left enough space between us so that I could reach up and touch her. I needed only to come into her body and stroke her a bit before she produced a shimmering climax. I had never met a woman so constantly responsive nor so abundantly moist. Was it real?

She let her weight down on me, little weight that it was, and I forgot about my question. We slept.

When I awoke, I found myself wrapped around her slender body. My thigh was pressed against her sex, and I could feel it throbbing against me. I probed her with my fingers. After my brief rest, I felt refreshed, so I was able to be forceful. As I moved in her, she suddenly cried, "Oh, you are so right!" Within moments, she came to me.

Afterward, as we lay entwined, she said, "I dreamed of you. I imagined you before I even knew your name."

I had no idea what to make of this, so I said nothing.

We lay there for hours, making love again and again. Several times I thought that I was spent, yet I continued to find the strength to repeat the act. Finally, sublimely satisfied, we lay side by side and shared confidences.

"You have pianist's hands," said Eva, inspecting my fingers.

"I play, though not as well as you do. They are surgeon's hands, really."

"You cut people open and look inside them?"

"You know I do," I said, amused that she could doubt this very important part of my life.

"And what do you find there? Do you see their souls?"

"Of course not. I see their organs, their connective tissue, their muscles and bones..."

"I'm disappointed."

I laughed aloud, which made her frown. "Not really? What did you expect?"

"May I see? May I watch one of your operations?"

The thought of Eva in my operating theater was highly amusing, but this time, I suppressed my laughter and affected a serious expression. "Perhaps I'll allow it. If you promise not to faint."

She was not taken in by my patronizing tone. "I'm stronger than I look," she replied indignantly.

As I regarded the determined look in her eye, I had no doubt of it.

"How did you become a singer?" she asked.

"I was always musical. When I was four, my mother had a miniature piano brought from Vienna and she taught me to play. She's quite a good musician herself. In fact, she plays nearly as well as you do. At my English school, I auditioned for the student choir. The choirmaster realized that I had a decent voice and encouraged my father to hire a voice teacher. When they sent me to the convent school at Obberoth—God, how I hated that place—the precentrix, who had once been a famous opera singer, decided my voice had potential and decided to train me."

"She has given the world a great gift."

"Eva, how you exaggerate. I have a good voice, not a great one."

"It is a great voice, and I've heard many. Such a shame you couldn't have a career but being noble-born can be a curse as well as a blessing. We are trapped in our gilded cages and often cannot do that which our hearts most desire. Music is your great passion. It means more to you than any-thing, even love." It was as if she had reached into my chest and clutched my heart.

When I recovered, I said, "If I could have done anything with my life, I would have chosen to be a musician. But as a physician, I do some good."

"No doubt, but as a singer you would bring the world much beauty, and that is also doing good."

This conversation had become far too depressing. To escape it, I sug-gested we rise. Eva left me to prepare myself for the evening, and I was ac-tually grateful to be alone. As I inspected the dinner dresses I'd brought for my brief stay, I realized that every one had been chosen with an eye towards Eva's opinion. I always listened intently to her comments and compliments on my clothing and stored the information for future reference. That I should even care what she thought was quite odd. I always dress to please myself first. Even as I put on my makeup, I didn't rush through my usual routine. Because I am always dressing and undressing for surgery, and a surgical mask is quite the enemy of cosmetics, I had become extremely adept at dashing on my "face" in minutes. Not so that evening. I applied the mascara, the rouge, the lipstick with great care.

The glow of approval in Eva's eyes when I joined her in the dining room was my reward, but it took second place to my hunger. I was ravenous, especially after depleting my energy in our afternoon pursuits. The meal featured an excellent beefsteak sautéed with green peppercorns and wine. As usual, my companion ate little. Eva began with a smaller portion but even so was unable to consume it.

My physician's antennae started to twitch, and I began to entertain the possibility of pathology. Sated, I gazed at Eva with different eyes and saw that she was thin and pale enough to be consumptive. However, I had never heard her cough, and when my ear was against her chest during lovemaking, her lungs sounded perfectly clear. Of course there was the possibility of myriad malignancies, but I had been over every inch of her body and had found no lumps or thickening anywhere. Our adventures had taken me places that I wouldn't ordinarily probe with a new lover, but our time together was brief and not to be squandered on propriety. In short, I could attest to her apparent health everywhere my eyes, mouth, and hands had been able to roam.

"What are you thinking?" Eva asked, perceiving that I had left the conversation to dialogue with myself.

"I was considering the fact that you are so thin but realized you are apparently healthy."

She laughed. "Do you always think like a doctor?"

"Yes, of course. It's an essential part of my personality. I can't turn it on and off at will."

"That surprises me. You have such self-discipline and control, I would expect you to change roles as easily as you change clothes."

"It's not quite that tidy," I replied, stirring crystals of brown sugar into my coffee. Ordinarily I drank my coffee without sugar, but the strong Italian coffee defeated even my tolerance for bitterness.

"Everything about you is tidy, Margarethe. Your perfect life in Berlin, your career, your brilliant management of your family fortune. You could do with some chaos to keep it interesting. All true creativity comes from the dark."

"Dusky Dionysius, spurn not your fair brother, Apollo," I mused. "No, thank you. Chaos comes without bidding. No need to invite it."

She smiled her little knowing smile. "But you have. Otherwise, you would not be here." Mercifully, she changed the subject. "Come, let's finish our coffee in the music room." She clapped her hands to summon a servant. She asked him to relocate the coffee service and bring us grappa.

Naturally, she expected me to sing. "But this time you may sing anything you wish," she said, sitting down at the piano.

I gave her a deep, mock bow. "How gracious of you, Lady d'Allessandro."

She waved me off with a flick of her wrist. "Stop. I merely wish to see what you will choose."

"Another study of my soul, my dear?"

"But of course. What else?"

"You probably won't know how to play the selections I choose."

"So you play," she said, getting up from the piano. She made herself comfortable in a wing chair and looked quite like a queen enthroned.

"My keyboard skills hardly approach yours. Can you tolerate it?" I asked, exchanging places with her.

"Stop being modest, Margarethe. It doesn't become you. Go on. You play and I'll listen." I played a few runs of scales to warm up while I considered what to sing. I could tease her by choosing pieces that meant nothing to me, but even then, she would say I had revealed something. I decided to indulge her and began to play "*Gestillte Sehnsucht*." It was written for an alto and posed no great demands on my voice. Eva closed her eyes while I sang, apparently swept up in the music.

"Exquisite," she said, when I'd finished.

"It's really much better with the string accompaniment. My son plays it very well."

"Your son? You never speak of your children. How old is he?"

"Twenty-two now. A medical student in Munich."

"Show me a photograph." Even I, the most negligent of mothers, always had some pictures of my children. I asked a servant to fetch my bag and located my son's photograph in the miniature album. It showed him in his Oxford robes. "Wilhelm Frederich," I said, handing Eva the photo. "'Willi' to us."

"Oh, Margarethe, he's magnificent! What a beautiful mouth. *So sensual*," she said with great feeling. "Twenty-two, you say? You must have been a child when you gave birth to him."

"Why do you say such things? Having looked me up in the *Almanach*, you know precisely how old I am."

"Yes, but you don't look it."

My face flamed at the compliment. Usually, I'm immune to flattery, but when it came from Eva, I basked in it. Why had I allowed her such power over me?

"What next?" she asked.

"Schubert?"

"Oh, dear. Another German night." She waved her hand to indicate that I should proceed. The song I sang described my experience with Eva's ever-present perfume. Like a drug, it left me helpless.

"Schubert is so very modern sounding at times," she remarked, when I'd concluded. "He occasionally makes the moderns seem like romantic anachronisms. *Winterreise* amazes me."

"I sang it once," I said with great bravado.

"But it's written for a baritone!"

"So? I can invoke a male persona when I have a mind to."

"Yes, I've noticed. Well then, my darling, sing something heroic."

I thought for a moment. "This piece wants orchestral accompaniment, but I shall do my best." I chose a Mahler song that demanded a great deal of the singer, from *pianissimo* melancholy reflection to a stentorian declamation at the conclusion.

"*Brava*, Margarethe! There is my Valkyrie!" From the tone of her voice, I wasn't sure this was a compliment. I closed the cover over the piano keys.

"One more," she begged. "Just one."

"Did you have something in mind?"

"No, you choose. It's your program."

So I sang "Marietta's Lied" from "Korngold's *Die tote Stadt*. It was on the higher end of my range, but I could manage it now that I had been singing for a while and my voice had warmed into flexibility. When I reached the high notes, I needed the air so I released them as I would in a concert hall rather than the containment of Eva's music room. The last melancholy phrases of the coda faded away. I looked up and saw tears glistening on Eva's cheeks.

"It can never be," Eva said in a mournful voice. "It can never be…"

I knelt beside her and put my arms around her. As she wept silently against my shoulder, the scent of her perfume rising from her warm hair was intoxicating. I kissed her forehead, her eyes, hoping to elicit an explanation or at least a response. But she was nearly limp in my arms. Finally, she sat up and gazed at me with a puzzled look. She allowed me to ease her to her feet. We went upstairs, but she resisted my attempt to steer her towards my room.

"No," she said, "I must be alone." The strange expression on her face told me this was no time to argue. So I kissed her forehead and found it chilled. She left me standing in the hall as she headed to what I surmised to be her quarters. I stood watching for a long moment, futilely hoping she might change her mind.

Chapter 7

When my head found the pillow, I instantly fell asleep, exhausted from travel and exuberant sexual activity. Fortunately, the ability to fall asleep on command is one of my talents, an invaluable skill in a surgeon, for sleep is so often interrupted. For the same reason, I can be alert at the lightest touch of a hand or a whispered word. So, I was completely astonished to awake the next morning around five, my usual waking time, and find Eva in bed beside me. Her hair was unbound and covered the pillow in a dark cascade. Her distinctive perfume filled my nostrils. She lay at the very edge of the bed with no covering. She was as still as the dead.

I rose on my elbow to confirm that she was still breathing. She was, albeit with the shallowest of breaths. I had never seen her asleep. For the first time, I was not at the mercy of her judgments, nor anxious that she had discerned some aspect of my personality that I would prefer to keep private.

Eventually, she stirred. "Oh, *mia carina...*" she murmured.

"When did you come in?" I asked, kissing her.

"Not long after we parted," she said with a yawn, "but you were sleeping so beautifully I couldn't bear to wake you."

I put my hand on her arm and found it cold. "Get under the covers," I ordered. "You're chilled."

She got up so that I could pull up the duvet. I was surprised to see that she was wearing a white nightgown so simple, one might find such a thing in a convent.

Once I was sure she had gone back to sleep, I got out of bed. I drew myself a bath, not bothering with the maid because it was so early, and really, I preferred to be alone. After bathing, I dressed in linen trousers and a cotton blouse and went out to the little sitting room overlooking the garden.

My intention was to look over my paper one more time for grammatical errors. While I can speak Italian quite well, writing it, especially writing in medical language, had proven to be far more difficult than I had expected. It was completely a self-made challenge. The conference officers had offered to take the paper in German and have it translated, but I had insisted.

Presently, I felt a gentle hand at the back of my neck, followed by the press of warm lips. "Good morning, *cara*," Eva breathed into my ear.

By then, the sun had risen in the sky. Hours had passed since I'd first sat down to work. I suddenly remembered my glasses and whipped them off, not wanting Eva to see that I'd reached an age when I needed them.

I sat up to receive Eva's kiss. She caressed the inside of my thigh. "Trousers, this morning. How chic!" She stood back and gave my blouse a critical look. "You have too many buttons fastened. Here like this." She undid two of them. I wasn't wearing anything beneath, so the cleavage between my breasts was now visible. "Much better," she said, reaching into my blouse to give me a caress. "Much better, indeed." Then she sat down beside me. "I've ordered some breakfast for us. You will take coffee with milk in the morning?" At the mention of food, my stomach growled in eager anticipation.

"What are you writing?" Eva asked, snatching the paper out of my hands. "Good heavens, Margarethe, who can read this scribble?"

"I can," I said defensively and reached for it.

"No," she said, blocking my hands. "I want to see." She spread out the sheets on the table. "This is wrong, my love," she said pointing to a word on the second page. "You don't 'make after the first cut.' You say, 'After making the first cut, etc.'"

"I mean *Einschnitt*," I said, opening my Italian-German medical dictionary.

"Oh, *incision*! That's something different." She picked up my pen and made the correction before I could find the entry in my dictionary. Then she went through the rest of the paper and did the same, finding a few horrors in the process. It had never occurred to me to ask her to read it.

"I can't vouch for all the medical terms, although I can guess their meanings from the Latin or the Greek, and they seem to be used properly," she said, handing my pen back to me. "Otherwise, everything is correct."

"Thank you," I said, capping my pen.

"I would like to come tomorrow. May I?"

"You won't be bored?"

"I've read the paper, and I wasn't bored. Not at all. And, I want to see what you do when you are a doctor."

"I'm flattered…and honored. But of course."

I cleared away the papers into my briefcase. By that time our breakfast had arrived. It was served on a little bistro table on the balcony, where we could see the garden and inhale the delicious scents of the late season flowers. We drank coffee with steamed milk. Eva nibbled on one of those sweet pastries the Romans call *cornetti dolci*. I was treated to a proper German breakfast of rolls, cheese, cold meats, and the obligatory soft-boiled egg.

"I love to watch you eat," said Eva, watching me with a smile. "You enjoy it so much. You consume life. That's what I love about you." She laid a hand on my thigh and began to stroke it gently. "What would you like to do today, *cara*?"

"You mean, apart from making love?"

She smiled indulgently. "That we can certainly do, but what else?"

I craned my neck so that I could see over the rail of the balcony. "I'd very much like to see your garden and to speak to your gardener. Horticulture is one of my interests."

She laughed softly. "What doesn't interest you?"

I thought for a moment. "Politics. I despise it."

She sighed. "So do I. It's all Pietro speaks of, and it is so complicated, I've given up trying to follow what he's saying. So I don't listen any more or think about it. Besides there's nothing I can do about it, so why should I worry?"

"My sentiments exactly," I replied. "But I could do something about it. I have influence through my holdings, and many of them—the steel plant, the chemical plants, and the coal mines—are of strategic interest to the government. I try to give them just enough in the hopes that they'll leave us alone. My great fear is that they will attempt to nationalize everything." I was surprised to hear myself say so much about the subject. I was rarely so frank with Konrad.

She pointedly cleared her throat, which made me think she understood that I hadn't meant to say so much. "Allow me time to dress, and then we shall walk in my garden."

I met her on the lower-level terrace. She was again wearing a white dress, a wide-brimmed hat, sunglasses, and she was carrying a parasol. "I hate the sun," she explained as she opened the parasol. "And you, my sweet, should be careful of the sun too. Not even a hat?"

"I despise hats," I muttered.

"Which surprises me. You're so careful of your dress, and a woman is not quite dressed without a hat."

"They're silly," I said, "Like plumage on a bird. Unnecessary."

"But they're so delightful. What a pleasure to find a new hat!"

I ended the conversation about hats by taking her arm and saying, "Come. Show me your garden."

She asked a servant to locate the gardener and soon he joined us on the path. He was dressed carefully and surprisingly clean and neat for a gardener. Their type always seems to carry a bit of the earth they love around with them. He patiently explained the principles behind the garden's design and the horticultural demands of the plants. Eva hung back a little, listening to our conversation. I wondered if she cared at all about what we were saying or was simply exploiting another opportunity to observe me and draw conclusions.

At the end of our tour, we rested on a bench. Eva, ever anxious to avoid the sun, sat on the shaded side. She lightly stroked my arm, which caused me to shiver. "I love this pale hair on your arms," she said. "Your skin is so golden and the hair nearly white."

"My hair bleaches in the sun. It makes the white hair less noticeable."

"You worry so about your age, Margarethe. You are still beautiful and appear much younger than you are."

"But I'm older than you and very conscious of it."

She laughed. "I never think about it! Why do you?"

I knew the answer, but I couldn't say it, not even to myself. Admitting that I needed her approval would be too humiliating.

"There are some things in the city I wish to show you today," Eva said, diverting me from further self-indulgence. "I'll wait for you while you change into street clothes."

❊❊❊

We drove into the city with the roadster top raised because Eva refused to tolerate the wind disturbing her hair. I suggested a scarf, but she cocked a shoulder at me. She took me to a shop on the Via Condotti that offered men's as well as women's hats, an odd combination that one would never see in Berlin. All the hats in the shop were pressed from the finest felt. Evidently, she was known to the staff and chatted cheerfully with the head clerk. However, when it came to business, she asked to see the owner.

A short, bearded man came out from the back. When Eva explained what she had in mind, he gazed at me with some alarm. The reason, of course, was his height—and mine. He needed to stand on a stool to measure my head. Of course, I could have sat but that would have been an even greater insult. He gave quick instructions to the head clerk and presently two hat boxes appeared. He opened the first and produced a classic fedora in camel hair. He placed it on my head and invited me to inspect myself in the mirror. To my surprise, the hat suited me. It gave me a kind of rakish charm that was fairly irresistible.

"Too light," declared Eva. "We need something darker."

The man opened another hat box and handed me a black version. If the camel hair hat made me look quite the roué, black enhanced the effect. It was perfect. My only worry was that it might recall the infamous British novelist, Radclyffe Hall, whose trademark was a black fedora. Of course, her notorious obscenity trial had taken place ages ago and surely no one remembered it now.

"So," said Eva as we left the hat shop. "Now you have a hat you like and you have no reason to go bare-headed this winter."

"I'm surprised you care."

She stared at me. "Of course, I care, Margarethe, more than you can imagine." She gave me an indignant huff and headed down the street in the direction of the motorcar.

After I settled myself behind the wheel, I aped the role of a chauffeur. "I await your orders, Madam. What is our next destination?"

"First to the confectionery and then to the Forum."

We went to the chocolate shop where Eva purchased two truffles covered with white chocolate. Each was crowned with a dot of pink raspberry crème. They looked exactly like miniature breasts.

"I prefer dark chocolate," I said.

"These are not for you." She gave me a little pinch on the thigh. "But I cannot bear to deprive you." She instructed the clerk to add another truffle to the box, this one covered in dark chocolate.

We headed to the Forum and parked near a plot where they were excavating the ruins from ancient times. Eva hiked up her skirt and, without a moment's hesitation, stepped over the fence. Fortunately, it was Sunday and there was no one about. I glanced at the sign which clearly forbade trespassing and stared with dismay as she boldly pranced into the excavated area.

"In Germany, when a sign says, 'Keep out,' we do," I scolded.

"Yes, I know. Germans are very good at following rules. But come on, Margarethe. Don't be a coward!"

How dare she dare me like that! Now, I had no choice but to follow her. She sat down on a large fragment of marble, evidently part of the ruins, and motioned for me to sit beside her. She opened the box of truffles. "Chocolate wasn't invented in her time, but I am sure it is very dear to her." In answer to my quizzical expression, she explained, "Venus is here. This is where her temple stood in imperial times." I surveyed the ground but saw only the line strung to indicate the perimeter of a structure.

She held the delectable chocolate under my nose. "Now kiss it." I grinned mischievously and she quickly snatched it back. "Don't eat it, Margarethe. A little kiss, that's all. Be quick or the *carabinieri* may turn us out!" She glanced anxiously at the policemen at the far end of the street, but they were busy talking to one another and seemingly ignoring us.

I gave the little chocolate breast a quick kiss and she did the same to the other. She opened her bag and removed a small folding knife, which she used to open a small hole in the earth. She carefully inserted the two truffles. Set together, they looked, as intended, like miniature breasts with their rosy nipples pointing to the sky.

Her eyes closed. "We must pray, my darling," she said taking my hand, "We must thank her for favoring us with her pleasure…and we must ask to know the blessing of desire until the end of our days." She covered the hole with soil and rested her hand on it for a moment. I guessed she was adding a secret intention of her own. "We must wait until we return to the villa to complete the prayer," she said. I did not require an explanation of that part.

She made a beeline to the barrier and was over it in an instant. I hurried to catch up with her.

"Now, my love, this is only the beginning," she said. "Are you willing to learn more?"

I was intrigued. "Let's see."

On our way to our next destination, the National Museum, Eva said, "I am her gift to you. She has told me so."

"Has she now?" I asked, with more mockery in my voice than I'd intended, but I had been suppressing laughter during the entire bizarre ritual.

"Oh, Margarethe, don't be such a skeptic. I know you are a scientist, and worse, a German! But there are many things to learn in this life and they don't all yield to your precious logic. You must open your eyes and see!" She took the remaining truffle from the box and offered it to me. "Here, little girl, you may have your sweet now."

We arrived at the museum and Eva, although obviously impatient to show me something in particular, allowed me to study the exhibits. Finally, we entered the room that Eva intended me to see, but not through the correct door, which upset her. She took me by the arm to escort me to the proper entrance. I wanted to take in the statuary near the door, but she tugged me along. "Never mind that," she said impatiently. "There is only one thing you need to see. We can come back later for the rest."

She led me to a reclining female nude who lay on her belly, evidently asleep. The statue was a study in physical perfection. The face was so classical, it was neither female nor male.

"Touch it," Eva encouraged. I glanced at the guard at the door, but conveniently he turned around and looked the other way. I ran my fingertips along the cool marble, so smooth to my touch.

"Except for the temperature, it could be alive!" I exclaimed.

"It is alive," she said. "This is you."

"I?" Actually, I saw a resemblance, less in the face, but in the form of the body—long limbs, well-muscled, but not overly so, the buttocks well defined, but still soft.

"Come here, my love, and you will see what I mean." She took my hand and gently pulled me around to the other side. I admired the perfect angle of the head, the definition of the shoulder muscles, the lovely curve of the breasts, but then I saw it. Between the legs was a perfectly formed penis.

"A hermaphrodite," I whispered, finally perceiving the facts. "You think I'm this?"

"Yes. It is you. As you truly are. Hermaphroditus was so beautiful, men and women killed themselves over his beauty."

"Apart from my husband, all of my lovers, male and female are still alive. At least I hope they are," I said with a quick, nervous laugh. "Good God, Eva! A hermaphrodite?"

"Don't make light, Margarethe. This lesson is essential."

"Essential to what?"

She emitted a string of invectives in Italian. Quite a few I didn't understand. It was, however, abundantly evident that she was exasperated with me. "Margarethe, pay attention." She reached out and touched the statue's penis. "You think you don't have this, but you do. Except it's not between your legs, it's here." She reached up and touched my forehead with her fingertips. "This is true of all of us, but most perfectly in you."

"I am a woman."

"Of course, you are. Most obviously so, at least in your body. But you see, you are both. The perfection is to be both at once, as it is in you." She looked, if possible, more frustrated than before. "Tell me that you understand, my darling. I don't know how better to explain it."

"I do understand."

"No, you don't! You're thinking about it!"

In fact, I understood completely, and her insistence was annoying. "As you have probably observed, I am not lacking in intellectual capacity."

"It is not a matter of intellect. Wisdom requires no thinking. The truth is instantly apparent. 'Self-evident,' as your philosophers would say."

"Why do you show me this?"

"So that you can see yourself as you are. There is nothing more erotic than to be able, as you are, to be both male and female. You love with such strength and aggression and yet you swoon for your lover like any woman." She took my face in her hands. "Margarethe, please tell me you understand!"

I was growing uncomfortable, most especially because the guard had heard our raised voices and was staring at us. "Let's get out of here!" I snarled.

I was sullen as we drove back to the villa. It was enough to participate in her ridiculous ritual in broad view of anyone who might happen by, but the temerity to suggest I was mentally a hermaphrodite was beyond the pale! For the span of our drive, I thought only of how much I hated her.

When we arrived at the villa, she went off and left me to my own devices. I was still in a temper, so I was glad for the privacy. I went to my room to read and then decided I'd rather have a nap. Not long after, the door opened.

"Are you finished with your little fit of pique?" asked Eva.

"Are you finished with your ridiculous lessons?"

"Perhaps. You're not ready to learn. Why force you?" She turned to leave, but I jumped out of bed and caught her arm, holding it more firmly than I had intended. She regarded my hand with a frown. "Margarethe, why are you being so difficult?" She twisted her arm out of my grasp. "Stop. I despise pain except when it is meant for pleasure."

The idea that I had caused her pain distressed me. "I never intended to hurt you."

"You forget your own strength. You are large and powerful. You are unaware of the boundaries of your own body."

I saw the opportunity for a seduction. "Perhaps you will teach me."

She laughed. "I'm trying, but you are a most unwilling student. You must always be in control. Relax, *cara*. No one here is going to hurt you." I attempted to kiss her, but she turned her head. "Are you quite done with your anger?"

"Yes," I assured her, "it's passed."

"That's good, because we cannot make love with your ire between us. I won't allow it."

Soon, we found ourselves between the sheets to renew our passion. We took our time, deliberately drawing out the pleasure because we knew we would soon be parted. Afterwards, Eva nestled in the crook of my arm, while I lazily stroked her hair.

"You belong to me now," she said. "Though you may leave me, you will always be mine."

This remark puzzled me, but I said only, "So I shall be yours."

"You don't know it yet," she replied. "You are still learning."

We went downstairs to have our supper. Once again, the expenditure of so much energy had left me famished. I demolished a plateful of Osso Bucco, a bowl of pasta, and a great dish of Roman artichokes. "Delicious!" I declared, sitting back from the table.

Eva gave me a bemused smile. "There's more in the kitchen, I'm sure."

"I'm always hungry. This body requires so much fuel."

"Then eat, my love. You must remain strong for me. I have plans for you later in your bed."

Such activity would have to wait. After dinner we went into the music room. I was an audience of one as Eva played Chopin and Fauré. Then she gazed at me shyly and announced, "I've written some songs for you."

"Really?" I asked, delighted. "Let me see."

She handed me the manuscript. As I sight-sang the composition in my head, I saw that she had written me an elegant song cycle. She had taken the text from Catullus, including some of my favorites. However, she had omitted the poem that best described my feelings for her, the one I had remembered at the air field. I hummed one of her songs. The infectious melody was perfectly charming.

"I would never have thought to use a Latin text for a modern song."

"Why not? Your Carl Orff used the *Carmina Burana*." She looked uncharacteristically shy when she asked, "Will you sing them for me?"

"Play them first and let me hear. You've given me a few high notes I wouldn't have expected."

"But you can reach them. I've heard you."

"Always trying to make me stretch, aren't you?"

"Of course."

I sang her songs, as well as I could, despite the stretch. It was a competent first reading. Even Eva had to agree.

"I had no idea you were a composer," I said, making notes on my copy of the score.

"Oh, I'm not. I dabble from time to time. But I was inspired to write these by your longing. You're always singing of longing. *Sehnsucht, Sehnsucht, Sehnsucht*! Like Goethe, you're always pining for the Eternal Feminine."

"Yes. The longing. The imperative of desire. It is *everything*."

She smiled. "So, you do understand."

Chapter 8

When I woke the next morning, I was painfully aware that my time with Eva would shortly come to an end. I would soon return to Berlin and my life there—my arguments with Katherine, my disaster-prone charges at the Charité, and my duties as the mistress of the House of Langenberg-Edelheim. For a brief moment, I dearly wished that I could be locked forever in Eva's villa, where I could drug myself with her perfume and drown in her ever-flowing moisture.

It was impossible. In fact, it was barely imaginable. Even that very day, I would don my dark suit so that I could deliver my paper at the Institute. In the face of losing my soul to Eva's charms and learning her painful lessons, which exposed my personality like a shockingly unforgiving photograph, I cheerfully welcomed the duties of the day. I rose and bathed. Then I went out to the balcony, where I could practice delivering my paper to the garden. When I finished, I turned around and saw I had another audience.

"*Brava*," said Eva. "Your accent is perfect, but you sound so solemn."

"Breast cancer is a solemn matter," I replied, bending to kiss her.

"I'm sure, but even your shoulders droop when you speak of it. Stand tall, Margarethe. You have a military background. Good posture should come naturally to you."

"I sometimes wonder what I might have been, had I been raised otherwise."

"But you are, as you are. I am, as I am. You had so many opportunities. You went to Oxford. You became a physician. How I envy you."

I hardly knew how to respond to this, but I said, "You're an intelligent woman, who's made the most of her resources."

"Have I?" She emitted a long sigh. "I'm merely the wife of a minor diplomat, and my education has been as I could find it," she said with a bitterness that surprised me. "I once thought I might like to be a physician. But of course, it was out of the question. My family had engaged me to Pietro when I was barely a woman. But medicine has always interested me. I studied the anatomical texts, and they have enriched my appreciation of art. I follow the medical developments in the newspapers, which is how I first learned about you."

I was intrigued but said nothing in the hopes she would say more. Fortunately, she was in a story-telling mood and went on.

"One of my husband's duties is coordinating international medical conferences. So, I scan the newspapers and clip interesting items for him. I found a story about you and your conference in London on breast cancer. I was fascinated by the photograph printed in the paper. You looked so serious, as always, and so perfectly German—blond, nobly featured...striking. But it was the look in your eyes. I saw that you had a soul, something I can't say about all Germans. I put the clipping into Pietro's correspondence folder so that he would find it, but then I took it out to look at it again...and again. Finally, I just snatched it away and hid it in my jewelry case."

"I'm flattered," I said, although the idea of someone venerating my photograph in that way was a bit troubling.

"Imagine my surprise when I came to Berlin, and I saw that I could read about you in the society pages, day after day. 'Countess Stahle entertained Maestro Strauss and his wife, Pauline. Countess Stahle will be the mezzo soloist in Bach's *B minor Mass*...' Imagine my delight when I realized you were one of us and a musician as well! Once I discovered that you sang regularly in the cathedral, I became a devout Catholic. When you gave concerts to benefit your hospital, I attended every one, dragging Pietro along, although he hates music and sitting for concerts especially. He once asked me why I was so fixated on you. I said, 'she has the most amazing voice and I *must* hear it.' He merely shook his head. Of course, he understood nothing, being a man with little imagination."

"Why not simply call at my house and introduce yourself?"

"I had no idea what I wanted from you."

"But now you know?"

"Yes."

I waited for her to tell me, but she did not elaborate. Meanwhile, I had been so absorbed in the conversation that I'd neglected to remove my glasses. I hastily whipped them off.

"Oh, don't hide your glasses, Margarethe. I know how old you are. But, *cara*, it doesn't matter. I love you exactly as you are."

This declaration seemed to require a like response. "I love you too."

A shadow of sadness passed over her face. "You don't love me. You need me. You need me because I know who you are. But you don't love me." Her eyes began to glisten with unshed tears. "But no matter."

"How could you bear these days together when you think I don't love you?" I asked.

"Because I'm selfish. I wanted you to myself." I tried to approach but she shook her head and retreated into the house.

There was no time to reflect. It was closing on seven o'clock, and the conference began in two hours. I went inside to don my professional attire and organize my papers.

After our difficult conversation, I expected to go to the conference alone, but when I came downstairs, Eva was waiting for me in the entry hall. She was striking in a dark-green suit. In such a tailored look, she could easily pass as a professional woman.

"We must go," I said. "I mustn't be late, and I don't really know the way."

"Don't worry. Paolo will drive us. He knows."

We got into her motorcar, a large Mercedes, much like mine at home, and her man drove us to the headquarters of the Institute.

Some of the members knew me from other conferences, and they greeted me with great warmth. When I introduced Eva, they looked curious that a non-medical person should wish to attend. Some of the films would be quite graphic. I wondered whether Eva's sensibilities could tolerate them, but she listened attentively to the proceedings, never flinching nor turning away. When my turn to speak came, she gave my hand a little squeeze and wished me luck.

I conveyed the greetings of the Charité, whose study results I would report, and of my mentor, Ferdinand Sauerbruch. This was met with warm applause, for the professor was known all over Europe. I began to read my paper. Whenever I came to a place where Eva had made a correction, I glanced at her. Each time, I was greeted by her knowing smile and a nod.

I thought to myself that she would make the perfect wife. Her mate would always shine in her eyes.

When I sat down, she whispered directly into my ear, "You were excellent, *cara*. Your accent made you sound like a Roman. But most of all, I found your ideas very interesting."

"You understood what I was saying?"

"Some of it. More, now that I've heard the entire conference."

There was a break after the next speaker. While he'd been talking, an idea had occurred to me. "Eva, you could study medicine," I said during the intermission. "I could put in a word at the university. The dean is a..."

"It's impossible. Pietro would never allow it," she said, cutting me off. Then she put her hand to my lips. "Speak no more of it, my love. Don't break my heart."

At that moment, I felt a hand clap my shoulder, and I turned around to see Charles Calder. I was completely disarmed because his name hadn't been on the roster of attendees.

I took refuge in bravado. "By Jove, it's the man himself. Why didn't you tell me you were coming?" I asked, throwing myself into his open arms.

"It was a last-minute decision, really. And I wanted to surprise you."

He hugged me with great enthusiasm, and we thumped one another on the back like old school chums. Finally, I remembered my manners. "Eva, I'd like you to meet one of my very dearest friends. Charles Calder and I were surgical fellows together at Barts. Now he's chief of surgery there."

I introduced Eva, producing such facts about her as I could, which only served to tell me how little I actually knew about her. Charles thrust out his hand and grinned. He was a delicate man, which his coloring, dark hair, pale skin, and absurdly blue eyes, accentuated. He had the ruddiness that so suits the English. Just the cheeks blush, leaving everything else delightfully pale. Eva offered her hand.

"I am delighted to meet you, Dr. Calder," said Eva in a astonishingly good English. I had no idea that she could even understand the language, never mind speak it. Of course, wives of diplomats are expected to be as multilingual as their husbands.

"Countess, the pleasure is all mine," said Charles, kissing her hand. He wasn't usually given to ostentatious displays, but she was the kind of woman who inspired such old-fashioned manners. "I do hope you're keeping Meg out of mischief." This remark caused me to blush to the very roots of my hair. Fortunately, Charles was so taken with Eva, he had eyes only for her.

"Margarethe, perhaps your friend would like to join us for lunch?" Eva suggested.

"I don't mean to impose," said Charles. "But I had to say hello to the old girl. You understand."

"It's no imposition," replied Eva. I fear I stared, realizing that her English was far better than her German. I wondered why, despite my ear for languages, I had never guessed. "I would be pleased to offer the hospitality of my house to one of Margarethe's friends."

So it was agreed. We moved down a chair, and Charles took a seat beside me. After the closing remarks, we headed off forthwith, although Charles and I had been invited to a reception. In the motorcar, Charles and I conducted our usual post-mortem on the conference, a dissection of the proceedings, and most especially the response to my paper. We decided that it had been well-received.

After Charles and I exhausted the medical topics, we exchanged information about our families, eventually approaching the subject we both dreaded. "How is Alex?" I finally asked.

"Oh, she's still angry with you after her last visit to Berlin."

"That was quite a scene," I said, glancing over to Eva, who seemed uninterested in the conversation. Now that I knew her English was perfect, I was anxious about what she heard.

Charles sighed. "I fear the situation has not gotten better. Mother's looking after her in my absence. But I worry about Alex's health." He tapped his temple with his forefinger.

Now it was my turn to sigh. "Can nothing be done for her?"

"I haven't a clue where to start."

"You're not a psychiatrist, Charles. Engage one at once! It's essential."

Eva suddenly asked, "Who is Alex?"

"Forgive us, Countess," Charles said. "Alexandra is my sister, and she's been quite ill. Meg and Alex were once very close."

Eva turned her eyes on me, and I realized she was putting the pieces together. There was no judgment in her expression, save a raised a brow. After that, Charles and I talked of our old friends at Barts, particularly our former mentor, Harry Abrams, who had suffered a recent spell of poor health. During this conversation, Eva genuinely lost interest and took in the view from the window.

As much as I was glad of my chance encounter with Charles, I was also glad when he departed. My time with Eva was drawing to a close. I hated to waste a single moment, even for so close a friend as Charles. When he announced that he was ready to leave, Eva offered her driver to take him back to the city. I walked him out to the motorcar.

He looked me directly in the eyes. As we are the same height, this gesture is especially effective. "Come now, Meg. What are you up to?" He waited for me to answer, but I continued to engage his gaze and remained silent. "Does Katherine know you're here?"

"Yes, of course."

"Well, then," he said with a shrug and averted his eyes. "You're a big girl. I trust you know what you're doing and can look after yourself."

"Please keep this between us, Charles," I said as he got into the motorcar.

"Of course." He smiled. "What is there to say?"

When I returned to the solarium where I had left Eva, she said to me, with a wink, "*Cara*, you look very tired. I think you could use a little nap."

After making love, we lay in one another's arms and mused. Eva remarked on the downy hair that ran along my lower spine to my buttocks. She described my scent to me, using wine vocabulary, which amused me. She explored my interior, asking questions about the anatomical structures her fingers found. She listened to my answers intently.

"Does it excite you to examine a woman?" She asked, "or a man for that matter?"

"No," I replied bluntly.

"How can that be? Surely, if a beautiful woman appeared in your consulting room, you would notice."

"Of course, I would notice, but I would put aside any attraction I felt for her. It's one of the first things we learn in clinical work—detachment and unfailing attention to modesty. Otherwise, the reverse could be true. An ugly patient could cause revulsion. Either way, it would impair objectivity and interfere with the doctor's judgment."

"But what of the reverse? Do your patients ever fall in love with you?"

I shrugged. "No one's ever said, so I have no idea."

"I would fall in love with you."

I kissed the top of her head. "Then I'm grateful you're not my patient."

✽✽✽

After dinner, I sang the songs she had written, better this time, and she was pleased. I sang no German music, only some French songs she requested, and then we went to bed. I succeeded in mustering the strength for the act once more.

I lay awake, but Eva instantly fell asleep. She slept so quietly that several times I reached out to touch her to assure myself that she was alive. I had never known anyone to be so still in sleep, barely breathing. At one point, I put my ear to her chest to listen to the air exchange. She was breathing, but so lightly, I wondered how her lungs could inflate. And she was cold to the touch. Her body temperature dropped precipitously in sleep. Combined with her extreme pallor and thin frame, her sleeping state was reminiscent of the final stages of consumption or cancer, when the body is still animated, but only a thin thread of life separates it from the tomb.

With a chill, I turned my mind from such thoughts. Instead, I reflected on the day. I reviewed my presentation at the Institute and decided that I had done a creditable job. By then, I was close to regaining my usual state of mind, which comforted me, and I fell asleep.

✽✽✽

I was awake before Eva and followed my now usual routine of getting up to bathe and dress before she rose. I have never been very good at leave-taking.

I despise it, actually. In my career as a rake, I seldom spent an entire night with a lover. My usual strategy was to slip away in the gray light of dawn before he or she awoke. I now wished that I could simply be off in my little hired Alfa on my way to the airfield, but Eva awoke while I was bathing, and she ambushed me on the way to the dressing room.

"You must eat something, my love, to be strong for your travels." This injunction, so practical and caring, touched me. She caught me around the waist. "Were you able to find what you came for?" she asked.

I really had no answer, for I had no idea what I had sought, save an opportunity to be alone with a woman whom I desired. That had been achieved. But for all the rest, all the unexpected revelations, I'd had no expectation. "Yes," I answered, "I suppose so."

"There is so much more I can teach you. Perhaps another time. We must plan it." She gave me one of her sly smiles and went off to dress.

Shortly, our breakfast arrived on the little table on the balcony. We sat together over coffee with steamed milk and a flash of cinnamon on the foam. Eva fed me bits of her *cornetto*, so that I might linger on her fingertips.

"You must consider Signore Gürtner's invitation to sing Octavian."

"Oh, it's sport between us. It's been going on for years."

"It's not a game, *cara*. You have the voice and it's time."

"No," I said, "The time has passed. I'm too old to sing Octavian. How can a woman past forty sing the role of a boy who's only seventeen?" Even as I said this, I kept the truth from her, that I had already signed the contract to sing the role. This was a rather large lie of omission, but I desperately needed to reserve something from Eva, some part of me that remained private, despite her incessant probing of my psyche.

"You're not too old," she said caressing the inside of my thigh. "It's exactly the right time. You're at an age when you can understand both Octavian's love song and the Marschallin's. You must tell Signore Gürtner you will sing. When you do, I'll be in the audience *every* night."

Even as we tarried over our coffee, I was aware of the clock ticking away, devouring the remaining time with my lover.

"I'll accompany you to the airfield," said Eva.

In truth, I was looking forward to a solitary ride so that I could make the transition to my other life, my real life. Eva pouted at my long consideration of the idea. In the end, I couldn't deny her.

She explained the arrangements as we got into my little hired car. A taxi would bring her into the city, and then her chauffeur would fetch her from the shopping district. She had planned it all down to the last detail, including the street on which her driver would meet her.

While I drove, she rested her hand on my thigh to remind me of her claim. She stopped me from driving directly to the place where I had agreed to meet the lease agent. "Pull over here," she instructed, and I did. "One more time, *cara*. One more time for remembrance," she said, and guided my hand under her dress. So I made love to her in broad daylight in the middle of the car park of the Rome airport. When she had given me what I sought, she reached into the pocket of my suit coat to find the perfectly pressed linen handkerchief my maids always stowed for me and offered it to me to cleanse my hands. When I had, she replaced it whence it came. "So that you can remember me when we are apart."

I started the engine and drove to the appointed place. Our farewell was brief, an exchange of proper kisses on the cheek. Then I consigned her to the lease agent, who had already engaged a taxi, and I headed off to the plane.

The pilot was perfectly professional, not at all like the engaging Baumert on my inbound flight, so I sat in the passenger compartment to watch the quick dance of the propellers through the window. When we were in the air, I removed my handkerchief from my pocket to inhale the scent. I was amazed to discover that it smelled only of laundry soap and my own cologne. Nothing more.

Part III

KATHERINE

Chapter 9

Margarethe was reserved when she returned from Rome. She crept into the house and immediately retreated to her quarters. Perhaps she was unaware of my presence, but I was at home, having returned early from the hospital to spend time with my daughter. It was Krauss who alerted me to her arrival, perhaps expecting that I would go to her at once, but something told me to give her privacy.

Our first opportunity to speak was at dinner. I tried to draw her out by asking about the conference.

"It was a success. Yes. Very much so," she said and went back to her meal, although she'd only been picking at the fine roast lamb, one of her favorite dishes.

"Was your holiday enjoyable?"

"Yes, it was splendid," she said, but her frown belied her words. More worrisome still was the pinched look around her mouth which always indicated that her mind was burdened. She looked pale, although her skin is usually the healthy, golden color that true blonds enjoy. Margarethe loves to be outdoors, yet despite the warm weather in Italy at that time of year, her complexion showed not even a kiss of the sun.

After a few more abortive attempts to open a conversation, I filled the silence with stories of my afternoon with our daughter. I had taken Fiona to the zoo, which she always enjoyed, no matter how many times we visited. She had a special fascination with the reptiles, particularly the snakes.

"Margarethe, we must plan a family outing soon. The zoo, perhaps, or perhaps even a visit to your mother at Edelheim. We really shouldn't neglect her."

The mention of her mother merely caused Margarethe to sigh and increased the depth of the furrow between her brows. So, I chatted on through dinner about an interesting gynecological procedure I had done that morning. Lately, Becher had been involving me more deeply in his surgical cases, which I knew would please Margarethe. However, she only grunted from time to time merely to acknowledge that she had heard. After suffering through coffee with me in the drawing room, she excused herself and went upstairs.

I sat alone, nursing the glass of port that I had only accepted to please her and wondered how we had grown so distant. We still had medicine in common, although her constant advice, especially in my specialty, often put me on edge. Ironically, my role as a doctor had only intensified our difficulties. Nearly every day, I saw pregnant women or delivered some other woman's infant, which only made me long for another child of my own. For years, I had spoken of having another child, but Margarethe always advised, gently at first, and then more strenuously, that I wait until my career was better established. At thirty-seven, I was certainly not getting any younger and as an obstetrician, I knew the risks of a mid-life pregnancy all too well. I was also aware of the relentless ticking of the clock. If I were to be a mother again, it must be soon or never.

A part of me still believed that I could persuade Margarethe to expand our family. She absolutely adored Fiona. Her own children were grown and needed little attention. If necessary, I could simply force the issue by becoming pregnant. I was confident that she would, as before, accept the child out of love for me, but before I resorted to such draconian means, I would give the art of persuasion one more go. Fortunately, an opportunity soon presented itself.

❊❊❊

Margarethe's charges at the Charité—her "boys" as she called them— were always getting themselves into trouble. Not long after she returned from Rome, she needed to jump into an especially difficult case that required long hours in surgery. The operating tables at the Charité, as in most hospitals, are set at a comfortable height for the majority of the surgical team. Margarethe, being taller than most of her colleagues, has to bend. Combined with the tension that inevitably accompanies a challenging procedure, this posture often causes pain in her neck and shoulders. In such cases, a therapeutic massage is exactly what the doctor ordered. I say with no immodesty that I am quite skilled in this art and use it to my advantage when there is need. After one of my massages, Margarethe is willing to give more than usual patience to a difficult topic.

As I rubbed Margarethe's shoulders, I enjoyed the simple pleasure of touching her. So many weeks had passed with barely a quick kiss or embrace exchanged between us. As my fingers danced over her warm skin, I began to long for more and was suddenly inspired to take off my night gown. Seating my naked self on the back of her thighs, I became even more aroused. A deep sigh from Margarethe told me she was experiencing a similar effect.

"Katherine, are you attempting a seduction?" she asked in an incredulous tone, a bit muffled for she was prone and her face was pressed against the mattress.

"Why? Does that trouble you?"

"Not at all, but I am a bit surprised."

"I've missed you. And I do have needs, you know."

"You do?" she asked in a sarcastic voice. "I was beginning to have my doubts." I pinched her, and she flinched with great exaggeration. "Enough of that," she said, rolling me off. As soon as she began to kiss me, I yielded without protest.

Our moment of bliss recalled the happier times in our union when we would lie abed for hours, making love and sharing secrets. I tried to remember exactly when this period had ended. Naturally, our physical intimacy had suffered a brief hiatus in the last months of my pregnancy when I was confined to bed. However, the decision to keep my child had unintended benefits. It delayed the completion of the training required for my panel certification, thus providing a welcome spell of leisure, something other women of my class simply took for granted.

Margarethe, who had endured her pregnancies only for the sake of ensuring her line, seemed to enjoy my sheer delight in the wondrous changes. Always the scientist, she took great interest in my empirical observations, as if she couldn't remember her own experiences. More likely, she had purposely forgotten. Eventually, she admitted to finding my changing figure a great source of erotic inspiration. How patient she was and considerate, almost worshipful. I felt like a goddess of old attended by a priestess.

Yes, we quarreled when I announced my decision to nurse Fiona. Margarethe was adamantly opposed, aggressively arguing that a woman of our class *never* fed an infant from the breast. "That's what wet nurses were once for," she declared, "but now we have *the bottle!*" Why should I feed my daughter from a bottle when I could give her my breast? At first, Margarethe expressed her dissent by electing to be absent during feeding times. Then she would come feigning the need to discuss an important matter. Of course, the matter and its importance were as fabricated as those necessitating our silly conversations when I was still a nun. But I was relaxed and dreamy with the smell of milk and the new skin of my wonderful daughter, a miracle in my eyes. Margarethe's strong arms enclosed us both. I'd never felt so without care and so perfectly cared for.

As I lay in my lover's arms in the present, I sighed. "Remember how happy we were those first years?"

She stroked my hair. "Oh, Katherine, it's so for all new lovers. The mind is dulled, and the desire is great, so the mating will take place."

"…and produce a child." Margarethe instantly tensed, but I held her tightly against me. "Listen to me. My love for you is so deep that I want to raise children with you."

"Katherine," she said, sitting up, "I cannot make you pregnant. If that is your wish, consult your husband, not me."

She shrugged off my arms and hurried off to her dressing room. I heard the door close forcefully. She was hiding, as she often did when she could not face something.

***

Perhaps I read too much into what she'd said, but I also heard the implicit permission to do what I needed to do. I must turn to my husband if I wished another child.

In a few days, I menstruated, so I had the marker I needed to begin charting my fertile time. I rang Konrad in Bochum. "My dear, the time has come to put the plan into action."

He politely cleared his throat. "What plan is that?" he asked in a maddeningly innocent voice. One needed to be canny when dealing with Konrad. He was just too clever for his own good.

"Oh, Konrad, how can you have forgotten!"

"Oh, that," he said with a sigh so deep, I imagined the air being sucked out of my ear through the telephone.

"Yes, that. Now be a good fellow and do your husbandly duty."

"Dear God! Grethe will have my head on a silver platter!"

"Darling, you're not John the Baptist. Your martyrdom must come in another form." I instantly bit my tongue. Despite all my scientific training, I still cling to the Irish superstition that even a jest can turn out to be an unwitting curse. "Have no fear. She will forgive you. She always does. She loves you."

"She may forgive me, but what about you? You tried this trick before. Can you get away with it twice?"

"First of all, it was no trick the first time, as you well know. It was simply an accident."

"My point exactly. This time it's totally deliberate," he declared, followed by another suffocating sigh.

Despite my attitude of breezy confidence, I too had some reason for concern. Regrettably, my seduction of Margarethe turned out to be a one-time event. Our relationship rapidly reverted to its usual chilly state. I continued to be overwhelmed by my work, and now she was distracted by preparing for her debut as a professional singer.

Night after night, she disappeared into the music room to practice, sometimes until ridiculous hours of the morning. The house reverberated with the sound of her powerful voice and the superb Bechstein on which she played her own accompaniment. Sometimes she sang without the piano, and it was amazing to hear those astonishing arias *a capella*. She said it was the one unfailing way to learn to stay on key. Why she worried, I don't understand. She has perfect pitch.

Occasionally, after her practice, she slipped into bed beside me, supposing me to be asleep. Of course, the depression of the mattress under her weight always woke me. I am a light sleeper. During these secret visits, she never touched me. Nor did I acknowledge her presence by speaking. After a few minutes, she would get up and leave. Once or twice, I thought of calling her back, but then lost heart, fearing rejection.

Meanwhile, I pursued my own project with enthusiasm, making a great task of keeping track of the data. Mercifully, my menstrual cycle had righted itself after my first pregnancy. Now, it was as predictable as clock-work. Nevertheless, I did the clinically correct thing and took my temperature every day, carefully noting the results on a little chart, which I hid under the blotter in my study. I was quite alone in my pursuits. Consulting my mentor, Dr. Becher, was out of the question. Not only was he loyal to Margarethe, who had been his colleague when she was the chief of surgery at St. Hilde's, he was a devout Catholic. Human experiments on artificial insemination, conducted at the instigation of doctors prominent in Nazi circles, were in direct opposition to the teachings of the Church.

My plans for the project evidenced a deliberation that Margarethe would have admired. I secured several sterile, capped collection cups of the kind used for testing sputum for tuberculosis and put aside some catheter-tip, sterile syringes. I also carefully planned how Konrad would achieve the one necessary step. In the obstetrics laboratory, hidden in a cabinet to keep it from the nuns, we had a small collection of pornographic magazines for the occasion when an anxious husband was required to give a sample of sperm for examination. My husband's erotic inclinations were unconventional, so I sought out a purveyor of pornographic books cater-ing to esoteric tastes. The bookstore clerk stared at me when I asked for magazines with photographs of naked men.

"I am a physician doing research on homosexuals," I explained.

The clerk narrowed his eyes, clearly weighing the validity of my state-ment. Homosexuality was illegal in the Third Reich, and I could have been a Gestapo spy. To reassure him, I showed him my papers, which clearly in-dicated my profession. Finally, he coughed behind his hand and produced a few magazines wrapped in brown paper. He looked away while I opened them and examined the contents.

The week before Margarethe's debut at the Deutsche Oper, my

thermometer indicated that I would be fertile within a few days. I rejoiced in the fortunate happenstance. Konrad had already planned to come home for the opening night of *Der Rosenkavalier*. I asked Konrad to come directly to the hospital when he arrived in Berlin.

❀❀❀

Konrad was dapper in one of his Savile Row suits when he appeared at the hospital that afternoon. The nuns at St. Hilde's knew he was my husband and came in turn to greet him. I watched with faint disgust, remembering from my convent days how exceedingly deferential nuns can be in the presence of a handsome man. Many times, I'd seen them fawn over a young priest, the poor man having no clue that he'd just happened into a nest of female insects.

As soon as I could, I hurried Konrad off to my office. He'd been there many times before. Nonetheless, he made a great show of inspecting the place.

"You've changed the wall color."

"No," I said, "It's the same."

"Quite cheerful," he observed.

I allowed him a few moments to acclimate himself to his surroundings. Then I prepared him for his task. "It's really very simple, my dear. All you need to do is ejaculate in this cup. I'll handle the rest."

"There is a simpler way," he said with a wan grin.

"I didn't think that would interest you," I replied with an equally defective smile.

"No, not usually. But given all this fuss, it sounds almost appealing."

I opened the drawer and gave him the magazines. His brows shot up. "Good heavens, Katherine, you've thought of everything! Always prepared, just like my cousin."

"Let's not speak of her…just now."

"Of course not. How insensitive of me." I handed him a sterile collection cup and showed him the way to the lavatory. "That's all?" he asked. "Not even a kiss?"

That flustered me. I usually greeted him with a kiss, but in my nervousness, I had simply forgotten. With a quick kiss on the cheek, I sent him off to his task.

While I waited, I engaged my mind in writing up notes from my recent cases. Konrad was in the lavatory an inordinately long time. Finally overcome by curiosity, I knocked on the door. "Is everything all right?" I asked.

He opened the door and gave me a sheepish look. "How do you expect me to do this with you sitting right there?" he asked, nodding towards my desk.

"Would you like me to go elsewhere?"

"If it's not too much trouble."

"Very well. Meet me in the doctor's dining room when you've finished. Leave the specimen there on the sink. I'll come for it later."

"Thank you," he said, looking greatly relieved. He closed the door and engaged the lock.

I headed to the doctor's dining room. After helping myself to coffee from the ever-flowing urn, I settled myself at a corner table to read medical journals.

Presently, I looked up and saw Konrad looking a bit lost. When he saw me, his face brightened.

"It's done," he said with a dramatic sigh and took a seat across from me. "I've left it where you asked."

"Thank you," I replied.

"Now, don't waste it!"

"I assure you I won't."

After Konrad left, I returned to my office. The collection cup was on the sink in the lavatory, just as I had instructed. I held it up to the light, musing over the fact that the milky fluid was teeming with life invisible to the eye. We only needed one of those intrepid swimmers to get me with child. In the process, thousands of others would go to a noble death. But poetry was the furthest thing from my mind when I locked myself in the examination room and inserted the syringe with the aid of a speculum and a mirror.

Chapter 10

"But it will injure her beyond imagination!" exclaimed Konrad. His hovering as I put on my makeup had put me out of sorts. He toyed with a tube of lipstick, repetitively screwing it up and down until he caught my disapproving gaze in the mirror and finally stopped.

"There will be three performances. Why must it be this one?"

"This is her professional debut, an event that can only happen once!"

Near tears, I tossed aside the little pad I'd been using to blend the rouge and covered my face with my hands. "Can't you see how tired I am?"

He rubbed my shoulders sympathetically. He had already heard my complaints about being kept awake until dawn by a woman in labor, so I did not repeat them. "Please, darling, make the effort. You simply must or she will never forgive you."

I sat up straight and studied myself in the mirror. Unfortunately, I looked every bit as awful as I felt.

"If you give me some privacy, I might be able to finish dressing." Finally, he left.

After I completed my makeup, the maid helped me put on my dress. It was a sea foam green similar to the color of the first evening gown Margarethe had chosen for me after I'd left the convent. I'd bought the new dress hoping to trigger the memory of that long-ago event. The effort failed. Margarethe's only remark was to say the color suited me.

"Are you feeling better now?" Konrad asked, when I joined him in the entry foyer. Actually, I was beginning to revive. With a bit of effort and luck, I might even succeed in remaining awake through the performance.

We took our seats in the Stahle box at the opera house. The performance was completely sold out, even the standing room. The glittering crowd had come to hear Lotte Lehmann sing one of her most beloved roles, perhaps for the last time in Berlin. It was rumored that Lehmann was leaving Europe for America.

I would have liked the opportunity to see Margarethe and wish her well, but she never allowed visitors into her dressing room, not even me.

She always suffered from severe anxiety before she sang in public. How odd that someone so otherwise confident could have stage fright.

Konrad saw some of his former political associates and instantly abandoned me. I took the opportunity to study the program. How handsome Margarethe looked in her cast photograph. Adorned in a white wig, she perfectly evoked a young aristocratic man of an earlier time. The central twist of the opera—a woman singing the role of a man, who masquerades as a woman, made it especially amusing to those of us who knew that Margarethe could impersonate Konrad with great success.

Finally, the audience settled down and the house lights dimmed. There was a palpable excitement in the crowd as the overture began. Konrad took my hand and squeezed it. "Now, tell me. How could you have missed this?"

I have always enjoyed *Der Rosenkavalier* because it is an opportunity to see public affection between women. Many who sang the role of Octavian tried to conceal the passionate kiss in the first act behind a discreetly placed hand. I wondered how Margarethe would address this issue.

Finally, the curtain opened, and we found Octavian with "his" hand in the Marshallin's nightgown tenderly caressing her breast. This was bold indeed, even for Berlin. Now came the kiss. I held my breath. Octavian kissed the Marshallin with a realism that shocked even me. I felt a slight ripple of feeling in the audience but saw no sign of disapproval or discomfort, although my eye caught sight of a small, slight woman leaning over the rail in a box near the stage. One of Margarethe's many female admirers, I assumed. After a performance, Margarethe often received love letters from the likes of her.

Fortunately, Margarethe's stage fright always passes once she is on stage. She sang superbly. The remainder of the first act, with its many diversions grew tiresome. I dozed, but the applause woke me in time to see Margarethe come out for a curtain call. There followed the traditional long intermission for a glass of champagne or a quick supper in the *Opernterrassen*. Konrad was hungry so I kept him company while he ate.

My little nap during the first act had refreshed me, but once the theater was dark, I nodded off again. However, the excitement on stage preceding

Octavian's arrival woke me. I roused myself quickly because that evening, the much-anticipated Octavian would be my own Margarethe. The doors of the set opened, and Octavian ascended the stairs. His splendid costume, a dazzling white coat, embroidered in silver, reflected under the stage lights like a thousand tiny mirrors. Awe moved like a wave through the audience, even in that sophisticated Berlin house. Applause stopped the music. Whatever our recent disagreements, I would never begrudge Margarethe her moment of triumph. A few tears of pride came to my eyes.

During the third act my fatigue once again got the best of me. I nodded off. Then Madame Lehmann arrived, and the applause woke me. The great trio began. Having heard Margarethe rehearse her part many times, I knew every single note, but there is nothing to compare when it is accompanied, as intended, by two great sopranos. Once again, the action had to be stopped to wait out the applause. Finally, Octavian and Sophie blended their voices in the concluding duets and kissed sweetly. Even I sighed.

By the fifth curtain call, my hands ached from clapping. Margarethe was pushed in front of the curtain to stand alone, appropriately to cheers of *Bravo* rather than *Brava*. She remained squarely in character, playing the shy and awkward young man. As she gave a deep, courtly bow to acknowledge the shouts of acclaim, a single white rose fell at her feet. Margarethe picked it up and mimed smelling the fragrance with great feeling, just as Octavian had smelled the silver rose in the second act. Her eyes scanned the ring of boxes. Once again, I noticed the small woman in the front box. The brazen creature threw another white rose and then a kiss. In response, Margarethe raised her fingers to her lips and nodded.

The whole scene left me feeling very uneasy. I tapped Konrad's arm.

"Who is that woman?"

"Which woman?" he asked, attempting to align his gaze to my pointed finger. He squinted in that direction and then bent to speak in my ear because the sound of clapping around us was nearly deafening. "I don't actually know her. But I believe the gentleman beside her is attached to the Italian consulate. Why do you ask?"

"She seems very interested in your cousin."

"Oh, you know how it is. They're all interested in her," Konrad pronounced breezily, but out of the corner of my eye, I saw him studying the woman in question with great scrutiny. He knew Margarethe better than anyone, having been her accomplice during her wild youth.

When the house lights came up, we headed to the *Opernterrassen*, where a reception was being held for a select group of invited guests. Gürtner was sponsoring the party, and it had all the stamps of an impresario's flair. The champagne flowed freely and there was a generous table of rare foods, including a ridiculously large bowl of caviar, a veritable log of pâté, and an ice sculpture in the shape of a rose.

The principals appeared in their costumes from the final act to receive their well-wishers. Lehmann, in her magnificent hooped, satin gown, filled the room with her magnetic presence. The Sophie, Elisabeth Schwartzkopf, was demure and elegant. Octavian towered over them and looked very dapper in a green riding coat, white breeches, and tall, black boots. Ironically, Margarethe had to wear a wig to complete the costume. Her own hair was too short to gather into a ribbon at the base of her neck.

Konrad, with me in tow, threaded his way through the knot of well-wishers. He planted himself directly in front of his cousin and gave her a kiss. "My darling, you were simply superb!" he declared. He elbowed someone out of the way to let me come forward.

"What a triumph," I said, kissing her. "Congratulations."

"My voice has darkened. I had to reach a little…"

I put my hand on her arm. "Stop this minute. You sang superbly."

"For an amateur," she said, frowning.

"For anyone! It was glorious!"

Gürtner came up and thumped her on the back. "I thought for a moment you might actually run the Baron through. I know you're a champion fencer, but it's supposed to be *mock* swordplay. Now, come over and make amends."

Margarethe laughed and excused herself as he spirited her away. Konrad handed me a glass of champagne.

"Oh no," I protested, "if I drink alcohol, I'll be done for the night."

"Sip it," he advised, "just for effect." He leaned over and added in a confidential tone, "...and smile. Everyone knows you belong to her. Act the part and look radiantly proud."

I bristled at the unsolicited advice and even more at the suggestion that I was *owned* by Margarethe. Konrad downed his champagne quickly. Then he caught sight of Nigel Calder and disappeared.

Fortunately, I saw Mitzi von Treppen across the room. She and Margarethe had once been lovers, but it was far in the past, and we had developed a warm friendship. She could always be counted on for "girl talk" and scathingly accurate assessments of everyone at a party.

"Oh, look at her," she said, nodding in Margarethe's direction. "How she loves this, being in male clothes, acting like one of them. It makes one wonder if it's really an act at all." I looked at Margarethe and saw that everything from her wide-legged stance to the way she held her champagne glass was convincingly masculine.

I also saw the small woman who had been leaning over the rail of the box during the curtain calls enter an orbit around Margarethe. I now observed that she was slender to the point of emaciation and had no figure to speak of. Her complexion was unhealthily pale, accentuated by her dark hair and the intense shade of lipstick she wore. Yet for all these flaws, she was also striking—as pretty as a carefully painted corpse. This gave me a moment of relief. I couldn't see anything in this creature to compel Margarethe's interest.

"Who is that?" I asked Mitzi. "Do you know her?"

Mitzi frowned a little. "Actually, I do. That is Eva d'Allessandro, the wife of the Italian under-consul." So, this was the friend whom Margarethe had visited on holiday.

"What do you know about her?"

"Oh, she's just another bored wife," said Mitzi lightly. "She collects musicians like some people collect coins or stamps. She fawns over them while they strike her fancy and then..." She made a throwing gesture. "... just tosses them away. She's quite the musician herself. It must all be vicarious pleasure. But what do I know?"

"She seems rather interested in Margarethe," I observed with exaggerated nonchalance.

Mitzi studied the scene. "Yes, so it seems. She tried to persuade me to introduce them."

"Really?"

"Yes, but I never got around to it. Actually, I deliberately forgot about it. I don't really care for her."

"Why not?"

Mitzi shrugged. "No reason in particular. I just don't like her. I certainly wouldn't go out of my way for her. Besides, I hardly see Margarethe. Why should I share her when I do?"

"I fear I'm to blame. We seldom entertain. I've been so occupied with building my practice."

Mitzi pinched me lightly on the arm. "You must take time for pleasure, Katherine. Otherwise, you'll become as serious as your friend there."

Across the room, Margarethe looked very serious. She frowned as she listened to the chorus master, no doubt having goaded him into giving a critique of her performance. I also noticed that Countess d'Allessandro was reducing her orbit in her effort to get Margarethe's attention. Mitzi, with her eagle eye, was also watching these machinations.

"Shall we get closer?" she asked with a conspiratorial arch of her brow.

We found a inconspicuous spot just within hearing range. When the chorus master left, Countess d'Allessandro made a beeline for Margarethe.

Unfortunately, they spoke in Italian. "Can you understand what they're saying?" I asked Mitzi.

"A little…. If only they would speak louder."

The tiny woman grasped the lapel of Margarethe's coat, opened it, and gave the line of her waist coat a critical look. She reached out for but did not actually touch Margarethe's breast. Then she said something that caused Mitzi's eyelashes to flutter in dismay. "What a bold thing she is!" she exclaimed. "One cannot believe the things that come out of that woman's mouth!"

"What did she say?" I asked anxiously.

"Nothing of importance."

Her worried expression said otherwise. I grasped her arm. "Mitzi, please. You must tell me."

"She asked where Margarethe had hidden her lovely breasts. They are so full and beautiful. Had she bound them?"

I opened my mouth to speak but found I couldn't. Mitzi took my arm and gave me a sympathetic look.

I flew from Mitzi's side and searched the room for Konrad, finally finding him still chatting with Nigel. I interrupted rather rudely. "Pardon, Nigel, but I must speak with my husband," I said, yanking Konrad away from the conversation by the hand.

"Katherine, what are you doing?" asked Konrad, looking bewildered. He glanced at Nigel, whose little moustache twitched nervously.

"We must go. At once!"

"Why? The party's just beginning."

"Take me home. *Now.*"

"Very well, Katherine," he said, looking over his shoulder to see if anyone besides Nigel had noticed my agitation. "Try to calm yourself while I find someone to fetch our wraps and call the driver."

While I waited for Konrad to return, I was aware of my heart racing. I actually became light-headed and forced myself to take slow, measured breaths.

Our wraps were located, and we went out to the street. When Grauer brought up our motorcar, I dashed into the rear seat, tangling my skirts beneath me. I swore as I rearranged them. When I was finally settled, Konrad put his arm around me. "Now, will you please tell me what's the matter?"

"No, I'm sorry," I said. "I just can't."

Neither of us spoke for some time. Then Konrad said quietly, "I saw. But perhaps it's not what you imagine."

"You know her better than anyone. What do you think?"

He shook his head and looked away, confirming my worst fears.

At home, I retreated to my rooms and locked all the doors. I was unable to speak to anyone, not even my maid. The new dress had a complicated system of hooks. I could have used her assistance to undress, but I couldn't bear to see anyone. I forced myself to behave in an orderly way. I carefully took off my gown and hung it up. I removed my makeup. The familiarity of the evening ritual steadied me. For a few moments I was actually calm, but as soon I turned off the lights, I was once more suffocating with anxiety and rage. For a long time, I stared into the dark, imaging all manner of horrible scenarios and outcomes before fatigue finally claimed me.

✻✻✻

The next morning, I felt rested and quite well until I remembered the events of the previous night. It was as if sleep had been a mere respite from the nightmare. As misery flooded over me once more, I briefly considered taking an absence from the hospital. Then I reasoned that my ordinary routine might help calm me, so I bathed and dressed and went downstairs for breakfast.

As usual, Margarethe sat reading the newspaper. That morning she was reading the *Berliner Tageblatt* instead of the *The Times*. Of course, she wanted to see the notices on her performance. When the sound of Krauss pulling my chair away from the table drew attention to my arrival, Margarethe put down the paper. She smiled at me, "Good morning, my dear. I hope you slept well."

It seemed such an ordinary comment, as if nothing had happened. Nothing at all. And, in fact, nothing had changed except that I had gone from ignorance to knowledge. "Yes, thank you. I slept well, glad to have gotten to bed a bit earlier than I expected."

"Is that why you left the reception so early?" she asked, moving her spectacles down the bridge of her nose to look over them.

"I just couldn't stay a moment longer." It was the truth, after all. "What do the notices say?" I asked, attempting a smile.

She picked up the paper and read aloud to me: "'Countess Stahle played the role of Octavian with all the vigor that one would expect of a seventeen-year-old boy.' I suppose that's a nod to my advanced age. 'Her height and her grasp of masculine mannerisms made her performance extraordinarily convincing. As for her voice, this writer confesses to some skepticism whenever an amateur steps onto a public stage, but in this case, it is our loss that Countess Stahle has not pursued a professional career as a singer. Her voice is a wonder. Although she has been trained by the great Marie Ivogün, she sings in a naturalistic style that is refreshingly modern. She sang with enormous power and elegance and contributed genuine sweetness to the great trio and the duets.'"

"What a sparkling endorsement! Perhaps now you'll believe you are a great singer."

She thanked me for the compliment, put the paper aside, and signaled to the maid to pour more coffee.

"Any surgery scheduled today?" I asked.

"No, but I have my regular lecture at eleven o'clock." She poured cream into her coffee. "And you? The usual?"

"I have clinic duty this morning."

"You might consider cutting back on the clinic. It doesn't advance your career, and it would give you more time for Fiona. In fact, we might even find some time to spend together." She raised her left brow.

How dare she!

I wanted nothing more than to blurt out my accusation, but I'd been raised to be decorous in front of servants.

"Mariechen, a moment, please," I said.

Instantly, the maid vanished.

Margarethe looked at me with great curiosity. "What's the matter?"

"As if you don't know."

"I'm afraid I don't, Katherine. If it's my advice about your career, you always say you wish you had more time with Fiona."

I stared at her.

"Yes?"

"Margarethe, are you having an affair?"

Her face registered no emotion. None whatsoever. Her gaze was unflinching. "Whatever put that idea in your head?" she asked in a completely dispassionate voice.

"I saw for myself...last night."

"Saw what?"

"That woman!"

"Which woman?" asked Margarethe, reddening.

"That...that Italian countess, whatever her name is!"

Margarethe raised her chin a little, ready for any challenge.

"Deny it," I dared.

She merely continued to look at me with that steady gaze, the slightest frown puckering her brow.

"Please, tell me the truth," I implored. Then suddenly the damn burst, and I dissolved into tears. Ordinarily, Margarethe would have made an attempt to comfort me. Even in our most difficult moments, whenever I began to cry, she put her arms around me, smoothed my hair, and offered me one of her pristine cotton handkerchiefs. That morning, she simply got up and left the room.

I had my answer.

Chapter 11

My world was disintegrating before my eyes. The secure life I had enjoyed, despite my recent distance from Margarethe, had come to an abrupt end. I was in a false marriage. My lover had betrayed me, and my future was uncertain. I was able to come to this dismal appraisal only after days filled with blind anger and nights when I cried myself to sleep. I locked my door against Margarethe, but she never attempted entry, so it was pointless.

Until I decided what to do, it was imperative that I keep up appearances. I was determined to do this despite my perpetually reddened eyes and a sudden addiction to quiet, dark rooms. With others, I attempted to appear normal, especially at the hospital, where I found the routine soothing, the one sure thing in that chaos.

At home, I avoided making a scene because we had guests—members of the family who had come to Berlin to see Margarethe's performance in *Der Rosenkavalier*. Willi had traveled from Munich, where he was studying medicine. He was a strikingly handsome young man, blond like his mother and favoring her in every way, including height. Liesel arrived from Oxford on the arm of a very good-looking young American, a Rhodes Scholar, who was reading physiology before continuing his medical education at the University of Pennsylvania. Elisabeth indicated an interest in accompanying him to Philadelphia, much to Margarethe's disapproval. She had a low opinion of American medical schools. Obviously, there was a romantic connection between the two young people, and marriage was very much in the cards. Margarethe disapproved of that as well and made her opinion abundantly clear.

As much as I loved Margarethe's children, especially Liesel, I heartily welcomed another guest. Veronika, Baroness von Teten was a distant relation of the family and like Margarethe, born to the *Uradel*, the ancient aristocracy. We'd met while I was still a nun, and she was my patient. After I'd left the convent and found adjustment to life in Margarethe's house fraught with pitfalls, Veronika kindly helped me find my way. She gently instructed me in the vagaries of aristocratic life. It is no exaggeration to say that without Veronika's guidance, my relationship with Margarethe would have ended before it had even begun.

When Margarethe learned that I was pregnant, she gave me an ultimatum: she would end our relationship unless I gave up the baby for adoption or married the father. It was certainly a dilemma. I would never give up my own child, but as a devout Catholic, I was appalled at the idea of taking false marriage vows. It was Veronika who convinced me that marriage to Konrad was a good idea and the best solution, considering the circumstances. I am forever grateful for her wise advice.

Veronika embraced me warmly, clucking that I looked tired. After tea with the family, she invited me to her room for a little chat. The maids were still about, busy unpacking her things. Veronika has no idea how to travel light. She always brings a complete wardrobe, even for a few days' visit. She was once a renowned beauty and knows how to make the most of the latest fashions. She always looked chic and supremely elegant. She was once a redhead like me, but now that she was well past sixty, the color had begun to fade. I often think that I would like to age so beautifully.

While the maids continued their work, we spoke of trivial matters—Veronika's new gowns from Paris, her husband's latest gambling losses, the early cold weather…. As soon as we were alone, Veronika took my hands in hers and gazed at me intently. "Dear Katherine. You're ghastly pale. Are you ill?"

I shook my head. "No, not ill."

"My darling, this is your old friend, Veronika. Tell me what's wrong."

Her sympathy unleashed the flood of sobs that I'd stopped up for days. Veronika took me in her arms and held me against her ample bosom. "Oh, my dear, dear Katherine," she murmured as she stroked my hair. The siege went on for some time. Finally, nearly suffocating from the tears, I had to sit up. I dried my tears with my handkerchief and replaced my hair pins which had come undone. "I can't go to pieces now. I need to put on a good face for the children."

"Oh, dear. You've been living with Margarethe too long. Always worried about appearances." She sighed. "I've noticed the tension in this house. But all couples go through their difficulties, no matter male and female or two of a kind. Try to be patient, my dear, and keep a good heart. This too will pass."

"No. Nothing can ever be the same again!"

"Why? What's happened?"

"Margarethe has betrayed me," I blurted out.

She frowned. "Oh, no. I always feared this day would come."

I swallowed my fury at this remark. Everyone knew of Margarethe's wandering eye. I myself had witnessed it when I was still a nun. Years before, Veronika had tried to warn me, but I'd refused to believe her.

"I've been living an illusion," I said with a despondent sigh.

"No, dear. Even I was convinced you had reformed Margarethe. At least...I was very hopeful." She touched my cheek. "You are so lovely, so very good for her. How could she even look at another woman? Or is it a man this time?"

I made a face. "Actually, it would be less painful if it were a man. She doesn't really care for them. They're merely another form of pleasure. A bit of *variety*," I said, mocking the way Margarethe emphasized the word when she spoke of sex with men.

"Is it serious?" asked Veronika, her green eyes wide with curiosity.

"Does it matter?"

"Yes. Very much. It could simply be an indiscretion. In which case, you could swallow your pride and look the other way, as we all do. It will be over soon, if not already. Persist in carrying on and you'll prolong it. You know how stubborn Margarethe can be." Veronika frowned. "I must admit to some surprise. Who is this woman?"

"She's an Italian countess and a musician. She gave a great deal of money to the hospital fund, which is how they met. She has striking looks, but she's skinny. No figure at all."

"Well, that alone will put an end to it," said Veronika glancing at my bosom. "You are certainly more to Grethe's taste."

"Mitzi von Treppen knows her and dislikes her intensely."

"Mitzi is an excellent judge of character. And despite what you may think, Margarethe as well. She'll tire of this creature very soon. In fact, it may be nothing at all." Veronika pursed her lips and frowned. "She hasn't admitted anything, has she?"

"There was no need for her to say a word."

"We always know, don't we?" said Veronika with a sigh. "Only the blind or the stupid fail to see the truth. And despite Margarethe's great abilities as an actress, she is as transparent as any man." Veronika leaned closer. "My dear, I hate to ask this question, and you must try not to be angry, but have you given her cause?"

"That's no excuse!"

"No, it never is…" She pursed her lips. "I know for a fact she loves you, and she loves you as she has never loved before. She will not end the relationship with you unless you give her sufficient cause. I am quite certain of this."

Out of a sudden need to confess, I told Veronika the entire story—how Margarethe and I had come to a stalemate over my desire for another child, how I had punished Margarethe by withholding intimacy, how I had allowed my work to engulf me. But I didn't need to hear myself report these missteps to know that I had sown the seeds of my own undoing. By the end of my tale, Veronika's delicate auburn brows were knit in a disapproving frown.

"What is more important to you, another child or your love for Margarethe?"

"Why must I choose?"

"Life is full of choices. You can't have everything. I could understand if you had no children, but you have a lovely daughter. You have a successful career. You have the love of a truly remarkable woman. You live in grand style in a fashionable district. You even have a title through your husband…."

I suddenly felt the need to unburden myself and needed to be quite explicit because Veronika was ignorant of recent medical advances. I described the plot and Konrad's role in it.

"Why that's idiotic!" she cried. "I'm sorry, Katherine, but you deserve to be switched like a naughty, willful, little girl!" I swallowed hard to keep back the tears, but I couldn't. They rolled down my cheeks. Veronika offered me her handkerchief as mine was now sodden. "I'm sorry," she said, patting my arm. "I'm being too harsh. Besides you know all this. Why must I beat the horse?" She gave my arm a little squeeze. "Come now. Pull yourself together and we'll go down to the others. Otherwise, Margarethe will know you're here spilling your heart to me."

"I'm sure she already knows."

"Of course, she knows. But we can play the game too," she said with a wink.

***

In the coming days, Veronika and I had many conversations of this sort. We planned and schemed. Finally, she suggested I attempt a seduction.

"I couldn't!" I declared. "I'm furious with her."

"Forget all that. Swallow your anger and your pride, Katherine. If you want your lover back, you must fight for her!"

I was willing to entertain this strategy except for one thing. "I've never been very good at seductions," I admitted.

"Nonsense," retorted Veronika, "you are naturally seductive. Even when you were a nun." Veronika rolled her eyes at my look of shock.

"But Margarethe prefers to initiate lovemaking."

"Even better. You'll have the element of surprise in your favor."

So we set our trap. Veronika went through my lingerie to help pick the right thing for me to wear. Years ago, when she had been enlisted in putting together my first wardrobe after the convent, we had purchased exquisite nightgowns trimmed with Belgian lace. These had long since been stored in tissue paper in favor of more serviceable night wear. Veronika chose the most revealing of all, one with the lace nearly transparent through the bodice and open at points to reveal strategic bits of flesh. She sighed as she held it up to me. "How I envy you the ability to wear such lovely things."

Next, we designed the set. By then I was beginning to enjoy the game.

I'd never been much for intrigue, considering myself too truthful, but we concocted a clever plan. We chose satin sheets that hadn't seen my bed for ages. We rearranged the lamps to create the perfect lighting on the scene. Satisfied with the effect, we proceeded to the next step—contriving how to get Margarethe to visit my bedroom at the proper time.

"It must seem extremely casual, given all the emotion at the moment," said Veronika. "After you've retired, I'll announce that you are ill and prod her to look in on you. As you know, our favorite physician can never neglect her professional duty."

But we needed to wait for the right opportunity. The plan could not be executed with all the visitors in the house. Finally, Konrad left for Bochum. The children returned to their respective universities, although not before Elisabeth dropped a bomb. She had been secretly engaged to her American beau for some time, and they took the occasion of the family gathering to announce their intention to marry in the spring. This precipitated a fierce row between mother and daughter.

Naturally, Margarethe would have preferred that Liesel marry someone of her own class, and Peter, however decent, was an American, and therefore classless. This was made all the more complicated because there were specific rules governing the inheritance of titles, although nowadays, only genealogists actually cared about such things. The fight was not done by the time Liesel departed, and Margarethe continued to scowl over it for days.

This new wrinkle made me doubt our plan could be put into action, but Veronika disagreed. "Don't be ridiculous. The quarrel with Liesel has nothing to do with you."

We continued our preparations. Veronika demonstrated how to amplify my makeup to make me look more enticing. "Creating the glamour is one of women's great mysteries," she said as she set out the little pots on my vanity. "You've become quite skilled, but this is a special occasion." She also passed along the secret of dabbing a bit of perfume between my thighs. I blushed at the suggestion. That made her chuckle. "Sometimes you still act like a little nun. But don't ever change, my dear. It's charming."

Unfortunately, on the day we decided to execute our plan, Margarethe was late to dinner, detained at the hospital until nearly eight o'clock. I began to fear our plot would unravel. In a surly mood, Margarethe came directly to the table in her street clothes, although evening dress was still the custom in our home. Margarethe ate rapidly, catching up to us by the third course. I could see that she was distracted by whatever had gone on at the hospital. Ordinarily, she would have discussed it with me, but with Veronika at the table, she chose more general conversation. Gürtner, pleased with Margarethe's success in *Der Rosenkavalier*, was attempting to persuade her to take another role, the composer in *Ariadne*.

"Will you do it?" Veronika asked as the dessert, a rich chocolate cake was passed. Margarethe chose a large piece, evidently forgetting her vow to forego sweets. The business at the hospital had definitely put her out of sorts.

"Of course, I won't do it," said Margarethe in a disparaging voice. "I'm a surgeon, not an opera singer."

"Grethe, I think you're disappointed your mother has not disowned you over your Octavian," observed Veronika, stirring the obligatory six lumps of sugar into her coffee.

"My mother cannot disown me," replied Margarethe. "So she's cold to me for a time. I'm accustomed to her frost."

After supper I followed the script and excused myself, explaining that I was suffering from a headache. Margarethe gave me a perfunctory kiss on the cheek and then went on chatting with Veronika.

As I put on the extravagant nightgown, I felt dreadfully exposed, but I could not argue with its virtues. I retouched my makeup per Veronika's instructions and adjusted the scene as planned. By the time Veronika looked in on me, everything was in place. "You look perfect," she said. "Irresistible." She kissed me carefully so not to disturb my makeup. "Think of this as the beginning of a new era in your life with Margarethe. Take her lead, but steer as well. Be imaginative, and don't deny her anything you think will please her." She winked at me and then was gone.

I trembled as I waited, and yes, I prayed as well. It seemed a very long time before I heard Margarethe's footfalls in my sitting room. She came into the bedroom and surveyed the scene, noting the changes. "Veronika tells me you're ill. Evidently, she's mistaken." She gestured around the room. "Is this in my honor? If so, I'm flattered. But I'm afraid to kiss you and spoil your beautiful work."

"If you don't kiss me, then all my work will have been for naught."

She laughed softly. Finally, she kissed me, and in a matter of moments all the trappings became irrelevant. The beautiful nightgown was flung to the floor along with Margarethe's clothes. She was wild, probing me with great strength until I couldn't bear it any more and gave her what she wished. She allowed me to make love to her, but it was quick, because she was so excited. Afterwards, she lay beside me and complimented me on my ingenuity in setting the scene.

"I had help," I admitted.

"As I surmised." She chuckled. "Dear Veronika. She means well."

I nestled into the crook of Margarethe's arm and inhaled her scent, no cologne since she had come from the hospital, but her own dear and familiar smell. "My darling," I said putting my arm around her waist, "can we begin anew?"

"If you are willing..."

"But I must know that I am the only one."

She perceptibly tensed. "Katherine, please don't drive me away with your worry and suspicion."

"Tell me you're not having an affair."

"Why do you persist on this topic?"

"Because I need to know."

"Some things are best left unsaid," she said, slipping out of my arms and sitting up.

"I cannot go back to the way we were without knowing the truth."

"The *truth*," she repeated with great sarcasm. "What is the truth?"

"Only you know it."

"You know it too. And you won't like it any better said aloud."

I pushed her away. "Get out," I said. "Get out and go to your skinny, little Italian. See if she puts up with the likes of you."

Margarethe dashed out of bed, grabbed her clothing, and completely naked, strode out of the room. She left the bedroom door open, making it necessary for me to get out of bed to close it. I slammed it very hard so that she would hear it even through her closed door.

I was now out of my wits with rage. I pushed a lamp off the table. It shattered on the floor, shooting sparks. Stupidly, I ripped the cord from the wall, without a thought to the very real danger of electrocution. I picked up a little crystal vase from Waterford and flung it across the room. It was the one thing I owned of my mother's. When I stared at the poor, destroyed thing, which had once been so dear to me, something inside me broke as well. Everything was ruined. *Everything.* I picked up the shards of glass, managing to cut myself in the process. Though not a deep cut, the wound bled profusely staining the carpet at my feet.

The sight of the blood shocked me back to sanity. I went into the lavatory for something to bandage my hand, but I could only find a sanitary pad. I clamped it around the wound and sat naked on the toilet to weep. I sobbed so hard my entire body shook.

Then I stopped crying. My mind was suddenly so lucid, the clarity of my thoughts stunned me. I had dealt the death blow to my relationship with Margarethe. It was over now, and there was no going back. I stared at the cut in my hand. I had put so much pressure on it, the bleeding had completely stopped, frightened, as it were, to show itself to the madwoman from whom it flowed. I got up and went into my dressing room to find something to wear. When I couldn't find my dressing gown, I put on a day dress.

In a short time, there was a knock at the door. Thinking it was Margarethe, I was prepared to send her away.

"It's Veronika," called my visitor through the door.

I opened the door for her. She came in and stared at me with a frown.

"I made a muck of it," I declared. "Go on. Say it!"

"I have no wish to add to your misery." She noticed the blood stains on the carpet. "Are you hurt?" she asked anxiously.

"No, perfectly fine. I have to be. I have to think now. I have to decide what to do next."

"You needn't do anything at the moment. Margarethe has left the house."

"I would have expected that. She always runs away."

Veronika gave me a hard look. "She has a violent temper. When she is unable to control it, she leaves. Rather wise, don't you think?"

I shrugged. "Has she gone to her Italian friend?"

"Nothing of the kind. She's gone to the Continental to have a drink. She has a room there and may choose to spend the night."

"You spoke to her?"

"Yes. She apologized for making me a witness to your row."

"I needed to know the truth," I protested.

"And now you know it. Does it make you feel any better?"

I shook my head. Of course, not. In fact, I felt worse, much worse, and I began to tremble.

"Sit down," Veronika ordered. "You're a doctor. You must have something to calm your nerves."

"In my medical bag…in the sitting room." Veronika went to fetch it. I found the bottle of Chloral Hydrate solution and filled a syringe. I gritted my teeth against the stick of the needle. Although I am a physician, I loathe injections as much as anyone.

"Perhaps it will prevent you from making matters worse," said Veronika, observing my grimace.

"Can it be any worse?"

She sat down and eyed me. "Oh, yes, I think so. Right now, Margarethe is angry, but she will get over it. You are angry, and if you want her back, you will get over it."

"I will never get over it. What she did is wrong!"

"In your eyes, perhaps, but you know it is our way. It is the only means by which many people of our class have any love."

"Oh, yes, you know very well. You had Margarethe's father for years."

Her face darkened. "Katherine, I understand your anger. She's hurt you. But it's unlikely it was intentional. It may not even have anything to do with you. That's not what you want to hear, but you mustn't take it personally."

The Chloral was beginning to work. I felt drowsy. "That's impossible."

"My dear girl, put it out of your mind for now and go to sleep. Tomorrow it will all be clearer." Actually, I dreaded the morning and its clarity. "Come," said Veronika. "Get undressed and back into bed." She glanced at the Belgian lace nightgown that I'd flung to the floor in the moment of passion. She took it away and returned with my usual formless, cotton gown. I was like a child, unable to do the least thing for myself. I climbed into bed and Veronika tucked the covers around me. "I'll stay with you until you fall asleep," she said, sitting down on the bed beside me.

"It won't be long now," I replied in a sleepy voice.

"However long it takes," she replied. "I want to make sure you stay put for the night." She gave my hand a little squeeze. "I used to think that Margarethe was the daughter I never had but longed for. Now I see it's you. You are stormy, so like myself when I was young, and the smallest upset seemed a great tragedy. You must learn to take things in stride, my volatile Irish princess."

"My father always called me his princess," I said, nearly dreaming now.

✳✳✳

The next morning, the clarity that Veronika had promised shone into my mind like a spot light. Under it, I saw every event of the previous night—as if a cinema played in my mind, and I watched another hapless woman make a fool of herself. In the light of day, the wound in my hand was insignificant, not even worthy of a bandage. I also felt nauseous, which I ascribed to the Chloral. The very few times I had taken it, I was left with a hangover. Although I was unsteady on my feet, I succeeded in making my way to the bathroom for a shower. Once there, I changed my mind and settled on a hot bath.

Although I'd risen late, I dressed and applied my makeup with care. Everything must be as usual when I came down for breakfast. Veronika rarely rose before ten o'clock, so if Margarethe was there, we would likely be alone. However, Veronika's pleasant chatter would have provided some distraction.

Margarethe was sitting in her usual place at the head of the table,

sipping her coffee and reading *The Times*. This was the scene I had witnessed nearly every day of my life since I had moved into the villa. It was so
ordinary, I wondered if I had been dreaming. Hadn't the entire world been
rearranged by the events of the previous night?

"Good morning," said Margarethe, setting aside her newspaper. "Are
you feeling better?"

"Much," I replied, taking my place at the opposite end of the table.
The maid poured my coffee, and just as I had for years, I poured in a little
cream and added two lumps of sugar. As I stirred my coffee, I thought I
must be mad. Everything was perfectly regular. Externally, nothing had
changed, yet inside, I felt entirely different. My trust in Margarethe, the
rock on which my life was built, was shattered. My world could never again
be the same.

Margarethe cleared her throat. I thought she was about to say something, but she merely asked for her coffee cup to be refilled.

"I believe I owe you an apology," I said tentatively.

"Why?" she asked. "You've done nothing wrong."

"I created a scene."

Margarethe gave the footman a side nod and he quickly vanished.

"We both created a scene," said Margarethe neutrally. "Now, let's close
the curtain on it. Agreed?"

"It's not that simple," I said. "There are things that need saying."

Margarethe put down her cup and sat up straight. "Don't you think
we've both said enough? I think a period of quiet is necessary to allow the
dust to settle."

"No," I said, surprised to hear myself protest. Usually, I went along with
Margarethe's suggestions because it was easier. "I need to have some assurances if I am to continue living here." This was pure bravado because I had
made no plans, and I certainly wasn't prepared to carry out the threat.

Margarethe looked uneasy. "What do you wish me to assure?"

"That your affair with the Italian countess is over and done."

I held my breath while I awaited her answer.

She gave me a hard look. Finally, she said, "It is over and done."

Chapter 12

My work distracted me from the dreadful intrusion into my personal life. I threw myself into my medical practice with renewed enthusiasm, taking on more problematic maternity cases and leaving the run-of-the-mill deliveries to the midwives. Dr. Becher had lately been involving me in his most challenging gynecological surgeries because he found me an able assistant. The change of pace stimulated me, and I enjoyed returning to the operating theater. Had Margarethe been one iota less adamant, I might have become a surgeon.

When I returned from surgery one morning, I found Mother Monica, superior of the Berlin convent, waiting in my office. We had known one another since I was a medical student in Heidelberg. It was she who had taken me in when, devastated by my mother's death, I had arrived unannounced on the convent doorstep.

Although nuns are discouraged from having friendships with seculars, Monica often came to call on me at the hospital. At first, she came to reassure me that I was not an outcast because I had left the community. When I'd first returned to St. Hilde's Hospital after my residency at the Charité, some of my former sisters shunned me. Sisters Berthe and Anna, my colleagues from my term as head nurse in 1931, were as warm as ever, but the others showed their fear and distrust of a defector by shutting me out. Monica tried to set an example by warmly welcoming me back to St. Hilde's. That act of generosity sealed our friendship forever.

Monica allowed me to embrace her despite the convent prohibition against touching others unnecessarily. I invited her to sit. "I understand your practice has expanded immensely," she said as she settled into one of the visitors' chairs. Although she had no role in the hospital, her primary responsibility being the administration of a convent of over forty nuns, she made it her business to stay current on hospital affairs. "I know you are very busy, so I won't take but a few minutes of your time." I sat back in my chair to show that I was unhurried while she surveyed me with the quick, measuring glance of a long-time superior.

"You're looking well, Katherine, though a bit tired."

I nodded. "I never thought I would be so in demand."

She chuckled. "You must have known. You were an obstetrics nurse for many years before you switched to surgery."

"Yes, but one forgets. Besides it's quite different for a nurse with a regular schedule."

"But you're happy in your work?"

"Exceptionally so."

"That's good," she said with a warm smile. "Happy physicians make happy patients." This was exactly the sort of thing nuns liked to say. When I was a nun, I was also a font of platitudes.

"I have a great favor to ask," she said and began to describe the plight of a middle-aged woman who was near term and confined to her bed to prevent early labor. "She is a Jew. Her husband was taken a few months ago, leaving her alone with two children. Fortunately, they are nearly grown and some help to their mother. I've tried to persuade her to come to St. Hilde's. Despite my reassurances, she doesn't believe that she'll be safe here."

The convent teaches nuns to avert their gaze for the sake of modesty, but Monica's gray eyes held mine with a determined look. I instantly understood her expectation.

"Please write down her name and address," I said, handing her a block of paper, "I shall call on her." As Monica wrote the information I admired her perfect penmanship—a nun's hand. Mine had once been equally neat, but it had been corrupted by the speed at which I needed to write as a physician. I noted that the address was in Halensee, one of the most obviously Jewish districts in Berlin.

"With the fetus presenting in breech and very large, there could be complications. The last time I visited, I brought Marthe." Sister Marthe was our best obstetrics nurse and a credentialed midwife. "Marthe attempted version, but to no avail. You must be prepared for the possibility of a Caesarian. The birth is imminent. All the necessary instruments and supplies will be delivered to Frau Gerstein's apartment tomorrow."

"If a Caesarian is a possibility, she ought to be in hospital."

"I certainly agree, but she won't leave her children. She's afraid for them, and unfortunately, she has good reason to be." We nodded in mutual sympathy over the horrors we were unable to stop. "Katherine, you must be very careful. There are rumors of a demonstration against the Jews this week."

"I'm not afraid," I said bravely, although I was frightened. I had witnessed several Nazi demonstrations, including the infamous burning of "un-German" books in the Opernplatz in 1933. Margarethe, who abhorred censorship of any kind, had dragged me along to watch as uniformed thugs threw the works of Mann, Freud, and Remarque into the flames. I can still see the Brownshirts' leering faces illuminated in the fire, the sparks shooting into the night sky, seemingly dancing to the rhythm of their obscene Nazi hymns.

Monica spoke, bringing me back to the present. "I knew I could rely on you, Katherine." She reached for my hand and gave it a little squeeze. "Rebecca and I grew up together. She is like a sister to me."

"I'll do my best for her."

"I know you will. And I'll keep you both in my prayers." Given the real threat of danger, it behooved me to pray as well.

***

I dared not tell Margarethe about my plans. She would never condone my putting myself in danger, although she herself sometimes took risks on behalf of the Jews. Of course, she thought she was more able, having been trained by her father in soldierly arts. She always carried a gun.

She had offered to teach me to shoot while I was working in a clinic in the rough district of Wedding, but guns terrified me. During a visit to her family estate at Edelheim, Margarethe had insisted that I fire her pistol. The ear-splitting noise and the recoil wrenching my wrist terrified me. I vowed never to touch a gun again.

It disturbed me to know that our home was full of them, everything from high-powered hunting rifles and shotguns to diminutive revolvers. I could not even bear to be in the same room when Margarethe cleaned her horrid guns, which she did from time to time to make sure it was done properly. But gun or no, if the rumors of a demonstration against the Jews proved to be true, no one would be safe in a Jewish neighborhood.

After my office hours were done, I drove my little BMW to Halensee to look in on my new patient. I easily found the address. The imposing building had once been majestic, although it had clearly suffered in recent years, partly from neglect but even more from vandalism. I knew I was in the right place because a small sign in the lobby read: "*Hermann u. Rebecca Gerstein, Zahnärzte.*" Husband and wife were both dentists. I noted the number of the flat.

The lift had ceased to function or had been shut down for lack of someone to operate it. A prominent sign ordered: "Keep Off." The anteroom was scribbled with all manner of hateful graffiti against the Jews, some of it lewd. I averted my eyes as I searched for the stairwell. I walked up the four flights to the Gersteins' floor. When I located the correct apartment, I had to ring several times before someone came to the door. A boy of about fourteen finally opened it a crack but left the safety chain attached.

"Excuse me, but who are you?" he asked in a polite voice.

"I am Dr. von Holdenberg. Mother Monica of St. Hilde's Hospital has sent me to look in on your mother."

He studied me for a long moment. "Let me tell my mother. A moment, please."

He closed the door. I heard the lock engage. After some time, the door opened again, and now the chain had been withdrawn. "My mother says you may come in." He gestured for me to enter. "Please. This way."

He was a good-looking boy, but hunger and worry had left him with dark circles around his long-lashed eyes. I decided that he was actually younger than he looked for he was still in short pants. "What is your name, young man?"

"I am Josef Gerstein, and I am pleased to make your acquaintance, *Frau Doktor,*" he said and made the formal Prussian bow with heel clicks. I was touched and amused at the same time. At least, decorum had survived, despite the misery the Nazis had brought them. "Come. Mother is in the bedroom. This way."

As we walked down the corridor, I noticed two well-equipped dental surgeries. The cabinets stood locked and everything was covered with sheets to ward off dust. Each surgery had a separate entry to a large room, which had evidently been the waiting room for the patients. Like so many professionals, the Gersteins had once made their practice under the same roof as their living quarters.

Josef opened a door and we entered a large, richly furnished room. My patient, enormously large with child, lay on the carved mahogany bed. The poor woman struggled to rise, and the boy sprang forward to help her. He added another pillow behind her back so that she could sit more comfortably. Once she was settled, Frau Gerstein brushed the hair from her face and gave me a warm smile. "Thank heaven! Luise promised to send a doctor." It took me a moment to realize that "Luise" had been Mother Monica's name before she entered the convent.

Frau Gerstein, beneath the bloating and stress of her pregnancy, was an attractive woman. She had dark hair, exotic eyes, and porcelain skin. Dressed and groomed, she would be a beauty.

In a formal tone, Joseph made the introductions. I approached and extended my hand.

"It is a pleasure to meet you, Dr. von Holdenberg," said Frau Gerstein, taking my hand in both of hers. She turned to her son. "Seffele, fetch *Mutti* a glass of water, will you?" It was obviously a ploy for privacy, but the boy cheerfully went off to do his mother's bidding.

"Delightful boy. How old is he?"

"Thirteen."

"No school today?" I asked casually.

"He's not allowed. His school reached its quota of Jews, so he was asked to leave. I've been teaching him at home, that is, until my pregnancy forced me to bed. My daughter, the elder, is still allowed at school." She saw the puzzled look on my face and answered my unspoken question. "My father was a Catholic, though my mother was a Jew, and my husband's mother was Christian. By some bizarre arithmetic that qualifies my children to be half Aryan, which still counts for something. Thank God for small favors,

I suppose." She gestured to a chair, and I took a seat. For a long moment, she studied me. "How wonderful that Luise sent me a female. I've always preferred a woman for these things."

"I do as well. I understand you are a dentist."

"I *was* a dentist," she said, "…until the law forbidding Jews to practice dentistry. How amazing that one can study diligently, earn a credential, and work to build a practice. Then one day it's all gone, just like that," she said, snapping her fingers. I tried to imagine how I would feel if I woke up and read in the newspapers that I could no longer practice medicine. "My husband and I treated our own people, long after the insurance refused to pay. But Hermann has been gone for almost four months, and as you can see, I am confined to my bed."

Josef returned with the glass of water. "Thank you, *Schatzi*. Now go to Frau Rabinowitz to see if she will give you some lunch. Tell her I'll send the money tomorrow." This made me wonder how they lived, deprived of the income from the dental practice. The faded grandeur of the flat suggested that they had once been wealthy. Perhaps they were selling their belongings to survive. "Go on, Seffchen," urged his mother. "You must be hungry. It's very late."

"I'm not hungry," protested Josef.

"*Frau Doktor* and I have things to discuss. Not a conversation for boys." He glanced at me and I nodded.

"Go on, Josef. I'll look after your mother."

He left and I heard the outer door close behind him.

"My neighbors have been very kind. Paula, my eldest, can cook a little, but you wouldn't want to eat it." We both chuckled, although my cooking wasn't very palatable either. My life from earliest childhood had been directed towards medicine, so unlike my sisters, I had been spared my mother's cookery lessons.

Despite Monica's quick summary, I actually knew very little about the case, so as I prepared for the examination, I tried to fill in the gaps.

"How old are you, Frau Gerstein?" I asked.

"Forty-six. Obviously, this child was not planned. Herman and I were looking forward to having the flat to ourselves soon." She sighed. "Life never seems to go according to plan."

I smiled. "One doesn't always plan for a child."

"Do you have children, *Frau Doktor*?"

"Yes," I said. "I have daughter. I'm hoping to have another baby soon."

We exchanged a conspiratorial smile.

"Good luck to you," she said. "Is your husband agreeable to the idea?"

How to answer this question?

"Yes, in the main."

Rather than get too deeply into this topic, I arranged the instruments for the examination. Frau Gerstein was quite impressed with the ingenious, portable blood-pressure cuff that Margarethe had recently given me as a gift. I took my patient's blood pressure and found it quite elevated, her pulse was rapid, both worrisome signs. Fortunately, the fetal heartbeat was normal.

The pelvic examination confirmed Sister Marthe's diagnosis of breech presentation. It was unusual because the child was very large and breech position is more likely when the fetus is smaller. I attempted to reposition it so it would face head down but was unsuccessful. It was clear that Frau Gerstein was uncomfortable, so I did not persist. However, I was encouraged by the fact that the fetus was in frank breech, that is, with the legs folded flat up against the face. A vaginal delivery could be successful. Despite Mother Monica's great confidence in me, attempting a Caesarian section outside the controlled and sterile environment of a well-equipped operating room was unwise. Once Frau Gerstein relaxed a bit, I made another attempt to turn the fetus, but it simply refused to budge. "It's not working, is it?" she asked, grimacing from discomfort.

"No, I'm afraid not." I didn't wish to alarm her, but because she was a medical person, I felt I could be more frank than usual. "These are not the best circumstances, as you know. You would be perfectly safe at St. Hilde's."

"Sheltering a Jew would put your hospital at risk." Fortunately, it hadn't yet come to that point. "And I won't leave the children alone. Who knows what would happen to them." She didn't elaborate, but I could imagine.

"We'll do the best we can," I said taking her hand.

I remained a few minutes longer simply to chat because Frau Gerstein was so clearly lonely for adult company. By the time I was ready to leave, Josef had returned and solicitously asked his mother if she needed anything.

On the way to the door, we passed the dental surgeries again. "Just a moment, Josef." I snapped on the light and went in. The surgery was exceptionally large and well-equipped. It was properly vented and lit. The dental chair moved aside, and a table put in its place, and the room would be quite adequate. I found a functional autoclave and surgical instruments in the cabinets. There was even a nitrous oxide canister on a rolling stand in the corner. It was still filled with gas.

The boy stood watching me as I surveyed the room. "Papa is gone. Mutti is no longer a dentist. We have no use for these things now."

"Oh, we may yet have a use for them." I looked under the sink where I found a bottle of antiseptic detergent. "Can you find me a wash bucket and fill it with hot water? Also, a sponge and a brush, please."

He went off to find these items. I took off my hat and coat once more and rolled up the sleeves of my blouse. I hadn't scrubbed a floor since I was a novice at the mother house in Obberoth. Manual labor was part of our training in humility, but I have never minded hard work. I enlisted Josef's aid in moving the heavy dental chair to the corner of the room. Fortunately, it was on bearings. We carefully dusted the room, aired it with the vent to remove the flying particles, and then scrubbed the place from top to bottom with antiseptic. The whole flat soon stank of it.

Frau Gerstein managed to waddle down the hall. "What are you doing?" she asked, peering curiously into the room.

"We are making an operating room," explained Josef proudly.

"I see," she said with a knowing smile, "the patient won't go to the hospital, so the hospital will come to her. Very clever, *Frau Doktor*."

"Thank you, but you should go back to bed. Josef, help your mother."

It was actually easier to complete the work alone than to have the boy underfoot, but I asked his help in carrying a cot and mattress into the adjoining consulting room. Mother Monica would no doubt send sterile sheets along with the other supplies, completing our tidy little surgery.

After we finished our task, I locked the door. "No one must enter this room," I told Josef. "It's sterile now and must remain so. Do you understand?"

He nodded gravely.

***

By the time I returned the following afternoon to look in on Frau Gerstein, the carton of supplies sent by Mother Monica had arrived. I took the box to the little consulting room adjacent to our makeshift surgery and examined its contents. Monica had sent sterile linen as well as two full sets of surgical garb, including gowns and masks. There was also a complete set of obstetrical instruments, wrapped in sterile paper, for both a vaginal delivery and a Caesarian. At the bottom of the carton were drugs: sodium pentothal, procaine as a local anesthetic, sulfa powder, phenol for disinfecting hands and washing the skin. I carefully arranged the items in the former dental surgery. Satisfied that I was now prepared for any eventuality, I went down the hall to look in on my patient.

Frau Gerstein squeezed my extended hand warmly. "Welcome back, *Frau Doktor.*" She looked somewhat better than the day before and her pressure was closer to normal, although still elevated. Perhaps knowing that she was being looked after had brought some relief. "How nice it is to have the company of another professional woman," she confided after I examined her and we both agreed that it was probably not the day for her labor to begin. "Tell me about your practice, *Frau Doktor.*"

I explained that my medical career had been interrupted. She assumed the cause to be marriage and the hope of a family. I said nothing to alter the perception. I described my role as Dr. Becker's junior partner and under-chief at St. Hilde's. Then I spoke of my concerns about my daughter. Of course, Frau Gerstein understood the challenges of building a new practice, and the burdens it put on a family.

"It's very hard to manage a career with young children. No matter how wonderful the child's nurse, one always feels guilty because *Mutti* wasn't there to dry the tears after a head bump or when the little one has a belly ache. Sometimes, I just missed the feel of the baby in my arms, especially when they were infants."

I commiserated with Frau Gerstein, reflecting that I had never met a working mother who hadn't regretted the time away from her children. None, except Margarethe. She was happy to hand off her children to the charge of a nurse and get on with her interests. Of course, her attitude was not unique among the upper classes, whose women found childbearing the one unpleasant duty they couldn't avoid. Nonetheless, as the children grew older, even Margarethe began to have doubts, so even she was not deaf to the siren of maternal instinct.

I was anxious as I wrote out my private telephone number and gave it to Frau Gerstein, wondering what I would say to Margarethe if the Gersteins called me at home. In fact, Margarethe never asked me to explain my comings and goings. My anxiety was simply bad conscience over keeping something so important from her.

At dinner that night, I became even more anxious. When the footman left the room to fetch something from the kitchen, Margarethe confided in hushed tones, "I overheard some of the Nazi medical students talking today. There's to be an action against the Jews this week." The footman returned, and Margarethe quickly changed the subject to a medical matter.

❖❖❖

Josef called the next morning around eleven. I left the *prima para* I was attending to take the call in my office. "I think my mother has gone into labor," said Josef, sounding very worried.

"You think? Has your mother asked you to call me, Josef?"

"No," the boy admitted.

"Josef, your mother knows more about these things than you do. She will tell you when to call me, which should be when the contractions are about ten minutes apart. Is there a watch you can use to time them?"

"Yes," he said proudly. "I have my grandfather's watch. It's gold."

"Good. You can help your mother by making her comfortable. Talk to her to pass the time. Read to her, if she likes. If there are any sudden changes, call me at once."

"Yes, *Frau Doktor!*" he said. I could imagine him snapping to attention like an anxious recruit.

When he called me again, his timing was more favorable. By then, my hospital patient was proudly holding her newborn, and my consulting hours were finished for the day. I called Krauss to let him know I would be late at the hospital. A twinge of guilt chafed my conscience because this was an outright lie. To give it more credence, I left my motorcar parked at the hospital and took the U-Bahn to Halensee.

Josef's sister, Paula answered the door. She was very thin and pale, with reddish hair and warm brown eyes. Once again, Josef went through formal introductions. "My father insisted that I learn proper manners," he confided afterward. "I was picking up rough language and bad habits from the boys on the street. Otherwise, he wouldn't let me play with them. Now many families have moved out of the district, and there are very few boys my age."

I patted his arm in sympathy.

"Will you join us for supper?" Paula asked. She was cooking a mysterious stew that smelled as unappetizing as it looked. The main ingredient appeared to be cabbage, which even I know never improves with additional cooking. There was no polite way to refuse, so I agreed.

While we awaited supper, I sat down at the table with Josef who was frowning over a mathematics problem.

"*Frau Doktor*, can you help me?" he asked. "Paula is an idiot when it comes to geometry. She failed it." Paula turned around and gave her brother a filthy look, which he returned and stuck out his tongue for emphasis.

"Let me see," I said, taking his copy book from him. He had most of the solution, so I only needed to explain the last steps. After that, he had many more questions. For the next hour, between brief visits to Frau Gerstein's room to monitor her progress, I found myself immersed in the geometry of solid figures. I needed to reach deep into the recesses of my brain, for it had been ages since I had studied formal mathematics.

Eventually, a steaming bowl was placed before me. In it was a watery mix of cabbage, noodles, and unidentifiable chunks of meat. When I glanced up from the unappetizing ragout, Paula said with an expectant smile, "I hope you like it." I couldn't think of a graceful way to refuse, so while Josef and Paula quickly devoured their meal, I mentally held my nose and put down as much of the horrible muck as I could bear.

Our dinner was interrupted by Frau Gerstein calling for me. She'd tried to turn herself and her water broke. The bed was completely soaked, so I asked Paula to help me get her mother up so that we could change the bedding. When I returned to the kitchen, I found Josef eyeing what remained of my stew. "Go on," I said. "If you're hungry, finish it." He needed no further encouragement and began wolfing it down.

We continued our vigil. While Paula sat with her mother, Josef brought out a pack of cards, and we played a few rounds of German Whist. Around eight o'clock, I went in to check on my patient. I was glad to get up and walk. The long spell in those high-backed chairs had left me stiff. From the window of the hall one could see the courtyard below. All was dark, save a few lights in the windows in the opposite building. It was eerily quiet.

Frau Gerstein had raised herself up in bed when I came in. "The contractions are about three minutes apart now," she said, and I realized it was time to prepare. I summoned the children and the three of us helped Frau Gerstein down the hall to the surgery. Rather than put her up on the table, I settled her on the cot in the consulting room.

I had no sooner begun to scrub, when I heard shouts from the streets. There was a loud crash followed by the tinkle of falling glass. I unlatched the window and looked out. Below a large crowd had gathered. Some carried torches; others, pocket lamps. They moved en masse, smashing all of the windows facing the street one by one, all the while singing that hateful Horst Wessel Song. I shut the window and turned back to my patient. She was ashen. A few seconds later, Josef opened the door. He looked purely terrified.

"Josef," his mother said calmly, "Make sure all the doors are locked."

"Yes, *Mutti.*" he replied in an equally calm voice, but he was visibly trembling.

Cries and shouts echoed in the courtyard. A door slammed. Within the building, there was the sound of running feet pounding up the stairs and through the corridors. I heard a loud thud, followed by another, a rhythmic, steady beat. The air was now filled with the tenor voices of young men, followed by the shrill wail of a woman in terror. I strained to make out words, but the voices were suddenly muffled. Then came a thunderous crash and the bright tinkle of broken glass falling to the pavement. The steady thud had resumed, followed by the distinctive sound of an axe splintering wood. Someone was breaking down a door on the floor below.

All around us, the building swarmed with activity. The ax blows continued. More footsteps pounded up the stairs. Someone in the flat above turned up the wireless very loud to drown out the noise. Incongruously, a Beethoven symphony was playing. Its sweet harmonies competed with the ax blows and the confused rumble of objects hitting the walls below us.

I decided to investigate, so I stepped out into the hall and leaned over the bannister. I couldn't see anything, but I heard a high-pitched moan from the stairwell, a feral sound, like a wounded dog. Tentatively, I descended the stairs. Near the landing door, an old woman was slumped against the wall.

"Are you all right?" I asked.

Slowly, the woman sat up and turned her head. Dark blood trickled from a cut on her forehead. I lifted her chin to inspect the wound. There was hardly any opening, just a little dark seepage, but blood was pooling under the skin. The wound appeared to be caused by a blow from a blunt object. "Let me help you back to your flat," I said.

"No! I can't go in there."

I glanced through the open door. The flat was a tiny, cramped place. The curtains fluttered around a broken window. On the floor lay a shattered curio cabinet with the memorabilia of a lifetime scattered on the threadbare carpet.

"Come upstairs."

"I don't think I can," she said, laboring to breathe. I helped her to her feet. Leaning heavily on my arm, she was able to get up the stairs. "I don't know why they're doing this to me," she moaned. "I'm not even Jewish. My husband was a Jew, yes, but I was baptized...a Catholic!"

Josef flattened himself against the wall as we came through and helped me bring the old woman into the kitchen. While I collected iodine and bandages from my medical bag, Josef explained that my new patient was Frau Rabinowitz, the neighbor who fed him lunch.

I became concerned as I inspected Frau Rabinowitz's injuries more carefully. Blunt force trauma could mean a fracture and intracranial bleeding. The woman ought to be in hospital where she could be carefully monitored. I considered calling an ambulance but, with all the disorder in the city, it could take hours for it to arrive. The best I could do for her was to clean the wound and watch for mental changes.

"Oh, Berthe, poor dear," sighed Frau Gerstein, when I explained the interruption. "She's too old for all this excitement."

I turned my attention to arranging the instruments for the birth. Occupied with my tasks and charting the intervals between the contractions, I failed to notice that the noises in the building had finally ceased, replaced by an uneasy quiet. The sound of the door bell ringing made us all jump.

"Don't answer the door!" Frau Gerstein ordered.

"They may break it down if they can't get in," I said.

"Oh, what a time for this kind of foolishness!" she exclaimed, grimacing with another labor pain.

Josef went to see who was at the door. A moment later, I heard a familiar female voice in the hall. My heart rejoiced and then instantly sank when I looked up into Margarethe's face. Although her expression was perfectly neutral, as it always was in a professional setting, I could feel her judgment as surely as if she had scolded me. She took in the situation in a glance, coldly assessing the room and the point to which the labor had progressed. Then she said, "How can I help?"

I wanted to fling my arms around her for her generosity and also because I hadn't realized how frightened I'd been until that moment. During the worst of the demonstration, fear was a luxury I could not afford. Now, I was actually trembling. I got hold of myself and began describing the case.

Margarethe silenced me with an upturned hand. "Never mind," she replied briskly. "Sister Marthe explained everything." She introduced herself to Frau Gerstein, then went to the sink to wash.

"So," she said, in a confidential tone as she scrubbed her hands, "all of your attempts at version have failed."

"Yes, but I think a vaginal delivery is still possible."

"Are you prepared for a Caesarian?"

I nodded in the direction of the instruments set out and ready. Gingerly, I awaited the advice she would offer, whether or not I wished to hear it. Usually, a surgeon chose to cut first and ask questions later, but Margarethe was also a credentialed gynecologist. I imagined the little war going on in her head between the dictums of the two specialties as she decided how best to advise me.

Finally, she said, "You should attempt a vaginal delivery. I shall assist you." This put me off guard. Margarethe *never* assisted. She always took over a procedure because she had the authority and because she was more skilled than anyone in the room. However, it had been ages since she had attended a birth, whereas it was my professional specialty.

To my surprise, Margarethe made a very able assistant. She followed my instructions without question, and despite all our concerns, the delivery went smoothly. The large, male infant gave loud, lusty cries without the need for encouragement. Thereafter, it was a textbook procedure. I was enormously relieved. Margarethe looked after washing the child and swaddling it, while I delivered the afterbirth and sutured the episiotomy. Frau Gerstein wept when the child was placed in her arms.

"We can't leave her here on this little cot," whispered Margarethe. "We must get her back into a bed."

"What do you suggest? We don't have a gurney."

Margarethe frowned as she sized up the situation. Frau Gerstein was actually slight, despite her still bulging abdomen "I'll carry her," said Margarethe, "You take the child." She grimaced as she lifted Frau Gerstein. "Dear God, I'll pay with a backache tomorrow!" Soon Frau Gerstein was comfortable in her bed, and I returned the child to her waiting arms.

"Come. It's time to go," said Margarethe stripping off her surgical gown.

"But I can't leave yet."

"You've done all that was needed. We must go to the Charité. The wounded will be arriving now that the evil deeds are done. We can use your hands."

"At least, let me tidy the room."

"Leave it," she ordered. "We'll send someone tomorrow." Her expression left no room for argument. She barely allowed me enough time to check on Frau Rabinowitz, who was having a cup of tea with Paula. I gave the girl instructions regarding the care of both patients, hurrying because Margarethe was already out the door.

She was waiting for me in the Mercedes with Grauer at the wheel. On the way to the Charité, she sat with her arms folded on her chest and silently gazed out the window.

"You're angry with me," I said, stating the obvious.

"You were very foolish to go out tonight. I warned you there would be a demonstration against the Jews."

"Yes, you did."

For the duration of the ride to the Charité, neither of us spoke. Grauer left us off at the emergency entrance of the hospital. We reported to the triage nurse to get our assignments. It had been years since I'd assisted Margarethe in the operating room, but in a matter of minutes, I fell into the familiar rhythm as if it were yesterday. When she neared completion of a procedure, she left me to close while she went on to the next patient. We treated dozens of emergency cases that night.

It was near two in the morning when we deposited our scrubs in the bin and headed out to the car park. We had to rouse Grauer, who was sound asleep behind the wheel. He had remained with the motorcar to prevent damage from any troublemakers who might still be roaming the streets.

I dozed on the drive to Grunewald and was near collapse by the time we arrived home. Margarethe, meanwhile, seemed quite fresh, although she too had been awake since before five. She had indefatigable energy, and emergency surgery always stimulated her. Afterwards, she often had difficulty falling asleep. I never had such problems.

Although I would have preferred to sleep alone, eking out what rest I could before morning, I invited myself into Margarethe's bed.

"Please forgive me," I said meekly to her back.

"You know how foolish you were to be in that neighborhood tonight. I needn't underscore it," replied Margarethe in a tart voice.

"I'm so sorry for causing you worry," I said rubbing her shoulder. "Please, forgive me," I pleaded. After a moment, she turned and took me in her arms. She brushed away the errant lock of hair that always escapes my braid and softly kissed my forehead.

"Promise me you'll be more careful," she said, strengthening her embrace. "I would die if any harm came to you." Despite the hyperbole, the statement pleased me. If nothing else, it reassured me that despite our recent quarrels and her unforgiveable indiscretion, she remained devoted to me. I began to doze as she gently stroked my back.

At first light, Margarethe quietly slipped out of bed. I tried to rouse myself so that I might speak to her, but I simply couldn't open my eyes.

Later, I discovered that Margarethe had gone back to Halensee to look in on Frau Gerstein and Frau Rabinowitz.

Part IV

MARGARETHE

Chapter 13

Grand rounds with my young charges were never without interesting moments. Our tour down the hall began in the usual way. We stopped at the bedside of each patient. The doctor in charge presented the case. My fellow, Sarah Weber, who was senior to the residents, interns, and students had a steadying influence on the others and set an edifying example. She had excellent patient management skills. She greeted each of her patients with great warmth and presented her cases in a quiet, matter-of-fact voice designed to reassure. Her summaries were always informative, yet tactful.

She was already such an excellent physician that I often wondered what she expected me to teach her. She had once confided that she'd hoped to learn "a way of thinking about medicine." As if any of us could think any longer! The Chamber of Medicine had recently issued a flurry of memos directing us to incorporate "racial hygiene" into all medical training. I wondered how I could bear to teach such spurious science to unwitting students and junior doctors. Not only would the military and SS students imbibe this intoxicating brew, but all the rest as well.

My concerns distracted me as we proceeded through rounds. Fortunately, the cases that morning were fairly humdrum: tubercular lungs, a mastectomy case, an appendectomy, and a young man suffering from an inguinal hernia. This condition had certainly caused him great pain in addition to being disfiguring. The hernia had progressed to the point where strangulation was a distinct possibility, which left no option but to repair it. In an earlier time, there would be no question that this man was as entitled to medical care as any other German citizen. This patient's case was suddenly under scrutiny for one reason alone. He was mentally defective.

The young man was affable, trusting in ways that a shrewder man might not be. He greeted us with great enthusiasm but had special words of warmth for Dr. Weber, who was overseeing the case. Despite the Reich's dim view of the retarded, this man was not a useless parasite on society as the Nazi propaganda would have us believe. He held a post as a messenger and supported himself rather well. He lived quietly with his mother, harming none and enriching the lives of many with his optimistic disposition.

Sarah began to present the case. While she was speaking, there was a private conversation at the back of the group between two Black Shirts.

"Dr. von Richthofen, have you something to say?" I asked in a loud voice, interrupting their conversation. Everyone turned to stare at me.

"No, *Frau Doktor!*" Richthofen replied, snapping to attention as SS members were taught to do when addressed by a superior.

"Then stop this rudeness at once and allow Dr. Weber to present her case."

"Yes, *Frau Doktor!*"

They were silent for a few minutes, but then the muffled conversation and snickers resumed. I was especially disappointed in this young man's poor behavior because he was a relative of one of our great war heroes. Not only had he dishonored our profession that day, he had besmirched a noble name as well. Sarah continued her presentation of the case, ignoring the discourteous behavior of her uniformed colleagues. Fortunately, our hapless patient was unaware and continued to beam at them all.

I waited until we were down the hall, well out of earshot of the patient, to raise the matter. I stopped the group at the coffee urn to allow them a break but also to have their attention outside of a medical setting. While they were drinking their coffee, I confronted them.

"Paulen, what is your issue regarding the Jenner case?"

The SS lieutenant I'd addressed snapped to attention. "I have no issue, *Frau Doktor*," he declared.

"Then what was all the conversation in the background?"

He glanced nervously at his cohorts. "We were only wondering why the retard needs his testicles. We certainly don't need his kind reproducing."

"And what kind is that, Paulen? He's a full-blooded Aryan, just as you and I are."

"But he's mentally defective. His mental deficit could be passed on."

"You are certain that such deficits are heritable?"

"No, *Frau Doktor*, but why should we take the chance?"

"In my experience, most defectives are created through birth trauma rather than genetics. Often the children of such people are as normal as the next man's." I wondered why I was troubling myself to make this rational argument to people who fervently believed the Reich's propaganda.

"But even so, how could he care for a child? He can barely look after himself."

"How do you know?"

"It is clear, *Frau Doktor*. Everyone knows."

"Indeed? And how would you feel, Paulen, were your testicle hanging halfway to your knees? Surely you would wish a surgeon to intervene?"

The young man blushed to the roots of his perfectly Aryan blond hair. He grinned at Sarah. "If my surgeon were Dr. Weber, I might consider it."

Sarah, to her credit, registered no expression in response to this lewd suggestion, but I had decided the conversation had gone quite far enough. "In that case, I would insist on being your surgeon, Paulen. Of course, I couldn't guarantee that my scalpel would be as steady as Dr. Weber's. One little slip and..." I made a little cutting gesture and winked to emphasize my point.

His uniformed comrades guffawed at his expense. The self-deprecation was meant to be ironic. My hands never shook. In fact, they called me "old iron nerves" behind my back.

Fortunately, the remainder of rounds proceeded without further incident, and I was frankly glad to be rid of them. I tried to remember that they were just young men, certainly no worse than most, and in many ways better. They were the brightest stars among the next generation of surgeons. Sauerbruch chose only the best for the Charité.

Heading back to my office, I became aware that someone in a hurry was following me.

"*Frau Doktor*, a moment, please?" Sarah paused to compose herself after her dash down the hall before adding, "Thank you for defending me."

"Defending you?" I asked, trying to keep my eyebrow from arching. A skeptical look is second nature to me and sometimes impossible to control. "I thought I was scolding your colleagues for their rudeness in front of a patient."

"Well, you certainly pulled Paulen up short. And what you said is true. The patient has a right to treatment."

"He does?"

She opened her mouth to launch into a speech, but I held my finger to my lips to stop her. One could never be too careful. "Hold that thought," I whispered, opening the door to my office.

Once the door was closed behind us, she began again. "That man desperately needs treatment. Why shouldn't he get it? Just because he's retarded?"

"Dr. Weber, you put me in a difficult position."

She frowned and gave me a long pensive look. "Surely, you don't agree with Nazi medical policies."

I scrutinized her face, wondering how far to trust her. My instincts told me that she was completely trustworthy, but these were strange times.

"What I say must stay in this room for obvious reasons."

"Of course."

"To answer your question: no, I don't agree with the concept of racial hygiene. However, I would be a hypocrite if I failed to admit that I have sterilized severely retarded women based on the assumption they were incapable of caring for a child."

"You weren't alone in that."

"In an institutional setting, where rape is a very real possibility or a hapless woman is easily seduced, it seemed a practical solution, but not a means for 'purifying the race.'"

"In such a case, it's reasonable and could be justified."

"Perhaps. However, I'm not so sure the end justifies the means." I invited her to sit. "In fact, I'm quite out of patience with this racial hygiene nonsense. It's spurious science, and yet I am forced to teach it. I think I must resign my post at the university."

She looked stunned. "But you can't. You have to stand your ground and be a voice of reason. It could make a difference."

I reminded myself that she was an American. Their devotion to what they called "freedom of speech" colored their perception of our politics.

When her fellowship year was done, she would sail home to the States, and all of the challenges we Germans faced would be but a fading memory.

"Perhaps it would make a difference to speak out, but my tenure would be rather short lived. Besides, the National Socialists would rather not have women in university posts. Female academics hardly fit the *Kinder, Kirche, Küche* model of the ideal German woman."

She looked bewildered. "How could this happen? I came to Germany because it was so progressive. This is a modern country. Women had professional freedom here while American women were still struggling for recognition."

"Things are not always what they seem," I replied. "And as you can see, conditions can deteriorate rapidly."

She gazed at the orchids on my window sill in a long moment of reflection. Finally, she said, "It's very discouraging to see you so negative. Are you really going to let them win so easily?"

"No, but in such times as these, one must play one's hand very skillfully, staying one step ahead at every turn."

"What will you do?"

"As I've said, they will probably be glad to see me go. I am the last female on the faculty of medicine. I'm not the sort of docile woman the new order prefers." I smiled ironically at this understatement.

Sarah continued to look grave. "Your resignation will make a statement," she finally said. "I hear Sauerbruch is moving on to a big government post and you're in line to succeed him."

"You mustn't believe every rumor, Dr. Weber," I replied mildly, although this rumor happened to be true. "Perhaps my resignation will signal a protest, but it will change nothing."

She frowned as she thought about what I had said. "I admire you for standing up for your principles, but it is a great loss to the faculty of medicine. Now there will be one less voice of sanity. Where will it end?"

"My dear, I fear it will become much worse before we see the end of this madness...if we ever do."

After Sarah left, her righteous indignation remained in the air like smoke. Her words gave me the impetus to take writing paper from my desk and compose my letter of resignation. Writing the actual letter proved to be difficult. It was an extraordinary honor to be a member of the medical faculty, especially for a woman, and I would truly miss teaching, although my role as the overseer of the rowdy, junior surgical staff at the Charité would give me ample opportunity for instruction. What I found most challenging was coming up with a plausible reason for my departure. Being entirely candid, especially on paper, would be unwise. In the end, I defaulted to the usual excuse—family obligations. God knows, they were legion. As I was sealing the envelope, I decided to deliver the letter in person. In order for my statement to have significance beyond releasing me from a position I now found untenable, I needed an opportunity to amplify its message. I called the office of the dean of medicine and set an appointment.

I'd often walked the short distance from the Charité to the Humboldt University campus distracted with thoughts of my impending lecture. This impromptu preparation had become something of a ritual. I seldom if ever wrote actual notes. As I entered the brick building where the offices of the faculty of medicine were housed, I realized that this might be my last visit to that place.

I ascended the stairs with a heavy heart. In the great hall on the second floor, bronze busts of famous faculty lined the walls: Virchow, Koch, Behring, Erlich and many other brilliant scientists and physicians, the heroes of the Charité and the University of Berlin. A few of the pedestals stood empty now, the nameplates removed, the busts taken away. Men once considered eminent were now discredited simply because they were Jews.

Professor Aretz and I were old acquaintances and had developed a good rapport. He had begun his tenure as dean not long after I was granted the post of lecturer. He read the letter in my presence. As he read, his face grew pale. I had assumed that the resignation of a troublesome, female academic would be welcomed. However, I had failed to consider how the departure of so eminent a medical person as myself would reflect on the university. Though I might be the wrong gender, I certainly had other criteria to recommend me, including credentials in two specialities, sheaves of published research, and university habilitation. Obviously, the dean was also very much aware that my wealth had allowed me to be a generous patron of the medical school.

Aretz stroked his salt-and-pepper beard and stared at the letter for some time. Finally, he looked up and gazed at me with a frown. "I don't understand, *Frau Doktor*. Your lectures are very popular, and you receive the highest ratings from your students. Clearly, you are a gifted teacher and you seem to genuinely enjoy teaching."

"It's not dislike for teaching, Aretz. It's reprehension for what I must teach." He looked alarmed to hear me speak so openly. "In this room, for your ears alone, I shall speak the truth. I cannot continue to teach lies to impressionable young minds. And this racial pseudoscience is most certainly a lie." At this, he looked even more distressed.

"*Frau Doktor*, we have already lost so many fine teachers..." He paused for effect rather than speak the reason aloud—they were Jews. "We are already overburdened and badly in need of senior physicians like yourself to share the benefit of their experience."

"Someone should have thought of that sooner, before turning out so many of our colleagues and forcing the rest of us to give up our academic freedom. Aretz, you cannot tell me you think we are still teaching *science*."

He gazed at me for a long moment before shaking his head. He rose and offered his hand, which I took. There was much unexpressed emotion in his face, as I'm sure there was in mine.

"Thank you, *Frau Doktor*, for your contributions to the university," Aretz said. "Your resignation is a profound loss."

I nodded and showed myself out. Another glimpse of the empty pedestals in the hall confirmed that I had made the right decision. But what if I had depended upon my teaching position for my livelihood—to put a roof over our heads and food in our mouths? This perception made me grateful to have the means to afford principles but also fearful for those who did not.

***

The morning post brought new confirmation that abdicating my teaching post was the right thing to do. I received a packet of pamphlets from the Chamber of Medicine, which included drawings of ideal Aryan physiognomies. There was a note enclosed instructing me to distribute these to my students and junior colleagues to aid them in distinguishing racial "types."

My first response was to laugh over the absurd renderings and deposit them into the rubbish bin, but then I saw myself in them and looked again. No, I hadn't been drawn by some Nazi artist unawares. It was only that I so embodied the physical type the party venerated. I too was blond and blue-eyed. My facial structure and features were so completely regular that in many ways, my face was unremarkable. I was the perfect image of the Aryan woman. One of the photographs on my desk, taken years before on one of our Garmisch outings, showed a tall, blond woman with two blond children, all rosy-cheeked and blue-eyed. Printed large, with a bit of cleverly designed typography, the image would make a perfect "Strength through Joy" poster.

My thoughts were interrupted by a knock at the door. "Come!" I called without enthusiasm, but I was pleased to see that my caller was Sarah Weber. She attempted an apology for disturbing me, but I interrupted her.

"You're not disturbing me, Dr. Weber. It's my duty to make myself available to you." In fact, I appreciated that she never presumed on my time because it made me feel more generous. I invited her to sit and listened while she described a situation requiring a difficult decision. The law required that we report our hernia patient as mentally deficient.

"His case is borderline," she said. "He's a bit slow, but is he actually retarded?" I realized she wanted me to make the decision because only an attending physician had the authority. I saw an opportunity for instruction.

"Then perhaps a report is unnecessary. What do you think, Doctor?"

She frowned a bit as she considered her answer. Her face was remarkably expressive, not always the best thing for a physician. So often we need to hide our feelings when delivering bad news or there is pandemonium during surgery. I was tempted to lecture her about minding her expressions more carefully, but I bit my tongue. I was a colleague, not a patient. There was no benefit to masking her feelings with me and why, after all, should everyone conform to my rigid standards of detachment?

A long pause elapsed as Sarah continued to ponder the question. To move the discussion along, I asked, "How do we define mental deficiency? By what measure?"

"By standardized tests. Logic. Vocabulary. Arithmetic."

"There are many people who perform well on such tests and yet are incapable of looking after themselves."

"True."

"Our patient, on the other hand, makes quite a nice life for himself. In short, I think competence should be the measure, not standardized tests. Will that answer solve our problem, Doctor?"

After a moment of reflection, she smiled. "Yes, actually, it does." It pleased me that one never needed to belabor a point with Sarah. Often, surgeons are brilliant technicians, but dullards about everything else.

I handed her one of the pamphlets that had come in the morning's post. "For you, Doctor," I said.

She scanned it quickly. "Tell me this isn't real."

"I'm afraid so."

"They all look like you," she said.

"And you."

"What does it mean?"

"Very little. It means that we have blond hair and pale eyes, and that our ancestors most likely came from northern or central Europe. Beyond that, nothing."

"What's the point?"

I shrugged. "There may be something scientifically useful to be derived from this, but not the conclusions our friends in the Chamber of Medicine have drawn."

This set us down the path of friendly argument. Watching Sarah's face become animated, pensive, sometimes red, fascinated me. I perceived how she strove for tact, not wanting to offend me, her elder, despite the fact that I egged her on, trying to force her out. This went on until I heard my stomach complain and glanced at my watch.

"Perhaps I could interest you in joining me in the doctor's dining room for lunch?" I asked.

Her face brightened so obviously that I was embarrassed for her. Was I ever so full of admiration for a mentor, even Sauerbruch?

❀❀❀

Heavy thoughts oppressed my mind during my consulting hours. I was still moody over my resignation and my conversations with Sarah. How had we come to this point? I hardly recognized the country in which I lived. Gone were the heady days of artistic creativity and intellectual innovation ushered in by the Weimar Republic. While my political conscience had been dozing, the most radical elements had taken hold in our country. The Nazis had promoted themselves as the party that would cure the ailing economy and restore Germany to its former greatness. Now that they had consolidated their grip on power, they were bold enough to show their true colors. They would purge our country of anyone who failed their rigid tests of racial purity.

Ordinarily, I would have taken myself to task for bringing my personal feelings into my consulting room, but my appointments that afternoon were all routine post-operative visits. I managed to convince myself that my distraction could cause no great harm.

Towards the end of the day, my nurse advised me that only one patient remained. Still out of sorts, I asked for a delay in order to smoke a cigarette and rearrange my mental landscape. I told my nurse that she could leave for the day. Before she agreed, it was necessary to reassure her that I was more than capable of managing the next patient on my own. I smoked my cigarette in blessed peace. Feeling better prepared, I opened the door to the reception area.

There sat Eva. Her dark eyes smiled with pretended innocence. Caught completely off guard, I couldn't stop my surprise and anger from showing. I felt the young secretary's eyes on me as I fought to get control of my face, forcing it to assume a look of dispassion in an effort to maintain professional decorum. I turned to the secretary and said, "Fraulein Hauptmann, you may go for the day."

"It's no trouble, *Frau Doktor*. I'm happy to wait until your patient leaves."

"I said, *you may go*," I said more forcefully than necessary. Clearly, my attempt to restore professional decorum was not succeeding. Only Eva could put me so off balance. The poor secretary looked injured and a bit worried, which made me regret my imperious tone, but I wanted her out of there as quickly as possible. There must be no witnesses to what might transpire. She hurried to arrange her desk and snatched her purse from the drawer. "Good night, *Frau Doktor*," she said in a brisk voice as she headed out.

Eva continued to smile with a subtle look of enticement. Of course, she expected a kiss, but my response was quite different.

"How dare you arrive here unannounced!" I demanded.

Eva gave me a look of elaborate indignation. "I have an appointment. Your secretary failed to tell you?"

"My secretary knows I'm not accepting new private patients."

"Yes, and so she said. But I convinced her that we are old friends, and she put me on your calendar."

This indicated the need for a little chat with my secretary, but to be fair to the woman, I had scolded her on more than one occasion for failing to recognize the personal importance of certain patients.

"My letter was quite clear."

"Clear, yes. Convincing, no. Can you really expect me to believe that career demands are keeping you from me? Nonsense. I came to see for myself."

"Really, Eva. I have no time for this. I must ask you to leave."

She gripped my arms. "Margarethe, I need the advice of a doctor."

My observations about her health returned to me in a flash. Perhaps her visit to my consulting room was justified. My attitude instantly changed from one of profound irritation to professional concern. "Are you ill?"

"Not exactly."

"What does that mean?"

"I'm with child."

Despite my surprise, I managed to make a polite response. "Congratulations."

"You don't understand. The child is not my husband's." The look in her eyes made me anxious. Would she dare ask me to terminate the pregnancy? In the past, I had come to the aid of my friends who found themselves in similar straits, but under the Nazis, performing an abortion had become extremely dangerous.

"Get your husband into your bed. He'll never know the difference. Maybe he can't count."

"Margarethe! How can you be so flippant! This is a catastrophe. I cannot bear his touch. It's been months since I've allowed that man into my bed."

"Then close your eyes and pretend he's one of your lovers."

"How can you be so hateful, when I love you so!"

"You've said it many times. I don't love you."

She began to cry, clutching me to her. "Please, my darling. I need someone discreet. You are my only hope. I need you!"

I found her dramatic pleas repulsive. Extricating myself from her arms, I spoke in an even tone. "I'm sorry, Eva, but I can't help you. You must leave. *Now*."

Her weeping ceased at once. "I made a mistake in coming to you," she said in a flat voice. "I won't trouble you again."

When she had gone, I found a file folder with her name on my desk. How had I missed it? I tore it and the notes form within into tiny shreds and fed the confetti to the wastebasket. Eva had never been there, never consulted me. If she found a solution more to her liking, I could deny any knowledge.

Chapter 14

I was instantly ashamed of myself. I had never refused any reasonable request for my advice as a physician, and a part of me sympathized with Eva. For the sake of wealth or land, many an aristocratic woman had been married off to a much older man whose touch she could not bear. I was able to broker my own marriage only because I would eventually hold my titles in my own right, and my father was such a forward-looking man. Of course, my parents made suggestions as to suitable matches, but in the end, I made my own choice.

Eva had never spoken at length about the emotional climate of the marriage, but I'd taken from her remarks that Allessandro was a possessive man. His men accompanied Eva everywhere. She was only allowed to roam so freely in my company because as a woman, I theoretically posed no threat to him. Perhaps expedience was the reason Eva had chosen a female lover. Now, expedience dictated that she get her husband into bed as soon as possible, or the news of her pregnancy could be her undoing.

Over the next days, my conscience chafed at the idea that I had violated my personal code of duty, both as a professional and as a friend. Perhaps it was only my lesser self, attempting to justify a desire to see Eva, but I convinced myself that I must offer my assistance.

I chose to telephone rather than wait for a response to a note. Contacting Eva required three separate attempts. By the third time, I swore that it would be my last, but Eva finally took my call. As usual, she knew the exact limits of my patience.

I decided to take a neutral approach to avoid making apologies for the scene in my office. "Let's meet for lunch."

"Why?" she asked coldly.

"We must eat. Why not do it together?" This was not entirely true. I needed to eat, whereas Eva seemed to thrive on coffee, wine, and air.

We agreed to meet for lunch at the Continental. Out of habit, I arrived early. I ordered a glass of Pinot Grigio while I waited. The wine was sweeter than I usually prefer, but I was trying for a friendly, positive mood, and the thought of drinking something heavier did not suit it. We had agreed to meet at noon, but when the hour came, there was no sign of Eva. Another thirty minutes passed. I ordered another glass of wine. Eventually, I began to doubt Eva would come. It would not be the first time she had set an appointment and failed to appear. I was about to leave when she arrived, full of apologies.

She regarded my white wine with disdain and asked the waiter to bring something red. My stomach was already rumbling with hunger so I ordered my lunch before the waiter could get away. Eva ordered only salad. She was unable, as usual, to finish her meal.

"I loathe pickled vegetables," she said. "You Germans cannot prepare anything without vinegar."

"It's a preservative," I murmured. "Acid is an inhospitable environment for bacteria."

"Spare me the science lesson, *Frau Doktor*," she replied irritably.

"If you're still so angry with me, why agree to meet?"

"Why ask me to lunch?"

"To discuss your dilemma."

"A dilemma no longer. I finally succeeded in getting Pietro into my bed. At first, I thought he could never complete the act. Finally, he was able, although it required extraordinary measures." Fortunately, she did not elaborate, and I forbade my mind from imagining it. "Like most Italian men he thinks he is a fountain of virility. What a delusion!"

"At least now, he can think the child is his."

"He can think what he wants," she said bitterly. "I wanted this child. Pietro had given up the idea of an heir and wanted to adopt his nephew. Now I can do my duty to our family. Perhaps then he will leave me alone."

So, she hadn't wanted an abortion, after all. "So why make an appointment at my office?"

"You wouldn't take my calls or answer my notes. What choice did I have? And I've heard that you had excellent training as a gynecologist." Whenever I regretted this diversion in my career, it was because some woman was with child and needed my help. I was uncomfortably reminded of how Katherine had once ambushed me in my office as a pretext to announce her pregnancy.

"But I no longer actively practice that speciality. I haven't for years."

"You could make an exception in my case," said Eva.

"No, I could not. It's never wise for physicians to treat their intimates. Whenever I am tempted, it inevitably ends in disaster."

She sighed. "A part of me hoped you would take me as a patient. It would help me convince Pietro of the timing of the conception if my physician went along with the scheme."

This made me wonder how she had been able to get away from her husband's men long enough to find someone to impregnate her. "If your husband watches you as closely as you say, how were you able to meet your lover without being followed?"

"I told him I was visiting Dr. von Stahle. He allowed me to travel with my maid. She is entirely loyal to me." The idea of being an unwitting accomplice in the plot disturbed me. She smiled slyly and reached across the table for my hand. "I knew you would come back to me. I knew if I pleaded for your help, my dear Octavian, you would be unable to resist."

I withdrew my hand. "I'm here only as your friend."

"Nonsense, Margarethe, you belong to me now. You must always come back to me." She gave me one of her beguiling little smiles. "I understand you have a room here." Indeed, I kept a room at the Continental reserved for my mother's use during her increasingly rare visits to Berlin. I had long since given up the pretense that she would wish to stay in the Grunewald. "We could make good use of it," suggested Eva, gazing at me through half-closed eyes. I took a deep breath as I tried to concoct an excuse, but my mind went into instant confusion when she reached under the table and put her hand on my thigh. "Just this once, *cara*. Please. I need it. My soul needs it."

We went to the front desk so that I could get the key. While we waited for the lift, I wondered what kind of madness had possessed me. We rode to the sixth floor. In the mirrored walls as the lift opened, I was again confronted by the fact that I was ridiculously tall standing beside her. We walked down the hall at an unhurried pace. I dallied from reluctance; she from her usual patience.

There was no preamble, no conversation as Eva undressed at the bedside. I was reminded of the one and only time I had engaged a prostitute, on Konrad's dare, years before. She too was silent except for asking what I liked. As she demonstrated her skills, I felt nothing but pity for her. I gave her two hundred Marks and told her to buy herself a good meal. Konrad told me I had been far too generous.

Eva undressed until she was wearing only a camisole and garter belt. I watched her unhook her silk stockings from the tabs. She sat on the edge of the bed to await me. Mechanically, I removed my suit coat, stepped out of my shoes and began to open the buttons of my skirt. It was clear that I was procrastinating. I tried to muster more enthusiasm, stripping off the remainder of my clothing as I would to get ready for a swim. The thought helped a little, as it has always been easy for me to be undressed for athletic pursuits. Finally, I knelt beside her.

She caressed my hair. Her fingertips traced a path down to my cheek. I was curiously unmoved by her touch. To encourage me to action, she put her tongue into my ear before whispering, "Darling, I have wine for you." She lay down on the bed and her legs parted. I could see the moisture glistening on her sex, open and lush as one of the orchids in my hot house. "Come, my love. It's all for you," she urged.

Her scent made me light-headed, and I struggled to breathe. Suddenly, the feeling of suffocation became overwhelming—her potent, female smell filling up the space in my lungs instead of oxygen.

I sprang to my feet, snatched up my clothing, and fled to the outer room, where I dashed into my clothes. By the time I'd finished dressing, Eva was also dressed. She gave me a cold look before she left. I waited a good five minutes to make certain she had caught the lift ahead of me.

***

To attempt a return to rationality, I retreated to my Charité office and busied myself with dictating a long-overdue report. I was just concluding when Sarah flew into my office.

"Someone is here to take Jenner."

"What do you mean *take* him?"

"A man came to remove him from the hospital."

Quietly dismissing the secretary was a deliberate act meant to set an example. Sarah took the hint. She composed herself and explained more calmly: "There's a man here with official papers signed by the Chamber of Medicine. He says he's taking Jenner to a place in the country."

So, the day I had always feared had arrived. We had all heard the rumors about the "rest homes" in the country, where they took the mentally ill and retarded. The poor souls who were removed to such places were never heard from again.

"I don't understand. We agreed not to report his mental deficiency."

"I didn't report it, but it seems someone else did."

"Where is this man who intends to take Jenner away?"

"He's waiting in the visitor's room. I told him he couldn't take any patient without your permission."

The official who had come for Jenner had bland features and pale skin. He was tidy. His brown suit was pressed and clean, his shoes carefully shined. He was rotating his hat in his hand while he waited. He looked so absolutely ordinary.

He smiled when he saw me, and I was momentarily disarmed. "Good afternoon, *Frau Doktor*, I appreciate your time and apologize for interrupting. Your associate says you must sign the papers."

"Yes, but Jenner is due to be released tomorrow. He has no need of further medical care."

"Perhaps not, but his mother is elderly and cannot assist him during his convalescence. The state has generously offered to provide him with a few weeks of respite in the country. It's a beautiful place, really, near a lake. He'll enjoy the rest."

"As I said, Jenner does not require further care."

"It's a gift. To show the generosity of the Reich to its people."

"It is generous, but unnecessary to his health. What if I refuse?"

The man smiled patiently and spoke in a low voice. "You do understand, *Frau Doktor*, that refusal is not an option."

The official thrust a clipboard with the release form in front of me. Sarah shot me an anxious look. I was momentarily worried there might be a scene. When I made no move to sign the paper, the man handed me his pen.

"Thank you for your cooperation, *Frau Doktor*," he said, pulling the clipboard out of my hands. "The Reich appreciates it." He gave the Hitler salute. I did not return it.

We watched the man take Jenner away in a wheel chair. The poor man gazed at Sarah with an imploring look before the double doors swung shut behind him.

"Do you know anything about the place where they're taking him?" she asked.

"No, but I can guess it's not a place intended for his good."

"Then why didn't you stop them from taking him?"

"What could I do exactly?"

"I don't know. But I wish we had done something."

❖❖❖

At dinner, Katherine asked if I would attend Fiona's riding demonstration. This was her way of letting me know that the girl's riding lessons, which had been my idea, were now my responsibility. She had insisted that the girl was too young, but I believe it is never too early to form a good seat on a horse. I have been in a saddle since I was old enough to sit erect.

After I assured Katherine that I would attend the event, she went on telling me about her day. Everything about her annoyed me that evening— the dress she wore, her sniffling due to a slight cold, and her non-stop, idle chatter. I sat at the other end of the table, glowering at my food, yet she seemed not to notice that my mind was elsewhere. Instead, she continued on about Becher's latest paper, which I had read and thought woefully lacking in originality. I attempted to comment at appropriate times so that she would believe she had my attention. Then she asked me a pointed question, and my charade was exposed.

"You haven't heard a word I've said."

"Pardon," I murmured. "I have other things on my mind."

"As usual," she said testily and asked for her wine glass to be refilled.

I excused myself and went to the music room. Katherine followed me. My irritation over the invasion of my privacy was out of proportion to the offense. I interrupted the sonata I'd been playing and glared at her.

"Don't stop on my account," said Katherine.

"I've finished, really," I said, closing the keyboard cover.

She sat down beside me on the piano bench. "Margarethe, what's wrong?" she asked, caressing my arm. "We have a rare bit of time together and you're silent as a stone."

The resentment that had been bubbling just below the surface began to boil up. How dare she presume that because she had granted me an audience that I should wish to attend?

"I'm going up to bed," I said, rising.

"Good idea. I'll come with you." This was exactly the result I'd hoped to avoid, but Katherine took for granted that she was always welcome in my bed. Usually, I found her presence comforting, but that night, my bad conscience over seeing Eva was overwhelming. And I had no illusion that Katherine's presence in my bed meant anything more than sleep.

When I returned to my bedchamber after completing my evening tasks, Katherine's nose was in a book. It often amazed me that, in a house with over thirty rooms and a library that was the envy of any scholar, she found it necessary to read in my bed. "Will you be reading long?" I asked in a mild voice.

"Only briefly. Will the light bother you?"

"No, probably not," I said with a sigh and rolled over to sleep.

I was just beginning to doze when Katherine said, "Margarethe, what's troubling you?"

"Nothing!" I snapped. "I was just falling asleep!"

"My apologies," she replied, sounding defensive. I settled against my pillow once more. "You've been so distracted," she added.

"Well, if you must know, I was required to release a retarded patient to one of those 'rest homes' that we've been hearing about. The poor man will likely never return."

"Oh dear, Margarethe. That's horrible!"

"And I have resigned from the university."

"What!" she exclaimed with genuine shock in her voice. "When did you decide this?"

"Last Tuesday. I made an appointment with Aretz and told him."

No doubt, she was mentally calculating that nearly a week had passed since I'd offered my resignation. "And when were you going to tell me?" she asked indignantly.

"I don't know. Soon. I'd only just decided myself and you're never here. Now will you please turn off that bloody light and let me sleep?"

Finally, her bedside lamp clicked off.

The few moments of blessed silence were again interrupted. "I cannot believe you never thought to discuss it with me," Katherine said in a pained voice.

I thought about this. In an ordinary marriage, such an important topic would certainly be discussed. However, I'd never discussed my business affairs with Lytton during our marriage. He had no head for such things, nor had Katherine. There was a time when I attempted to explain these matters vital to my interests in the hopes of finding a companion with whom I could share my burdens. But Katherine had shown little interest or understanding. As the years went by, the list of matters that we did not discuss had grown longer still. Once I had shared all my personal feelings with Katherine. If I had a quarrel with someone at the hospital or felt a bit sad over nothing at all, I told her about it. If I ached with menstrual cramps, I went to her for sympathy. Now I kept these insignificant bits to myself.

"I'm sorry I failed to discuss it with you, Katherine. It's been a difficult decision, something I needed to come to terms with on my own. Can you understand?"

"No," she replied honestly.

"Well, then, let's discuss it!" I said, my voice brisk with anger. I sat up and pulled the lamp chain so hard that it snapped back and hit the bulb, nearly breaking it. "I've taken leave from the university effective immediately. I can't bear the meddling in my teaching any longer. Now, is there any more to say?"

"No, obviously not," Katherine replied in an equally brisk tone. She rolled over. As she adjusted the eiderdown, cold air rushed into the gulf between us.

***

The next day, I waited with Fiona until the last possible moment before departing for the riding demonstration. Finally, I rang the hospital. The ward clerk told me that Katherine was in the delivery room attending a birth. Prickling with anger, I headed off to the Grunewald stables with Fiona.

"When is *Mutti* coming?" asked the girl.

"She won't be joining us this afternoon."

"Why not?"

"*Mutti* is very busy with a lady who's about to have a baby."

Fiona's face adopted a thoughtful attitude as she considered this. For someone so young, she was extremely reasonable. "Why does *Mutti* have to work so hard?" she asked after a long period of reflection. "Aren't we rich?"

"Yes, we are. But *Mutti* is a doctor, and her patients need her."

"*Tante*, you're a doctor too, but you can come to my riding demonstration." Leave it to a child to see the obvious inconsistency.

"I've been a doctor longer and needn't work quite so hard." I felt plainly ridiculous trying to explain this to a child. For Fiona, this was an important moment, and she only knew that her mother would be absent. "You must make do with your *Tante* today." She moved closer to me on the front seat of the motorcar and leaned against me.

"*Mutti* doesn't know as much about horses. It's more important for you to be there." I was flattered for the space of a heartbeat, then saddened for Katherine, whose place it should have been.

Fortunately, I'd had the good sense to change into my riding attire before we left. After the charming little show, we left Fiona's pony with the grooms and took a quick ride on my horse around the Grunewald horse path. Fiona's little, warm body in front of me on the saddle comforted me.

We both stank of horses when we arrived home. I sent Fiona off in the care of her nurse and went up to bathe. Katherine had still not returned, so I invited Fiona to dine with me in my sitting room. Such private moments recalled my father, who used to steal me away from my nurse, sit me in his lap, and tell me stories. He reserved the foam of his beer for me. Then he would laugh at my white moustache and call me, *"Der Nicklaus."*

When Katherine finally arrived, she found us side by side on the sofa in my sitting room, sound asleep.

I woke to Katherine's scolding. "She should be in bed by now!"

I squinted at my watch and saw that it was half-past midnight. "It was not my intention to nod off," I muttered. "We were waiting up for you."

"We must get Fiona to bed. At once!"

Transporting the child to her room was my duty. Fiona was getting heavy, and Katherine could no longer easily carry her. As I collected the sleepy child into my arms, her head rolled on to my shoulder and a great mass of red hair came into my face. She half woke. *"Mutti,"* she murmured.

Katherine kissed her and I headed off with my little burden. The nurse was still awake, waiting for her charge, but it was I, who undressed Fiona and put her to bed.

When I returned from my errand, Katherine said, "You mustn't keep her awake past her bedtime, Margarethe. It disrupts her routine."

"It's harmless," I replied in a dismissive voice.

"It is essential that children be in bed at the same time every evening. Otherwise they cannot form good sleep habits."

I nodded and went into my dressing room to change into my pajamas. Katherine followed me. "I am so sorry I missed the riding demonstration."

I shrugged. "It wasn't my event. Don't apologize to me."

"It was a difficult labor. I couldn't leave."

"I understand," I said. "My only grievance is that you didn't telephone. I waited until the last possible moment before setting off."

"I'm sorry. I didn't think."

Katherine left to put on her nightgown. In a short while she returned, just as I was about to switch off the light. She kissed me, and said, "Margarethe, you are a very good mother. Probably better than I shall ever be."

After delivering this odd message, she left.

Chapter 15

S t. Hilde's Hospital always held quarterly meetings of the board of directors on the first Thursday of the month. Usually, I preferred to go on a mental holiday while we debated such critical issues as the brand of coffee to serve in the doctor's dining room. That morning I listened with polite attention as the members reviewed the qualifications of the proposed candidates for chief of staff. When my name was raised, the chief director gave me a little nod, and I excused myself.

I wondered what they would say about me in my absence. Would they debate, as they should, my relative merits versus those of other potential candidates? No doubt my grandaunt, a member of the board *ex officio*, would have made a strong recommendation that I succeed the incumbent. However, I hoped they would disregard her support and judge me solely on my credentials and experience. It was fantasy, of course. A person with social connections and money is never judged on merit alone.

While I waited in the anteroom, I chatted with the secretary, whose cleverly fabricated brassiere gave her significant breasts the distinctive profile of artillery shells. I regretted this crass thought when she was kind enough to offer me a cigarette, which I smoked slowly and deliberately in an effort to calm an unexpected case of nerves.

The discussion in the boardroom turned out to be brief. I interpreted this to mean that my candidacy had either been a foregone conclusion or had been summarily dismissed. In either case, I would have to wait until the selection committee convened at a later date to see if I would be invited to apply.

After I returned to the meeting, the board moved on to other critical matters such as the decorations for Christmas and the holiday party for the staff. Would we simply have punch or a wider variety of liquors? The room filled with smoke as everyone partook of the wooden box filled with cigarettes in the center of the conference table. An odorous cloud developed overhead.

During the discussion of the new x-ray equipment, the door suddenly opened and the secretary, looking very pale, gestured to me. I pointed to myself, and she nodded. Once outside the boardroom, I began to scold the young woman for the interruption.

"Please forgive me, *Frau Doktor*," she said, cutting me off, "but this is an emergency." She stood on her toes to whisper the nature of the crisis directly into my ear: "Dr. von Holdenberg has taken ill..."

"Ill? What do you mean *ill*?"

"Sister Marthe can tell you more. She's just outside."

Sister Marthe was indeed waiting for me in the hall. "Forgive me for troubling you, *Frau Doktor*, but Dr. von Holdenberg is in terrible pain, and she's asking for you."

"What seems to be the trouble?"

She hesitated. It was not a nurse's place to offer a diagnosis. "An ectopic pregnancy, I believe."

"What!"

"Please, *Frau Doktor*. You must come at once!"

I flew down the three flights of stairs with Sister Marthe at my heels. We dashed through the waiting area. In the sitting room adjoining her consulting office, Katherine lay on the daybed. Her legs had been raised to avert deadly shock. She was pale as a corpse.

"Call Becher," I said, speaking as quietly as I could to avoid telegraphing my alarm.

"We have paged Dr. Becher and telephoned his residence," said Sister Marthe, attempting to sound calm but not completely succeeding. As a credentialed midwife, she knew very well how dangerous this situation could be.

"Try again. Don't worry. I'm here to look after her."

Sister Marthe went into the consulting room to call Becher. Meanwhile, my fingers sought the pulse in Katherine's wrist. It was racing and she was growing paler by the moment. I raised her legs higher. Her dress pinched her as I attempted to reposition her. Without regard for her modesty, I rent it from the hem to waist. The sound of it ripping startled Katherine. "Relax, my darling. The dress doesn't matter," I soothed as I moved to palpate her abdomen. The localized rigidity indicated the possibility of internal bleeding. She wrenched away from my touch when my hand neared the left ovary.

"Was there any warning?"

She looked anguished. No doubt, the source lay beyond her physical troubles. "Yes, cramps today and yesterday. And spotting. Then the bleeding began."

Sister Marthe returned from her attempt to raise Dr. Becher. "I am sorry *Frau Doktor.* His man said he has gone out, and he knows not where."

"Where in Christ's bloody hell is that blasted man?" I exclaimed in English. Marthe stared at me. There was no need to understand the language to know that this was a string of expletives.

My thoughts came rapidly. If I did not intervene at once, Katherine might not survive.

"Please prepare an operating room. Call Sister Anna up from surgery and ask the ward clerk to round up some blood donors." My training allowed me to emulate a state of calm while I gave these orders. Within, I was purely terrified.

I took Katherine's hand now that we were alone. "Now, Katherine, tell me the truth. Could you be pregnant?"

"I used a syringe to…" Her mouth twisted and she was unable to continue. However, she had given me all the information I needed.

"Thank you for your candor." I gave her a kiss to reassure her that she needn't fear my anger.

Two orderlies arrived with a gurney to convey Katherine to the operating theater. I accompanied them down the hall. Her hand continued to hold mine so tightly that it actually became numb. Even when the nurses came to prepare her for surgery, she wouldn't let it go.

"Stay with me," she begged.

"Please, Katherine. I must scrub. We haven't much time."

"Come closer. I must say something…something personal." I put my ear near her lips. "If anything happens to me…"

"You mustn't even think such a thing!"

"Please, Margarethe," she said in a desperate whisper. "I love you. Please tell me you know it!"

I mouthed the words to her.

"Take her pressure," I ordered Sister Marthe over my shoulder as I headed off to scrub.

My mind raced as I tried to plan the procedure. It had been ages since I had done that kind of work, although I had once been quite adept at complex gynecological surgery. I tried to remember the steps, but it was as if my brain were in a fog or I was drunk. I simply could not think! What if we were unable to stop the bleeding? I wondered as I washed my hands under the too hot water and doused them with phenol. I was nearly reciting the textbook to myself as I dashed into the waiting gown and gloves and entered the operating room. Fortunately, when I stood at the table, I met Sister Anna's confident eyes and instantly felt steadier. Anna was always stalwart in emergencies.

I purely loathed the gynecological operating theater because it was not nearly so well equipped as the surgical suites below, but there was no time to move Katherine. The bleeding must be stopped at once. The nurses finished placing the drapes. Surrounded by sterile linen, the exposed area was totally anonymous, as if no real person lay beneath, only an expanse of skin waiting for my scalpel. Gritting my teeth, I made the first incision, going a bit deeper than I had intended. After steadying myself, I began to dissect down.

"Stahle, get out of here!" cried a loud voice. Becher stood just outside the sterile field, impatiently shrugging on a gown while Berthe desperately tried to place gloves on his waving hands. I ignored him, but within moments he was at my elbow. "Move over," he ordered.

"No."

"Don't be a fool. Let me in!"

I was occupied with cutting the peritoneum above the ovary. I could see the dark blood pooling beneath, seemingly buckets of it. As soon as there was an opening, Sister Anna deftly moved in to suction it.

"Stahle, get out of my operating room!" insisted Becher.

"I have privileges at this hospital." It was hardly a time to bicker, but I was incensed and actually glad because my anger trumped my anxiety. "How dare you speak to me in that fashion! I am a member of the board."

"I don't care if you are the fucking *Führer* himself. Get the hell out!" I had never heard Becher use profanity, not in all the years we had worked together, so it made an impression. After a moment of indecision, I handed off the instruments to him and moved aside.

"I shall remain to watch," I said, stepping back. Becher was an excellent gynecological surgeon. I always learned something from observing him at work, so my motives went beyond my concern for Katherine.

"Not on your life. Get out! Now!"

He nodded to Sister Anna who, handed off the instruments to Sister Marthe, and took me by the arm. "Come, *Frau Doktor*. Let's wait outside."

"But it was going so well," I protested as I allowed myself to be led into the scrub room.

"Yes," Anna agreed. "But why not leave it to someone with a clearer head? Someone who can maintain detachment. It's best for the patient." Anna accompanied me to the doctors' lounge. "Let's sit down," she advised.

"No. I can't sit. I'll go to the theater gallery to watch."

"*Frau Doktor*, I advise against it. Katherine needs you to be calm. We all need you to be calm." Did I look that disturbed? I caught a glimpse of my face in the glass partition and saw that it was ghostly white. My eyes were brilliant with fear. "Sit down," Anna urged gently. "I'll get you something to drink." She returned after a moment with strong tea and Mother Monica, the superior of the convent, who took my hands in hers.

"I've just heard. *Frau Doktor*, I am so very sorry." My mouth couldn't form the words to thank her so I merely nodded. "Dr. Becher is the finest gynecologist in Berlin," she added. "You can trust him to look after her." She nudged me towards a chair and applied gentle pressure on my shoulder. "Sit down. You look pale."

Evidently, they feared I might faint. It was unlikely; I have never fainted in my life. However, I was completely unprepared for what came next. Tears filled my eyes and rolled down my face. When I made no move to brush them away, Anna offered me her handkerchief. She gave my shoulder a reassuring squeeze. Whatever the nuns' prior suspicions, the true nature of my relationship with Katherine was now transparent for all to see. Of course, they had known for years. There had been rumors of an intimate relationship between us even before Katherine left the convent. It was the reason why my grandaunt had finally encouraged her to leave. Gazing into Monica's sympathetic gray eyes, I was grateful that I neither had to hide my feelings nor explain them.

After Monica sent Anna back to the operating room, she sat down beside me and took my hand. "Let's pray, shall we, Margarethe?" In private, Monica always addressed me by my given name. "I know how dear Katherine is to you," she said in a steady voice, which also served to confirm my suspicions about her knowledge. She pulled her rosary beads closer so that I might touch them.

"Please, no Aves," I begged, reclaiming my hand. I simply couldn't bring myself to repeat the dreadful words, "now and at the hour of our death..."

"Oh, but it is a prayer to the mother of us all. And you know how devoted Katherine is to her." In fact, Katherine kept a shrine to the Madonna with the centerpiece being the little statue of the Madonna I'd brought from Oberammergau when she was still a nun. However, Monica couldn't persuade me to say the awful words nor touch her ridiculous beads.

Perceiving that prayer was not the best means to induce calm, Monica attempted to distract me with talk of some staffing changes she wished to make. The rumors that I would become chief of staff were rampant. As the local superior, Monica would also have privileged information from my grandaunt, the superior of the order. I tried to focus on what Monica was saying, but a glance at the clock on the wall told me that Becher had been at work for well over half an hour.

"I must know what's happening," I said, attempting to get up.

"Stay here," said Monica, putting her hand on my knee to hold me down. "I'll ask."

As soon as Monica was out of sight, my mind instantly invented the worst. Katherine was dying but no one dared tell me. I sprang up from my seat, but Monica intercepted me before I could escape to the operating room gallery.

"The crisis is over," she said, "but she's lost too much blood. They're looking for more donors."

"Take my blood," I offered, rolling up my sleeve. "We have the same type."

Mother Monica urged me back into my seat with a firm hand on my shoulder. "Sit down, Margarethe. You're in shock over this tragedy. We'll find other donors."

"I insist! " I said in my most imperious voice.

Monica sighed and sent a nurse to fetch the transfusion apparatus. Sister Marianne, our champion phlebotomist, was elected to place the hollow needle. She found the way into my vein on the first try. I often envied her this knack. As the needle pierced my arm, I was reminded of the thorn pressing against the heart of the nightingale in Oscar Wilde's fairy tale. The story was one of Fiona's bed-time favorites. I could recite it by heart and sometimes did when she needed entertainment on a long drive. "Press closer, little nightingale," cried the Tree, "or the day will come before the rose is finished." I silently recited the fairy tale in my mind as I watched my blood siphon through the tube into the glass jar. My pressure was probably greatly elevated from anxiety, and the bottle filled in no time.

"Take all you need," I said with ridiculous heroism as they removed the needle.

"We'll do no such thing," scolded Monica, taping a lump of gauze over the needle wound. "You'll give a half liter like anyone else. In your state, we wouldn't dare take more."

In fact, it was some time before I could sit up without feeling dizzy. Mother Monica offered me sweetened tea. While she was talking to the duty nurse, I saw my opportunity to escape, slid off the gurney and slipped into the scrub room so that I could spy on proceedings through the glass. To my great alarm, Katherine was as pale as death as Becher labored over her. His blond brows were knit in worry. The nurse hung the transfusion bottle from a hook and placed the needle into Katherine's arm. I was moved by the thought that the blood filling her veins was mine.

Naturally, I couldn't stay out of the operating room. I scrubbed and slipped in quietly behind the sterile field. Sister Berthe looked concerned but offered me a gown and mask without question. Becher scowled over his mask when he realized I had entered the room.

"Stahle, I thought I told you to stay out of here."

I didn't answer, being more intent on surveying his work than listening to his annoying admonitions. I began to understand why the procedure had gone on so long. Becher had carefully excised the embryo, and with great patience, had reconnected the tube. I complimented him on this delicate and exacting work.

"Thank you," he growled. "Now get out and sit down before you *fall* down. You look like death."

Satisfied that everything was under control, I headed to the recovery ward to await Katherine. The dizziness that had overtaken me after the transfusion returned, so I was happy to stay seated and stationary.

Katherine was finally wheeled in on a gurney. She looked so extraordinarily pale that she could only be described as cadaverous. I was frightened to the point of panic. Then Becher came in, and his presence reassured me.

"She'll recover completely," he said, resting a comforting hand on my shoulder. "The tube may even heal to the point of being functional. It's difficult to predict." He gave me a sheepish look. "Stahle, forgive me for being so rude."

We had known each other for years, so there was no need for an apology. "You were entirely correct in ordering me to leave. But we couldn't locate you. Time was of the essence."

"I would have done the same in your position," he admitted. "I'll look in on her later. But call me at once, if there's any change."

As I sat waiting for Katherine to awaken from the anesthesia, I began to piece together what had occurred. Katherine had attempted to inseminate herself with a syringe. Konrad had most likely contributed the sperm. Of course, she had chosen her husband as the donor. Katherine was too proper to do otherwise. But the idea of this conspiracy was very disturbing. If they had only told me what they intended, I might have grumbled, but ultimately, I would have gone along with the scheme. Why hadn't they known this?

As I continued to examine my feelings, I discovered that anger had no part in them. If anything, I felt unspeakable remorse. My stubbornness had forced Katherine to the point of desperation. Perhaps it had also endangered her life. Artificial insemination had only been tested experimentally in humans. Because there was no research to speak of, there was also no way to determine whether the method had contributed to the ectopic pregnancy. Unfortunately, they were common enough when conventional means of conception were employed.

I looked at the beautiful hand I held. It was a good deal smaller than mine, but well made, with delicately tapering fingers. They were good hands, deft and sensitive—one reason why Katherine made a fine physician…and, I might add, such a good lover. Although she had lately been a stranger to my bed, I still desired her, and despite my ridiculous and unfortunate indiscretion, I loved her with my whole heart.

I kissed her. In her ether-induced sleep, Katherine sighed. Behind me, I heard the swish of drapes, followed by the sound of a female throat clearing. I looked up. Monica's calm, gray eyes gazed back into mine. I smiled to disarm any feeling on her part that she may have intruded.

"I came to see if she's awake," she said, taking Katherine's wrist in the reflexive act of a nurse arriving at a patient's bedside. "Good. Her pulse is steadier. Dr. Becher says that she'll make a full recovery. That should be of great comfort to you."

"Most certainly. And I must thank you for your prayers."

"We all pray for you, Margarethe. You are the patroness of the order and very dear to us…" She patted my arm. "…and very dear to me as well." She and Katherine were close friends, that I knew, but I was surprised to learn Monica had such warm feelings for me. "Get some rest now," she urged in a gentle voice. "I'll sit with Katherine until she wakes."

"Thank you, Monica, but this is a vigil that I alone must keep." She nodded in understanding and went out through the curtains.

After some time, the ether fog began to fade. Katherine stirred. I called for ice chips to feed to her. Finally, she opened her eyes. "My darling," she murmured, and she gave me a look of love such as I hadn't seen since our earliest days. "Thank you," she said, "for coming to my aid."

Why would she feel the need to thank me for doing what I would only consider my duty? Her warmth and generosity in the face of her own pain made me feel even more miserable for my selfishness.

"Tell me what they found," she insisted, "…please, spare no detail."

"It was ectopic. You lost the fetus, of course. But Becher repaired the isthmus very skillfully, and it may eventually be functional."

"Why should that matter?" she said with a sigh. "Now that you know, it can never be."

"We can talk about that later," I said, giving her hand a squeeze. "But tell me, how long were you aware of the pregnancy?"

"Just a few weeks. That's all."

"Why didn't you *tell* anyone?"

"I thought I could look after it myself." She often lectured me against the folly of treating myself, so I only needed to give her a firm look to make my point.

The conversation, however brief, had required heroic effort on the part of someone who had just endured profuse bleeding and invasive surgery. Katherine eyes began to flutter as the ether haze threatened to reclaim her. I squeezed her hand to bring her back.

"Once they bring you to your room, I'll make arrangements to stay the night."

"No," she said with closed eyes. "You must go home and see to our daughter." After that, she lost consciousness, so I had no opportunity to argue with her. She barely stirred when they moved her to a private room on the gynecology ward.

Becher came in to give her an injection of codeine against the pain. "We were lucky," he said to me on the way to his office. "A more extensive hemorrhage, and it might not have turned out so well."

One question continued to trouble me. I decided to ask it, although it meant betraying what Katherine would consider a confidence. "Could artificial insemination have contributed to the ectopic pregnancy?"

Becher raised his bushy eyebrows and rubbed the back of his head as he considered my question. He kept his head shaved and had lately been sporting a Charlie Chaplin moustache like Hitler. Becher never wore a party pin on his lapel, but I wouldn't be surprised to learn that he was a Nazi sympathizer.

"Well, we really don't have any research on artificial insemination in humans. I doubt it would make a difference how the sperm is delivered. So, yes, I suppose it could, but probably no more than ordinary conception."

I nodded. "Please never tell Katherine I asked this question. She would be mortified to learn that you knew."

"Not to mention your cousin," he said with a little grin.

"Nor he."

"You needn't worry. I'll never breathe a word of it."

Katherine remained unconscious for most of the afternoon. Fiona would soon be wondering why her mother hadn't come home. Katherine kept Thursday afternoons free to spend time with her.

I called Mother Monica, who came over from the convent at once.

"Of course, I'll stay with her, Margarethe," she said in a reassuring voice. "Go home and look after the child." When I hesitated, she added, "Please, go. And trust that Katherine is being looked after by those who truly care for her."

Fiona was waiting in the front hall for her mother. I took the child into my arms and rested her on my hip. "*Mutti* can't come to the zoo this afternoon, my little mouse. Your *Tante* will have to do."

Fiona studied me intently. "Is *Mutti* with her patients?" So often, this was the excuse we gave the poor girl, but I could not bear to lie to those eyes that looked so like Katherine's, blue with gold flecks in the irises.

"No, dear. Your mother has taken ill. She had a very bad pain in her belly," I said, giving her abdomen a little poke. "She must remain in hospital for a few days."

"May I see her?"

"Not just now. She needs rest to get better."

"When can I see her?"

"Perhaps tomorrow if she's feeling well enough."

"Can we still go to the zoo?" she asked hopefully, which made me laugh, the one light-hearted moment in a day fraught with anxiety and crisis.

"Yes, of course, my darling."

Grauer drove us to Berlin's famous zoo. Fiona was fascinated by the reptiles. Fortunately, they were housed indoors because the late autumn afternoon was raw. Miss Carter had bundled Fiona in a heavy wool coat with matching bonnet and leggings. I was not so warmly dressed and suddenly longed for my fur coat and Eva's fedora, which by my choice had never left the hat box.

Fiona especially liked the glass tank of pythons and could not wrest her eyes from the sight of the giant beasts, as thick around as my thigh, interwoven like a massive rope.

"How can they eat?" she asked. "They have no hands."

I explained how a python winds its way around its prey ever more tightly until the life is crushed out of it and demonstrated by encircling Fiona with my arms and giving her a little squeeze. "Then he opens his mouth very wide." I opened my mouth wide, made gobbling sounds, and pretended to eat Fiona. She squealed in mock terror.

After we concluded our tour of the exhibits, Fiona and I went to the Zoo Cafe for ice cream. She couldn't eat all of hers; it was an adult-sized portion. I consumed most of it without complaint, for Fiona shared my weakness for chocolate. The delicious sweetness soothed me until I thought about Katherine, weak and in pain in her hospital bed and felt miserable.

As we drove back to Grunewald, Fiona suddenly asked, "Will my mother die?" She had asked this question with such absolute dispassion that my blood ran cold.

"Fiona, your mother is very healthy and will soon be as fit as ever," I said in my most convincing voice, but the question had reminded me how close Katherine had actually come to death. I instantly banished the thought from my mind, knowing how easily adults can telegraph their worries to a child.

We ate supper in my sitting room. Afterwards, I told Miss Carter of my intention to keep Fiona with me for the night. The nurse looked distressed, as if this plan were somehow a reflection on her, which in this case, it was not. I was merely trying to reassure the child with my presence and attention.

Fiona and I ensconced ourselves in the canopied bed in my bedchamber, and I told her tales of mischief from my youth, despite knowing that I was doing Miss Carter's efforts towards discipline no favors. Fiona snuggled against me. Her presence comforted me, and I suddenly wondered why I had so strenuously opposed the idea of another child. If Katherine had followed my advice when her first pregnancy was discovered, we would not have our dear Fiona with her delightful curiosity about the world. There could be worse things than another child in the house. As the day had shown me, much worse, indeed.

***

The next morning, I headed to St. Hilde's to see Katherine before my consulting hours. Fortunately, her color had greatly improved, indicating that her blood pressure and red cells were returning to normal levels. The pain, however, was worse than the previous day as is common after surgery. I telephoned Becher to tell him of my intention to give her more codeine and then rang the nurse to bring me a syringe. Once the medication began to take effect, Katherine was considerably more comfortable.

I described my evening with Fiona. Katherine nodded thoughtfully. "You always doubt yourself, Margarethe, but you're very good with children. Despite what you think, you're a very good mother." She sighed. "I wish I had more time to be a mother."

"Perhaps you might ease up a bit on your career."

"My career has never been as important to me as yours is to you."

"I can see that now."

"You can?" she challenged. "I so wish we could have had this kind of frank talk earlier." She grimaced as she attempted to raise herself on her elbows. I adjusted the pillows for her.

"We should reserve this conversation for a more favorable occasion. You're in pain."

"Yes, but I want to talk about it while I have your attention…and we are both being so candid. Margarethe, if you had only listened to me, I never would have done this behind your back." Was she apologizing to me? If so, it was both ridiculous and pointless.

"Katherine, to be clear, I never forbade you to have another child. I merely argued against it."

She gave me a meaning look.

"I was giving advice. And it's not for me to decide. If it is your wish to have another child, then get on with it, but conceive it in the ordinary way, in your bedroom with your husband. I did the same when I needed children. At times, one needs to make concessions to nature, and this is one of them."

Katherine looked surprised. "Just like that?"

"What else?"

She sighed and covered her eyes with her hands. "I've been very foolish, haven't I? I've risked everything, even my life."

"Actually, we don't know if your scheme contributed to your ectopic pregnancy. As for the subterfuge, this trick worked on me once before. I allowed it the first time, so you had every reason to think it would work again. I'm the foolish one. I should have known better. Once you make up your mind to do something, you always find a way."

"Then you don't hate me?"

I began to perceive how truly cruel and insensitive I had been. "No, my dearest Katherine. I have never hated you. Quite the contrary." To underscore the meaning of my words, I kissed her temple at that vulnerable spot where the skin is so pale that a vein shows blue beneath.

Part V

KONRAD

Chapter 16

Naturally, people thought I ought to be apprised of my wife's distress. My cousin sent me a wire in Bochum, where she supposed me to be. But I was not there. Instead, I had gone to Prague to look after some business having nothing to do with the family enterprises.

When I received Margarethe's message, which had been forwarded to me via telegram by my loyal secretary, I had just returned from paying the rent for the little warehouse the *Pilze* used for storage. We always paid cash for the rent. It was Stahle money, of course, but no one must ever know the source, especially not Margarethe.

I had already exhausted all of my own cash. I couldn't sell off my securities because our brokers would certainly tell her. Instead, I was reduced to selling my jewelry—cuff links, and the like. The few gold bits fetched practically nothing. Eventually, I discovered how easy it was to write bogus purchase orders for equipment, which we may or may not ever need in one of our few remaining factories or mills. I later realized that this was even more clever, for it enabled us to ship the crated order under legitimate drayage forms.

In short, I had become a rather sophisticated smuggler, although the goods transported beneath the watchful gaze of the Reich's customs agents and the ministry of commerce had little worth. Certainly, they were not for my profit. No, the crates that arrived in our factories and mills, and which were immediately removed to another warehouse, were filled not with industrial equipment, but with paper. They were flyers and pamphlets with an urgent message specifically directed to our nation's Roman Catholics: Rise up now while there's still time!

We Catholics were a minority, of course, outnumbered by the two thirds of the country who were Protestants. But we were a strong enough minority to have elected a chancellor from our Center Party in 1930. Shortly after, the little corporal came to power, sweeping away all of our efforts, even the free clinic that Franz Borchert and I founded. At one time,

Katherine had been a nurse in that clinic—the nexus through which our lives intersected.

Franz and I had been collaborating far longer. In our university days at Ludwig Maximillians in Munich, we had our own little *Kreis* of intellectuals devoted to phenomenological philosophy and the liberal ideals on which the Weimar Republic had been founded. Franz and I became friends at once. He had a brilliant mind, and he was delightful to look at, being as fair-skinned and red-haired as Katherine. He had the most penetrating amber eyes, rather like those of a predatory forest creature. I worshipped him and his sleek body, which was also animal-like. Despite the physical attraction, ours was a noble love worthy of the ancient Greeks.

Then, without a word of warning, Franz abandoned me and ran off to a Jesuit seminary. In the beginning, his intention to become a priest meant little. He shared my bed whenever we could. After he took his vow of celibacy, he told me, "Never again." It depressed me to think I had lost him to the church forever, but as it turned out, I had nothing to fear. With very little encouragement, he could be induced to fall off the rails. Oh, I could describe the most splendid holiday we spent together in Margarethe's Alpine chalet in Garmisch, but Franz certainly wouldn't like that. He wants everyone to think he is serious about his vows, and certainly, he means to be serious.

For our rendezvous in Prague, Franz and I decided to meet in a different place from the usual because we liked to keep the authorities guessing. The tavern we had chosen was also ideal in another regard—it was often frequented by our kind.

I sat at a table near the front window to await him. As soon as I saw the flash of red hair in the street lamp, my heart began to race. Franz came into the smoky place. We wound our way around the rough patrons to a table far in the back. He threw himself into my arms, and I drew him into a shadow so that I could kiss him on the mouth. He laughed but then let me kiss him again. It always excited me to kiss him, not only because he was a priest and therefore forbidden, but because I had never fallen out of love with him.

"It's so wonderful to see you, old man," he said, squeezing my arms. I suddenly wished that I had taken more advantage of Margarethe's basement gymnasium. Franz kept himself in splendid physical condition by playing tennis and lifting weights. His biceps were hard, whereas mine easily gave to his touch.

We sat down to order some Pilsner and food. While we ate our meal of smoked ham, boiled potatoes, and cabbage, I told Franz about my recent journeys on behalf of the Stahle enterprises. He liked my stories of adventure in Louisiana and especially enjoyed my tale of the nocturnal boat ride and the alligators under the light of a kerosene lantern. Naturally, I reserved how like an alligator I'd felt waiting outside the stevedores' tavern in Spandau. There was no need for him to know, although I'd once confessed—in the ordinary sense, that is, not as to a priest—that my tastes were changing. I offered the rationale of getting older and finding it harder to be stirred by conventional sexual advances. He frowned a little, but there was no judgment in those beautiful eyes exactly the color of fine cognac.

"Perhaps you lack feelings for your partners, and that's the trouble," he finally said. "With love, all things are possible."

"Love would certainly help," I said, but as much as I wanted to tell him the truth, I simply couldn't. I still loved him and longed for him with all my heart.

After eating, we got down to business. I told him of the plan to deliver a crate to our warehouse outside Berlin. From there, the trunks inside it would be sent to *Pilze* members and distributed throughout the country.

"I think this should be our last printing," Franz said. "Pamphlets are only marginally effective, and the cost is so high. You know what they did to that poor man who was caught with a trunk." I'd heard of the terrible way the Gestapo had treated our comrade. They beat him within an inch of his life and carved a swastika on his cheek. He later died of his injuries, despite the efforts of the good sisters at St. Hilde's to save his life. Mother Monica later explained that the internal injuries required the intervention of a surgeon, and they dared not call one.

Franz responded to my thoughts as if he could read them. "We need a physician we can trust. Can we ask Katherine? She recently helped one of Monica's Jewish friends. And it was on *Kristallnacht*. What a nightmare!"

I had been in the Ruhr on the "night of broken glass" and the demonstrations had been just as ugly there. Caught in traffic as I tried to get home from the plant, I watched from my automobile as the synagogue burned to the ground. The beautiful old building had been standing in that same place for over two hundred years. There were fires everywhere, people screaming, and the glass from store windows all over the street. Behind the scene, like the sound track of a newsreel, was the steady sound of marching boots and the fervent singing of the *Horst Wessel Song*.

"Katherine is too innocent. I would never put her in such danger. We need someone shrewd and tough, who can mount a defense, if necessary."

"Someone like Margarethe von Stahle?" asked Franz, raising his chin a little because he knew this would be controversial.

"Well, yes," I agreed. "If we can convince her. She hates politics."

Franz frowned. "You must do the convincing. She's never liked me."

"Can you blame her? You're forever trying to convert her. Why can't you accept she's a confirmed atheist?"

"Because it makes no sense to me. How can anyone be an atheist? And it's a scandal that she, the patroness of Obberoth, is an unbeliever. The nuns are forever praying for her return to the faith. How can she resist?"

"You know why. Because you're all trying so hard to change her. One must be very sly with Margarethe. Give her room, and she will come to you."

He gave me an odd smile. "Are you still so familiar?" It took me a moment to perceive the meaning of his question.

"No, I gave that up long ago. Katherine forbids it, and for that matter, anyone else sharing her lover's bed."

"Good for Katherine," he said, nodding. "Margarethe needs someone to keep her in line."

I laughed. "Why are you so hard on her? It only makes her dislike you, and you're such a good and likeable fellow at heart."

He shrugged. "It's my role as a priest to enforce the laws of the church and to chastise sinners."

I threw back my head and roared with laughter. "Oh, Franz. You are such a fraud!"

Our amusement was short-lived because we moved on to planning our members' missions. We were the leaders of the *Pilze* and everyone looked to us to keep things running smoothly. Margarethe's money certainly helped. There were many petty officials who were easily bought. The cash also paid for forged papers, passports, and visas. It was abundantly evident that the Jews had to leave, but where could they go? We debated this for some time. Spain was merely a point of transit and had enough worries of its own. Only the very rich were able to relocate to England. America wanted nothing to do with Jews unless the refugee in question had mountains of money or excellent political connections.

Franz looked aghast when I told him that I was literally reaching into Margarethe's pockets to fund these activities. "What if she discovers what you're doing? Then what?"

"Oh, my dear, she'll never find out. I promise you."

"Why not simply ask for her help?"

"She still believes that the Kaiser will regain his throne and restore the nobility to its rightful role as the natural leaders of German society."

"Not really..."

"I swear to you! Oh, she's a realist, all right, and knows in her heart that the past will never return. But oddly enough, she's also a romantic and still believes in the natural right of the noble class to lead. I tell you, Franz, I've tried to analyze it, but it only makes my head hurt."

Franz laughed and pointed to our empty beer pitcher. "There's the source of your headache, I think." Then he sighed. "Yes, I remember her devotion to the noble ideal. In some ways she is as great an admirer of the *Übermensch* as the National Socialists." He looked into some distant place and recited: "Can you determine your own good and evil and hold your own will above yourself as a law? Can you be the judge of yourself and enforcer of your law? It is terrible to be alone with the judge and enforcer of one's own law. It is like to be a star flung into the void and into the frigid breath of solitude."

I sighed. "That was simply beautiful." I was even tempted to clap, but it would have attracted the attention of the rough trade in the tavern.

By then, we were both in our cups, and I was tired of talking about philosophy and the dark future we envisioned. I wanted to lose myself for a few moments and forget it all. So, we ordered another pitcher of Pilsner.

After we drank all the beer, Franz decided he was too inebriated to report, as planned, to the Jesuit house in Prague. Instead he agreed to accompany me back to my hotel room.

"We mustn't do anything," he ordered, wagging a finger under my nose as we supported one another to the taxi.

"Of course not."

I succeeded in undressing him and poured him into bed. Then I washed and looked after my evening chores. When I came to bed, Franz was snoring lightly. I stroked his beautiful red hair and pressed my lips to his forehead, thinking only to kiss him and then turn away to sleep. But he drew me to him and began to kiss me. Eventually, he invited me to touch him. I loved to run my hand down his hard belly where the red hair was dense like the pelt of a fox. Below was the great, strong manhood that always rose to my touch.

❖❖❖

I woke Franz the next morning by accidentally slamming the lid of my valise while looking for my shorts. He turned away, looking shy because I was naked, even though he had loved me so beautifully with his mouth the night before. I had allowed him into my body, holding him and loving him so completely because I knew he always held my heart with such care. The tenderness between us made me wonder how I could ever lust after the big men, who used me so brutally, when I had my dear Franz. But what I had with Franz was only occasional, depending on the alcohol he'd consumed and how long we'd been apart. We had collaborated in every way, yet for some reason I couldn't understand, we could never be a pair in the way that Margarethe and Katherine were. I fought back tears as I scraped my cheeks with the razor.

I heard him get up but dared not look at his magnificent body with its pelt of red fur. Somehow, daylight always made such things more egregious. I'm sure as he went down the hall to bathe, his vow was very much on his mind.

I dressed in an ordinary suit from one of our Berlin tailors, even though I had a beautiful English Savile Row suit in my luggage. In Czech lands, it wouldn't do to look too fashionable. They were a good people but a bit traditional, and it behooved me to do as I always did on a mission—blend in with the landscape.

But Franz had no intention of blending in. He put on his priest's clothes. I gave him a hard look to see if there was a meaning in this, but he merely said, "I'm expected to wear it at our Jesuit house." Despite this excuse, I knew the costume was intended to remind me of his station. His soutane and Roman collar, the most obvious outward signs of his priesthood, were like a medieval suit of armor against the feelings he had for me. A priest of his order could wear secular clothes, and Franz often did. A cassock doesn't quite suit a mountain hike. Certainly, he hadn't worn his uniform into the tavern the night before. But I accepted the message. I was tired of arguing with him, and I knew I could never win. His God owned him, and he was forever lost to me.

Before I departed Prague, Franz and I met to rearrange the cells in Cologne and Munich. We were strongest in Bavaria, which was ironic because the little corporal had used that province as his first stepping stone to power. During our debates in the tavern, we had come to the conclusion that we must alter our tactics. There would be no more pamphlets. The political cause was lost. Everyone was simply too frightened. When the state even colludes with children to report their parents, people have good reason to keep their opinions private.

We also realized that our organization must be a network of small, tight groups, whose individual members felt bound by personal loyalty to one another. We chose to concentrate our efforts in the most Catholic areas, where we would have access to sympathetic religious orders. There is no better place to hide someone than in a convent. Nuns are school teachers and wards of orphans, so we could easily disguise young fugitives as their charges. As nurses, nuns were in high demand to aid a people whose physicians were forbidden to practice medicine.

While the decision to focus on the South made perfect sense, it also made me uneasy. The majority of Stahle holdings were in the Ruhr, and of course, I would be expected to spend time in Berlin.

"Not to worry," said Franz. "You needn't be so personally involved. If you can only help us find the money."

"Actually, I know where there's a great treasure trove of that!"

"But really, Konrad, you are tempting fate by abusing Margarethe's trust. If she discovers what you've been up to, there will be hell to pay. You must tell her. I think she would be happy to help if she only knew how. Try to enlist her."

"Oh, Franz, believe me I've tried."

"You succeeded once before. She gave generously to your campaigns. Look, she funded our clinic, purchased the building, furnished it with medical supplies…she even paid the salaries."

"That was out of personal affection for me. This is different."

"Yes, this is different. The stakes are much higher."

"But one must have a political conscience to embrace such an idea. One must see it as a duty."

"Ah," said Franz smiling broadly. "How clever you are, my boy. I think you've just uncovered the compelling argument to use against your noble cousin. What Prussian can resist the call of duty?"

Clever boy, himself. I could instantly see how his Jesuit training had benefited both Franz and our cause.

Chapter 17

I took a circuitous route home to avail myself of the opportunity to visit the resistance cells. When I finally returned to Berlin, I learned that we would be departing for Edelheim the very next day. Margarethe had simply assumed that I would go along and had already ordered my things packed. "You need a holiday, my dear. We all need a holiday." She had also taken it into her head that Katherine needed country air to recuperate. Of course, it was December and the country air would be rather cold. But the cold never stopped Margarethe, nor anything else for that matter!

A trip to Edelheim, Margarethe's ancestral home, suited several purposes. Margarethe was due to look in on her mother, and at that time of year, there was another compelling reason to visit Edelheim—the great stag hunt in honor of the lady of the manor. Margarethe had never missed this event, not even while she lived in England. Ironically, because Margarethe held her titles *suo jure*, she was technically the lord. The lady continued to be the dowager countess, Lady Ursula, Margarethe's mother and my aunt.

On the evening we were to depart, the weather was ugly. Throughout the day, a chill rain had fallen, and after dark, a cold wind blew in. As we left the city precincts, the changed sound of the soft patter on the roof and windshield indicated the rain had begun to freeze. We stopped several times to scrape the windshield to keep the wiper blades from freezing. I offered to drive, but Margarethe wouldn't hear of it. She wouldn't allow Katherine to drive either, so she herself drove for hours in the miserable weather becoming increasingly grumpy in the process.

Finally, we turned into the drive to find the gates closed. They were nearly always closed since my uncle died. Still despondent and taking her widow's role seriously, my aunt received few guests.

The guard lumbered out of the gatehouse to unlock the gate. His greatcoat hung open, despite the weather, and he wore no hat. No doubt, our arrival had torn him from his favorite pastime, smoking his meerschaum pipe while listening to patriotic music on the wireless. He smiled as he approached, or rather the edges of his gray bush of a mustache curled up. As he bent to peer through the open car window, I could smell the schnapps on his breath. Well, why not? In that lonely gatehouse, he must have needed a nip now and then, just to keep warm. In the icy air, his breath was vapor.

"*Meine Gnädigste*," he said with a bow, addressing Margarethe. "They've been waiting for you." His speech was thick with the Polish accent of East Prussia.

"Close down and go home," said Margarethe. "No one else will be coming in tonight."

"Thank you, Lady Margarethe, but it would never do to leave my post. What would your father say?" The gatekeeper, like nearly every man in service at Edelheim, had once been a soldier under my uncle's command.

"I am Mistress of Edelheim now," Margarethe said lightly. "Must I order you?"

"No, *Gnädige*," he said, standing at attention and clicking his heels. "I shall obey at once!"

Margarethe rolled up the window and headed up the drive. The granite façade of the Schloss came into view. Why it was lit by spotlights I never understood. It was conspicuously ugly, enormous beyond imagination, and incomparably dreary.

To be sure, Edelheim is considered to be one of the great houses of Prussia, and I have many fond memories of the place. When I was a boy, my father sent me to my uncle to toughen me up. From the time I was seven, I spent nearly all my summers at Edelheim. Like a pair of young hounds, Margarethe and I loped after the Groß-Lichterfelde cadets who swarmed over the manor in summer. They indulged us in every way. We learned to ride and shoot and handle a sword with them, which is how Margarethe became such a devotee of the blade. And it was on the bracken in Edelheim's deepest forest that I lost my virginity to Margarethe at the age of sixteen.

Finally, we reached the house. I always find arrival at the Schloss very alarming. Within seconds, retainers surrounded our vehicle, tearing open the doors. Klowitz, the majordomo, who had once been an artillery officer, shouted brisk orders to the footmen regarding the destination of the baggage.

We trudged up the ridiculous course of stone steps and entered the great atrium with its polished floors of patterned Italian marble, the three-story columns of matching stone, and the immense staircase ascending to the upper levels of the house. Whatever the exterior of the Schloss lacked, the interior redeemed.

We were greeted by a long line of servants. Each, in turn, stepped forward to offer handshakes and words of welcome to the returning mistress of Edelheim. Margarethe dutifully greeted each in turn, returning the handshakes, occasionally offering an embrace or a kiss on the cheek. Some of these people had known her all her life. This old-fashioned ritual took at least twenty minutes, whereafter I finally delivered a very sleepy Fiona into the arms of our old nurse.

"Is my mother still awake?" Margarethe asked Klowitz as he brought glasses of brandy to warm us. It was nearing ten o'clock, so it was possible that we might be spared the trial of paying our respects to my aunt.

"Yes, *Gnädige*. The countess is in her sitting room."

If possible, Margarethe looked even more miserable than before, but she stood erect, as is expected of the daughter of a soldier. "I'll look in on Mother," she said, "You and Katherine make yourselves comfortable. Klowitz will see that you have something to eat."

"No, I'll come with you," Katherine said without a moment's hesitation. How loyal she was. I had personally witnessed my aunt's unkindness to her, and yet Katherine continued to be not only civil, but cordial for Margarethe's sake. Not to be shown up by Katherine's generosity, I tagged along.

We walked through the endless corridors to my aunt's apartment in the east wing. Like her father, Margarethe kept quarters on the other side of the house in the west wing. Though mother and daughter were separated by this remote geography, no physical distance would ever be enough. Finally, we came to the door of my aunt's apartment. I paused before the expanse of polished mahogany to wonder what Margarethe had been thinking to come to Edelheim for relaxation. In her mother's presence, she could not be more tense.

My aunt was sitting near the tile stove to benefit from its heat. Although the house had central heating, it was indifferent at best. The ceilings were too high, and there were so many windows to let in draughts. The heat simply could not be pumped in fast enough. On a chilly night such as that, the house never became warm enough for comfort.

"You're late, Margarethe," said my aunt, not looking up from her needlework. She jabbed the fabric as if she loathed it.

"The weather is foul," Margarethe explained, bending to kiss her mother's cheek. Lady Ursula looked up and grudgingly acknowledged my presence and Katherine's and suffered our kisses as well.

"Have you eaten?" she asked, turning to Margarethe. Of course, she would direct all of her remarks to her daughter. We were beneath her notice.

"No, there wasn't time," Margarethe explained. My aunt rang the bell beside her and instructed the footman to bring sandwiches and wine. I moved a chair closer so that Katherine, who was still looking pale from her recent trials, could sit. I moved near the tile stove to warm myself.

The extended silence was unnerving, so I tried to find a way into conversation. "Do you think the weather will break in time for the hunt?" I asked in a pleasant voice.

"Why do you care, Konrad? You never shoot anything," said my aunt.

What could one say to that? Ordinarily, I would have happily tolerated the silence that followed, but with Katherine present, it seemed plainly rude. Again, I cast about for a topic with possibilities. "Will you be going to France this spring, *Tante*?"

"You know I always go to Paris in the spring."

"Paris is beautiful in springtime," Katherine ventured bravely.

"It rains too often," my aunt replied in a tart voice.

Margarethe made the next attempt to open a conversation. "How is the work going on the new sawmill, Mother?"

"You know better than to ask me. I never trouble myself with such matters."

I was grateful when the sandwiches came because chewing gave me an excuse to avoid speaking. Katherine and I had our own chat in a corner of the room while Margarethe sat with her mother to discuss plans for the feast following the hunt. My aunt continued to stab her needlework. She made this pastime, which was intended to provide relaxation, seem like an act of violence. I winced every time I saw the needle forcefully pierce the canvas and finally had to avert my eyes.

After eating, I was finally able to escape with Katherine. "Are we cruel to leave Margarethe alone with her mother?" Katherine asked as we walked the absurdly long corridor to the other side of the house.

I considered her question. "Unfortunately, *Tante* is Grethe's burden and our sharing it will not make it any lighter."

Katherine nodded gravely. I could sympathize with her, having many times tried to lighten the load for Margarethe only to find my efforts entirely futile.

Katherine's illness inclined me to be a bit more attentive, so I accompanied her to the sitting room in her quarters to look after the fire. I added a few logs to the tile stove and poked in the fire to encourage a flame. "It will be much more cheerful when it's warmer. What a horrible night." I mocked a shiver for emphasis.

"Thank you for tending the fire," she said. "How kind." She sat down with a grimace, evidently still experiencing some pain from the surgery. Margarethe had assured me that it had been limited, but she'd cautioned there might still be pain.

"Was it horrible during your illness?" I asked, warming my hind quarters by the stove.

"The surgery?"

"Well, yes that. But I really meant our mistress's response."

"She would hate to know you call her that. But to answer your question, she was extremely anxious."

"Anxious, not angry?"

"Of course. She was relieved that I survived."

It finally dawned on me how precarious Katherine's situation had been. "You could have died?" I asked, trying to digest the information.

"Yes, certainly, from shock or loss of blood. An ectopic pregnancy is extremely dangerous."

I went to her and took her hands. "Dear Katherine, I am so very grateful you survived. While our relationship may not be what it appears to the world, I am ever so fond of you."

She stared at me for a moment. Evidently, she had no idea how to respond to this heartfelt declaration. Finally, she said the expected thing: "Thank you, Konrad. I feel the same."

I took a seat next to her on the sofa. Out of habit, my hand went into my jacket to find my cigarette case. Then I remembered whom I sat beside and changed my mind. "I keep waiting for the other shoe to drop. She hasn't confronted me yet."

"And it's unlikely she will. She told me we should simply get on with conceiving a child." This remark was accompanied by a sidelong glance with an unmistakable meaning.

"Katherine, you can't really be suggesting you want me in your bed, and we certainly couldn't do it in the house right under her nose. How awkward!"

Her smile faded and she looked away. "First, I must heal. It will be months before we can try again. And even when we do, the chances I can conceive are slim." She looked so discouraged. I felt obliged to put my arms around her.

"Don't give up, my dear. We can even try the nasty-magazines-in-the-bathroom route if you find it less burdensome." Certainly, it would be less burdensome for me.

"I wonder if the method contributed to the problem."

"Could it?"

"I don't know actually. The technique is so new. What I do know is this. An ectopic pregnancy increases the likelihood of another in a subsequent conception."

"Oh, Katherine," I said, strengthening my embrace, "then it's certainly not worth the risk."

She sighed. "As I said, I need time to heal."

By then Margarethe had escaped from my aunt. She came in to say she was going to bed, and I saw my cue to leave.

***

To my surprise and pleasure, the first part of our sojourn at Edelheim was restful. The weather cleared. Margarethe and I went riding every day. Katherine was too tender to sit on a horse, so she stayed behind with Fiona and *Tante* Veronika, who had also come for the hunt.

Soon the hunters and their families began to arrive. The peaceful atmosphere came to an end amidst boisterous billiard games and loud hunting stories told in clouds of billowing cigar smoke. It was for such occasions that Edelheim was so obscenely large. In the evenings, the long tables in the great hall were set for dinner, and there was dancing and after-dinner entertainment. Margarethe sang while my aunt accompanied her on the piano. When Lady Ursula pled fatigue, Margarethe cajoled Katherine into playing the piano. Katherine was shy about performing for an audience but played very well. Margarethe persuaded me to sing with her. Nothing too classical for me. We chose familiar university songs.

We were about to break for brandy and billiards, when one of the guests stood and began to sing *Frülingsgruß an das Vaterland.* Lately, it had become even more popular than when it had been written, over a hundred years before our time. With its martial tone and patriotic text, it had ominous implications in the present. Some of the guests, mostly veterans of the old imperial army, stood and began to sing along. Many among the old Prussian officer class were sympathetic to the Nazis, believing that Hitler would restore them to their former military glory.

Hospitality dictated that Margarethe and I join our voices with the others. Katherine, whether from conviction or ignorance of the tune, abruptly ended her accompaniment, so we sang *a capella.* Margarethe kept us all on key, her ringing contralto, soaring above all the male voices. We were all in our cups, of course, and feeling sentimental. Tears came to my eyes as I sang, and Margarethe sang with as much fervor as any of us. We were patriots, after all, no matter who ruled our land. No one objected, when our guest next launched into *Mein Vaterland*. At the conclusion, the audience applauded with enormous enthusiasm. We realized that we'd found a successful theme and continued with our student songs, less political ones, thankfully. Once we steered away from the nationalistic songs, Katherine suddenly remembered how to play the piano.

The entertainment ended. The card games and billiard matches would go on well into the night, but one by one the family members headed off to bed. Fortunately, the sound was contained on the first floor because it became quite raucous. A roulette wheel had been brought down from the attic and the dice were rolling in several of the parlors. Despite the casino atmosphere, everyone agreed that the most important wager was on the stag hunt. The purse passing through the rooms was soon filled to bursting. Whatever the sum, it would be matched by the family. Colonel von Lauer, the deceased count's closest army friend, was the favorite, followed by a young infantry officer, thought to be the best sniper in the Heer. Margarethe was only third in the lists.

While her marksmanship lacked for nothing, my cousin had never won the hunt in nearly three decades of competing. Winning the hunt required luck and timing in addition to skill with a rifle. Not only did one have to shoot the beast and bring it in before the other hunters brought theirs, the weight and the number of points on its antlers also counted. The wagers continued, and by the time I retired for the night, the purse was approaching twenty-thousand Reichsmarks.

I enjoyed one last cognac and smoked a cigarette before going up to bed. As I passed in the hall, I saw the light on beneath Margarethe's door, and I decided to pay her a visit. Margarethe was alone. Katherine, exhausted from the festivities and her performance, had decided to sleep in her own room. The circumstances were fortunate, for what I had to say to Margarethe must be said in private.

My cousin briefly looked up when I came in. I slipped off my shoes and climbed into bed beside her. "Grethe, darling, do you mind if we talk?"

"Do I have a choice?" she replied, placing a ribbon in her book and setting it aside. She clasped her hands on her lap and struck an attentive pose.

"I need money," I blurted out. Then wished I had given my request and its manner of delivery more thought, knowing how Margarethe loathes muddled proposals. At least, this one had the virtue of being direct and to the point.

"Money," she repeated. "I already give you a great deal of money."

"Yes, I know, but I've spent it all. I need more."

"Konrad," she said, leaning closer and looking concerned. "Have you been gambling?" This had never been one of my vices, so it was a wild guess. On the other hand, one could construe my adventures with the *Pilze* to be a sort of gambling.

"No, I haven't been wagering the family fortunes on the tables, if that's what you fear." At least that part was true.

"Then let me guess. It's for one of your causes, isn't it? When do you have time for causes? I thought I kept you busy enough to stay out mischief."

"Evidently not." I smiled a little, but she did not smile in return.

She crossed her arms on her chest. "Is it political?"

I considered equivocation but decided against it. Margarethe knew me too well and would instantly see through it.

"Yes."

"For or against the National Socialists?"

"You really need to ask?"

"No. But I will say this. Whatever you do must in no way implicate or harm the family. Is that quite understood?" I cringed as I thought of the crates of pamphlets shipped under Stahle drayage forms and felt profound guilt over the idea of betraying her trust.

"I understand," I said.

"How much money do you need?" she asked casually.

I remembered the old adage about fortune favoring the bold. "Fifty thousand will do for now."

She gave me a sharp look. "A rather expensive cause."

"The need is great, and the remedy, expensive. We need working papers and passports…"

"Never mind," she said, "I don't want to hear about it."

"I wish you would let me tell you. We could really use your help."

"Oh, now it's my help you want as well as my money."

"Yes."

"Ask me another time, when I'm completely sober and haven't been singing those old songs."

She picked up her book again, and I realized I had been dismissed.

❖❖❖

The knocking at the door had roused me, but it was still dark, so I pulled the eiderdown closer. In the frigid air, my breath came as vapor. "Wake up, dear. We leave in an hour," said Margarethe, opening the door. I pulled down the duvet a little and gave her a fish-eyed stare. "Here, I've brought you coffee." She switched on the bedside lamp. She was already dressed. Her boots reflected like black mirrors, no doubt having benefited from her personal attention. She loved to do soldierly things—shine her boots, clean her pistol, sharpen her hunting knife, even though she had servants who would be happy to do such things for her. She ripped away the duvet, leaving me to shiver in the cold. "Now get up, you old bag of bones. Everyone's already at breakfast."

Breakfast was a noisy affair. The hunters gathered in the great dining hall to feast on strong coffee, cold meats and smoked fish, soft-boiled eggs, and for those who needed more potent stuff to engender stamina, iced vodka. Margarethe ate hungrily, listening to the others at the table, who were still busy making their wagers for the contest. She glanced at the small notebook lying open on the table.

"What's this? I'm only third in the lists!"

Colonel von Lauer smiled across the table. "Lady Margarethe, has the sight on your rifle been adjusted?"

"It has, indeed."

"Then perhaps I'll reconsider my wager." The colonel began to tell the story of how Margarethe's father had won the rifle as a gift from the Kaiser during one of the stag hunts at Edelheim. Margarethe, as the others, was enrapt in the story and the hunting talk. She reveled in the company of men. Given the choice, she always preferred it to that of her own sex.

After breakfast, we walked down to the stables to choose our horses. Margarethe brought up a large chestnut mare for me. "She's very even tempered. She'll give you no trouble." The horses were all magnificent animals, perfectly groomed until their coats gleamed. Margarethe's father had loved horses, and Edelheim produced some of the finest Trakehner breeding stock in the world. Its hunters and saddle horses commanded high prices.

Margarethe gave me a "leg up" with cupped hands. I waited outside for the others. When everyone had been outfitted with a horse, our hostess finally emerged from the stables on her favorite mount, a bay Trakehner mare, bred from a long line of animals with Wagnerian names, this one "Helmwige," after the Valkyrie.

The hunt master sounded the horn, and we all set off towards the quadrant of the forest to which we had been assigned. The sound of the hoofs pounding on the earth was like the beat of ancient drums as the horses galloped across the grassy meadow. We entered the pine wood in single file. Droplets of water sprayed on our coats as we brushed past low-hanging branches. I felt a wave of awe as we rode into the darkness. It was like the primeval German forest of legend. One could smell the wonderful scent of oak moss and the lichen growing in secret crevices in the rocks and trees.

In many ways, it seemed like just another pleasure ride until Margarethe suddenly stopped. I brought my horse alongside.

"Look. Fresh tracks and deep," she said in a low voice. "A very large animal." She turned her horse and rode into a nearby stream bed. I let her ride ahead. She has always been a solitary hunter and really hates company. She would have happily been a team of one, but no other team would have me, so I had been assigned to hers. I followed by ten paces to avoid getting in her way. I loved to watch Margarethe hunt. She was like a predatory animal herself—alert, silent…deadly.

Finally, Margarethe stopped, slid down from her saddle and tethered the reins to a sapling. She took her rifle from its holster on the saddle. I dismounted too and found a hiding place behind a tree, downwind and out of sight. She bent to examine something on the ground. More tracks, I surmised. With great stealth, she moved along the stream, careful not to dislodge any stones in the process. With a single, smooth motion she moved behind a tree. With the rifle stock firmly planted in her shoulder she circled around.

The report of the rifle made me jump and rendered me momentarily deaf. I put my fingers in my ears and braced for another shot. Deer seldom fell after the first. But there was an extended silence. I gingerly relaxed and dared to look.

The buck had dropped where it stood, killed instantly, yet it continued to writhe. Margarethe took her pistol from her hip holster and shot the poor creature between the eyes. Finally, it lay still. Scarlet streams ran from the round wounds in its head and breast. The white fur at its throat was stained a deep red. The beast's black eye stared accusingly. Margarethe took off her silk scarf and tied it around one of the antlers, her claiming mark.

"Signal the hunt master," said Margarethe, glancing at her watch.

I fetched the horn from my saddle bag and blew the signal. By the time I returned, Margarethe was field dressing the stag. The rules of the hunt required this chore be performed by the hunter who had shot the animal. As this task required considerable strength, some hunters eliminated themselves at this point. Margarethe had taken off her hat and coat and rolled up her sleeves. She single-handedly pulled the dead buck on its back. With an enormous hunting knife, she gutted the beast, rending open its belly with a few deft strokes. She rolled the animal over, and the internal organs spilt out. They would be left behind, providing a feast for the forest creatures.

I signaled again with the horn to help the hunt master locate us. Time was of the essence. Finally, the gamekeeper's wagon rumbled over the rough ground. The men struggled with the heavy weight. They eventually succeeded in loading it into the truck. A trickle of blood ran out and spattered on the ground.

As we rode back to the house, I couldn't get the sight of the dead animal rent open out of my mind. My breakfast churned uneasily in my stomach, but I resisted the urge to vomit. Margarethe loathes squeamishness. However, she wasn't paying any attention to me. She was frowning and distracted as we rode back to the house. I could guess the cause. Although Margarethe had been hunting since she was tall enough to hold a rifle, she never liked the kill. The hunt, yes, but not the kill. She had once confessed that it disgusted her.

When we reached the Schloss, Margarethe and I went to the stables to see to our horses. The stable master offered us hot coffee laced with brandy. Chilled to the bone from our early-morning adventure, I gratefully accepted. We passed a good hour there, warming ourselves in front of a little tile stove. Margarethe was completely engaged in the horse talk. It bored me, but the stable master was nice to look at, so I didn't mind remaining a while. Eventually, one of the house servants found us and confided something directly into Margarethe's ear.

"Evidently, I've won the prize," she said, getting up from her chair. "We must go."

We walked up the hill. I was a bit stiff because I seldom rode in those days. We entered the Schloss thorough a subterranean passage—the shortest route to the door that adjoined the courtyard. The prize-winning buck was already hanging from the great tree in the center of the courtyard, where it would remain for three days. After that, it would be butchered and served at a great feast in Lady Ursula's honor. The other hunters, or at least those who had returned, gathered in the courtyard. Presently, Lady Ursula appeared on the landing with several other ladies.

"In your honor, Lady of Edelheim, a great stag for our feast," said Margarethe, reciting the traditional formula. With a little bow, she gestured to the poor, gutted animal.

Tall and majestic in a coat of silver fox, my aunt looked down on the scene. I tried to imagine it through her eyes. There stood her daughter, hair wild from the wind, her cheek and pristine white blouse splashed with blood, but a thrilling sight nonetheless—extraordinarily tall and handsomely made, hair as blond as wheat, cold under a winter sun, her eyes shining with pleasure in her triumph. Any other mother would be enormously proud, but not Lady Ursula. From her look of disdain, I could guess what she was thinking: *if only today's hero were a man, not my daughter, but a son.*

At first, it seemed my aunt would adhere to form. She called to a foot-man, who carried the bottle of aged brandy reserved for this occasion. Another brought up a tray containing the engraved, silver cup that would be the winner's prize in addition to the purse. "And to you, Margarethe von Stahle, the cup of the champion," said Lady Ursula, pouring the drink.

The crowd broke into cheers and applause as Margarethe ascended the stairs, but as she reached the top step, the cup suddenly fell to her feet, splashing the brandy over her perfectly shined boots. Whether it was an accident or not was difficult to tell, yet it seemed too perfectly timed to be mere coincidence. Servants sprang forward to clean up the mess, while Margarethe and her mother stared at one another in mutual contempt. Finally, my aunt turned and went into the house.

The muttering crowd began to disperse. "Grethe, I am so sorry," I said, meeting her halfway as she came down the stairs. "Why don't you take your mother to task for such abominable behavior?"

"And what would I say?" She shook her head. "It probably looked like an accident. Let everyone think so."

Katherine suggested we go inside and have a drink to calm our nerves. In the hall, we met Lady Ursula, who said in a cold voice, "Margarethe, take off that blouse. It's soiled."

❊❊❊

After lunch, Margarethe asked if I would go out for a ride with her. She was still moody over the morning's incident, so I agreed without question.

We rode through the forest to the bluff that overlooked the estate. The winding path was narrow, and it was a long way to the bottom of the ravine. I dared not look down.

We tethered the horses on a tree and walked up to the lookout. I took off my riding cap because the wind in that place was fierce, but now that the stormy weather had passed, the air was perfectly clear and the view, spectacular. One could see the Schloss, the surrounding compound of cot-tages, barns, workshops, all nestled in a patchwork of plowed fields and meadows. The manor included the "home farm" and the estate village with its own carpenter shop, blacksmith, and wheelwright, a granary, cottages for the servants' families, barracks once used for soldiers, now dormitories for the field hands. It was like a self-contained city.

Margarethe's brows were knit as she regarded the scene below. Clearly, something was troubling her. I decided not to ask her to explain. Instead, I gave her the gift of my silence until she finally spoke her concerns aloud.

"I am sworn to protect this. To keep it safe for my descendants," she said. Her voice was full of melancholy, but strong nonetheless. The wind was blowing her pale hair in every direction. She was ruddy from the cold and the wind. Her face was resolute, almost stony. She seemed more like a heroic creature from myth than my own dear cousin.

Then she stood erect and raised her chin a little, summoning a look of ascendancy and pride from some deep resource within. I suddenly saw that my mockery of her aristocratic code was wrong. Margarethe truly believed in her obligation to be of service and to protect those who served her. Her ideal of nobility raised the mundane to a higher plane by imbuing it with purpose. To her, those ancient ideals were sacred, and her beliefs gave her the conviction to do many things that I would never dare.

"I find it difficult to believe in the future," she said. "Everything we hold dear is at risk. And all of this." She raised her hand to the scene below. How beautiful it was, the multicolored fields, the vast forests, and Schloss Edelheim massively dominating the plain.

"Then help us," I said, seizing the opportunity. "Together we can rescue our world from the men who would destroy the very heart of our civilization."

"How?" she asked.

"Oh, my dear, I would be happy to tell you."

Chapter 18

I saw the chink in Margarethe's resistance on that afternoon, when we stood on that windy bluff and mused over the passing of our world. The Great War had stolen a generation of young men and along with them, our optimism. The notorious excess of the years after the war was like the giddiness of a drunk to mask his sorrows. We of the aristocracy had suffered great losses. My father, brother to Lady Ursula, had lost everything in the stock market crash. Although he held a baronial title and an estate, he had no means to support it. With nothing to hold him in Germany, my elder brother Richard had gone to Africa, where he grew rich growing coffee. Others of our class left too, abandoning ancestral homes overburdened by debt to speculators. What is the landed gentry without the land? The blow to our esteem stung nearly as much as the financial losses. Things would never be the same again.

As a class, a political force, and an idea, we were simply outlawed. After 1918, no one in Germany held political power through an inherited title. Our titles became merely part of our names. We could be addressed by them, but legally they meant nothing.

Margarethe had always put more stock in her professional titles, so that aspect meant little. What troubled her was the erosion of the ideals of nobility and *noblesse oblige* that had been drummed into her since childhood. Outwardly, Margarethe was a modern woman, emancipated, independent, and dedicated to science. She was even strikingly democratic at times. In her medical colleagues, her staff, and the employees of her enterprises, she always valued performance and skill over social position. Yet at the core, in her heart of hearts, even in her very bones, she was a countess of the *Uradel*. This, as Franz had been so clever to intuit, was our leverage.

It was some time before I could test this premise. I was sent to Silesia to put down yet another strike in the coal mines. It was especially hard because Christmas was coming, and I hated to turn anyone out before the holidays. I decided to put off dealing with the redundancies until the new year, and I returned to Berlin for Christmas.

Usually, we celebrated Christmas at Edelheim, but Margarethe had changed the venue, claiming concern over Katherine's long absence from her practice while she was ill. I knew the real reason for relocating our feast. Margarethe hadn't quite forgiven her mother for her behavior after the hunt, and frankly, I couldn't blame her. Besides, I liked the idea of staying close to home for the holiday. It allowed all of us to invite special guests without forcing them to make the long journey to Edelheim.

Sarah Weber was the first to arrive on Christmas eve. She was actually a few minutes early. Evidently, my cousin had schooled her in the importance of Prussian punctuality. Like most Americans, Dr. Weber made a virtue of being obnoxiously forthright. The first thing she said to me was, "Who are you? You look just like her."

The formal Prussian bow seemed the only way to respond to this impertinent question. "*Frau Doktor*, I am Konrad von Holdenberg." I took her hand and kissed it. Margarethe had praised Dr. Weber to the rafters. I studied her to see if she posed any threat to our domestic peace.

The woman wore an off-the-rack gown, yet she somehow managed to make it look it like an offering from one of Berlin's famous *Werderschermarkt* salons. Margarethe had once explained that surgery bestows an indomitable confidence on its practitioners. Perhaps that's why Dr. Weber could carry her cheap dress with such grace. She was the kind of woman, whose personality and spirit makes her very attractive—not so much pretty, as striking.

Katherine came in and I introduced them. "May I present my wife, Baroness Holdenberg. However, she prefers to be known by her professional title. She is a physician like yourself."

Sarah Weber looked Katherine up and down in an unabashed inspection. My wife is beautiful, and any woman would be justifiably envious, yet I intuited that these two would be allies not competitors. Dr. Weber took Katherine's offered hand. "Merry Christmas, *Frau Doktor*. Best wishes of the season." While Dr. Weber's German was accurate, her accent left much to be desired. Katherine and I switched to English to make her feel more comfortable. We invited her into the drawing room to have a glass from the

Wassail bowl. Margarethe had brought the tradition from England, and it was now a centerpiece of our holiday celebrations. In the great crystal bowl was a mysterious combination of many different liquors and of such great potency as to run a train.

Presently, the mistress of the house appeared, and I very much enjoyed Dr. Weber's reaction as she experienced the mirror effect when Margarethe and I stood side by side. "Good Lord, are you twins?" Dr. Weber asked.

"No," said Margarethe, kissing her on the cheek, "merely cousins. Well, not merely. We are more than three times cousins. That is, where we can trace the lines, but only once in the first degree."

"Where I come from that sort of inbreeding would raise a few eyebrows," replied Dr. Weber.

"I'm afraid it's rather usual among us," Margarethe explained. "Our inheritance laws require that nobles marry within their class. After a time, the pool of options becomes...rather limited."

"Sounds like the German aristocracy was practicing eugenics long before the Nazis ever got the idea," opined Dr. Weber rather tactlessly.

Margarethe pointedly cleared her throat. "Isn't it lovely to have snow for Christmas?" she remarked with an exaggerated smile.

Dr. Weber glanced at me, I assume to gauge whether we had taken offense. To reassure her, I took her arm and led her off to see Margarethe's amazing library.

Our other guests began to arrive. First came Mitzi and Christophe von Treppen, our long-time friends, then Ferdinand Sauerbruch, Margarethe's mentor since Munich, and his wife. We were also fortunate to have Maestro Strauss and his wife, Pauline, as well as Dieter Gürtner of the Deutsche Oper and his lover, Horst Geissler. Gürtner had advised us that he was bringing another couple.

When Gürtner's guests came into the drawing room, Margarethe looked plainly shocked, and all the color drained from Katherine's face. After she recovered herself, she exchanged a glance with Mitzi von Treppen. At once, I knew that everything I'd suspected was true.

"The Count and Countess d'Allessandro," intoned Krauss as he announced them. The woman was thicker around the waist than I recalled from the opera. She had been absurdly thin, so it was quite noticeable. She was pregnant, I realized with surprise. A glance at her elderly husband made me wonder how it was possible.

The wife went directly to Margarethe and reached out her hands. Margarethe, seemingly at a loss, was forced to play the gracious hostess. She touched cheeks with the countess. "*Cara*, I've missed you so," the tiny woman murmured, just loud enough for me to hear, but fortunately not Katherine. In any case, Katherine would not have understood Italian. But one had no need to know the language to understand that this was the greeting of two intimates. I began to feel rather dismal. The joyous and peaceful Christmas I had longed for now looked increasingly remote.

Our next arrival was Margarethe's daughter, Elisabeth, and her American fiancé, Peter Fischer. Margarethe had made it abundantly clear how she felt about the engagement. To be fair, the boy was handsome and earnest. He came from a distinguished family of American blue bloods, but none of their blood would ever be cerulean enough for the *Almanach de Gotha* nor for Margarethe, who actually believed in such things. Breeding was everything, whether for horses, hounds, or Stahles. Nonetheless, Margarethe was cordial to Peter, if for no other reason than he was an outstanding student of physiology and was soon to study medicine. But while she allowed for advancement through intelligence and effort, she simply would not allow that effort to be directed towards her daughter.

Could there be any more tension in the large drawing room where we had gathered to drink from the great Wassail bowl? I confess that in an effort to blunt my own anxiety, I imbibed more than was wise without more food in my stomach.

A short time later, our final guest arrived. He was very tall and blond, the very image of our hostess. The resemblance was not coincidental nor the result of many cousinly matings. He was Wilhelm, Count von Langenberg-Edelheim, Margarethe's son. How handsome he was now that he was fully grown, more than half a head taller than his formidably tall mother. His shoulders seemed to go on forever, and he had a trim waist and hips. His high, noble forehead telegraphed intelligence and his mouth was beautifully-shaped and sensual. Any man of my persuasion could not help but sigh over him. And he was especially handsome in that dashing, black uniform with the red piping and silver skulls on the collar, which demonstrated to all that he was now a lieutenant in the SS.

Katherine drew breath in an audible gasp when she saw him. Margarethe merely gazed at him with a calm that would have fooled anyone but me. It was quite obvious that she had not been apprised of this development. Nor did she approve.

"Merry Christmas, Mother," said the magnificent, blond giant bending to kiss his mother. She turned her cheek a little in disdain. Only I was close enough to hear her whispered response.

"How dare you!"

He stood straight and regarded her with a even look. "I thought you'd be pleased," he said, "Every man in our family has been a soldier."

"A soldier, yes. Not this." She took him aside, but I was still near enough to hear what they said. "What of your medical studies?" she asked.

"What of them? I'll continue my studies until I qualify as a doctor. I've joined the medical SS. I'm going to train in radiology in Halle."

"I thought you planned to be a surgeon."

"Not everyone can qualify for that deified specialty, Mother." He bent to kiss her again, but there was no Judas aspect to the affection as there had been with Countess d'Allessandro. I knew very well that Wilhelm genuinely loved his Mother. "Please, Mother. It's Christmas. Let's all be happy tonight. Who knows what lies ahead?" At this sentiment, I felt suddenly chilled.

Margarethe was not mollified by this remark. Not one bit. She gave Willi the cold shoulder for the first hour or so. Undaunted, Willi found more receptive company in Countess d'Allessandro, who smiled radiantly while they chatted on the other side of the room.

Krauss called us into the dining room for a Christmas Eve supper of salmon from the North Sea and other delicate seafood. Despite Margarethe's loathing for religion, she kept the Church's rules on meat abstinence for Katherine's sake.

After the meal, we moved the celebration into the music room to exchange gifts. Margarethe gave me a half dozen pairs of new cuff links, having noticed that mine had suddenly vanished. There was also a credit note at a Savile Row tailor for several new suits. But the gift with the most significance was a new .32 caliber revolver in a compact holster intended to be worn on a special garter on my leg. "Make sure you wear it," she said in a low voice. "Your adventures take you to some very dangerous places." She raised a brow and gave me a firm look.

The others began opening their gifts, which provided me with much vicarious pleasure. Despite Margarethe's professed disdain for shopping, she always chose remarkably appropriate gifts. My daughter, who looked like a little princess in a beautiful new dress from *Tante* Margarethe, delighted in a book identifying the reptiles of the world and a telescope to gaze at the stars. Katherine was the recipient of a diamond necklace with emeralds that Margarethe had inherited from her grandmother. "It complements your red hair," said Margarethe. "Green jewels were made for red heads." Sarah Weber received a gold-handled folding knife identical to the one Margarethe always carried. The blade was engraved with a little pun: *For she's a jolly good fellow.* For the gentlemen, there were fine new gloves, a fur muffler for Mitzi, an ebony, silver-handled walking stick for Richard Strauss and an elegant brooch for his wife. Even Peter, Elisabeth's intended, received a gift—a fine Zeiss microscope for his medical studies, exactly like the one Margarethe had given her daughter. Perhaps there was yet hope for a reconciliation.

But it was Wilhelm who received the most glorious gift that Christmas. Margarethe had located an ancient violin, not a Stradivarius, but one fashioned by a contemporary and no less fine than one made by the ultimate master. Wilhelm thanked his mother profusely, hugging and kissing her and showing the fine thing all around. Then he said, "Come, my friends. Let's give her a try." How much encouragement could that illustrious gathering of musicians need?

Gürtner and Strauss briefly squabbled over rights to the piano. Ultimately, the impresario yielded to the maestro, who began to play

Brahm's great Christmas song, "*Geistliches Wiegenlied.*" Pauline Strauss, now elderly, although once a great mezzo-soprano herself, encouraged her hostess to sing. Margarethe rose to sing and her son, Willi, played the ancient violin, spontaneously transposing the accompaniment to suit the higher voice of the instrument. Countess d'Allessandro wept, whether from emotion or for effect was difficult to know.

Music certainly was the common denominator in the gathering that night. As it turned out, even Sarah Weber had quite a nice soprano. She and Margarethe led the traditional carols, accompanied by the Maestro and Willi on his ancient Guarneri.

Finally, it was midnight, and there were kisses all around to greet Christmas day. I watched Eva d'Allessandro carefully as Margarethe offered Katherine a tender kiss and gazed lovingly into her eyes. Since their reconciliation, the two had been behaving more like new lovers than companions of long standing. This was one of those moments. The emotion I perceived on the Contessa's face was not quite jealousy. Instead, I saw a cold, dissecting stare directed at the two women. Soon after, the under-consul's wife expressed the urgent desire to leave. I overheard Margarethe telling Gürtner afterwards, "Never bring that woman into my home again. *Never.* Is that quite understood?" Gürtner's expression left no doubt that he had, indeed, understood.

Meanwhile, Willi and Maestro Strauss were greatly enjoying putting the old violin through its paces, and it was a marvel to behold. Fiona fell asleep in Margarethe's lap. I saw that my daughter trusted in her more than in anything else, even me, her father. Margarethe gently transferred my daughter to me so that she could rise to sing, at everyone's request, more Christmas songs. She induced Sarah Weber to sing a final duet with her.

As the last notes faded away, I knew that we had just passed our last year of peace, having the benefit of intelligence from Nigel and others who were in a position to know. I wept not from too much alcohol, as I sometimes did, but out of love for all whom I cherished and from fear that my time with them could never be long enough.

❋❋❋

I was glad for the bright light of morning streaming through my window. The storm had passed leaving a glistening white coat on everything. The winter sun shone brilliantly, sparkling in the ice crystals on the window panes. The sentiment and melancholy of the previous evening had miraculously lifted, and there was nothing but the clear air and light of a perfect winter day.

I bathed and dressed quickly. The family was had already gathered in the small dining room, and I was pleased to be in time for breakfast. To my relief, Wilhelm was wearing an ordinary suit rather than his black uniform. I took my usual place at the table, on Katherine's right. She always sat at the foot, opposite Margarethe. The conversation in progress had a controversial subject—Elisabeth's plans for a wedding.

"I won't have you eloping as if you were an orphan," Margarethe was saying as she spread butter on one of those crisp, little Berlin rolls.

"But Mother, we haven't the time to plan an elaborate wedding," replied Elisabeth. "We must leave Oxford in May. We could be married in the chapel before we depart for the States. Peter's parents will allow us stay in their home until the term begins in September, but we really ought to be married beforehand."

"Peter, dear, how do your parents feel about this hasty wedding?" asked Margarethe, giving the poor lad a penetrating look. "Surely, they don't approve?"

What could the boy say? He certainly didn't want to offend his future mother-in-law. Peter pulled at his moustache as he considered his response. He had sandy hair and hazel eyes. There would be more blond Stahles in the future. "I think they imagined something a little grander."

"Well, then invite them to Edelheim in April, and we shall have a modest wedding in our chapel. Elisabeth is heiress to an ancient title. She must be wed properly, not have it hidden away like a dirty secret."

Elisabeth pressed her lips together no doubt to prevent herself from saying the first thing that came into her head. I had often been an unwilling witness to the bitter sparring between mother and daughter, so I was glad that she held her tongue. Fiona, meanwhile, had interrupted my listening to ask if I might open her boiled egg, which I did with a sharp rap from my butter knife. The child seldom ate with the adults, but on special occasions like Christmas, we allowed it.

"Liesel, we've heard what your mother would prefer," said Katherine in a kind voice, "but it's your wedding. What would you like?" I was not surprised to see my wife intervene. She frequently needed to smooth things over between Margarethe and her daughter. Perhaps she succeeded because she could share ordinary, feminine things with Elisabeth, whereas Margarethe often found such matters baffling. Even I probably understood them better.

Elisabeth leaned on her hand as she thought about Katherine's question. "I'm actually not opposed to a wedding at Edelheim, as long as Mother doesn't invite every one of our cousins and all the neighbors to boot." She turned to her fiancé. "Peter, what do you think? Would your parents mind terribly?"

What could he think? Was this really a question? It was an enormous honor to be married at Edelheim. The boy shrugged. "We can ask."

"If I'm to have a formal wedding, I must have someone escort me to the altar."

"I'll do it," volunteered Wilhelm.

"I was really thinking of Uncle Konrad."

At the mention of my name, I looked up from my breakfast and nodded. "I would be honored, my dear."

Although Wilhelm bravely tried to mask his feelings, it was evident his sister's disregard had hurt him. They were as close as most aristocratic siblings, which is to say, not at all. They had shared the nursery for only the briefest time before they were sent off to their respective English schools. "But if your brother wishes to do the honors..." I added.

Margarethe abruptly changed the topic. "Willi, what inspired this sudden interest in radiology?"

He took a sip of coffee and cleared his throat. "My last clinical rotation. I hadn't realized there were so many possibilities. There is so much more that we can do with radiation beyond tumor reduction."

I feared they would all disappear into a medical conversation, abandoning me, the sole ignorant. "All right, then. Let's leave the medical talk for the surgery and get on with Christmas breakfast, if you please."

Wilhelm looked greatly relieved to be spared further interrogation by his mother. "Thank you, Uncle," he whispered behind his hand.

***

Margarethe never attempted to hide her contempt for Franz Borchert and all priests, but on rare occasions, she indulged me. She allowed me to invite Franz to Christmas dinner. She even suffered his blessing before our feast, the centerpiece of which was a noble roast from the prize stag. After dinner, Katherine was taken up with entertaining Elisabeth and Peter, and I saw the opportunity to lure Margarethe away for a private chat.

Within her earshot, I began telling Franz about the special port Margarethe's father had cellared in 1896 to celebrate his daughter's birth. Over the years that liquid gold had mellowed to perfection. Every year on her birthday, Margarethe opened a bottle, and then a few in between. Even at that rate, the stock would last well past her lifetime. As I waxed eloquent over its phenomenal qualities, the flattery succeeded exactly as planned. Margarethe invited us to her study for a taste. Tapping glasses, we wished one another a merry Christmas. At least, this was something on which we could all agree.

"What do you think of the port, Borchert?" Margarethe asked after he had sipped from his glass.

I wondered what Franz would say. He had sophisticated tastes. The good fathers of his order had access to excellent food and drink; only the very best was good enough for the Jesuit order.

"It's exceptional. But Margarethe, we've known one another for decades. Why can you never bring yourself to call me by my Christian name?"

Margarethe gave him a tart look. "Why can you never resist the temptation to convert me?"

"Touché," he replied.

"Not at all," said the most expert fencer I knew. "You wouldn't recognize a touché if your very life depended on it."

"All right then," I said, interposing myself between them. "Let's try to be friends. It's Christmas, after all."

"Very well," replied Margarethe, conceding with a bow. "In honor of the great feast of peace, I stand down." She eyed Franz tentatively. "What do you think of the port, *Franz*?"

His amber eyes smiled warmly, and she returned his gaze with equal warmth. Although they would never admit it, they secretly liked one another. My pleasure in this truce made me regret the necessity of bringing up business, yet opportunities like this, when we had Margarethe alone and positively disposed, were quite rare.

"Of course, we think the port is lovely, but we also want to thank you for your generosity to our cause." Since my chat with Margarethe at Edelheim, the *Pilze* had become the recipients of a small fortune consigned to numbered accounts in the Dresdner Bank.

"Hopefully, it will aid your work," said Margarethe.

"I know it's presumptuous to ask for more," I said, "but the need is truly great."

"More money?"

"That would be greatly appreciated, but, no, that's not what I mean."

"Ah," said Margarethe, understanding. "This is when it really begins to cost something." She frowned. "If not money, then what?"

Franz and I exchanged a glance, and it was clear that I had been elected to make the requests. "We often have need for doctors, especially when our associates have been injured. The sisters have always come to our aid, but there are times when we need a physician."

Margarethe sipped her port and looked thoughtful. "What you ask is very dangerous." She made a signal to me by tapping her upturned index and middle finger together to indicate that she wanted a cigarette. I opened my case for her.

"It *is* very dangerous," I agreed, "but lives hang in the balance. Sometimes we need aid in one of our safe houses. Other times we can transport the injured to a place where they can get care."

"Where do you take them?"

"To St. Hilde's Convent."

Margarethe gave me a sharp look. "My grandaunt would be concerned to know you are putting her nuns in such danger."

"She knows," said Franz.

Margarethe turned to me and asked, "Am I the only one who blithely goes about doing nothing?"

"You and millions of our countrymen," I replied.

She reflected for a moment. "What would you have me do?"

"The Jews are on rations. We can use food. They still have their own doctors even though they are forbidden to practice, but they have no access to medicines, bandages, syringes, not even the simplest things."

"Such things are easy enough to secure. And I could lay in additional supplies here. But we must be careful. I have no intention of being caught. There are too many who depend on me, and it would be irresponsible of me to take unnecessary risks."

"That's why we swear allegiance to one another," said Franz, stepping forward. "Will you swear to us before God not to betray us?"

"I will swear on my honor," said Margarethe. "It means more to me than your God." I began to see it was she who couldn't resist an argument.

"You must have a code name, Margarethe," I said, attempting to distract them from becoming engaged in another debate. "How is 'Chanterelle?'"

She chuckled. "An interesting choice. A ruffled, French mushroom."

"Well, at least, it's better than mine." She gazed at me expectantly until I confessed it. "Truffle." This so entertained her that she laughed aloud, I'm sure, as much to dispel anxiety as from amusement.

"What's yours, Franz?" she asked.

"*Steinpilz*," he replied sheepishly.

"So we're all mushrooms now. What a lovely ragoût we shall make!"

I cleared my throat to indicate that we needed to return to the subject at hand, especially before the others conceived of the idea to join us. "There's one more thing. We occasionally need escorts."

"Escorts?" she repeated, raising a brow.

"We often need to transport people from place to place to hide them from the Gestapo. In such cases, we need a person who can handle a gun.

"You expect me to shoot people?" asked Margarethe, arching her brow higher.

"If necessary. You are an excellent shot."

"Next you will be asking me to hide fugitives in the basement."

"Yes, we were going to ask. It may come to that."

"What about the servants?" asked Franz. "Can they be trusted?"

"They are absolutely loyal to me," said Margarethe, and I nodded my agreement. She drew on her cigarette as she considered what we had proposed. Finally, she nodded. "Very well, enroll me in your secret society. However, I cannot make a career of it, so choose your assignments wisely."

"Of course, we would respect your time and other obligations," said Franz.

Margarethe studied each of our faces in turn. "I can only hope that you are as wise as you are brave." She replenished our port and we raised our glasses to our pact. "To the *Pilze!*"

After the toast, Margarethe decided to join the others in the music room. Finally, Franz and I were alone. He was suddenly shy and averted his eyes.

"Can you spend the night at my flat?" I asked, kissing him.

He looked pained. "No, my dear. Not tonight. It's Christmas, and I'll be expected back."

"Please. Just one night."

"Don't plead. It breaks my heart." He drew me close for another kiss and allowed his fingers to linger on my cheek before turning away. "I'm sorry, but I must go."

I felt so bereft after his departure that I could not bring myself to rejoin the merriment in the music room. Instead, I asked Krauss to call a taxi. When the driver asked me where I wished to go, I chose, not my flat on Tiergartenstraße, but Spandau and the stevedores' district.

Part VI

MARGARETHE

Chapter 19

The red flag with the *Hakenkreuz* was hung on the Charité's old tower to celebrate the opening of the new offices of the *Reichsforschungsrat*—the Reich's Research Council, a rather innocuous name for the research arm of the SS. Once the flag was put up, it was never taken down again. Every day when I reported for duty, I saw this sad reminder of how deeply we were into the Nazi's evil business. For generations, the Charité had been the pre-eminent hospital in all of Germany, a model throughout the continent of forward-looking technical advancement, highly trained and skillful staff, and efficient administration. Now, the Chamber of Medicine wished to make our hospital a model of racial hygiene as well. The increasing demand to report defectives was becoming more than burdensome. Where once we were only required to report cases of venereal or contagious disease, any illness or condition with even the most remote genetic aspect must now be reported. I was once proud to be a senior member of the Charité staff. No longer.

When my grandaunt called again to encourage me to take the post of chief of staff at St. Hilde's, I was more than willing to give her a sympathetic hearing. The prestige of my Charité post had caused me to waffle, so she had stepped up her campaign to persuade me. The incumbent's term was swiftly coming to an end, and a decision must be made soon. The board was prepared to offer me the position. I need only say the word.

I was reluctant to discuss on the telephone why this idea was suddenly so appealing. One never knew who might overhear. In person, I would say, that despite my long defection from the church, I could see advantages in working in a Catholic hospital. There, I could hide behind the Church's dogma and by pleading conscience, disregard some of the worst imperatives of modern German medicine. The next step was to explain to Sauerbruch what I intended to do. He had been my mentor and supporter since the beginning of my career, and I owed him some advance notice.

Despite my affection for the man, I could not reveal my true motives. Sauerbruch was not merely sympathetic to the regime, he often espoused their ideas with great enthusiasm. He was a prominent member of the new Reich Research Council and involved in other Nazi business that I preferred not to know about. Although I was long past disappointment at seeing my god fall from his pedestal, it deeply saddened me to see such a basically good man go down this sorry path.

"I'd always hoped you would succeed me," he said after I'd laid out my plan, "but I also knew the day would come when your aunt would try to woo you back to that Catholic hospital. Of course, were the position anything less than chief of staff, I would try to dissuade you." He smiled to let me know that he still had my interests at heart.

"St. Hilde's is a small hospital, really nothing compared to the Charité."

"But you built that hospital, Margarethe. Don't belittle it. It has a fine reputation. In fact, I've been thinking we should create an alliance with other hospitals in the city. Many young doctors want to train at the Charité, but we can't accommodate them all. When you are chief you should consider implementing a training program. Then we could collaborate and exchange personnel."

Turning St. Hilde's into a teaching hospital *per se*, would take some effort, but it would raise its prestige and donations. The board would certainly like that idea.

"The Catholic Church has unusual views on some aspects of medicine," he continued. "It condemns the use of condoms, even to prevent disease. Won't you find its dogma too much interference in your practice?" I merely shrugged in response. How he could ask this question amazed me, especially as the Church's intrusion seemed so completely benign compared to that of our Nazified Chamber of Medicine.

He sighed. "I know when you make up your mind, there is no dissuading you. I'll very much miss you, Margarethe. But you have my blessing."

"We can still work together," I said hopefully.

"Yes, but when you are chief of staff, I can hardly call you on the spur of the moment to join me in surgery." He gave me a meaning look, and its message both pleased and saddened me—after being under his wing for decades, I had finally graduated to the status of equal.

When I returned to my hospital office, I sat down to draft my letter of resignation before I changed my mind. It would be some time before it could be delivered. The board would be required to deliberate, at least in principle, before my appointment could be confirmed. Meanwhile, there were many details that would need attention. Making a list of these items completely occupied my mind. I ignored the knock on my door. There followed another, much more forceful knock

"Come!" I called in a loud, surly voice, impatient at being interrupted.

Sarah Weber, looked apprehensive when she opened the door and leaned into the room, no doubt fearful to enter after my less-than-friendly invitation.

I attempted an apology. "Forgive my irritated tone. This task is unpleasant and requires concentration."

"I'm sorry to disturb you. I'm going off duty, and I wondered if you would check on one of my patients." She gave me a quick summary of the case and the reason she wanted me to look in on her patient. "I won't keep you. You look busy."

I nodded. "I am, but come in. And close the door, please." I gestured to a chair. She sat down and gazed at me expectantly.

Needing a few moments to compose my thoughts, I took off my glasses and polished them with my handkerchief. Of course, Sarah would be alarmed when she heard of my plan to leave the Charité. She would see my departure as abandonment, despite the fact that she was not technically my fellow. There was no way to soften the blow, so I just came out with it: "I am writing my letter of resignation." She looked at me as if I were quite mad, which in her eyes, I must have seemed. Why would any physician in his right mind voluntarily leave the most renowned hospital in Europe? "An attractive post has become available," I explained. "The chief of staff at my former hospital is resigning at the end of the month. I have been recommended as his replacement."

"And I would be left here without a mentor," she concluded anxiously.

"No, Sauerbruch must step in—you are his responsibility, after all."

"Professor Sauerbruch doesn't even say hello when we pass in the hall."

"The Professor respects you highly. It's only that his new government duties consume so much of his time." Her expression told me she was not mollified one bit by this excuse. She continued to frown.

Eventually, she said, "I could go with you. I could be your fellow at your new hospital." She gave me a hopeful look.

"Now, don't be hasty. A fellowship at the Charité has great prestige, even beyond Germany. Only Berliners have ever heard of St. Hilde's."

"I don't care."

"Think of your career, Doctor."

"I am thinking of my career. I have learned more from you than any-one. I'm not giving up my remaining time here to learn more."

I sat back in my chair to take her measure. Her jaw was resolutely set, and her gray eyes, full of determination. "It may be possible for you to come to St. Hilde's. Sauerbruch has proposed a collaboration, an exchange agreement with the Charité. Let's see what transpires." As I spoke, I realized there would be a need to filter the junior doctors we brought to St. Hilde's. Young men in black or gray uniforms lurking about would defeat my purpose in leaving the Charité. "I shall keep you informed regarding the exchange program. Meanwhile, please keep this conversation between us." Her expression indicated some displeasure that I should even think otherwise.

After Sarah left, I telephoned my grandaunt at Obberoth. As usual, it took some time for me to be connected. No one ever hurried at Obberoth. It was as if the motherhouse of the order were in another world, and in some ways it was. The foundation went back to the eleventh century, when its nuns were fully cloistered. Apart from running water and electricity, installed at my insistence, little had changed since. My aunt finally came to the telephone. The chatter of the local operators ceased and there was only the sound of her voice, surprisingly strong and youthful, although she was past eighty. The sisters said that she would live to be one hundred. I dearly hoped so.

"Margarethe, how pleasant to hear your voice," she said, and I could imagine her pale eyes, the color of an Alpine glacier, illuminated with warm affection. "To what do I owe the pleasure?" she asked, as if my call were so out of the ordinary. In fact, we spoke to one another by telephone often, and I wrote to her weekly. For important communications, we used the post, which was more secure than the telephone, despite the sensitive eyes of the Thousand Year Reich. Perhaps I was being overly cautious. My aunt and I knew one another so well that we spoke a kind of short hand, guaranteed to confound all but the canniest Gestapo agent.

"I've reached a decision," I said without preamble.

Without even bothering to ask what my decision was, she said, "Very good. I shall lay your application before the board. Naturally, you must absent yourself from the discussion." Nothing could be more obvious. By underscoring it, she was reasserting her traditional role as my elder and teacher.

"There is another matter, *Tante*. I wish to implement a training program in association with the Charité. It will make St. Hilde's a teaching hospital and confer great prestige. It would benefit our fundraising as well." She agreed this sounded like a good idea.

Our business concluded, my grandaunt turned the conversation to personal matters. "Why haven't you come to see me?"

I felt an immediate twinge of guilt and began to make excuses. "The weather has been so poor this winter, and Katherine's illness…"

"But I understand she has recovered. Some gynecological ailment…"

"You didn't know?" It seemed very odd that she wouldn't know, having been privy to Katherine's most intimate struggles before she left the convent. As a former nun under my grandaunt's charge, Katherine looked to her for spiritual direction and had always been candid with her. I was even more surprised that the nuns at St. Hilde's had kept Katherine's secret. The Rule required a nun's absolute candor with the superior.

"She had an ectopic pregnancy in autumn," I explained. "We nearly lost her to the hemorrhage. She never told you?" I realized from the extended silence that this was news. I had never thought to share it with her because I had assumed it was Katherine's place to tell her.

My grandaunt, who liked to answer questions with questions, played to type. "You're not troubled that Katherine wishes to be a mother again?" Of course, she would remember my adamant objections to Katherine's first pregnancy, so her question came as no surprise.

"It's not an ideal situation. She's not young. There is some danger to her health and that of the child. And this is a very difficult time in her career when she must expend great effort."

"That is you speaking as a physician, Margarethe, or as an administrator. Not as Katherine's most intimate companion."

"True," I admitted.

Fortunately, she let the matter drop. Instead she asked, "Will you come at Easter?"

"Perhaps. Let's see where we are by then. Katherine and her husband mean to try again when she is healed."

"Oh dear," replied my grandaunt. "How will you deal with that?"

"I endorsed it. We only need to see whether the damage can heal well enough to make it possible."

"May I say, when Katherine and I speak again, that I know the nature of her illness?"

"Perhaps it's better left unsaid," I replied after a moment to consider.

"As you wish, my dear."

When we rang off, I reflected that so much remained unsaid among so many. Lies of omission, I have been taught, are the least egregious kind.

❋❋❋

The hospital board met the following week. As before, I was asked to absent myself from the proceedings while they debated my suitability. When the discussion went on for more than half an hour, I began to become anxious that something had gone awry. Perhaps my grandaunt had been over-ruled, or in a last-minute fit of conscience, the board had decided to shy away from such blatant nepotism. I was in a state of high anxiety bordering on panic, when Katherine appeared.

"Good," she said, "I was hoping to find you here. Actually, I was hoping it would be over by now."

"So was I," I muttered.

"Don't fret, Margarethe. They're only doing their duty. Reverend Mother would want it so. Perhaps they're debating the amount of your salary." We exchanged ironic smiles. Whatever salary they decided would be returned to the hospital as my gift. "They must go through the motions. No need to worry." She handed me a very official looking envelope. "But I do want you to have a look at this. And as my new chief, tell me what to do."

"Even assuming all goes well, I won't be the chief here for weeks."

"Never mind. I need your advice."

I opened the letter. It was like all the others from the Chamber of Medicine, dictated by the chairman, and written in memo form. It outlined the latest directive. All obstetricians and midwives must report each and every birth defect. Moreover, it defined a birth defect narrowly and included conditions as innocuous as a port wine stain. Birth traumas were also lumped into this category, ostensibly because they could have long term effects on intelligence.

"Oh, what rubbish," I said, refolding the paper and replacing it in the envelope. "Ignore it. It's simply ridiculous." I handed it back to Katherine.

"But I'm not the only one in the birthing room. There will be nurses, sometimes other physicians."

"Don't worry. The sisters certainly won't report you. That's why you are lucky to be here and not at the Charité where the administration is so bloody determined to impress their Nazi masters." I glanced around to see if anyone had heard, but we were quite alone. My anxiety over the deliberations next door had inclined me to be less circumspect than usual.

Mercifully, the door to the boardroom finally opened. *Professor Doktor Rackow*, the chairman, emerged with the other members in tow. I perceived from his broad smile that my fears had been completely unfounded. He shook my hand and kissed me on both cheeks. "Congratulations, to our new chief of staff," he said. There was applause and cheers. We shook hands all around. Although it was only half-past ten, Dr. Geller, the chief of medicine, produced a bottle of champagne, and we all had a toast, including Katherine and the secretary. After the celebration was done, and the board members had drifted away, Katherine took my arm.

"Walk with me to my office," she said.

We took the stairs rather than the lift because after the long spell of sitting in the board meeting, I decided I could use the exercise.

"Will you be pleased to have me back?" I asked when we were in the stair well.

"Of course. It means we'll be able to see more of one another," said Katherine. "And it's always advantageous to know someone in high places." She winked to let me know she was only joking about the last bit, but I stopped and gave her a firm look.

"Now, Katherine, you know I would never treat you differently from the others."

"Of course not" she replied, nudging me forwards. "You are a paragon of objectivity and fairness, but you would certainly give me as sympathetic a hearing as any member of your staff. A less confident person might be inclined to be harder on a friend, but not you." As I listened, I realized that she was gently instructing me on how I should behave towards her in my changed role.

We walked down the hall of the obstetrics and gynecology department to Katherine's office. As under-chief, she had a small office, which had become rather cramped in an effort to fit in all the furniture, including a divan for the many nights when Katherine needed to get some rest during a lull in a patient's labor. My impulse was to give her a more generously appointed space once I took over as the new chief. I cut off this thought at once, realizing it to be exactly the sort of behavior that could upset the delicate balance of our professional roles.

"Sit for a moment," Katherine said. As I took a chair on the other side of her desk, I imagined the many anxious patients, who had sat there to receive Katherine's sensible advice on how to deal with their pregnancies or hear gently delivered bad news about an illness. To my surprise, Katherine took not her usual seat behind the desk but selected the chair beside me. For some time, she smiled at me without speaking. I recognized this ploy from long experience. No doubt, she had already carefully prepared her message, but she wanted me in a positive mood for whatever she had to say, hence the smile.

"Is there something on your mind, Katherine?" I finally asked, "or are you merely detaining me for the view?"

"Yes, actually I do have something to discuss. I'm quite certain now that my healing is complete. I'm ready to try again. It will soon be a favorable point in my cycle."

Caught off guard, I couldn't hide my dismay quickly enough.

"Please, Margarethe, don't tell me that you've changed your mind!"

"Not at all," I replied, striving for a more neutral expression. "It's only that we have such a short time to prepare. Konrad is in the States, as you know, and it will take more than a week for him to arrive. We must wire him at once."

"I've already seen to that," said Katherine, looking very satisfied at being so efficient. She knew how much I valued this trait, and perhaps she thought her actions would impress me. They did, but not in the way she intended. "Konrad will be home tomorrow."

"I'm surprised he never told me. Usually, he keeps me apprised of his travel plans."

"I swore him to secrecy so I could tell you myself."

More subterfuge, I thought. No one had lied. They had simply withheld the facts. I continued to smile pleasantly, although I found the idea disturbing.

"Have you told Becher? If you are successful, he'll need to make arrangements for your replacement, especially if this pregnancy goes as your first." I was already thinking like an administrator, worrying over the personnel issue rather than the patient. I justified it by telling myself I was showing optimism for Katherine's benefit.

"Yes, I've told Becher. Actually, I asked him to confirm my readiness for another pregnancy."

"Very wise of you to consult him," I said with a forced smile. I needed some privacy to think, so I looked for an excuse to leave. "I must return to the Charité to dispatch my letter of resignation." I said, springing up from the chair and heading towards the door.

In fact, I couldn't be out of that room quickly enough.

Chapter 20

They made a solemn pair at dinner, as if they were about to commit some guilty act, of which I had no knowledge or had not condoned. Certainly, there would be no pleasure in it, if they felt so tense. I urged more wine on them in the hopes of encouraging them to relax. Konrad imbibed freely and was soon giddy. He made a few off-color remarks, for which I wanted to kick him under the table. Katherine, lost in her own worries, seemed hardly to notice.

In an attempt to create a "normal" setting, we went into the music room, where Katherine played the piano while I sang to her accompaniment. Finally, when we could find no further reason to procrastinate, the long-wedded couple trudged off to bed. As I watched them ascend the stairs, I wondered if I had been wrong to encourage them. Sometimes, even the most admirable and generous intentions result in disaster.

Before heading to my quarters to prepare for sleep, I waited a respectful interval, occupying myself with playing the piano. Finally, I went upstairs. As I removed my make up, I was reminded of Katherine's oft-repeated remark that I look boyish without it. As I never leave my rooms without my war paint, it is only in the privacy of the bedchamber that one can actually witness me in this state.

It is also in such moments of naked truth that my resemblance to Konrad is most apparent. It had been years since I had masqueraded as my cousin, not since that fateful outing at the opera. Afterwards, Katherine made me swear never to impersonate Konrad again. As I gazed at myself in the mirror, I saw the likeness that astonishes everyone, yet I also saw our differences. Anyone with the least sensitivity must see that my face has the bones of a female, and my features are more delicate than his. Even when Konrad wore cosmetics, his face was hard.

After donning my pajamas, I settled down to read, my mind all the while distracted by thoughts of what might be happening in the next room. Eventually, I became engaged in my book. The novel was called *Of Lena Geyer* by the American writer, Marcia Davenport. It featured a female opera singer stalked at every turn by a woman. For obvious reasons, I found the theme sympathetic, but there was otherwise much to recommend the tale. I had barely gotten through the first two chapters when the door opened and Konrad entered. "Surely, you haven't finished already." I was especially surprised because I knew that Katherine required a long and careful approach.

He sighed and rolled his eyes. "We haven't even begun. It was going very well, but then she touched me and I...." There was no need for him to complete the sentence. I knew exactly what had happened. His look of profound dismay suggested that this was a novel occurrence, one that greatly distressed him. "Of course, it's been ages since I've been with a woman, and it's no criticism of Katherine. She was ever so gentle and patient. But the very thought that I must perform, that the performance was the very point, so absolutely essential, left me cold."

I got up from my comfortable chair and clapped him on the shoulders. "Don't worry, my dear. It's happens to the most virile of men, especially at our age."

"Oh, stop! It's not age. It's this awful position in which I find myself. I feel like one of your prize horses at stud." At that, I couldn't resist laughing. Fortunately, neither could he, which dispelled some of the awful tension. "You don't understand," he murmured. "It was quite a feat to rise at all."

"Perhaps you had too much wine."

"It's not the wine," he said, shaking his head. "I've simply lost my taste for women."

I touched his cheek. "Really?"

He gave me a quick, guilty look. "You're the exception."

I took him by the arm to walk him back to Katherine's room. "You must go back to our Katherine and speak gently to her. She must be equally miserable, thinking she did something to cause the problem."

"Grethe, I swear. I've tried everything, but now she keeps weeping. I can't say or do anything right!" he exclaimed, looking distraught. "You must try to comfort her."

I had no wish to interpose myself in this situation. At least, when it was something going on in another room, I could pretend to ignore it.

"My dear, this is exactly the time to rely on your diplomatic skills," I advised, nudging him in the direction of Katherine's door. "Tell her how beautiful she is. How she excites you. For goodness sake, Konrad, you have seduced more lovers than I can ever imagine. You know what to do!"

"It has nothing to do with seduction and everything to do with her feelings for you. She feels this is a betrayal, and it's put a curse on the act."

"That's absurd," I remarked dryly, but I knew how superstitious Katherine could be. Thanks to her devout Catholicism, she could be consumed with guilt over matters that I would never even give a second thought.

"If you don't reassure her," said Konrad, "it will never happen. I promise you."

My instincts told me that if I insinuated myself in this scheme, I would regret it. On the other hand, if I did not do something and quite soon, the whole enterprise would collapse, and I would never hear the end of it.

"Come. Let's see if we can soothe poor Katherine's feelings," I said, pulling him along by the hand.

Katherine was as Konrad had left her, turned on her side with her face in her hands. Her weeping was muffled by the eiderdown. Only her pearl-perfect shoulders were bare. I felt a stab of tenderness for her as I saw the abundant, faint freckles that covered them. She was still as beautiful as the day I had first uncovered her. Despite maternity, she had recovered and kept her youthful figure. Her lovely breasts could still cause me to wax poetic. Any man would surely find her inspiring. Any man, that is, except her husband.

I pulled aside the duvet and crept into bed behind her. "Katherine, my love," I said kissing the back of her neck and her shoulders. "What's the matter?"

"I can't do this," she mumbled into her hands.

"Now, my darling, we agreed that this is the best way. We all want the making of this child to be a happy occasion. Certainly pleasant. Not a cause for tears."

"I can't…He can't…."

"Come, my dearest." I urged her to turn around with a gentle tug at her shoulder. After a moment's resistance, she turned into my arms. "Now, now," I said, kissing her tear-stained face. "There's nothing wrong here. Konrad is your husband. He has a right to be in your bed, and you have a right to be here with him."

"Margarethe, you know that's utter nonsense!" she replied bluntly. "I simply can't go through with it."

I sighed with exasperation. "Yes, you can," I insisted. "All that gloom before you went to bed. No wonder you can't make love. You need to create the right mood." I glanced at Konrad, who merely gave me a sheepish look. Certainly, he wasn't going to be of any help. I nudged Katherine's face up from my breasts, where she had sought refuge, and kissed her. At first, there was little response. Finally, her lips grew pliant, and she began to sigh.

When I opened my eyes, I saw that hers had lost all their mist of worry. I also saw an expression that I had come to treasure. When she truly wanted me, she looked so very vulnerable, so infinitely trusting, that it made me ache. I kissed her again, if only to hide from that awful look.

While my goal was to arouse her sufficiently so that she would be receptive to Konrad's overtures, it now seemed that I was also succeeding in arousing myself. Katherine began to unbutton the coat of my pajamas. I glanced over at Konrad. Although we had sometimes been *à trois* with men or women in our randy youth, I did not relish his being a spectator while I made love to the woman with whom I shared my life.

"Stay with us," whispered Katherine, turning my face back to her.

I was startled by the request. But despite my persistent objections to the goal of this process, the variation on the means was in no way unappealing. It seemed so logical a solution, I wondered why I hadn't thought of it myself. I had assumed Katherine's conventional ideas about sex would preclude even the idea of it. Now, I saw that my presence would not only encourage her to relax but would also reassure her that nothing she was doing was against my wishes.

***

One would never know from observing the properly-attired pair seated at the breakfast table what had transpired during the night. Konrad, impeccably dressed in one his Savile Row suits, was calmly reading that useless excuse for journalism, *Frankfurter Zeitung*. I loathed it, but we always had it on the breakfast sideboard when Konrad was "in residence." At the head of the table, I read *The Times*, as usual.

We had left Katherine deep in slumber. My hunger had awakened me not long after my usual time to rise. After such strenuous activity, I was positively famished and had nudged Konrad out of bed because I wanted company.

I waited until Krauss refreshed our coffee and had gone off to refill the carafe before comparing notes on the previous night's activities.

"Did you enjoy yourself?" I asked Konrad from behind my newspaper.

"Rather much," he replied, also not emerging from behind his newspaper. "It was something of a novelty to be with women after all these years, which made it all the more exciting. Do you suppose we succeeded in our mission?"

"Hard to say. It will certainly be a few weeks before we have any proof." After such long acquaintance, I could easily intuit my cousin's plans. I finally put down the paper to engage him. "You're not thinking of leaving already?"

He set down the *Zeitung*. "Well, yes. If you recall, I really need to get back to Silesia to see about the strike at the mine."

I smiled. "Only Stahle business or other business?"

He smiled in return. "Both."

"Then I won't ask."

"Good idea. Actually, it's quite difficult to leave the party. After all, it's only just begun."

The idea that he might wish to repeat the night's events briefly worried me. Our delicate domestic balance could easily be tipped by the forces we had invoked during the night. While a bit of wine and expedience had induced me to join them in bed, the bright light of day demanded that I grasp sensible ordinariness and cling to it with all my might.

"But, Konrad, it's like any party," I said, attempting a breezy tone despite my worries. "One can have the same host, the same venue, the same food and drink, and still not have the same experience."

"So true, my dear. Unfortunately, so very true."

After we finished our breakfast, I went upstairs to look in on Katherine. Usually she was a light sleeper, but she had been the object of our efforts in nearly every joining. It was no surprise that she was exhausted. Although I tried to wake her with a kiss, I needed to shake her arm to achieve a response.

She woke with a start and sat up looking around. "He's gone?"

"Not yet, my dear, but he's packing to leave for Silesia this morning."

"I should get up to say good-bye," said Katherine, attempting to rise.

I held her down by the shoulder. "No, you shouldn't. Standing won't aid your cause, and a horizontal position most certainly will. I would also avoid bathing until tomorrow." She wrinkled her nose at this idea, although as a physician, she knew it was wise advice. She fell back against the pillow and rubbed her eyes. "You could sleep longer," I suggested.

"I don't think I could sleep now. Perhaps I'll take a little nap later." She inspected me. "You look rather tired yourself."

I chuckled. "It was an active night."

This understatement seemed to amuse her, but the merry look in her eyes quickly vanished, replaced by one of anxiety. "You weren't shocked by my knowledge of how to please a man?"

Now it was my turn for amusement. "Good heavens, Katherine. You specialize in a branch of medicine dedicated to the female reproductive organs. I certainly hope that you are well versed in all the possibilities regarding sex, if for no other reason than the sake of your patients." Despite my reassuring remarks she began to blush. "For myself, I am pleased to see that you've gotten beyond your convent modesty."

She grasped my hand and held it tightly. "I don't want Konrad in our bed *ever* again. *Ever.*"

"Then let's hope we've achieved your purpose."

Chapter 21

My mind was only too happy to draw the curtain on the scene. Too many other matters demanded my attention. First, I needed to conclude my duties at the Charité and put things in order for my successor. I also needed to make arrangements for the first three members of the exchange program between the Charité and St. Hilde's—an obstetrician to work with Katherine, a pediatrician, and the gifted Sarah Weber.

St. Hilde's new physicians were, not coincidently, all female. I had deliberately chosen them because both the Chamber of Medicine and the certification panel were increasingly putting pressure on women of child-bearing age to leave the profession. Allowing some of the best breeders to be occupied with a demanding profession did not suit the Reich's plan to create a formidable new generation of healthy, blond warriors. In the Nazi's view, successful female professionals set a poor example for other women. They were proof positive that a career was an alternative to the traditional role of wife and mother.

Sarah had witnessed some of this official misogyny and it distressed her. One morning, she came to me so incensed that she could barely speak.

"What's the matter?" I asked, gesturing for her to sit when she showed herself in my doorway.

"Have you seen the latest issue of *Die Ärztin*?" she asked, waving her copy under my nose. In fact, I had long since stopped reading the journal because it had ceased to be an advocate for female physicians. Instead, it had become an organ of the regime like every other publication in Germany. "It says that the calling to be a wife and mother supersedes our duty as physicians. And it cites statistics claiming that over seventy percent of medical women are mothers."

I considered this for a moment. "That statistic is probably true. I, myself, am the mother of two."

This fact seemed to fluster her all the more. "So I should abandon my career to be a mother? No one demands that men become fathers!" She finally sat down. "I can't go along with this."

I shrugged. "Soon you'll be back in America, and all this will be but a memory."

"How can you be so nonchalant?" she demanded in an agitated voice. "It's dangerous when people are constantly exposed to a negative idea. It starts out being the eccentric opinion of a few. Then more people believe it, and more, until even the government officially sanctions it. Doesn't that worry you?" Her assessment perfectly described how the Nazis had used their propaganda to sway German citizens to their ideas.

"People adopt their neighbors' views because they desire acceptance. The need is very strong, especially here, where conformity is highly valued. Germans venerate authority. We have little experience with democracy or free speech. Many people find the philosophy of the National Socialists compelling. Anti-Semitism runs deep in our culture. And it's very seductive when people constantly tell you how superior you are…that it's your destiny to rule the world."

She stared at me with apprehension. "You can't really believe that."

"That I am superior? Actually, I've been taught so for my entire life. It's essential to the concept of a noble aristocracy. The idea that all men are created equal isn't universal. In many ways, it is peculiarly American. In fact, not everyone is equal—some are rich, and some are poor, some are intelligent, others not. But under the law, everyone ought to have the same rights. Even we Germans understood that concept. That is, we did."

"What will you do?"

"Do?" I repeated. I hoped that my increasing impatience over this interrogation wasn't written all over my face. "I assure you that I do what I can. Now, Doctor, you really must put these issues out of your mind in order to focus on your work."

She hardly seemed mollified by my explanations. Still frowning, she took her copy of *Die Ärztin* and left. Not long after she departed, I noted in my review of her files for the transfer, that it was her birthday. I called my florist to have flowers delivered to her flat. Perhaps they would cheer her and help her to forget her anger, if only for a moment.

***

When I returned to Grunewald that evening, I found that for a change, Katherine had arrived before me. I was delighted, and even more so when I came into the music room and found her with Fiona. The child was performing an early Mozart harpsichord allegro. The music teacher I had engaged was proving to be quite satisfactory, for she was not only challenging the child to attempt fairly difficult pieces, she had also succeeded in teaching her the rudiments of dynamics. I applauded when Fiona concluded her little recital, and she ran to me.

"*Tante!*" she exclaimed, hurling herself into my arms. "Did you hear all of it? If not, I can play it again." I hugged her, but she sprang away, a little bundle of energy that defied containment. In this child with bright red hair and pale freckles, I saw a younger Katherine. Fiona would be far taller than her mother and had just gone through a growth spurt, which left her looking older than her six years. In fact, she was now just able to reach the piano pedals if she sat forward a bit on the bench.

I couldn't truthfully assure her that I'd heard the entire recital. She took my hand and tugged at it until I accompanied her to the piano. Out of the corner of my eye, I could see Katherine watching this scene indulgently. Fiona insisted that I sit beside her on the bench. "Very good, Fräulein von Holdenberg. I shall turn the pages for you."

She played the piece without a single error. I applauded, as did her mother. Fiona slid off the bench to take a gracious bow. The girl's sudden maturity made an impression. This important transition had been lost amidst our myriad professional and domestic dramas.

After Fiona's nanny had taken her off to the nursery and we were alone, Katherine embraced me. "What do you think of our young musician?"

"She's quite talented. And she's grown into quite the little lady. She's suddenly so tall."

"She gets that from you."

"Hardly from me."

"Well, then from the genes you share with your cousin."

"Let's avoid conversation of genetics, or medicine or anything that can remotely relate to the Reich's Chamber and its insufferable policies."

"Oh, dear, another new directive? I never had time to read my mail today."

"No, it was an article in *Die Ärztin*. It profoundly offended Sarah Weber, and it took some effort to calm her. I'm not certain I was entirely successful."

Katherine listened sympathetically while I described my conversation with Sarah. "It's impossible to know how much to say to young physicians without creating a climate of danger for them or ourselves," she said. "Can you trust this American?"

"Oh, yes, I think so."

"But her father was Sauerbruch's friend. Perhaps he shares his views as well." Katherine knew how much I disliked discussing the topic of Sauerbruch's conversion to National Socialism. Fortunately, Krauss arrived to bring me a martini. As I sipped that icy perfection, I allowed the alcohol to help me forget the miseries of the day.

✳✳✳

Our dinner was interrupted by Krauss. In the many years since he'd become my majordomo, he almost never allowed his feelings to show, but when he entered the dining room that evening, I instantly knew that something important had happened. I signaled to him to come forward. He bent to whisper his message directly in my ear.

"*Gnädige*, pardon the interruption. Father Borchert is here to see you." Since this could only be *Pilze* business, I was worried. I was even more worried because Borchert had brought danger right into my home.

"Where is he?"

"In your study."

Katherine gazed at me with a questioning look. I returned it with a reassuring smile.

"No emergency, dear. I have a visitor I must see. I'll be but a moment."

Borchert looked grave and deathly pale. "I know this must be urgent for you to come personally," I said closing the door.

He nodded. "May I have a drink?"

"Of course." I took a bottle of my best Scotch from the credenza and measured out a generous portion for each of us. He downed his drink in a gulp. After I refilled his glass, I rummaged in my desk drawer for the packet of cigarettes I'd secreted there. From the look of Borchert, I knew we would need fortification beyond alcohol.

"Who is it this time?"

He looked at me with imploring eyes as if to ask forgiveness for what he was about to say. "Your cousin."

"Dear God!" I exclaimed in horror, but while this news greatly disturbed me, Borchert looked completely shattered. I took his hand. "Franz, I am so very sorry. I know how close you are." He stared at me. How could he think I wouldn't know of their liaison?

After a moment and a deep breath, Borchert seemed to get hold of himself. He reclaimed his hand, which gave me an opportunity to open the packet of cigarettes. "Tell me everything. And I mean, *everything.*"

"I actually don't know very much. What little I know comes from our informant in the Moabit. That's where they've taken Konrad. Fortunately, his arrest had nothing to do with the *Pilze*, although I understand the Gestapo has been shadowing him for months."

"Franz, I am totally confused. Konrad has been in Silesia working out a new contract with the miners."

"He was in Silesia. He returned to Berlin by the afternoon train yesterday."

"Damn him! He's supposed to tell me his plans in advance. I keep telling him so!"

"You must forgive him, Margarethe. He's only trying to protect you and the family. The less you know about our activities, the better."

"But if he wasn't arrested because of the *Pilze*, won't they release him?"

Borchert swallowed hard. "I fear the charges are equally serious." He hesitated so long, I wanted to throttle him to get the rest out of him.

"For Christ's sake, Franz, just tell me!" The profanity, combined with my aggressive posture, got his attention.

"He was found *in flagrante delicto*, fellating an undercover Gestapo agent. He went to one of those Spandau taverns where the stevedores go.

The Gestapo were rounding up the lot of them. Such raids are very common now."

I turned away to light my cigarette because I didn't want Borchert to see the profound anxiety I felt. "It doesn't matter," I said. "That's a trivial charge. We can persuade them to release him. No one is immune to bribes, not even the precious Gestapo. I am willing to pay whatever is necessary. Find out who and how much."

"I'll do my best. It would be different if Konrad were merely another patron in the tavern. But he was caught in the act with a very credible witness."

"If he's so credible, why was his penis in Konrad's mouth?"

Borchert looked startled at hearing me state the facts so bluntly, but I wasn't surprised to hear the Gestapo had infiltrated the homosexual clubs or had our kind among their ranks. When Hitler purged the SA in '34, they found their leader, Röhm in bed with his male lover. The Night of the Long Knives was supposed to purge homosexuals from the party elite. Evidently, they had retained a few for other purposes.

"Franz, I must see him," I said. "Can you arrange it?"

"We can do nothing tonight. Tomorrow, I'll attempt to enter the prison as a priest. You may come along but not as Countess Stahle or even Dr. von Stahle. Disguise yourself as a pious parishioner, one who makes a charity of prison visits. Wear ordinary clothes, something a middle-class matron would wear." If I could successfully impersonate Konrad, I could surely make a convincing church woman. My mind was already devising a plan. I would borrow a suit from the kitchen maid who was nearly as tall as I, and a hat with a veil from Katherine. Although I despised hats and hated wearing them, I needed to hide my resemblance to Konrad. "I must go," said Borchert. "The *Pilze* will be anxious once they hear the news."

I finally found my hospitality. "Have you eaten?"

"No," he said and drained his glass. "But I have no appetite."

For the first time in the more than two decades of acquaintance, Borchert and I embraced. With the man we both loved in danger, there was no room for differences.

"Not to worry," I said, as I held his arms firmly. "We shall find a way to help him."

He managed a brave smile, but I could see the sincere doubt in his eyes.

By the time I returned to the dining room, Katherine had gone upstairs to see Fiona to bed. Krauss reheated my dinner. While I finished my supper, I considered how to address Konrad's dire situation. Certainly, there must be someone in the prison system or the courts who could be bought. Unfortunately, the person best able to investigate the possibilities was Konrad himself. I was momentarily discouraged by the thought that I must now learn to navigate the intricate workings of the Third Reich on my own. Then I remembered Borchert was also well connected. Perhaps I would have a use for him after all.

When I went into Fiona's room to kiss her good night, I realized that we needed to be circumspect about Konrad's absence. While she was accustomed to his being away for long periods, she worshipped her father. If anything happened to him, she would be crushed.

Katherine accompanied me to my sitting room and, to my surprise, accepted a glass of *Halb und Halb*. She rarely drank anything stronger than wine. Perhaps she knew from my grim expression that there would be bad news.

"All right," she said when we were both sitting down. "Who was your visitor? Krauss wouldn't tell me." Loyal Krauss would never reveal anything about my personal affairs, not even to Katherine.

"It was Borchert."

"What could he want at this hour?" she asked anxiously. For a long moment, I debated how much to tell her, but Katherine gave me a hard look. "Margarethe, don't you dare try to hide the truth! I can smell cigarette smoke on your clothes. Something is wrong. Very wrong. This has to do with Father Borchert's little club, hasn't it?" I was startled to hear her say such a thing and turned my head so fast that I had a twinge in my neck. "Tell me, Margarethe. Tell me at once!" She added in a defiant voice: "And don't you dare try evasion. I am also a member of the *Pilze*."

"No," I said in shocked denial. When I recovered myself, I demanded proof of her words. "What is your code name?"

"*Russula*." I could immediately envision how the name of the strikingly beautiful, red-capped mushrooms perfectly suited my red-headed lass. So, she was a member of the *Pilze*. How had she kept it from me so long? The answer was the clever organization Konrad and Borchert had put in place. The cells, apart from their leaders, never knew more than two or three members at a time. In fact, by revealing our identities to one another, Katherine and I were violating a cardinal rule of the group.

"And yours?" she asked.

"Chanterelle."

"I knew it! Why didn't you tell me?"

"I could certainly ask the same!"

She nodded. "I very much wanted to tell you. I was among the first members. Mother Monica recruited me."

"Katherine, you mustn't be involved in this. It's too dangerous. You have responsibilities. You're a mother and perhaps a mother-to-be."

"Nonsense, Margarethe. I take great care. You're a mother too, and you have responsibilities to all of us."

"Were you aware that Konrad was a member?"

"I suspected as much," she said. "He and Father Borchert have collaborated on so many schemes on behalf of the Center Party." Or what used to be the Center Party, I thought glumly. It was outlawed now. "I take it that Father had a mission for you," said Katherine.

"No. He came to deliver bad news."

She gave me a quick anxious look. I allowed her a moment to prepare mentally. However, she guessed before I could say a word. "Don't tell me that Konrad has been taken." Her face contorted in anguish. "On what charge?"

"It's not really something he would want you to know."

"Margarethe, I am his wife—as you have lately been so fond of saying. I want the truth. *Now!*"

I moved closer to her on the sofa and took her hand. "My darling, you must steel yourself for what I am about to tell you and for what lies ahead." She gripped my hand more tightly. "Konrad was taken in a tavern where there is rough trade. He propositioned a Gestapo agent and was engaged in the act when the place was raided. He, along with the others, have been taken to the Moabit."

Katherine grew pale. Her eyes glittered with anxiety. "You must help him."

"I shall do my level best. In the morning, I shall consult my attorney and investigate the legal possibilities. Perhaps we can bribe an official in the justice system to offer Konrad leniency."

"Can we see him?"

"It's unwise to involve yourself at the moment, but tomorrow Borchert and I shall attempt to visit Konrad in the Moabit. Borchert, wearing his priest's collar, will pretend to be on an errand of Christian mercy, and I'll masquerade as a pious parishioner. Would you be kind enough to lend me one of your hats?"

At this, she began to laugh peals of anxious laughter, but they rapidly devolved into tears. "Oh, Margarethe, this is dreadful. Poor, dear Konrad. We must help him!"

I put my arms around her. "I swear to do everything possible."

❀❀❀

The next morning, I borrowed a suit from the kitchen maid. It was too big in the bust and too short in the sleeves, but an ill-fitting garment played to my déclassé charade in an ideal way. I also decided to adopt her name, Ute Salzberger, as my alter-ego. Katherine's hat presented something of a problem. My hair was simply too short to hold a hat pin, so Katherine helped me secure it with some of the springy fasteners she used to contain the short hairs when she wore an upsweep. I endured her amusement with as much patience as I could muster at that early hour.

Borchert met me at Konrad's Tiergartenstraße flat. Konrad's man had been loyally serving him for decades. We could trust him, but for his sake, the less he knew, the less danger to everyone. We sent him to make coffee while we finalized our plan.

"Margarethe, you are a superb actress, and your costume is very convincing, but this a serious matter. You must remain in character, even when you are tempted to revert to your true identity and intervene," said Borchert, instructing me in a manner that I found most irritating. I resisted the impulse to argue with him because I knew his advice was sound. This was no opera nor idle amusement. It was truly a matter of life and death.

We took the U-Bahn to the Moabit, rather than my motorcar. All of our actions were directed towards stepping into the characters we intended to portray. Of course, Borchert needed no rehearsal to be a priest on a pastoral mission. He was the chaplain of St. Hilde's convent and assistant pastor of the Jesuit church in Kreuzberg. However, it took effort to muster the mental attitude to become Ute Salzburger, widow and pious church member. At least, I came by the widow aspect honestly, and the ill-fitting suit helped me conjure the spirit of the character. In the end, it is all illusion. The eye sees what it expects, and the mind invents the rest.

The anteroom to the prison chaplain's office, a dreary little room with benches along the walls, probably saw many anxious supplicants—family members trying to use the influence of the Church to gain access to a prisoner. Of course, Dr. Moeller represented the official Lutheran Church, not Catholics. Even so, he showed great respect and collegial warmth for Borchert. Evidently, they were well acquainted.

Eventually, the two men emerged from Moeller's office. Borchert introduced me as a member of his parish, a woman who gave of her time for errands of mercy. I tried to emulate Katherine's convent modesty, and her conscientious "custody of the eyes," reasoning that my usual direct gaze and confident attitude might give me away. In fact, my efforts seemed to make little difference. Moeller barely took notice of me. He probably saw me merely as Borchert's insignificant appendage, which only served to remind me how women of little consequence are viewed by society.

We walked the long corridors lined with cells, and it was a horror. The Moabit has a long and ignominious history. The prison was synonymous in every Berliner's mind with "the clink." After the many purges and pogroms against the Jews, the place was filled to near bursting. Cells designed to hold four prisoners now housed six, leaving two to sleep on the floor. Although I tried to keep my gaze focused ahead, my physician's eyes took in a surfeit of ailments—bruises, bandaged limbs, abrasions and lacerations on the verge of suppuration. Where was the prison doctor and why had he not looked after these people?

Borchert spoke my thought aloud. "What have these people done to be kept in such squalor?"

"They are Jews," Moeller whispered. "They will be transported within the week."

"To where?"

"Sachsenhausen."

"Can nothing be done for them?" persisted Borchert.

Moeller shook his head. "I'm afraid not."

We entered another wing of the prison. I was relieved to see that conditions here were marginally better. There were only four men to a cell, and most looked physically sound. Yet, here and there, one heard the deep, phlegmatic cough of tuberculosis. The inmates watched us with dull eyes as we passed.

We came to a cell near the end of the block. When I dared to look up, I saw a sight that stabbed my eyes. Konrad sat on one of the double bunks, his head leaning against the post. His knuckles were scraped and red with abrasions. His fine tweed jacket, a souvenir of our holiday in Donegal, was torn in several places, one sleeve nearly ripped out at the shoulder. He cherished that jacket because it had been a gift from Katherine when we had visited her family in Ireland. Its sorry state would no doubt cause him much grief.

Eventually, he became aware of the three of us gawking at him as if he were a specimen in a zoo. As he raised his face, I saw the prominent bruise on his chin. One eye was nearly swollen shut with another bruise. There was a crust of blood on his forehead and a dried rivulet down his cheek. Dear man that he was, he managed a weak smile when he saw us. He had also lost a few teeth. Of course, he wasn't taken in by my disguise and even succeeded in raising his undamaged right eyebrow in our little signal of skepticism. I did the same with my left.

Moeller spoke to the guard who went away for a moment and then returned with a key. "Holdenberg, come out," called the guard gruffly. Then he escorted the four of us to a little room with a table and several chairs, although not enough for all. Moeller stood. The guard locked the door.

"*Herr Baron*," Borchert said, "I've brought Frau Salzberger from our parish. She's a trained nurse." A nurse! How very insulting! However, I banished my indignation in favor of dismay over the lack of medical supplies. Why hadn't Borchert thought of this before now? Why hadn't I? "What do you need to help the baron, Frau Salzberger?" asked Borchert, turning to me. "Perhaps Dr. Moeller can fetch it from the infirmary." I realized Borchert had been improvising all along, and this was a brilliant ploy to secure some privacy as well as bandages and antiseptic.

"Of course," said Moeller. "Just tell me what you need."

Borchert shot me a quick warning look that plainly said, "Be careful. Don't be too fancy or you'll reveal yourself."

I stated my requests: "Sterile gauze and tape, phenol. If possible, novocaine and a syringe. Some light sutures. Sulfa powder."

"I'll see what I can do," said Moeller and knocked on the door for the guard.

Finally, we were alone. Konrad looked from my face to Borchert's and his eyes filled. "Please forgive me for bringing this on us."

"Stop now," I ordered. "There will be time for penitence later. You must tell us everything, so we can advise your attorney."

His story was quite simple. He had returned from Silesia. Weary from his travels, he had taken a nap. When he awoke, it was dark. He meant to telephone to let me know he had arrived but then decided the call could wait until morning. After his supper, he'd taken a taxi to his favorite haunt.

"There was already talk of a raid when I arrived, but there are always rumors, so I ignored them. A man came in. Tall and very handsome. He had a dark beard and piercing eyes. He was dressed like all the rest in an old jacket and a high-neck sweater. I thought he was just another dockworker. He smoked a meerschaum like they all do. He kept staring at me, staring and smiling. Finally, he gave a little wag of his head to indicate that he'd meet me in that back room. The one set aside for...ahem...quick business. It's a foul-smelling place. All kinds of things go on there." A glance at Borchert told me he found this description greatly disturbing. Konrad continued, "He opened the buttons of his trousers. He responded with great enthusiasm, so I was distracted when the door flew open. Someone kicked me in the chest, then threw me up against the wall. I tried to stand straight, but someone punched me. For some time after, I knew nothing. Then I heard the bearded man laughing as they carried me out."

"He was a Gestapo agent," said Borchert. "They mean to close down all the taverns that cater to homosexuals."

"What idiots!" exclaimed Konrad. "New ones will open."

"I'm sure," replied Borchert, "but they mean to make an example with this raid, which will make it all the harder to do anything on your behalf. And they suspect you for other reasons."

Konrad turned sharply. "But I've been so careful. We've all been."

"Evidently, not careful enough. I hear they have evidence against us."

"Impossible."

"You must be very strong, Konrad," said Borchert. "You may be beaten, even tortured."

Konrad's eyes widened in terror. "I don't know how much I can take. I loathe pain."

"I know." Borchert reached into his pocket and removed a small cardboard box. It was a chemist's box of the kind used to supply powders in gelatin capsules. He discreetly passed it to Konrad under the table. Konrad looked forlorn. He covered his eyes with his hands.

"Don't worry, my dear," I said quickly, grasping his wrist. "My attorney is already at work seeking both a legal solution and someone we can bribe."

Konrad gave me a sad smile and bravely replied, "I know you will do your best."

Moeller returned with our supplies. Fortunately, he had other business to attend to and left us alone. "Just knock on the door when you're done, and the guard will show you out." He leaned over and said to Borchert in a confidential tone, "It's probably a good idea to be quick rather than annoy the guards. They always take out any offense on the prisoners afterward."

I needed little encouragement to hurry. Unfortunately, Moeller was unsuccessful in securing everything I had requested. I was able to clean all the wounds with the antiseptic he'd brought, but there were no sutures. I succeeded in taping closed the head wound. There was nothing I could do for the broken teeth. The contusions on the chest from Gestapo boots covered a few broken ribs, but I could do nothing for them either. I felt quite useless.

"We must go," urged Borchert. He reached across the table and gave Konrad's least damaged hand a little squeeze. He mouthed the words, "I love you."

"Don't worry," I said to Konrad "I'll do absolutely everything in my power to get you out of here."

As we rode the U-Bahn back to Tiergartenstraße, Borchert was silent.

"What was in the apothecary box you gave Konrad?" I asked when the train halted to take on passengers.

"Surely, you know."

"But the church is opposed to suicide."

"There is too much danger to too many if we are exposed. If he uses the pills, it is an act of charity. Remember our Lord's words: 'Greater love hath no man than this, that a man lay down his life for his friends.'"

Chapter 22

"When will they release Konrad from that awful place?" Katherine asked every day until my stony expression warned her not to ask again. She could not appreciate the gravity of the situation because I had not been entirely candid with her.

At first, there seemed little reason to upset her with facts that worry could not change. Naively, I assumed that the matter would be resolved within a few days, so extended explanations were unnecessary. Under other circumstances, such confidence would be warranted. I had never met a public official who could not be bribed. This was especially useful when one of my ventures met with legal resistance. In the Weimar Republic, bribery had simply been another cost of doing business. As my lawyers were so fond of pointing out, things had changed. The Gestapo, and the courts under its influence, believed completely and absolutely in their mission. There is nothing so intractable, and so frightening, as a true believer.

As the days passed, my attorneys became increasingly pessimistic that Konrad's case would ever go to trial. He was never arraigned, nor brought before a magistrate. Two weeks passed, then three. I asked Borchert if we should consider another visit to the Moabit. He shook his head. "As much as I would like to see with my own eyes that Konrad is all right, we must reserve our visits for those times when it will really make a difference." We were, however, able to send Konrad some clothes and edible food through Moeller.

Amidst all the anxiety, there were some happy developments. Although it was still quite early, signs indicated that Katherine might be pregnant. She was overjoyed, but I urged caution and patience until it could be confirmed.

Katherine, meanwhile, was busy helping Elisabeth plan her wedding. Elisabeth asked Katherine to stand as matron of honor. Katherine protested she was too old and carrying a child, which would certainly be more evident by the time of the wedding, but Elisabeth demonstrated a refreshingly modern outlook and dismissed such protests as absurd.

The marriage to an American still vexed me. To assuage my worries about the succession, Peter had paid a very large sum of money to trace his ancestry to an obscure count in Thuringia. This information was forwarded to the editors of the genealogical books, who were still trying to confirm it.

Whether or not it turned out to be true made little practical difference. I could arrange for Elisabeth to inherit Raithschau through my lawyers. The main issue for me was that I simply could not adjust to the idea of my daughter marrying an American. Although I was fond of Sarah Weber, I found many of her countrymen to be ignorant and uncouth. The thought of my daughter raising her children among them was repellent. Of course, my mother had strenuously objected when I'd decided to marry an Englishman. At least, Lytton was the son of a Marquess, so there was no question of his nobility, and whatever one thinks of the English, they are a civilized people.

Elected Elisabeth's co-conspirator in planning the wedding, Katherine in turn, enlisted Veronika and my mother to make arrangements at Edelheim. Borchert volunteered to solemnize the vows. Now that Konrad was unavailable, Elisabeth had invited her brother to lead her to the altar. He responded with a charming display of brotherly affection, but not before we had a fantastic row over his wearing his formal SS uniform. Fortunately, he relented. Never again would I allow a Nazi uniform to be worn in my house by any member of my family.

Despite enrolling everyone in the family to help plan her wedding, Elisabeth never asked me to do a single thing. I took no offense as these bridal concerns interested me not one bit. I was more than happy to leave the details to the people who actually cared about them. Although I remained aloof from the pre-nuptial frenzy, I found myself surprisingly touched by Elisabeth's request to be married in my wedding gown. It was sorely out of date, having been made before the Great War, but to my daughter that seemed of little consequence. The dress was finally located in Edelheim's cavernous attic. After being properly cleaned, and the lace and pearls made right, it was acceptable.

We entertained Peter's parents in Berlin for a week before the event.

Katherine had suggested that our Berlin home would feel more comfortable to modern Americans than an ancient, overly-large Prussian Schloss. While it was a sensible idea to invite them to Berlin, the visit did not go as well as Katherine hoped.

Although I had never met the Fischers, I decided I didn't like them simply because I objected to the match. I regret to say that my behavior was proof positive that aristocrats can be not only downright rude given the right opportunity, but also quite nasty. I affected boredom and yawned behind my hand when Agnes Fischer described her many and mighty social connections in Philadelphia. She described the creations of her dressmakers and showed me a few of her rags. Afterward, I let her have free run of my closet full of Schiaparellis and Chanels. Then I took her on a little excursion to the *Werderschermarkt,* our justifiably famous clothing district. Karl Fischer told me he liked billiards. I tried not to crow as I beat him in every game. He raised race horses. I showed him the nag I kept at the Grunewald stables, one of the daughters of a Trakehner grand prize winner my father had raised. Fischer's brows rose when I told him that she was valued at a quarter million Marks.

No, I wasn't the most gracious hostess. Not at all.

Katherine scolded me for my mean behavior. She tried to persuade me that I ought to make an effort for Elisabeth's sake. Of course, Katherine's arguments fell on deaf ears and made me even more determined to create mischief.

Eventually, even I grew tired of my antics. I allowed myself to see that the Fischers were intelligent and kind. To my great surprise, I found myself warming to them, so much so, that I invited Karl Fischer to my study after dinner for a glass of my birthday port. We compared notes on our offspring and the political situation in America until well into the night. Our little party would have gone on even longer had Katherine not come down to encourage me to go to bed.

The day of the wedding approached, and we moved the scene to Edelheim. After greeting my mother, who was unusually charming, as she can be in the presence of guests, the Fischers and I occupied some time with a tour of the house. We ended it in the hall of ancestors, where portraits of my family line the walls. As any aristocratic child, I had lived daily with these ghosts from the past, and my grandfather had made certain I knew them all. I could, on request, recite their lineage, dates of birth and death, and the names of all their descendants, even the junior and cadet branches.

"They all look oddly alike," Mrs. Fischer noted.

"That's because we are all related beyond the obvious ways. For example, Uncle Richard here, was cousin to my grandmother on my father's side. Twice cousins, actually, and my great grandmother, Sofie Anna, was also a cousin to her husband, the Landgrave of Moravia…" As I continued in this vein, Mrs. Fischer's eyes began to glaze over, and she looked very alarmed. "Not to worry," I assured her. "There are no heritable defects in the line. At least, none of which I am aware. But that's also why we so love Peter. *Fresh blood*!" I pursed my lips to hide my naughty smile. Katherine pinched my arm rather painfully.

The next day, Elisabeth was married in the little chapel in Schloss Edelheim. The village church was Protestant, of course, but the pastor had offered its use out of loyalty to the family and friendship with my late father. In the end, we all agreed the intimacy of the Schloss chapel was the right setting for the wedding I'd promised—small but fittingly grand for the daughter of one of the oldest houses of Prussia. I confess to shedding a few tears at seeing my daughter grown enough to be married. With all the last-minute hurrying about, I'd forgotten my handkerchief. Veronika passed me hers and gave my waist a sympathetic squeeze.

The preparations for the event had distracted me from Konrad's predicament. At the wedding festivities, I found myself imagining him, dapper as ever, turning his young cousin around the dance floor. The thought of him lying, broken and miserable, in the Moabit was depressing, and I drank more alcohol than was wise. Afterwards, I was unable to sleep. While Katherine dozed quietly against my shoulder, I devised a plan to take a more active role in securing Konrad's release.

***

"*Herr Doktor* Schlemmer, I would like you to make an appointment for me," I told my personal attorney on the morning after we returned to Berlin. He had agreed to meet me on very short notice and seemed somewhat flummoxed by the request. "I wish to pay a visit to the Gestapo commander."

His eyes widened. Then he assumed a very grave expression. "*Gnädige*, I strenuously advise against it."

"Why? Nothing you've done has advanced our cause. Not one iota! How long do you expect Baron Holdenberg to rot in that jail?"

"But, *Gnädige*, it's rather complicated. Evidently, they are no longer holding him on the primary charge, but on a secondary one they cannot prove. They are waiting for witnesses to come forward so they can charge him with collusion to undermine the Reich." This was cause for concern. Perhaps Konrad had already been forced to betray the Pilze.

"Witnesses? Who?" I asked anxiously.

"Associates from the Party—from the era when the Catholic Center Party held power." I was relieved to hear they suspected Konrad's former political allies rather than *Pilze* members. Fortunately, apart from Konrad, none of us had ever been directly involved in politics.

"Schlemmer, my father was one of the great heroes of the imperial Reich. Surely, I can trade on his name for something."

"Your father is still venerated in certain circles. But I do not advise involving the family name in any way."

I couldn't understand why Schlemmer was being so overwhelmingly timid. How could he ever hope to win a case with such a passive approach? Surely, this matter required an effort on our part rather than simply waiting around for some action by the authorities. "When your enemy fails to act, provoke him," my father always said. I chose to remember that part of the lesson and conveniently forgot the rest: "But first consider all outcomes."

"*Herr Doktor*, make an appointment with the Gestapo commandant." Schlemmer gazed at me with alarm. "I can be available to him…" I flipped open my diary. "…on Wednesday. Please convey to him the greetings of Countess Stahle von Langenberg-Edelheim."

"As you wish, *Gnädige*," he said in an excessively obsequious tone.

Schlemmer followed my orders and got me on the calendar of the Berlin-district Gestapo commandant, Marcus Schmidt, for ten o'clock on Wednesday morning. In the intervening time, I considered how to present myself. Should I conjure the imperious Countess Stahle and appear in a brightly colored couture costume? That was my first impulse, of course, to attempt to intimidate the man with glamour. Fortunately, I succeeded in remembering that the Nazi ideal of beauty was the simple peasant maiden, unadorned and natural. Makeup was considered something for prostitutes, and I had modified mine to suit to the current style. I finally decided to revert to the role I most easily played—a professional woman.

❋❋❋

Schmidt was not at all as I expected. He was quite young, perhaps not even thirty. When I was shown into his office, he gave me a lazy Hitler salute, just a flip of the wrist to show his palm, the words muttered and seemingly inconsequential. He was not wearing a uniform, as so many did now, but an ordinary suit with a party pin in the lapel. The suit was nicely cut and showed some taste. I took this as a positive sign.

He was a good deal shorter than I. Some men find a woman towering over them threatening, so I slouched a bit as I shook his hand. He gestured to the chair on the opposite side of his desk. He allowed himself a long moment to take my measure, and I returned the inspection. I could see from his humorless expression that social amenities would be lost on this man. Fine, we would get directly to the heart of the matter. I cleared my throat pointedly.

"I have come on behalf of my cousin, Konrad von Holdenberg. He has been held without charges for over a month."

"I am familiar with the case," he replied matter-of-factly.

"The baron is a respected member of the community. He was a member of the Reichstag. His family needs him. He has a young daughter, and his wife is expecting another child."

He smiled slightly, but his eyes revealed that he was not amused. "We know he has a wife and child. Were you hoping to convince me that the sodomy charge is false?"

Fortunately, I was prepared for this. "I have no idea what went on in that tavern, but I have known Konrad von Holdenberg since he was a boy. I can scarcely believe he would associate with such riffraff."

"That riffraff was my lieutenant," Schmidt replied with poker-faced deadpan.

"Was your lieutenant on an official assignment or does he usually frequent such places?" My abrupt candor took him by surprise. He frowned.

"I usually ask the questions, *Frau Doktor*. The others, who were arrested that night, have been released. Being caught in the act was unfortunate for Herr von Holdenberg. But that is only a small part of our interest in him. How much do you know about your cousin's political activities?"

The time had come to make liberal use of my acting abilities. I stared at Schmidt with a shocked expression. "Political activities? He gave up politics years ago."

"So you were unaware of the subversive pamphlets he was distributing?"

There was no need to feign surprise, because this came as news to me. "Pamphlets. What pamphlets?"

"May I suggest you look into the activities of your chief manager? We discovered his involvement after finding a crate destined for one of your factories. All of the markings had been removed, except one on the bottom, evidently overlooked."

"That's impossible."

"I assure you, *Frau Doktor*, that everything I say is true. However, it took us some time to make the connection to Holdenberg. We traced the drayage forms and found his signature."

Idiot! How could he be so foolish? He could have had anyone sign the freight documents. Certainly, the discovery of the crate could implicate me, even though I had nothing to do with the pamphlets.

Showing the least hint of my fear to Schmidt was dangerous. Instead, I boldly asked: "If you are so certain of my cousin's guilt, why haven't you charged him?"

He smiled ironically. "You really think your cousin could print and distribute those pamphlets without help? There were certainly accomplices."

I made a quick assessment of the situation. My lawyers had been correct in guessing the Gestapo's strategy. If Konrad were tried for the relatively minor charge of sodomy, he would be under the supervision of the courts. He would also have access to an attorney on a regular basis and be protected from further interrogation or worse. The Gestapo intended to let him languish in the Moabit, while they worked on him to expose the identities of his collaborators. Konrad, despite his proclivity for brutal sexual encounters, actually loathed pain. I could not imagine how he could possibly stand up to aggressive questioning, especially in a weakened state. If they succeeded in breaking Konrad, we would all be in great danger.

I needed to show resolve or risk suggesting that I had been intimidated. "Then charge him with subversion and be done with it."

"We want the others. All of them," he replied bluntly. "Until your cousin gives up his friends, he will enjoy our hospitality."

He rose. The interview had been concluded. For the first time, Schmidt smiled. "As a matter of fact, Countess Stahle, I am a great admirer of your father. He was a true hero of the Fatherland." This time, he gave me a more assertive Hitler salute.

I acknowledged it with a nod, but I did not return it.

***

I had already come to the cheerless conclusion that my visit to Schmidt had been a mistake, when Borchert flew into my Luisenstraße office. I had kept the lease on the private office after I left the Charité because it gave me a place to see patients without interruption from hospital business. It also gave Borchert the privacy to speak to me in a tone that I found shocking.

"Are you insane, Margarethe? What in God's name were you thinking!" Since little more than a few hours had passed since I had called on Commandant Schmidt, I wondered how Borchert could know.

"Moeller told me," he explained without my needing to ask, "and he's very angry because now none of us can help Konrad."

"Why not?"

"Because they plan to move him to Buchenwald within the week." He sighed and threw up his hands. I understood from his frustration that this must be serious, but I failed to perceive the degree.

"Why there?"

"It's a concentration camp." Even I, who liked to insulate myself from all things political had heard about such places—nothing good, to be sure.

"You don't think my call on the commandant actually caused them to move him? Why, that's spiteful!"

"You think the Gestapo isn't capable of spite?" he said, reddening once again. "But no, it's not spite. It's only that you called attention to Konrad. We were hoping he might simply get lost in the system until we could find a way to get him out. They are so intent on rounding up the Jews, there was a real possibility he would be forgotten. But that's also contributed to the problem. The Moabit is now so overcrowded with Jews, there's no place to put common criminals." He covered his face with his hands. "Dear God, Margarethe, this is a disaster!"

"We mustn't jump to conclusions," I said in my "doctor's voice," trying to calm Borchert. "Perhaps it's not as bad as you think."

He stared at me. "You have no idea, do you? They work people to death in those camps, and Konrad is not the strongest as it is."

"Can Moeller help us get into the prison before Konrad is moved?"

He sighed deeply. "I'll see what can be done."

"We can use Katherine as a justification. Surely it makes sense that his pregnant wife should wish to see him."

"Katherine is with child?" said Borchert with surprise. Then he smiled for the first time since his arrival. "That devil. He never said a word."

"He doesn't know. We only recently confirmed it ourselves."

"But how will she take seeing him in this state?" he asked, rubbing his forehead fiercely as if a terrible headache had suddenly asserted itself. "*I* can barely stand to see him this way."

"Katherine, as you well know, is a physician and very strong. I think we should have no concerns in that regard." I spoke confidently, but I realized I must prepare her.

My effort to do so had to wait until Fiona had gone to bed. I asked

Katherine to take a seat in the library and exiled the servants to their quarters. While I spelled out our assumptions regarding the Gestapo's strategy, Katherine listened with a frown. She waited until my report was completely finished before speaking.

"You and your soothing lies, Margarethe!" she said in an accusing voice. "Why couldn't you just tell me the truth?"

"There seemed little need to worry you over this, and especially not in your condition. We both know that early pregnancy can be a delicate time, especially for someone with your history."

"That's no excuse!"

In my mind, it was. I had been scrupulously monitoring Katherine's health for any warning signs of an ectopic pregnancy. I dreaded an encore of the fall's anxious moments, and for a woman of Katherine's age, there was also the real possibility of miscarriage. I had been tip-toeing around her to create a calm and orderly atmosphere. Perhaps my concern over the pregnancy was excessive, but it provided the consoling illusion of control, whereas Konrad's situation left me feeling completely helpless.

Katherine asked me to describe Konrad's physical condition in great detail. She was particularly concerned about damage to his eye. Because I had lacked instruments during my visit, there had been no means to evaluate his injuries beyond a cursory examination. Fortunately, as a physician, Katherine could justifiably carry a medical bag.

❋❋❋

Despite all my careful preparation, Katherine wept openly when she saw Konrad. Moeller placed a paternal hand on her shoulder. Konrad played up his role as the doting father-to-be, touching her pregnant belly, although at such an early stage, there was nothing to be felt. Perhaps this tender display was more than pretense. Konrad adored Fiona and was extravagantly happy when we told him that he would be a father again.

Konrad looked far better than when we had seen him after the horror of his beating. The swelling on his face had receded. The wound over his eye had closed with no sign of infection. His color had returned, and he had gained a bit of weight from inactivity. When he smiled, his broken teeth gave him a strangely affecting and charmingly imperfect grin.

Moeller remained through the entire visit. We had brought our own medical supplies, so there was no pretext to send him on an errand of mercy. His motive in remaining probably had less to do with insinuating himself into our privacy than a wish to provide pastoral comfort. To his credit, the man stood aside to allow us our final farewells.

"Please tell my Fiona that Papa loves her," said Konrad, blinking back tears. He kissed Katherine. Then he and Franz exchanged a long fervent look, clasping one another's hands so tightly, the tips of their fingers blanched. "And thank you, dear Frau Salzburger," he said, kissing me on the cheek. He whispered into my ear: "I love you."

Chapter 23

In late June, the lindens began to bloom along the great avenues leading to the Brandenburg Gate and in the Tiergarten. The air was filled with their heady and intoxicating perfume. To a Berliner, it is the signal that summer and its sultry weather will soon be upon us. Usually, the scent of the lindens filled me with joy, but in 1939, it was a sad reminder that Sarah Weber would soon be departing for home.

Sarah had adjusted swimmingly to St. Hilde's. The nuns simply adored her. I had put her in charge of the medical students w'ed brought on for rotations, and she had proven to be an exceptionally able leader. This opened interesting possibilities. Zimmerling, the chief of surgery had lately been making noises about retiring from hospital administration and opening a private practice. I began to see Sarah as his replacement. In the interim, or in case he changed his mind, Sarah would make a perfect under-chief. It was largely a selfish wish to have her join my staff. With Sarah at the helm of such a critical department, my burden would be significantly lightened.

I invited Sarah to Mattke's to press my suit. We settled in to consider the menu. Of course, I didn't need to study it—my order was always the same—but I required a moment of reflection before I laid out my proposal. While I scanned the familiar list, I felt her eyes on me.

"How do you do that?" she asked.

"Do what?" I asked, not looking up.

"Go from being the imperious mistress of every junior doctor's fate to a relaxed and urbane Berliner."

"Because I am," I replied with a shrug.

"Which?"

"Both."

"You're amazing," she replied and gave me a long, admiring look. I cleared my throat and went back to staring at the menu. It had been the same since my grandfather's time but pretending to read it allowed me to avoid Sarah's appreciative gaze.

"You must tell me what you think of the wine," I said as the headwaiter poured Sarah a glass. She tasted it tentatively, then nodded in approval.

"Not as sweet as most German wines. Actually, it's really good."

"It's from my estate in Franconia. I think I may finally have gotten it right. The first few vintages were quite undrinkable." I made a face at the memory.

"You make wine too?" she asked, cocking her head and regarding me with undisguised awe.

"Yes, among other things." I wanted to flog myself for having brought up this subject. Clearly, Sarah's hero worship needed no encouragement. As I was still in the role of mentor, at least until her term was done, I decided to offer some gentle advice. "My dear, it's generally better to avoid showing how impressed one is. Leave something to the imagination. And in any case, healthy skepticism is always in fashion." I winked to soften the criticism, but she colored and went back to deciding her meal.

I was happy to turn the conversation away from me and focus it, as I had intended, on her career. "What are your plans once you return to the States?"

"Oh, I suppose I'll join my father's practice. It's what he expects, of course. But life in Maine will seem pretty boring after living in Berlin."

"With your excellent education and training, you must have other opportunities."

She sighed. "Well, yes, but Dad expects me to take over the practice when he retires." I was reminded of Augustine Tierney's ambitious plans for his daughter, Katherine, and how circumstance had made them all go awry. At least, Tierney had finally reconciled to Katherine's living in Berlin. Perhaps Sarah might also be saved from the burden of following in her father's footsteps. "Dad really wants me back. He already had an architect draw up plans for expanding the office."

I shrugged. "Even your father would admit another experience might be wise before you settle into private practice."

"Oh, I definitely have a vacation in mind."

"I meant something of longer duration. Perhaps a staff position."

She leaned on her hand and gazed out the window at the passers-by on the street. "I've thought of going back to New York. I went to medical school there but never had any time to do or see anything. It's been the same in Berlin. All I see is the inside of a hospital."

"Well, then you might like to extend your stay."

She frowned. "How? My fellowship is over at the end of the month and so is my lease at the doctors' residence."

"Perhaps you would consider being under-chief to Dr. Zimmerling."

"You're kidding, right?...me?...really?"

"Why not? You're a fine surgeon. You've demonstrated excellent leadership in handling your colleagues and the medical students. Zimmerling wants to go on to private practice. It's likely you would be chief before long."

"Chief? Wow! Do you really think I'm ready for that?" Her artless reaction was charming, but I worried about her need to hear my assurances. She needed to draw confidence from her own reserve.

"Sarah, you have the makings of a fine leader, but you must learn to trust yourself."

She hadn't heard a word I'd said since making my offer. "Wow, under-chief, maybe chief before long. Holy shit! That's goddamn amazing."

"If you are interested, you must let me know very soon so I can make arrangements."

Her excitement evaporated and she frowned. "Don't think me ungrateful, but I really need to think about it."

"Of course, you do."

"I mean, I could go to New York and try to make a name for myself. I have friends at Presbyterian, schoolmates who stayed on for residency there. Or I could go back to Hopkins."

From my point of view, it seemed a very haphazard way to manage a career, but I didn't want to injure her by saying so. "Have you made inquiries?"

"No. Because I really need a long vacation before I settle down. I haven't had time off since I started medical school."

An idea suddenly occurred to me. Konrad had returned the Garmisch chalet to my ownership not long after demanding it for the wedding settlement. He'd found it too expensive to maintain, which anyone could have predicted, knowing how burdensome the costs were.

"I don't know if this interests you, but I have a chalet in Garmisch. The caretaker's wife is quite a good cook. I doubt I can get away for a mountain holiday this year, especially now that I've become chief at St. Hilde's. You could stay there as long as you wish. You'd have the place completely to yourself."

"That's very generous, but I couldn't even think of accepting."

"Why not?"

Sarah leaned forward and spoke in a confidential tone. "At any other time, I'd jump at the chance. I love the Alps and mountain sports, but there's going to be a war."

I sat back and gave her a skeptical look. "You're so sure?"

"Everyone knows war is coming."

I assumed a neutral expression to avoid telegraphing my concern, especially because I had privileged information regarding the increasing demand for steel and coal.

"I don't want to be caught here if there is a war."

"Well, war isn't being declared tomorrow. You could still enjoy a mountain holiday. Invite some friends if you wish."

"I don't know..."

I interrupted before she could finish. "Think about it but let me know before your term is done."

By then, the headwaiter had approached to take our order. Sarah chose something I knew she probably wouldn't like, but having been scolded often enough for dictating what others should order, I said nothing.

Sarah glanced enviously at my meal as we ate, but she never complained. I shared some of my salmon so that she could taste it and was intrigued when she ate it directly off my fork. It gave me a strange feeling because it seemed so intimate.

I ordered another bottle of wine because Sarah seemed to be enjoying it so. When she began to giggle at remarks that were not remotely funny, I knew she was sliding into her cups. I urged coffee on her, but it had little effect. Discreetly, I signaled to the head waiter and asked him to call a taxi.

"Perhaps you'd like the afternoon free, Dr. Weber?"

"Hell, yeah," she said with a chuckle. "That wine of yours went right to my head."

"We should probably leave now," I suggested.

"That would be a damned good idea."

On the way to the door, I offered my arm to steady her. She continued to lean on it as we waited on the street for a taxi. Yes, the alcohol had definitely gone to her head. "I could use a nap right about now," she said.

"I'm sure you could. I recommend aspirin and bicarb before your nap, that is, if you don't mind my advice, Doctor."

"Sarah," she said, "Please call me Sarah." In my mind, I had always called her by her given name, but our relative positions required a certain formality, which must continue until her term was done, so I did not return the favor.

The taxi pulled to the curb, and she suddenly took my hands in hers. "Oh, *Frau Doktor*, you've been so good to me, and I'll miss you so much!" Had I allowed it, she surely would have embraced me there on the street. I succeeded in reminding myself that alcohol often makes one effusive and generous. Decorum must be especially scrupulous at such times. I retrieved my hands and opened the door of the taxi for her.

The wine had gone to my head as well. Fortunately, I had no substantial duties that afternoon and retreated to my hospital office to hide my compromised state from others. I was reviewing the mortality and morbidity reports, when Katherine appeared in my doorway. She had lately been so busy that I rarely, if ever, saw her in the hospital. Our attempts to set luncheon dates in the physicians' dining room were always frustrated by the demands of the mothers-to-be under her care. So much for our hope that my return to St. Hilde's would allow us more time together.

"My dear, what a delight. To what do I owe the pleasure?" I closed the file to indicate she now had my complete attention. "Come in and sit down." I gestured to a chair.

"I haven't much time," she said, continuing to stand. "But I thought you'd want to know that Eva d'Allessandro was delivered by Caesarian this morning. A son." My surprise at hearing her speak so casually about Eva made it impossible to think of a quick response. "She was your friend," Katherine continued, "so I thought you might want to know."

"I had no idea she was your patient." Actually, it made no sense because Katherine scrupulously avoided cases where her emotions could interfere with her judgment. Despite her basic kindness, Katherine had a long memory and found it difficult to forgive those who injured her. She had never forgiven her favorite uncle for concealing the facts about her mother's death. For that reason, her relationship with her Irish family remained attenuated.

"She's actually Becher's patient," Katherine explained, "but I'm looking after her now that she's postpartum."

I attempted to be artfully disinterested, but I was curious from a professional point of view. "Why Caesarian?"

"Her son is enormous. She could never have delivered him vaginally. I find it very odd because she and the father are so small."

I shrugged. "We really never know who the father is, do we?"

"I know the father of this one," she said, patting her abdomen, which had lately begun to swell a little. It made me think of Konrad and wonder how he was faring in Buchenwald. My attorneys continued to press for his release, or at least a trial. So far, they'd made no progress.

"Thank you for the news," I said, attempting a little smile.

"The gas has worn off. She's awake and asking for you. I said I would tell you."

After Katherine left, I wondered if she was giving me permission to see Eva. If so, why invite trouble? Any meeting with Eva was bound to be fraught with drama. Of course, this rational debate lasted mere seconds. I conveniently remembered that I had a plausible reason to visit the obstetrics department. Becher had asked me a question in a meeting that morning, and I'd promised him an answer before the end of the day. I could have telephoned but instead, I went down to his office and chatted with him for a while. I was especially interested to hear his take on Katherine's health. From my point of view, everything seemed to be proceeding normally, and he agreed. We talked about bringing over two obstetrics residents from the Charité to lend a hand, especially as Katherine's pregnancy came closer to term and she took leave. Eventually, I ran out of things to discuss with Becher. I should have returned to my office and the business of the day, but I suddenly found myself at the nurse's station to ask the location of Eva's room.

Eva was dozing when I entered. I was surprised to see that despite the surgery, she looked quite comfortable. I don't know why I was surprised. Katherine is exceptionally able where pain management is concerned, having made it a special professional interest of hers since the misunderstanding about her mother's death.

I took a moment to read the chart. Becher kept a separate office for seeing private patients, which explained why I hadn't seen Eva in the hospital for prenatal visits. From the chart, I also learned that the infant was two weeks premature. Even so, the child, mildly described by Katherine as "enormous," was nearly ten pounds in weight and twenty-three inches in length. My son had been about that size, but I was far larger than Eva and had been able to carry him to term and give birth to him in the ordinary way.

My hand automatically sought the pulse point in Eva's wrist, which had the effect of waking her.

"*Cara*," she murmured, waking. "I knew you'd come."

I instantly withdrew my hand. "Congratulations on the birth of your son," I said in a formal tone. Unable to think of something else to say, I stood stiffly beside the bed, hands in my pockets.

"What? No kiss? Not even from affection?"

I bent to touch my lips to her forehead. She reached up and put her hand on the back of my neck, gently holding me down. "Oh, *cara*, I've missed you so," she said, and I instantly melted into a pool of desire. I kissed her offered mouth, lingering perhaps a moment too long. When our lips parted, she smiled. "So, you missed me a little. I knew you would." She patted a place on the bed. "Sit down, my love, and stay with me a while." She winced as my weight depressed the mattress.

"Are you still in pain?"

"It's fading now. Your Dr. von Holdenberg was here just a moment ago to give me some medicine. She is very kind and has a gentle touch. I can see why she is such a success with new mothers." I was not about to discuss Katherine with Eva, so I shifted the topic.

"That's quite a *bambino*, Eva. His father must have been a very large man."

"Not large, but extraordinarily tall and very handsome. I was smitten by his beautiful mouth and the way he plays the violin."

"Ah, you have such a weakness for musicians."

"Oh, when I chose a father for my child, it was essential that he be a musician. My child must have musical talent or I couldn't bear it. I want him to grow up to be the composer I can never be."

"Was the poor man aware of how deliberately you chose him?"

"Were you?"

My mind rebelled against remembering the earliest days of our affair, and yet, as I sat beside Eva, I found her as compelling as ever. It would be so easy to fall under her spell again.

"The father has other desirable traits," Eva continued. "He is a physician like you, exceptionally well educated, and he comes from a very old family. Perhaps his child will even be blond. But perhaps not. Dionysius usually wins over Apollo, especially when it comes to coloring."

Despite the drug of her dark eyes caressing my face, for Eva was certainly my rival as a mesmerist, my brain began to weave the threads of her description into a pattern. I forced myself to remain calm. "An old family, you say?"

"Yes, and quite well known in musical circles because of a particular member, especially now that she has made her debut." She smiled because she could see from the appalled look on my face that I was beginning to draw conclusions.

"My family perhaps?"

"That's what I love about you, Margarethe. You are so quick!"

I jumped up from the bed as if it were on fire. "How could you!" I demanded. "How did you find him?"

"You gave me all the clues when you told me he was in Munich studying medicine. It was easy to find the address. The Lehel villa, where he lives, is in your name." She did not stop talking long enough to allow me a response, although, in fact, I was speechless. "How handsome he is in his black uniform. How like you in every way. But it's you I want. You, *cara*. I want to hear your wonderful voice and give you my wine." She reached out for my hand.

"Why us?" I asked, stepping back, out of her reach. "Why not some other family you found in the newspaper?"

"Because you are a musician, a great one, and your son as well. Oh, *cara*, he is so beautiful and so sensitive…so like you."

I dashed out of the room. On my way to the lift, I did not even glance into the nursery. If the child, whom Eva claimed to be my grandson, lay there, I never wanted to know.

❀❀❀

Fortunately, the work day was nearly done so I left for home. I drove my roadster with the top down, racing through the streets toward Grunewald. The scent of the lindens blooming everywhere was oppressive. My agitation left me feeling nauseous, and the extra wine hadn't helped. I moderated my speed to avoid vomiting the remnants of my lunch in my motorcar.

Fiona was at the door to meet me. I had promised before I left that morning to take her to the stables for a ride. Despite my dark mood, I reluctantly changed into my riding clothes because I know how important it is for an adult to keep a promise to a child.

While Fiona's pony was being saddled by the groom, she took the opportunity to badger me with questions. I think she saved them for such opportunities.

"When will Papa come home?" she asked. Konrad traveled often, so his being at home was a novelty rather than the routine. Until now, we had been able to use this as an explanation of his extended absence.

"I have no idea," I said curtly without fully considering my words.

The child gave me a brief, curious look. "But don't you tell him where to go." This served to tell me that Fiona, despite her youth, understood more about Konrad's role in my business affairs than I'd imagined.

"Yes, I usually do, but not this time."

"Why not?"

"He has made a problem for himself and must remain where he is until it is solved."

"You could solve it for him," she suggested.

"I would, if I could, my little mouse. But this is beyond my control."

She nodded. "Papa is very smart. He'll find a way to come home. I know he will."

The conversation during the remainder of our ride was mercifully less grave for we talked about ponies. Fiona explained that she was quite done with them and wished to have a horse now, specifically a white horse, or perhaps, a black horse with a white star on its forehead. We briefly debated these choices.

Accompanied by a distinctively equine scent, we made our way home. Katherine wrinkled up her nose when we arrived. Although she is an excellent rider, Katherine finds the smell of horses repellent.

"Off with you to the bath!" she ordered, instantly banishing Fiona. Despite the aroma of my clothes, she invited me for a glass of aperitif. I took off my mucky boots and in stocking feet followed Katherine out to the terrace.

"I heard from the nurses that you visited the countess."

"Yes, does that trouble you?"

"Not at all. You told me the affair was done, and I believe you."

I could hear a hidden imperative in the statement—a subtle warning that if it weren't done, then *it bloody well ought to be.*

"I have no further interest in the woman," I said, putting my foot up on the chair opposite mine.

Katherine turned her eyes on me. "My, my, aren't we a bit snippy on this subject?"

"Don't read into it," I replied neutrally.

"What happened? You rushed to her bedside only to be rebuffed?"

"Katherine," I said in an increasingly annoyed tone, "I said, it is done, and I have no wish to speak of it. I visited her today merely from courtesy because she requested it. Now let it rest."

"Then I suppose you don't want to hear the details of the birth. It's actually quite an interesting case. Clearly, the child's father was a much larger man than the countess's husband, and a normal birth would have..."

"Katherine, for Christ's bloody sake!" I snarled. "I said, let it rest!"

She stared at me with exaggerated concern and some feigned injury.

"Pardon," I said, although it galled me to apologize when I had clearly warned her away from this topic. "It's been a trying day."

I realized that my overstated response had genuinely upset Katherine. She perceptibly withdrew and sipped her wine in silence, which gave me the opportunity to retreat into my own concerns. Her needling me about Eva was peripheral to the real cause of my distress. I could never speak of the parentage of Eva's child, not to Katherine, nor even to the father himself. Then it occurred to me that my beautiful son could have made many conquests, and I could have other little bastard grandchildren scattered about. What an unnerving thought!

"'Will you have more wine?" Katherine asked. Having apparently gotten over her hurt, she was now demonstrating her willingness to make peace by playing the attentive wife. My glass was nearly empty, so I agreed to have it refilled.

"How was your talk with Sarah Weber?" Katherine asked, mercifully changing the topic.

"I doubt she'll take the post. She wants to go home. She says there will be a war."

Katherine sighed. "So everyone says. What do you think?"

"Now that the allies have found some spine over Poland, I think it's rather inevitable."

I had the benefit of knowing how much of our steel and coal the government was drawing, and it seemed that everyone was now in uniform. Some of the doctors at St. Hilde's had joined the medical corps of the various military services. The idea had even been suggested to me, despite the Nazis' contempt for female physicians.

My father's old army friend, Colonel von Lauer, accompanied the officer who came to offer me a commission as *Oberstabsarzt* with the rank of army major. The Heer wanted the propaganda benefit of my family name as much as my medical skills. Sauerbruch had put them up to it, thinking it would advance my career as well as please me. Long ago, I'd confided to him how much I had longed to be a soldier like my father. It was during the Great War, when my father was at the front, and I was stuck in Munich as a surgical resident. I might as well have been an army surgeon, with all the war wounded that came our way.

I had mixed feelings as I declined the offer. They couldn't compel me to accept it, of course, because as a woman, I was not subject to conscription. Colonel von Lauer, who had known me since I was a girl, watched me carefully. He knew that becoming a soldier had once been my fondest dream. As I deliberated, he could undoubtedly sense my ambivalence. Hopefully, he understood that I would have proudly served as a surgeon in the imperial army. However, I would die before wearing any uniform bearing the Nazi Swastika.

"I hear that nothing can stop it now," Katherine said, bringing me back to the present. "Hitler is only looking for an excuse to attack." I stared at Katherine, surprised to learn that she was so informed about politics, but now she had a rich source of information in the members of the *Pilze*.

"We must invite Nigel to supper and see what he thinks," I suggested.

"Yes, do," said Katherine, "It's been ages since we've seen dear Mr. Calder."

Chapter 24

It was some weeks before we could find an open slot in Nigel's calendar. Now that Molotov had become foreign minister in Russia, there seemed a higher likelihood that Germany would sign a pact, not an alliance exactly, but an agreement to avoid war between us. The idea had the British very nervous, and the foreign office sent Nigel, their finest expert on evaluating military preparedness, to Russia to do a broad assessment. Given his central role in events that could literally affect us all, I felt fortunate that we were able to make a dinner date at all.

In the meanwhile, domestic events continued to unfold, bringing some positive developments. Katherine had passed the most delicate stage of early pregnancy. We were well past the risk of ectopic implantation and even miscarriage was less likely. She was able to maintain a full schedule of duty, and I was glad to have her. Managing St. Hilde's had proven to be far more demanding than I had expected, and I was grateful to have at least one department fully staffed and functional. The obstetrics residents we brought over from the Charité were certainly kept busy.

Choosing personnel for the staff exchange meant walking a fine line. It was difficult to weed out the Nazis and sympathizers. Not everyone was obvious about their politics, even when it could be a professional advantage as it had been at the Charité. Perhaps people still feared the disapproval of their colleagues and friends if it were known they belonged to the Party.

To no one's surprise, except perhaps my own, for I was hopeful to the end, Sarah Weber ultimately declined my offer of a post at St. Hilde's. She had decided to return to the States as soon as possible, explaining that she wanted to spend the remaining weeks of summer at her family's summer home on the coast of Maine. She had accepted a staff position at Presbyterian Hospital in New York starting in September. I was glad that she had chosen another professional assignment before joining her father's practice. She was far too talented to disappear into a private practice in some backwater. However, I had reserved my advice and allowed her to come to that decision completely on her own. At least, I'd learned that much from the disasters resulting from my meddling in Katherine's career.

As any overworked young physician, Sarah was overjoyed at the prospect of leisure time. She was especially looking forward to spending time at her family's summer home in Boothbay, Maine. "It's beautiful there," she told me as we lunched at Mattke's on the day she was to depart by train to Bremen. From there she would take an ocean liner to New York and was already booked on the Queen Mary. "You must come for a visit sometime. You'd like it, I'm sure." She gave me a broad smile. Her generous mouth always seemed broader when she smiled fully. Once again, I admired her strong, expressive face—patrician, to be sure. Her pupils enlarged in response to my appreciation of her looks. Were she still my charge, I would have averted my eyes to avoid any confusion. Now it was unnecessary, but neither did I return her frank look of attraction. I merely smiled and asked her to tell me more about Maine.

"The water is so cold there, you can't swim in the ocean until mid-July unless you're a native, but it's a wonderful place. Do you like lobster?"

"Unfortunately, I've never had the pleasure."

"You would love it!"

"Someday, I'll come to Maine, but only if you promise to come to the Alps with me."

Sarah looked full of regret and lowered her gaze. "I'll be back one day. I promise."

This time, Sarah turned down the headwaiter's offer of a menu and let me order for her, my usual: poached salmon with green sauce. "Goethe adored this green sauce, he ate it with everything," I explained as the waiter served her meal. "I'm sure it's not as exotic as your American lobster, but it's one of my favorite meals."

"I wish I had known about this place before."

"We could have eaten here more often, but the role of mentor can be… delicate."

She nodded, understanding. "I'm so sorry I couldn't take the post at St. Hilde's. I'm just not cut out to be an ex-pat. I guess I'm just too goddamn American."

I smiled. One of the things I would miss about Sarah was her penchant for profanity, which made me feel nearly virtuous by comparison. I was musing over this thought when she gave me another smoldering look.

"I'm really going to miss you," she said with great emotion as she reached over to take my hand. I squeezed hers to demonstrate my feelings.

After lunch, I drove her to the Anhalter Bahnhof in my roadster. Her luggage had been sent ahead, so she carried only a small valise. Courtesy dictated that I wait on the platform until her train departed. We had a few minutes before she needed to board, and we were suddenly awkward in our extended farewells. Sarah kept checking her watch. She avoided my gaze. Perhaps she was simply anxious to get on with her journey. More likely, the heartfelt moment in the restaurant had unsettled her.

Finally, the conductor called for all passengers to board. "I have to go," Sarah said, extending her hand. "Thank you, *Frau Doktor*. It's been a pleasure working for you."

I took her hand but instead of merely shaking it, I used it to draw her closer and kissed her, not as intended, on the cheek, but on the lips. Our eyes met in a mutually questioning look. Then she clutched me in a powerful embrace and clung to me. When she finally let me go, she said, "I'll be back. I promise." She picked up her little valise and walked towards the train. Before boarding, she glanced in my direction and blew me a kiss.

I have always prided myself in keeping my emotions in check, but a few tears stung my eyes as Sarah waved from the window of the moving train. I couldn't quite understand why I felt so strongly about her. Occasionally, a junior doctor or a student became infatuated with me, but none had been so affecting as this young American. For Katherine's sake, I would never dare explore whether my feelings for Sarah had another dimension. I had already done enough damage to Katherine's trust in me.

***

The one area of our lives in which there was no change was Konrad's legal troubles. As my attorney had concluded, there would be no formal charge and therefore no trial. I began to make inquiries to see if there was the possibility of visiting him in Buchenwald. When Borchert heard about this, he told me unequivocally to abandon any such efforts. "You mustn't draw attention to yourself, especially not after they found the Stahle labels on the crate. You could put your entire family and everything you hold dear in danger. And you won't do Konrad any favors either." I hated to concede that he was right, but he was.

Because of the cloud of suspicion, the *Pilze* shunned me. Up to the point of Konrad's arrest, my sporadic assignments had been conveyed by a cryptic handwritten note or a similarly mysterious whisper from a visitor to the hospital. Twice, I was called to St. Hilde's convent to perform emergency surgery on a wounded comrade, although they seldom lived long enough to get that far. More often now, individuals from all walks of life simply disappeared. After we knew the drayage forms had been discovered, I continued to pass along medical supplies and food to St. Hilde's clinic and replenish the funds drawn on the group's numbered accounts, but I was given no assignments. I began to think the *Pilze* had forgotten me.

Then one night, a man came to call on me in Grunewald. We had just finished supper. I left Katherine in the dining room while Krauss showed our uninvited guest into my study. As I headed there, I was plagued by the memories of Borchert's visit just a few months before.

The young man had the look of a conspirator—restless, earnest, and dressed for a journey. He anxiously rotated his visored worker's cap in his hands. In another time, such hats were favored by the communists to show solidarity. Evidently, the *Pilze* were broadening the membership beyond Catholics.

The man told me to call him *Semmelstoppel*, "hedgehog mushroom." We never used names, so I never asked his.

"Father asked me to fetch you," he said in a whisper after Krauss had left the room.

"Where are we going?"

"Spandau. A transport. We need an escort who knows how to use a gun."

"I see, but I must change first." I said, although it went without saying that a dinner dress was inappropriate for an armed mission.

"Of course," he said, "but be quick. We haven't much time."

Reasoning that I would look more formidable as a man, I removed all trace of makeup from my face, oiled my hair, and combed it back. In Konrad's room, I found a pair of his trousers that fit quite well. I put on one of his shirts, a tweed jacket, and even appropriated a pair of his gum-soled shoes. They were only slightly too large, so I wore thick socks. I strapped on an ankle holster to carry a 9mm pistol and put another pistol in a shoulder holster under the jacket. The snub nose revolver I usually carried in my handbag fit neatly in the jacket pocket. I stuffed a roll of twenty-Mark notes in the pants' pocket and threw a box of ammunition and a hunting knife in a small knapsack.

When I returned to the study in Konrad's clothes, Hedgehog looked rather surprised to see me in male costume, but he cleverly perceived the rationale and gave my disguise an approving nod. "You look just like a man."

"That was the idea," I replied dryly.

I led him through the basement to the garages where I started the engine of Katherine's motorcar. It was smaller and would be less conspicuous than either my grand Mercedes or the roadster.

"Where are we heading?" I asked as we sat waiting for the engine to warm up.

"The convent of St. Hilde's."

"Oh, those bloody nuns. Up to their old tricks, I see."

My irreverence failed to coax even the slightest smile from my companion's stony face. Instead, he began to explain our mission in a completely dispassionate voice. "The sisters have two Jewish families hidden in their basement. We can't keep them there any longer. We'll bring them to the river, where they can meet a boat bound for England."

First, we needed to get our transport vehicle, a large van. The devices painted on the cargo hold indicated the van delivered bread and rolls from a famous Berlin bakery. I wondered how the *Pilze* had come by it. Was it stolen? Perhaps my funds had been used to create a facsimile.

Once inside, Hedgehog handed me a sheer silk stocking and explained that I was to put it over my head. It would compress my features, rendering them unrecognizable. I found the make-shift mask uncomfortable, but I could see through it quite well. "No one must ever see our faces," Hedgehog explained. He also gave me a black wool watch cap to wear, even though it was July and unbearably hot. My costume completed, I looked like a seedy bank robber or burglar, but this was no theatrical nor idle game. I was on a "real" mission with the *Pilze*. If guns were involved, it could be extremely dangerous. My heart raced at the thought, more from excitement than fear.

While Hedgehog drove the short distance to the convent, I used the time to load the backup magazines for my pistols.

"Do you carry a gun?" I asked Hedgehog.

He pulled a .38 revolver out of his jacket.

"Good. I'd hate to think I was alone in this. But why does *Steinpilz* think we'll need weapons?"

"The last time we attempted this, the police were waiting for us. We lost some people in the fight."

"How could the police have known?"

"We think we have an informant in our cell."

Mother Monica met us at the door to the convent basement. Her *Pilze* name was *Hallimasch*, "honey mushroom." It suited her, for she was the kindest person I have ever known. She recognized me despite my male disguise and the silk stocking over my face. I pulled off the prickly hat and the mask, grateful to finally be able to breathe normally again, never mind that it was a hot night, and I was sweating like a spent horse.

"Margarethe, this is very dangerous," Monica said, grasping my arms.

"If all of you can risk your lives, so can I." I pulled up my trouser leg so that she could see the holster. "And I can defend myself."

She shook her head. "Never mind. You must promise to be very careful." I promised and she embraced me. "I shall pray for you," she whispered into my ear. For once, I didn't resist the offer of prayers, for having seen the sincere worry in her eyes, I was beginning to feel anxious myself.

Our "cargo" was two Jewish families, minus their men who had been taken away in one of the recent pogroms. Monica explained that the women's husbands had been prominent. One man had been a banker, the other, a successful attorney. They always took the civic leaders first to throw the community off balance. Anyone or anything that gave heart to the Jews must be eliminated.

Monica took a large key ring from her belt and unlocked a storeroom door. The tiny space was outfitted with bunks and a table with benches. A bare light bulb cast harsh light and shadows. The people within drew back as the door opened. They clung to one another. The women were pitifully thin. All had dark circles under their eyes. Although some of the Jews still had wealth, the food in their neighborhoods was restricted, especially fresh vegetables and milk. The children—five girls and a little boy—all looked underfed. Two of the girls were fair haired and could easily have passed for Aryan. The boy had red hair and freckles like our Fiona.

All the lights in the courtyard adjoining the basement door were extinguished before we moved our charges into the van. The youngest girl began to whimper. "Hush, my dear. You must be very quiet," I said, raising my finger to my lips. She looked startled to hear a female voice. I realized I needed to adopt the lower register I used when I disguised myself as Konrad. At the thought, I felt close to him, disguised as I was in his clothes. His familiar scent rose from the lining of his jacket whenever I moved. It was almost as if he accompanied us on our mission.

Hedgehog drove at a moderate pace to Spandau. Of course, a bread van would not be racing through the streets, but the longer it took to arrive at our destination, the more apprehensive I became.

I occupied my mind with reviewing my father's instructions to the Groß-Lichterfelde cadets regarding small arms combat. I envisioned myself in the double-handed, stiff-armed, knees-flexed posture one used to shoot accurately with a 9mm semi-automatic. "Crouch and stick out your behind!" the drill master would bark as he went down the line of cadets. He would roughly rearrange my posture. "Stick it out or someone can knock you down. Stance is essential!"

"Have you ever shot anyone?" Hedgehog asked, interrupting my mental drill.

"No," I said. "Have you?"

"No, but I hear you're deadly."

Eventually, we reached our destination and not a moment too soon. By then, my anxiety had reached a high pitch. Hedgehog backed up the van to the pier where a small cargo boat lay docked. He hopped out of the cab and whistled sharply. A middle-aged man with a scruffy, gray beard came out of the boat's cabin and ran down the gang plank.

"Have you seen anyone about?" asked Hedgehog in a low voice.

"No," replied the skipper in an equally hushed tone. "It's been very quiet tonight. Too quiet. Let's get them boarded so I can push off." We hurried the women and children out of the back of the van and up the gang plank.

In a flash, Hedgehog and I were back in the van, heading towards Templehof. We decided to avoid major arteries. Instead, we took the back streets. When we were nearly at our destination, Hedgehog glanced in the side mirror. "We have company. That automobile just turned with us. We're being followed."

I could see the headlights in the mirror on my side. "Now what?"

"I'll stop the van near an open alley. You jump out and run."

"And you?"

"I'll drive past a few more streets, stop the van, and I run too."

"Shouldn't we stay together and fight them?"

"No, we're outnumbered. It's better if we separate. Then they must decide which of us to follow. It will buy us some time." He was leading the mission. It wasn't my place to argue, but I didn't like the plan and there wasn't time to think about it. "Prepare yourself...Now!" said Hedgehog, bringing the van to a screeching halt in front of a dark alley.

I flung open the door and jumped out. Once my feet hit the pavement, I ran as fast as I could, all the while blessing the sure footing Konrad's gumshoes provided. I passed a row of rubbish bins and ducked behind them for cover. I was perspiring heavily, so I ripped off the itchy cap and stocking mask so I could breathe. In the July heat, the contents of the rubbish bins stank. My stomach roiled in protest, but I forced my mind to block out the stench, just as I must during bowel surgery. My chest was heaving from the sprint, and I desperately needed some air.

I sat on my haunches behind the foul-smelling rubbish bins. Nearby, the doors of an automobile slammed. I heard footsteps and the low murmur of voices. Either our pursuers had come back for me, or they had sent reinforcements. I pulled my pistol from the shoulder holster and disengaged the safety. The voices came nearer. I held my breath. There were footsteps in the alley, two pairs of feet. As the sound came closer, I dared not even think of breathing. Then the footsteps moved away again, towards the entrance to the alley. Doors slammed. I heard the motorcar drive away with a roar. Finally, I took a deep breath. I was safe. I silently murmured a prayer of thanks to whatever deity would have me and rose to my feet.

A thin man in a trench coat stood less than four meters away. The streetlight cast shadows on his face, but otherwise I could see him clearly. He could see me equally clearly. He reached into the coat, but before he could take out his hand, I took aim and fired. The report of the pistol echoed loudly in the alley. The man fell back without making a sound.

I crept around the rubbish cans to make sure he was dead. I had shot him cleanly through the head. He couldn't possibly survive such a wound, but I checked the pulse at his neck to be sure. I also searched his coat for a gun to assure myself that I hadn't shot an unarmed man. His HP was still clutched in his hand inside his coat.

I secured my pistol in the shoulder holster. Then I ran and never looked back. The opposite end of the alley was blocked by a high chain-link fence. The adrenalin pouring into my blood gave me the strength to scale it with little effort. I ran east in the direction of Templehof. Fortunately, it was late and there were no pedestrians on the streets, which meant no witnesses. But the deserted streets also meant the Gestapo could instantly identify a lone runner as the culprit. I slowed my pace to a rapid walk. Hoping to throw them off my trail, I ducked into the first tavern I found. The smoky haze inside burned my eyes as I threaded my way through the crowd. I peeled off a twenty note from my money roll and tossed it on the bar. The barkeep finally came down to ask what I wanted to drink. I ordered a Pilsner, and he slid a foaming mug of Schultheiss in my direction. My thirst, after my dash through the streets, was fierce, but first I raised my glass in a silent toast to Hedgehog.

I had nearly finished my beer when a man ran into the tavern and shouted, "Someone's been shot!" The tavern rapidly emptied as the patrons raced out to have a look. In an effort to appear unconcerned, I finished the remainder of my beer before following the crowd out the door. Outside, we parted company. The tavern patrons headed one way, while I walked at a brisk pace in the opposite direction. When I came to a crosswalk, I cut over three blocks, where I succeeded in hailing a taxi. I directed the driver to take me to St. Hilde's Hospital with all possible speed.

Slouching in the back seat of the taxi to keep out of sight, I was finally able to take in what had transpired. The mission had gone wrong. Very wrong. Someone had betrayed us. I had shot a Gestapo agent, and Hedgehog was possibly dead. I only hoped that our passengers had been able to get away safely before everything had gone awry.

The taxi drove up to the emergency door of St. Hilde's hospital. I pretended to head inside until the taxi turned the corner. Then I adjusted my route to take me to the convent. Sister Marthe opened the basement door. Borchert was there, engaged in fretful conversation with Mother Monica.

"Thank God, you're safe!" Monica exclaimed and flung her arms around me. "I besieged heaven every moment since you left. Good heavens, you're shaking like a leaf!" She clutched me tighter. "Are you hurt? Dear God, Reverend Mother would never forgive us if any harm came to you." Her nurse's eyes gave me a quick inspection to make sure there were no obvious injuries despite my assurances that I was sound.

I took Borchert aside so that Monica couldn't hear my grim news. "I had to kill a man," I said to him in a low voice. "He had a gun and he saw my face. I had no alternative." The scene replayed in my mind like a bit of bad cinema while I described every nightmarish detail to Borchert.

"Call it self defense," Borchert concluded, after listening to my story with a frown. His newfound, practical approach to morality surprised me, especially coming from a man who once liked to split theological hairs.

The telephone rang. Monica answered but then put Borchert on the line. His anxious expression as he listened to the caller's message indicated the news was not good. "The boat got away, but Hedgehog is dead," said

Borchert in a solemn voice. The thought of the poor boy, barely older than my son, lying still and cold in some alley was painful. "They caught up to him and shot him in the back as he tried to run away," Borchert explained further. "What a terrible night!"

"My God, I could use a drink," I murmured.

"So could I," agreed Borchert.

"I still have some of that very old Scotch you like so much. Come home with me."

Borchert nodded his agreement. He reached out and touched the lapel of my coat. The tweed jacket had always been one of Konrad's favorites. "My God, you look so much like him. It almost hurts to look at you," he said. To underscore this message, he averted his eyes.

We said our good-nights to the sisters. "I'm so sorry, but I only have a little sherry to offer you," Monica apologized at the door. That made me laugh—anxious laughter, to be sure. "Thank God, you're safe," Monica murmured as she embraced me.

Borchert and I walked to Katherine's little BMW, all the while careful to stay out of the light from the street lamps. As we headed to Grunewald, I took a most circuitous route and watched the rear view mirrors carefully to make sure we weren't being followed.

Borchert was conspicuously quiet, no doubt anguished over the night's losses. Absorbed in his thoughts, he startled when I spoke.

"Would you consider giving me absolution?"

"Will it ease your conscience?" he asked.

"Probably not."

"But you would like to hear the words."

"Yes," I admitted.

He proceeded to say the formulaic Latin words granting me the absolution of the Church. They did, in fact, comfort me—a little.

We entered the house through the garages, making every effort to be quiet. It was well after midnight and everyone, even Krauss, would be asleep. In my study, I poured two glasses of my best single-malt Scotch. Its complex and peaty flavor was meant to be savored by connoisseurs. Borchert had sophisticated tastes and could appreciate it.

"Ah," he said after taking a sip. "Now that's what I call a drink. Just what the doctor ordered." He raised his glass to me. "To you, *Frau Doktor,* and to our mutual friend, who cannot be with us." We touched glasses and drank to Hedgehog. Then we drank to our other mutual friend, Konrad. That led to sharing reminiscences of our university days, when we often drank too much watery beer and indifferent wine. We were comparing recollections of the time we had stolen Konrad's clothes after he'd passed out from too much brandy, when the study door opened.

Katherine modestly clutched her dressing gown at the neck when she saw Borchert. "I had no idea you were here, Father."

Borchert scrambled to his feet and made a little bow. "Katherine, please forgive the intrusion."

"I invited him," I said, feeling it necessary to take responsibility for his presence.

"I thought you were at the hospital," said Katherine, giving me a penetrating look. My alibi made no sense, of course. As chief of staff, I would only be called to the hospital if there were a major disaster requiring all hands or the buildings were literally burning to the ground. Moreover, I was dressed as a man, which begged other questions. "Evidently, you were on some other mission," Katherine said, raising an auburn eyebrow.

"Will you join us for a drink?" I asked brightly.

She wrinkled up her nose at the sight of the bottle on my desk. She had once pronounced my prize Scotch to be the "filthiest poison" ever created.

"No, thank you," she said, shaking her head. "While you two are busy doing such manly things, I shall take myself back to bed." She turned and gave me a kiss. "Margarethe, you should invite Father to spend the night. It's very late. The linens are fresh in Konrad's room."

"You're welcome to stay, of course," I said after Katherine had left.

"Thank you. I think I shall." He took a cigarette pack from his jacket and offered it to me. I refilled our glasses. After that, I was feeling tipsy and decided to disarm myself before I shot anyone else that night. Borchert watched uneasily as I took the revolver out of my pocket and unstrapped the holsters. "You certainly were prepared."

"I should have stayed with Hedgehog. Maybe the two of us could have held them off."

"Don't be an idiot. You would have been outnumbered. They would have arrested you, and what a disaster that would have been! Isn't it bad enough we have Konrad rotting in that filthy camp?"

The reminder depressed me. "It was my stupidity that put him in that camp, my foolish pride and insistence that only *I* could make things right."

"Nonsense. He would have landed there or a place even worse. It was his own doing. He knew they were planning a raid." I was surprised to hear Borchert criticize Konrad so openly until I realized he was jealous and hurt that my cousin frequented such places.

I poured another round of Scotch for Borchert. I had a board meeting in the morning, so I decided to leave off the alcohol. I lit another cigarette, now that I was sure Katherine was down for the night.

"I never imagined a time when you'd ask me for absolution," mused Borchert. "...or that you and I would be chatting like old friends."

"I never imagined a great many things that have come to pass." My eyes filled with tears, brought on by the rapid consumption of potent alcohol and the maelstrom of emotion still swirling within—the fear I'd needed to repress, the awful guilt over taking a life, but most of all, the unspeakable longing for the man who was the reason for our connection. Borchert sensed the change. He reached out and took my hand.

"He'll come home soon, won't he?" I asked, hoping to be reassured.

"God willing," he replied.

"Do you really think God has anything to do with it?"

"Truthfully, sometimes I wonder...."

***

Borchert was gone before I came down to breakfast. Undoubtedly, he wanted to slip into the Jesuit house before anyone noticed his absence. Krauss told me of his departure when he brought me my morning coffee and the newspapers.

I scanned the *Berliner Morgenpost* for any mention of the shooting of a Gestapo agent but found none. In fact, there was no mention of any killings that night—and I only knew of two! This led me to wonder if the Gestapo was trying to conceal any signs of resistance to prevent giving encouragement to other resistors.

Presently, Katherine arrived at the table. She looked especially lovely that morning in a blue linen suit the same color as her eyes. Pregnancy agreed with her, making her skin lush and her red hair thick and lustrous. She still wore it long, winding it into an artful series of knots for professional appearances. In the privacy of our bedchamber, she let it fall loose because I especially liked the feel of it on my skin.

She sent Krauss off to fetch her favorite jam, obviously a ploy for privacy. "Margarethe," she said, as she buttered her toast. "You're making yourself very obvious." She tried for an expression of disapproval, but her eyes conveyed another message.

"My interest troubles you?"

"Yes, because we can't do anything about it. I can't be late this morning."

"Neither can I. There's a board meeting."

Krauss returned with Katherine's jam. It was the famous plum jam made by the nuns of Obberoth. I often wondered if she preferred it because it reminded her of her convent days.

"I forgot about the meeting," she said. "We must find a better way to organize our calendars. You mustn't forget that Nigel is coming to dinner."

"No, I remember. But even if we coordinate our calendars, there will be surprise visitors, like Borchert last night."

"Whatever was that about, Margarethe? Are you up to mischief again, masquerading as your cousin?"

I sighed. "Nothing so innocent, I fear."

Her frown told me that she understood. "I saw your miserable guns on your desk this morning. You must keep them in a safe place, so Fiona doesn't find them and hurt herself."

"You're right. How stupid of me."

"I hope you haven't had occasion to use them."

How could she know? I wondered as I watched her serenely spreading jam on her toast at the other end of the table. Yet Katherine had always had an uncanny sense of the state of my soul. Even more than our physical relationship, it was a sign of our profound intimacy.

"Krauss, would you kindly secure my weapons? They are on the desk in my study." This request obviated the need to dismiss him for the sake of privacy. There were few I trusted more than Krauss. However, there was no need to expose him to information that he might later be required to repeat under duress. "The Browning could use a cleaning," I added.

"As you wish, *Gnädige.*"

Once Krauss had closed the door behind him, I broke a cardinal rule of the *Pilze*—I discussed a mission with a member who had not been a part of it. "Unfortunately, I *was* forced to use my pistol last night."

"Oh, dear," said Katherine, putting down her knife. She stared at me with alarm. "Was anyone hurt?"

"As you know, I am a very good shot."

She got up and came to my end of the table. "Oh, my darling, you must feel dreadful!" she said, hugging me around the shoulders.

As I inspected my inner state, I discovered that I actually felt a strange, almost other-worldly calm. I could remember the startled look of my victim, his eyes rolling up as he fell back, then staring skyward. I recalled the large, curiously regular hole in his forehead. There was little blood save a rapidly spreading puddle beneath his head. What used to be a man was simply a dead body, an object quite without other meaning.

Was this the lesson we were all learning under our new masters?

Part VII

KATHERINE

Chapter 25

Although Margarethe insisted that she felt no emotion over the incident, she was moody and introspective for days. I knew better than to pry. She always resented my intrusion into her emotions, so I reserved such "fishing expeditions," as she called them, for those times when I could no longer bear her silent pain.

Actually, I was hoping that Nigel's visit would cheer her. Like Konrad, he could engage Margarethe in brilliant duels of wit. He was also the one man, whom I have ever known, to have a truly good sense of color. Indeed, on the evening of our little dinner party, his cravat was deep lavender with a pattern of olive diamonds worked into it. He wore a perfectly pressed, white linen suit and two-toned brogues, an entirely appropriate casual elegance, for Margarethe had declared that our dinner party must be informal. Weather permitting, we would eat on the terrace. She had also specified that Nigel be our only guest, because she wanted him to feel comfortable sharing confidences.

Naturally, we couldn't pounce on him regarding the political situation as soon as he walked in the door. First, we must have the expected social chatter. We began with martinis. I accepted one simply because Krauss made them so perfectly. Besides, they are thirst-quenching in a way that wine is not, especially on a hot night such as that. The famous *Berliner Luft* was nowhere to be found, and the sultry air was stifling. Despite the benefit of the alcohol and the forced heartiness, we were unable to steer away from dreary topics.

"How is Alex?" Margarethe asked. I always tensed when this subject was raised. I knew their liaison was still going on when Margarethe first showed an interest in me. But Margarethe is unfailingly steadfast in her friendships. Actually, her loyalty is one of her most endearing traits, even if it gets her into trouble from time to time.

"Oh dear, I was afraid you might ask," said Nigel, smoothing down his pencil moustache. "But I'm happy to report that she's actually improving.

Charles took your advice and consulted a psychiatrist. Evidently, Alex suffers from a mental disease called 'manic depression.'"

"I've read of it," said Margarethe with a nod.

"Really?" I asked, genuinely surprised. "Margarethe, I thought you loathed psychiatry."

"I do, but now that I have an entire hospital under my charge, I must take an interest in all branches of medicine." She turned to Nigel. "Unfortunately, there seems to be no effective treatment save some kind of barbaric shock therapy or worse, a lobotomy."

"As you can imagine, Charles would never stand for that," replied Nigel. "He's always been devoted to Alex. Fortunately, a regular routine and familiar surroundings help to reduce the episodes. My parents have taken her in again. Jonathan's been posted to Indonesia this time."

"I hear that war is brewing in the East as well," remarked Margarethe, replenishing his martini glass. "Will one olive do this time? I shall have to ask Krauss to bring more."

"Yes, one olive will do." Nigel sighed. "And I fear there's some truth to the rumors about the east. The Japanese are assembling quite a military force." I always found it amusing how those two could carry on several simultaneous conversations. My role in such discussions was merely to sit back and listen. "To get back to Alex, she asks for you all the time. You really should go up to London for a visit. And soon."

"That must wait 'til fall. I'm overdue for a visit to my mother, although I dread it. And my grandaunt hasn't seen me for more than a year."

"My dear, how did you manage to get away with that?" he asked. "Last I heard, she practically had you taking vows yourself."

"Oh!" exclaimed Margarethe, as if she'd been pinched. "I don't think Katherine would care for that. And as you can see, the old girl is expecting again, and was made quite ill in her first attempt. And there's the matter of Konrad, which remains unresolved." Once again, the multiple conversations, and this from two people whose thinking was usually so orderly!

"Oh, Meg, God knows I've tried to help him, but information is impossible to get. Everything about those camps is so bloody secretive. And I understand they are building more. Many more."

"What do they intend to do with them?" I asked. "Imprison all of Germany?"

"No, Katherine, I don't think so," Nigel explained patiently. "They're meant for Jews or the people of the East, whom the Nazis seem to think are fit only for slavery."

"Then it will be Poland," said Margarethe.

Nigel nodded. "Where else?" In fact, the papers had been full of talk about the tense negotiations for weeks. "The dispute over Danzig cannot be settled in any other way."

"When?" asked Margarethe with a penetrating look.

"Soon. Before summer's end," he said and emptied his martini glass in a swallow. "But keep this to yourselves. No one must ever know it came from an official source."

It went without saying that we would keep his confidence. Margarethe sighed and called Krauss to bring another pitcher of martinis and more olives. "There's nothing we can do about the political situation," she said as Krauss went off to see to her requests. "Let's eat, drink and be merry. If the last war is any indication, there will be privation ahead."

After that there was no more political talk. We ate our supper on the terrace as planned, just ahead of a fast-moving thunder shower. Afterwards, I accompanied Margarethe and Nigel at the piano while they sang duets. In their student days, they had each been stars of the Oxford Gilbert and Sullivan Society, although not concurrently, as Nigel was my age and Margarethe had been a very young Oxonian. To amuse themselves, they switched parts. Margarethe sang tenor to Nigel's falsetto soprano, and we laughed ourselves silly.

Fiona came down from the nursery looking for my attention. By the time I returned, Nigel had left. Margarethe refused to reveal anything beyond what had been said in my presence. I persisted until she finally said in frustration, "The only sane course is to prepare for the worst!"

***

I cannot imagine any way in which I could have prepared for what happened next. Not long after we hosted Nigel, I had a few days free.

Margarethe rearranged her schedule so that we could take Fiona to the beach at Wannsee. My childhood had been spent in Galway, Ireland, and in the sweltering heat of summer, I often longed for the ocean. In landlocked Berlin, Wannsee was the closest thing we had to a beach. Margarethe liked to swim for exercise and made frequent use of the swimming pool in our garden, but she was no devotee of beaches. Any long spell of idleness made her fidgety, so this holiday was a concession to my wishes and to indulge Fiona, who was game for any activity that afforded her our attention.

The prior evening was full of bustle as we packed the voluminous trunk of the Mercedes with our beach apparatus: a little folding cabana, beach chairs, an umbrella, and of course, bathing suits. I'd found one with a little skirt that was flattering despite my rapidly expanding figure.

We rose with the sun. It was bright that morning, a perfect day for the beach. We began our holiday with an early breakfast on the terrace. Margarethe often drank tea with lemon and ice on hot summer mornings. She sat with her ankle on the opposite knee, looking cool and stylish in short pants. They showed her long legs to great advantage. She'd had her toenails colored, which I always found very erotic. I doubt that Margarethe had done it for my benefit, but she surely remembered how a lazy day on the beach could affect me. The sun and the warm air, combined with a blessed state of relaxation, always stoked my libido. When Fiona's nanny had taken her off to finish dressing, I reached over and grazed Margarethe's leg lightly with my fingernails.

"Never mind that," she said, looking up from *The Times*. "We want to get an early start."

"We can be quick."

Her left brow rose in exaggerated surprise. "You say you don't like it when it's quick."

"Today, I could be persuaded to make an exception."

She gave me a rakish smile. "All those hormones coursing through your blood, no doubt. Later. I promise."

The front door bell rang. Although it was not even seven o'clock, we hardly took notice. In our busy physicians' household, it was not unusual to have such an early caller. Margarethe often had x-rays delivered in advance of a procedure. Messengers called at all hours to deliver the results of medical tests. Margarethe was so unconcerned, she never looked up from the newspaper. She was reading the financial pages, which always compelled her attention.

Krauss came out to the terrace with a small parcel on the silver tray he used to deliver messages or urgent mail. "This came for you, Lady Katherine," he said proffering the tray.

The package was about the size of a shoebox, tightly wrapped in brown paper and tied with cord. The wrapper bore at least a dozen swastika and eagle stamps, indicating that parcel was of government origin and had passed through many official channels before being released. There was no return address. I cut the cord with my butter knife and was opening the wrapper when Margarethe finally peered over her newspaper.

"Katherine, NO! Don't open that!"

Too late. I had already removed the cover of the box. Inside lay a sealed envelope and beneath it, a metal container.

Margarethe snatched the envelope out of the box. She tore it open by running her finger under the flap rather than waiting for a letter opener. She succeeded in giving herself a paper cut and needed to hold her napkin against the cut to stop the bleeding. Compromised in this way, she struggled to extract the letter from the envelope. She quickly read the message, then took off her glasses and wiped her eyes.

"It's Konrad."

"What about him?" I asked stupidly.

"He's there. In that box."

"What!"

"Those are his remains."

Margarethe handed me the letter. It was cruelly brief, addressed to me, of course, as the wife. It expressed the condolences of the Reich's Minister of Justice and explained that my husband had taken his own life on August 16, 1939. In order to expedite the return of his remains, the commandant of Buchenwald had taken the liberty of having his body cremated. Herewith were his ashes.

At that moment, Miss Carter returned with Fiona. Margarethe waved her away, which was fortunate because after a moment of shock, I dissolved into tears. While Konrad and I had never been husband and wife in the ordinary sense, he was a good man and hadn't deserved such an end. Margarethe held me as I wept. I felt selfish for making such a scene. I was shocked and saddened, but how must she feel, having loved him like a brother and more?

"I always feared this day would come," she said, giving me her handkerchief to tidy my face. "In a way, it's almost a relief. Now we know for certain that his suffering is over."

I began to realize she knew more about his situation at the camp than she had ever let on. I insisted she tell me everything. After much prodding, she revealed what I guessed was only a small fraction of what she knew about his plight. "There were rumors of electric shocks to the genitals to 'cure' homosexuals. Surely, he took his life because he was afraid he would finally break." She told me about the cyanide capsules Father Borchert had given Konrad on their first visit to the Moabit.

"Maybe they killed him," I said bitterly.

"Either way, they killed him," she replied. "Come, sit down. We must tell our friends."

She asked Krauss to bring the telephone and to remove the little box from the breakfast table. I stared vacantly at my half-eaten roll while Margarethe called Father Borchert.

"Franz, I fear I have bad news." She paused, allowing him a moment to prepare. "Konrad has returned, or at least, his remains. Can you come at once?"

Meanwhile, Fiona had escaped from Miss Carter and was demanding to know when we would depart for the beach. At the sight of my tear-stained face, she stopped short. "*Mutti*, what's wrong? Why are you crying?"

The rational part of my mind told me I ought to set an example of strength for Fiona, but I couldn't stop the tears. Margarethe picked up the child and carried her back into the house. I trusted her to find the right words to explain that Konrad would never be coming back. I could not even imagine how to say such a thing.

Father Borchert arrived shortly dressed formally in a black soutane and Roman collar. Meanwhile, Margarethe had also changed into a dark suit. Only I, still wearing my sundress, looked as if I expected to set off for a day at the beach.

❋❋❋

Margarethe surprised me by consulting me about the plans for the funeral. She always took over any matter of importance and informed me of the details later. In the beginning, this disturbed me. I felt incompetent and would try to insinuate myself. Eventually, I found it easier to go along for the sake of peace.

In this instance, Margarethe asked whom I would like to invite and asked how large a gathering I wished. She even asked for suggestions about the music. She listened thoughtfully and then spent long, lonely hours in her study planning the event. She asked my opinion about the idea of burying the little box of ashes in the garden. "I think he would have wanted us to keep him near," she said and I agreed. We were the closest thing to a family he had. Margarethe found a mason to create a stone recess in the garden wall.

"And when I die, will you bury me in the garden?" I asked as we inspected the mason's work.

"Hopefully, that is far in the future. And you're younger. You may very well outlive me. In any case, I shall be buried at Obberoth, as are all the Countesses Raithschau, with you beside me."

Although he was not truly my husband, I spent many tears over Konrad's death. I had great affection for him, the father of my children. I loved him like the brother I never had, and his likeness to Margarethe inclined me to love him all the more.

As before, when Margarethe had lost someone dear, she refused any attempt to comfort her. She stoically went about planning the funeral, never shedding so much as a single tear in my presence. I wasn't fooled. I knew Konrad's death profoundly affected her. However, I only realized the depth of her grief when I went into her rooms to look for my car keys and heard her weeping in the bath—great horrible sobs and wails that tore at my heart. I would never dare invade the privacy of her bathroom. This was a private grief, and she would be disturbed even to know that I had witnessed it. She once told me that she couldn't share her pain because she'd been raised to put on a good face for others. I think the real reason is that her mother always fell apart in a crisis, and Margarethe hated the idea of being like her in any way.

Our own grief was so strong that we nearly forgot about the youngest member of our household. Poor Fiona was shut away with her tutor or her nanny while the adults dealt with grown-up matters. It was Margarethe who managed to remember that Fiona was grieving too. She kidnapped the child and brought her down to the music room to play the piano and sing with her. Music was the way that Margarethe expressed her deepest feelings, and she was trying to use the same means to help Fiona cope with her loss.

While they sat at the piano, I overheard Fiona ask, "Why did Papa have to die?" The question wrenched my heart because I'd asked it myself—many times.

"He died to protect his friends," Margarethe explained gently, putting her arm around Fiona. "Jesus says it is the greatest love of all—to lay down your life for your friends. Your father was a very noble and brave man. You must always remember that."

Finally, the day of the funeral arrived. Mother Monica, and many of the nuns attended, as well as other staff members from St. Hilde's and the Charité. Father Borchert wore green vestments instead of the traditional black. "I wear green today because it is the color of hope. My friend, Konrad von Holdenberg was ever hopeful for a better world and worked tirelessly to make it so," he explained during his homily. He spoke eloquently, but there were times when his voice cracked, and he needed a moment of recovery before continuing.

Fortunately, Margarethe had no such issues with her voice. As the communion meditation, she had chosen Bach's "Delightful Rest" from Cantata 170. When she had practiced this remarkable aria in the days preceding the funeral, I often sat and listened because I found both the text and the rich sound of her voice very comforting. During her practice she often sang *a capella*, but now she was accompanied by a chamber orchestra organized by Gürtner. The performance moved many to brush tears from their eyes, some to weep openly. I had already spent most of my tears, so I gazed up at the perfect summer sky and thought of dear Konrad. At the end of the Mass, Margarethe sang "Fall asleep, you weary eyes" from Cantata 82, a sweet and comforting meditation, almost like a caress. There was not one false note in her rendition, not a single warble of uncontrolled emotion. I thought back to her performance of the Mozart Requiem for her grandmother's funeral so many years before. As then, I marveled at her amazing strength and discipline.

After our guests departed, we changed into more casual attire. Margarethe chose short pants and I, a sundress, for the afternoon had grown very warm. We found Father Borchert, in shirtsleeves, his collar and soutane removed, sitting in the garden. The servants had moved bistro tables and chairs near the new grave so that guests could linger and say their last farewells. Krauss had left wine chilling in a bucket on the table. We all took a glass to toast our departed friend.

"It seems very strange to turn my garden into a cemetery," mused Margarethe, sitting on the garden wall. "But Konrad always loved it here, especially the rose garden."

"He's with us, of course," said Father Borchert.

"Oh, Franz," chided Margarethe, "you're an educated man. You don't *really* believe in life after death, do you?"

"Of course, I do. Don't you, Katherine?" he asked, looking to me to support his position. I could feel one of their infamous arguments brewing and thought it best not to interpose myself.

"I believe that Konrad is in a better place," I said neutrally.

"Actually, and perhaps only for today, I find the idea of an afterlife appealing," said Margarethe. She got down from the wall and poured her wine into the earth near the little tomb. "Here, you old bugger, a libation such as the ancients might offer. May your paradise be full of fine English suits, excellent drink, and beautiful, young men."

Father Borchert laughed. "Margarethe, that's irreverent."

"Oh, really, Franz. Wouldn't you have the same wish?"

He thought for a moment. Then his eyes filled. He offered a brave smile, but when he spoke, his voice was hoarse.

"I have only one wish—to see my friend again."

***

Nigel had been unable to attend the funeral because he was traveling, but he came the following evening to pay his respects and give us his news.

"I'm being sent back to London. The embassy will be shut down except for essential personnel."

Margarethe and I exchanged a look, for we knew exactly what this meant. "Oh, Nigel, we shall miss you," said Margarethe, gripping his arms.

"Darling, you must leave," said Nigel in an insistent voice. "Both of you. Come to England with your family. Charles will have you back in a heartbeat, and I'm sure he could help Katherine find a position at Barts. Just say the word, and I shall make arrangements to put your townhouse in order."

Margarethe gave him a hard look. "Nigel, you can't really think I would leave my country in time of war."

"But Meg, I know you don't support this horrible Führer and his gang of thugs. You loathe these people."

"Yes, I do. But I can't leave."

"Why not?"

"Because it is my duty to look after my family, my mother, our lands."

Nigel shook his head. "Why am I wasting my breath? You remained for the last war too."

"There was no alternative. My father was an officer in the high command. How would it look if I, his daughter, remained in the country of the enemy?"

"Meg, your father is long dead. You were educated in British schools. You chose a British nobleman for your husband, which made you a British subject. You spent almost half your life in England. For pity's sake, you are nearly as English as I am!"

"If you think so, you know me not at all," replied Margarethe, frowning.

"Never mind. You are, without doubt, the most stubborn person I have ever known."

"Thank you. I shall take that as a compliment."

"Do, you pig-headed old fool!"

I knew the insults were just for show. They adored one another. Each in their own way was trying to lighten a conversation about a very serious matter, but their anxiety was palpable, as was mine.

"How long will it be?" asked Margarethe. I shuddered because I knew exactly what she was asking.

"Not long now," Nigel replied evenly. "The tension has to break."

Before he left, Margarethe gave Nigel a letter and some books for Alexandra. At the door, he took each of us in his arms. "May God bless and keep you both until we meet again."

After Nigel had departed, Margarethe poured herself a double whiskey and went out to the terrace. Krauss handed me a glass of wine, and I followed her out.

"The rats are leaving the sinking ship," Margarethe muttered when I joined her.

"Perhaps we should take his advice and leave as well."

She turned to me and stared coldly. "I'm not holding you here. Leave, if you wish. I'll ask Nigel to open the London house. Go wherever you choose...home to Ireland or to America with Elisabeth."

"Margarethe, I'm not leaving."

"Don't ever think I'm forcing you to remain."

"I don't feel forced. I would never leave you."

Chapter 26

We all pretended to settle back into our ordinary routine, but once I had seen Konrad reduced to ashes in a steel box, nothing would ever be the same again. Wherever I went, I endured an endless stream of condolences, which became increasingly tiresome as time went on.

I complained to Margarethe, who suggested the perfect solution: "Let's get out of Berlin. It's high summer and the whole city stinks like a rubbish heap. Perhaps the mountain air will do us good." I thought she had the Garmisch chalet in mind and mentally began packing dirndls for myself and leather breeches for her, but as it turned out, I had completely the wrong idea. "It's been ages since I've seen my grandaunt or visited Raithschau," said Margarethe. "I have a sudden need to commune with my elders."

I was delighted to think that I would soon see my dear friend, Reverend Mother Scholastica. I dearly missed the woman who had figured so largely in my decision to enter the convent and ultimately to leave it. It was she who'd put me in Margarethe's path, perhaps knowing we would form an alliance. She liked to say that there is no such thing as coincidence, and I don't think she meant the will of God. She once said to me, albeit after I left the convent, "Desire has its own imperative." It is a curious philosophy for a nun, although perhaps not for one who is reputed to be a great mystic.

We arrived in Obberoth, and Reverend Mother received us in her study with a warm smile. She was nearly as tall as her grandniece, and there was a strong resemblance between them. The one exception was the eyes. Margarethe's were dark blue, whereas her grandaunt's were as pale as mountain ice. Although Mother Scholastica was past eighty, her face was unlined. She touched her cool cheeks to mine in the usual greeting that one nun gives another on meeting after a long absence.

"Where is your daughter?" she asked. She loved children, despite her reputation as a firm schoolmistress.

"We left her at Raithschau with the caretaker's wife," said Margarethe. "We thought to spare you the crankiness of a seven-year-old who's spent the better part of the day in a motorcar."

"You may remember we have a school here and are accustomed to the behavior of young girls. You must bring her tomorrow." It was an order, not a suggestion.

"Yes, Mother," I said without question.

Reverend Mother sighed. "I so miss the days when you stayed here during your visits."

I felt a twinge of guilt, for I was the cause of the change. When my departure from the convent was new, Margarethe decided to spare me the embarrassment of facing my former sisters by insisting that we stay at Raithschau. Once the Russian émigrés had moved on, Margarethe had renovated the old castle, enlarging the living quarters and making the entire place comfortable and modern. It made a perfect base when we came to visit, but I knew both Reverend Mother and her grandniece missed the times when Margarethe would stay in the convent among the sisters and the two of them would have their philosophical debates late into the night.

After tea, Margarethe declared her intention to take a walk. I was glad to have some time alone with Reverend Mother, who invited me to sit with her in the window alcove in her study, the perfect place for a more intimate conversation. The sun streamed through the window and the view of the Franconian hills was perfect. Reverend Mother gazed at me with great affection. In such moments, it felt like former times, when I was a nun under her charge, and she was my beloved superior.

"It is quite evident you are with child," Reverend Mother said, glancing at my belly.

"Will it disturb the sisters?" I asked anxiously.

She shook her head. "No, my dear. Seeing an alternative to their lives will either confirm their commitment or call it into question. Either way, confrontation can be a good thing. Faith without question is simply blind and no gift to God." She took my hands. "But how did you convince Margarethe to agree?" With this remark, she indicated that she had known of our disagreements, which infuriated me until I realized her awareness of the situation saved me the trouble of elaborate explanations.

"I nearly had to die first."

The smile faded from her face. "Then you would have paid a high price to be a mother again."

"Motherhood is not for the selfish."

"And now you are without a husband."

"Oh, it was never a conventional marriage, as you know, but I was always fond of Konrad, and in a way I loved him, not because he was so like his cousin but so different. He was her alter ego…as if in their being opposites, they completed one another."

"Yes, I fear the impact of his death is yet to be felt," she said with a sigh. "They were always very close."

"Margarethe blames herself because she went to see the Gestapo commandant. Father Borchert told her that's why Konrad was sent to Buchenwald."

"Borchert cannot know why young Holdenberg was sent to Buchenwald," scoffed Reverend Mother. He is merely speculating, which is neither useful, nor helpful." She took my hand. "My dear, you must put aside these heavy thoughts and create a condition of peace for your child."

"It has begun to stir." I placed her hand on my belly. "There. Can you feel it? A little kick."

Her aged eyes were filled with delight, and she laughed a surprisingly girlish laugh. "A miracle." She allowed her hand to linger a moment longer, nodding and smiling.

"Margarethe tried to use my pregnancy to forbid me from working with our friends." Reverend Mother was in my *Pilze* cell, so there was no need to say more.

She gave me a sharp look. "Child, were I still your superior, I would forbid you as well. Look at you. You are growing unwieldy. And if your life is taken, two lives will be lost. I agree with Margarethe."

"Yes, Mother," I said, lowering my eyes from the scolding as if I were still a nun.

"Besides, my grandniece has a soldier's training. She is able to defend herself."

"She had to shoot a man," I blurted out, then glanced around nervously, although I knew the ancient convent walls were thick and no one could hear.

Reverend Mother's eyes betrayed her alarm. "Dear God! Did he survive?"

I shook my head. "But it was self-defense. She was being pursued. She had to kill him or be captured."

"That must trouble her greatly." She shook her head. "I never condone the taking of life, but in these trying times, one cannot be too precious about principle."

"Sometimes, I think it would be easier to give in to the Nazis. Their bizarre racial ideas are everywhere in our medicine. I am required to report the names of all children born with a defect even those that can be repaired through surgery, such as a hair lip or a club foot, but the Nazis see a genetic aspect to everything. But what troubles me most is what happens to these children once their names are given to the Chamber of Medicine."

Reverend Mother, nodded gravely. "Margarethe tells me they are taken to special institutions."

"Where they are euthanized, we think, although we have no proof. It's all so secretive." Suddenly the accumulated anxiety overwhelmed me, and tears came to my eyes. "Oh, Mother, there are times when a child is so defective that we can do nothing but make it as comfortable as possible until it dies. We all agree that it is a blessing that God takes it, but to deliberately kill anyone… And not just children, but the retarded or insane."

"Is it true that the psychiatrists were the first to aid in this horrible program?"

"Yes, there is hardly a psychiatric inmate left at the Charité, save the politically powerful or very rich. Anyone with chronic or severe mental disease has already been sent away to one of those places. 'Life unworthy of life.' How can any of us make such a determination?"

"This is the very reason why Margarethe left the Charité and chose to stop teaching."

"It's only because she has become chief of staff that I can continue to practice obstetrics. Otherwise, I would completely eliminate it from my practice—out of conscience."

"But that too would be wrong." Reverend Mother squeezed my hands a little. Her own, once proud and beautiful like Margarethe's, were now gnarled with arthritis, but no less strong. "My dear, by retreating from the enemy, you give them victory. Once all people of principle abandon their positions, it is simply a rout, and evil can do whatever it wishes." She touched my face gently because I had begun to cry more openly. She drew her handkerchief from her enormous sleeve and dabbed my face. "Dear child, you must be brave. We must all be brave and steadfast in our faith."

Somehow, I couldn't explain that my emotion came as much from the tides of pregnancy as from worry over my profession. When I had dried my face, I asked to be excused.

After I tidied my makeup, I went to find Margarethe. I searched the entire convent, looking first in the infirmary, where she often went to offer her services to any sister who wished the attention of a physician. Her available times and mine were noted on the bulletin board outside the refectory and any sister wishing to consult either of us could give her name to the infirmarian to schedule an appointment. Sister Clothilde, who had replaced me as infirmarian, told me that Margarethe had already come and gone. The librarian had not seen her, nor the portress. Thinking Margarethe might be hungry after our long journey, I went to the refectory, but Sister Cook had not seen her either. Finally, I happened upon Sister Elfriede, the mistress of the convent choir, and she provided a clue to Margarethe's whereabouts.

"She has gone to lay flowers on her grandmother's grave," the old dear informed me.

I recalled the day I'd first met Margarethe. Her grandmother had passed and had been laid to rest in the crypt below the abbey chapel. Nowadays, I no longer needed an oil lamp to find my way in the crypt. Margarethe had it electrified as she had every other part of the convent. Despite the electric lights, it was still quite dark in that place that never saw light from outside, but I could easily see Margarethe, standing near her grandmother's tomb.

"Ah, still approaching by stealth, I see," she said, her voice echoing eerily through that cavernous place. "Have you come to spy on me again?" It had become something of a joke between us, how I had followed her into the crypt on the day of her grandmother's funeral. Margarethe had looked ill, and I only wanted to help. I was but a novice then. Over fourteen years had passed since that day.

There was a great bouquet of wildflowers on the grave. "What beautiful flowers!"

"The field will soon be mown for hay. It would be a shame to waste them." Nearby, she paced off a rectangle heel to toe. "Look. Wouldn't this make a perfect place for our tomb?"

"What!"

"Here. Beside my grandmother. She would make good company for eternity. She was quite witty and very well read."

I swallowed my horror and replied, "You ordered us to avoid morbid thoughts on this holiday."

"Yes, but this isn't morbid, merely practical. Even Grandmother had her tomb built before she died. And after we've seen what's become of Konrad, who knows what lies ahead? It's best to be prepared and not have such worries when the time comes."

The idea of looking at my own grave was chilling. "If you think it necessary," I said with a shudder.

I took her arm as we left the crypt, needing the comfort of her near in that dreary, airless place. I was grateful when we ascended to the chapel above and clean air and light. Margarethe switched off the light in the crypt and closed the heavy door.

"It seems that I have no patients among the sisters this afternoon," she said. "Everyone has requested *you*."

I smiled to reassure her that it was no reflection on her reputation as a physician nor lack of affection from the nuns. It was only that I had lived among them for many years, and they felt more comfortable with me.

She glanced at her watch. "After your infirmary duties, we should get back to Fiona. She has been ever so anxious since her father died." I felt a twinge of guilt because Margarethe had remembered Fiona whereas I had not.

"Yes, we must get back. She will be anxious."

In the infirmary, I found the usual complaints—red eyes and scratchy throats because the late summer grasses were blooming, menstrual woes, infected lacerations or abrasions—certainly nothing of consequence. In some cases, I think my former sisters simply wanted an excuse to visit with me. They seemed intrigued by my pregnancy, and some asked to touch my belly. Country people still believed that it brought luck to touch a pregnant woman's belly and bless it.

When my infirmary duty was done, I found Margarethe occupied in Reverend Mother's office with the account ledgers, so I went to the chapel oratory where the infamous Madonna of Obberoth stood. Margarethe had brought the woodcarving to the convent over two decades before. This very unconventional image of the Virgin Mother was arrayed in red, white and black, instead of the usual blue, but most unusual of all was her figure—she was unmistakably pregnant. Although I had a replica of this image and kept it on a little altar in my room, it was even more moving to be standing before this nearly life-sized version, especially as I was in the same stage of pregnancy.

I had always been devoted to Mary, and it never mattered to me that Margarethe had something other than the mother of God in mind when she'd asked the carver to create the statue. To me, the image represented the blessed presence of a feminine power larger than my own to whom I could always turn for solace.

I dared not kneel at Reverend Mother's special prie-dieu. Instead, I took a position at the altar rail. At first, I wanted to be quick about my prayers, because Margarethe would likely arrive soon. She is an atheist and scoffs at religious devotion. Then I decided my faith was no concern of hers, and I should express it as I chose.

First, I prayed for the child within me, that it should come to full term and be healthy. I prayed for Fiona, most especially that no permanent harm came of her father's death. And I remembered him too. He had been a suicide, and the church taught that there was no redemption from such a sin. Yet he had bravely given his life to protect his friends. Surely God would take his sacrifice into account. I would miss the man who had agreed to be my husband and had given his name to my children. I would miss him for more than his generosity and kindness. Konrad could always be counted on to cheer me. He always had something deliciously vicious or witty to say, even in the darkest times. The times ahead would certainly be dark.

As every day, and as when I was still a nun, I prayed for Margarethe, the patroness of the order, especially for her swift return to the Faith. Of course, after all those years, it seemed unlikely that these prayers would ever be answered, but I would never give up. Next, I offered an intention for all those who were oppressed in the Third Reich—Jews, of course, but also the physically and mentally ill considered to be *Lebensunwertes Leben*—"life unworthy of life." There were so many others at risk in the Third Reich: homosexuals, gypsies, the peoples of the East considered inferior and only fit for slavery. It troubled me to think of the vast numbers of people who fit these categories. In fact, I was one of them and so was Margarethe, the most Aryan woman I knew.

Finally, I prayed for myself to have courage in the coming days to be a good physician and to make prudent choices that would enable me to continue to practice medicine with a clear conscience and a good heart. Once I had laid out all of my intentions, I took out the miniature rosary I always kept with me and began to recite the Ave's.

Not long after, I heard Margarethe's footsteps behind me. I expected her to tap me on the shoulder and tell me it was time to go, but she didn't. Instead, she knelt beside me at the altar rail. She raised her face to gaze at her statue, and then to my surprise, she clasped her hands and bowed her head.

She was praying.

There is a legend among the nuns. They say that Margarethe once had a vision in that very place. Of course, Reverend Mother, her grandaunt is reputed to be a mystic, but surely, that kind of thing isn't passed down through generations. Or is it? Margarethe has never told me much about that event, saying only that she can't find the words to describe it, but the nuns say Margarethe saw the Madonna of Obberoth come to life before her very eyes. Knowing Margarethe, she had conjured an ancient goddess instead of Mary, the Mother of God, although Margarethe would probably say they are one and the same.

****

After supper, we put Fiona to bed and returned to the convent. Margarethe had accepted the offer of an after-dinner drink from Reverend Mother's little cabinet. My stomach was too queasy for alcohol, but I was glad that Reverend Mother had allowed herself dispensation from the Great Silence so that she might entertain us at that late hour.

It was just a few minutes before nine, when the telephone in Reverend Mother's study rang. We all jumped because it was very unusual to have such a late call at the convent. It turned out to be Krauss ringing Margarethe.

Her brows were knit as she listened to his message. "Yes, thank you, Krauss. I shall do so at once," she said and replaced the handset. "Krauss says we must listen to the wireless. There's been an incident at the Polish border." Margarethe opened the doors of the large console Telefunken radio in the corner of the study, but when she switched it on, only faint scratchy sounds emerged from the speakers. She turned up the volume, but despite her patient attempts to find a signal, there was nothing to be heard but loud static.

"It hasn't worked since the storm last month," said Reverend Mother. "I meant to tell you."

"Probably the antenna blew down. I'll take a look in the morning."

"Margarethe, can't we tune in a station from your Mercedes?" I asked.

Their eyes turned to me. "Very clever of you, Katherine," said Margarethe. We all hurried down to the motorcar in the courtyard.

Margarethe carefully worked the dial. In that mountainous place, there were a few anxious minutes before she was able to tune in a strong signal, but then there it was, the booming voice of the announcer: "Once it became evident that the shots had originated from the Polish watchtower, the army crossed the border into Polish territory. The border guards who provoked the incident have all been killed or taken into custody. German troops will continue to occupy the area until it is secured." The announcer began to rant about the audacity of the Poles to provoke such a thing, especially while deliberations over a solution were so delicate.

Looking very grave, Margarethe switched off the radio. She took a deep breath. "I doubt there was ever a shot fired from that Polish guard tower."

"I must gather the sisters in the chapel," said Reverend Mother. "They must be informed of this development, and we must pray that it does not come to war."

✿✿✿✿

When I woke the next morning, I felt refreshed because for the first time in weeks, I had enjoyed a full night's sleep. Margarethe had loved me tenderly during the night, which always puts me in the right mood for a restful sleep. I'd hoped to join her at breakfast, but she was nowhere to be found. Neither were the servants. I called through the house, but no one answered. Finally, I located them in the servants' quarters, huddled around a wireless. From it came a chilling and familiar voice, the Führer addressing the nation.

One of the maids spied me and sprang up. At once, they all stood, looking very guilty at being discovered neglecting their duties. The head butler bowed and explained, "Lady Katherine, our troops have invaded Poland. They crossed the border early this morning."

My heart began to hammer at the thought, but I knew I must set an example of calm. "Let's listen to the speech and hear what the Führer has to say." A footman pulled up a chair for me.

I listened with growing anxiety as the news announcer reported that the Polish cities of Warsaw, Lodz, and Krakow were being shelled.

"Does Lady Margarethe know of this?" I asked the head butler.

"Yes, Lady Katherine, the countess has been listening to the wireless since dawn." How like Margarethe to listen to the broadcast before anyone rose so that she might be fully informed and able to answer any question.

The maid succeeded in pulling herself away from the wireless long enough to prepare me a breakfast of soft-boiled eggs and toast. I asked her to serve it on the tower patio so that I might enjoy the splendid weather. During the renovation, Margarethe had created a lovely place to have al fresco meals. From there, I could see the vineyards and Obberoth in the distance. As I stood at the wall to enjoy the view, I noticed a little open-topped motorcar approaching the Schloss—Margarethe and Fiona returning from the fields.

Margarethe, who had eaten at dawn, agreed to a second breakfast and afterward sat sketching on large sheets of grid paper. It was breezy, and she needed to anchor the papers with a plate. "What are you drawing?" I asked.

She turned the paper around to show me. Margarethe is no artist, but she is very adept at technical drawing. The sketch was tightly rendered with the dimensions written in architectural block letters. I instantly recognized what it was, and a chill passed through me.

"Margarethe, why are you suddenly so obsessed with building a tomb?"

She paused to erase and correct a measurement on her drawing. "None of us know what will happen. Look at Konrad. Dead at forty-three. There will certainly be a war, and you know what that means."

***

That afternoon, while Margarethe consulted the mason about her plans, Reverend Mother and I entertained Fiona with a walk through Obberoth's school. There was no lack of girls Fiona's age at Obberoth. The fine academy, known for its excellent classical education, attracted aristocratic daughters from all over German-speaking Europe.

"You could leave her with us," said Mother Scholastica as we walked with Fiona through the first-form dormitory, where the girls her age were settling themselves for the semester. "In this remote place, she would be safer if there's a war."

"I don't think Fiona is ready to be away at school. We'll have at least another year of the tutor, and then perhaps she'll be ready for Obberoth."

"It's not Fiona who is unready, but you," chided Reverend Mother.

"Oh," I sighed, "I'll never be ready. I can scarcely imagine being parted from her for a night, never mind a school term. But I think that Margarethe means to send her to an English school."

"You are her mother, after all. You must be the one to decide," Reverend

Mother said as she waited for me to open the door for her, so that we might go outside to see the playing fields.

"It's not quite that simple, I fear."

"You mustn't let my grandniece dictate how to raise your child, Katherine. She can be forceful, but she is also susceptible to a well-reasoned argument. I know. I trained her myself."

"Yes, but it takes so much energy to argue with her."

"Then you must find the energy if you want to manage the outcome."

My mind strayed from the topic of my daughter to one causing me more immediate anxiety. "Why is she so obsessed with this tomb?"

Reverend Mother smiled her little knowing smile. She always seemed to look as if she knew some secret that she just might tell you if you were patient enough.

"You know exactly why. When Margarethe is troubled, she needs a project to occupy her mind. It makes her feel she is in control. Remember how she labored over the translation of the Raithschau-Obberoth letters while you struggled with your religious vocation and your love for her?"

"You understand exactly how our minds work. Why are you never tempted to intervene, to sway the course of events to achieve a better outcome?"

She pursed her lips as she considered this. "Tempted? Yes, often. But we are all given this life to learn lessons. Interference can be a great disservice. I am here only to guide, not to direct."

"There will be another war. Where is the lesson in that?"

Reverend Mother nodded in response to my question and yet still managed to catch a ball flung in her direction. She handily sent it back to the field where the older girls were playing.

"I don't know exactly. But it will be a lesson for the world, and for all of us as individuals. Some of us will have courage. Others will be cowardly and follow those who wish to perpetrate evil. Some of us will live, and others will die."

"Konrad is already dead," I said for no reason other than the mention of death.

"Yes, but Konrad von Holdenberg chose his destiny, while so many will simply be swept along with the tide. That's what we must avoid for ourselves. We must all choose, or it will be chosen for us." Her words both stirred and frightened me. "One thing is certain about times such as these. They can make heroes of cowards and demons of ordinary men."

"We are women," I said. "What can we do to stop any of this madness?"

"My dear, while the males tramp off to war with dreams of glory, we are the ones left to maintain order and to protect the children who are the future. Men are very full of their self-importance, but women keep the world from falling apart."

Fiona suddenly ran into my arms. "*Mutti*, may I go with the other girls to have biscuits and milk?"

"Certainly, my darling. If Reverend Mother will allow it."

My daughter turned imploring eyes on Mother Scholastica, who nodded her approval. Fiona ran away with her new friends.

Margarethe's splendid voice sounded from the chapel. "Ah, I hear that my grandniece and Sister Elfriede are conspiring again."

Elfriede and Margarethe were indeed conspiring. I went to the chapel to listen. They had come up with a most soothing program for Vespers, first Bach's entirely appropriate aria "*Gott hat alles wohl gemacht*" from Cantata 35, then "*Schläfert allen Sorgenkummer*" from Cantata 197, followed by Schubert's sublime "Ellen's Gesang" known to the world as "Ave Maria." Margarethe always insisted on the original text by Sir Walter Scott, not the pious Latin version, and like Sister Elfriede, she preferred a faster tempo more appropriate to the agitated cry of a young woman in distress, petitioning the Queen of Heaven. I rested my hand on my belly and imagined my child enjoying the pleasure of the exquisite music along with me.

When we went to retrieve Fiona from the first-form mistress, we found my daughter reluctant to leave. Tempted by her success with the milk-and-biscuits experiment, she shyly asked if she might join her new friends for supper and spend the night in their dormitory. Other children were such a novelty to her. I was surprised that she got on so well with them. I also saw that while I might be unwilling to part with my child, she was quite willing to part with me.

"Well, so much for worrying about our lack of attention," said Margarethe with a shrug. "Obviously, she doesn't need us."

My pain over this realization was soon supplanted by another thought. Fiona's absence would provide me with an opportunity to spend the evening with my former sisters. What a pleasure to join them at Vespers and to hear Margarethe's rich voice filling the chapel with Bach and Schubert. Afterwards, we sat with the sisters in the refectory. Margarethe, as patroness of Obberoth, always sat at the high table with me beside her. After the blessing, Reverend Mother rapped on the table and announced, "The Countess von Raithschau will read this evening. Please give her your attention." I turned to Margarethe with a look of surprise. She smiled, touched my hand, and then went up to the podium. All eyes turned to her.

"Thank you, Reverend Mother," said Margarethe with a little bow in her direction. "My dear sisters, the lives of my family and those of the sisters of Obberoth have been entwined for many centuries. Long ago, my grandmother, many times great and also called Margarethe, befriended the prioress of this convent. Tonight, I wish to read to you from their correspondence. This letter was written by Mother Mathilde on this very day nearly seven hundred years ago. By remarkable coincidence, it was also on the eve of war." Margarethe put on her spectacles and began to read:

My Beloved,

We may agree that save to defend one's family or homeland, there is no such thing as a just war. Yet war is again upon us, and so it makes little difference whether or not it is just. What can we do? We must be brave and steadfast and allow our principles to guide us—honor and charity above all. Here at home, you and I must set an example for those who look to us for leadership. We must be steady though our hearts may be fearful. We must be patient when anxiety prompts us to lash out at others. War brings death, but we must preserve life, even if it means nursing the enemy's wounded. After all, they are God's children, just as we are.

You are probably thinking, how glibly I instruct you, safe as I am behind the convent walls. You, however, must send your husband and your son into battle. Of course, the boy strains at the bit to gallop off into the fray, to hear the clanging of swords and the smell of blood. All young men lust for glory even more than for the bodies of women. That is because

war is one of the ways that men reckon their place among themselves—
who is high and who is low. We women are less consequential in their
eyes because they know we will be waiting at home for their return.

Yes, you are right to fear that your son may die. He may die, as will
many mother's sons, or they will be maimed for life. How wrong that so
many young lives will be squandered, and for what? So that one man's
belief may triumph over another's? There is no making sense of it. All we
can do is our duty.

Dearest Margarethe, I shall pray that your menfolk safely return
to you. And you should pray too, for the world can never have enough
prayer. Most of all, let us pray for peace with all our hearts.

                    I remain yours ever,
                    Mathilde of Obberoth
                    2 September, A. D. 1259

"And so, my dear sisters," Margarethe said, "you will observe that little
has changed. In fact, Margarethe von Raithschau's son perished in that war,
and his father as well. In this coming war, many young men will also die.
Please remember them in your prayers." As Margarethe paused to scan the
worried faces of the nuns, I found myself thinking of young Wilhelm and
felt cold dread.

Margarethe replaced her spectacles in her pocket and then took her
place beside me to finish her meal.

❊❊❊

After dinner, we declined Reverend Mother's generous offer of drinks
in her study. It had been an anxious and busy day, and we needed a respite.

We returned to the Schloss and went up to the tower patio to drink
Raithschau wine and gaze at the stars. In that remote place with little ambi-
ent light, the heavens were aglow with tiny pinpoints of light. We took a
seat on one of the stone benches built into the wall, and Margarethe put
her arm around me.

"We are childless tonight," she mused, "a rare and special event."

"Yes, it's a delight, really. Perhaps we should enroll Fiona in the
Obberoth school. She will be safer here if there's a war."

"If there's a war… I expect a declaration by tomorrow. But, please, let's speak of something else," Margarethe said, kissing me on the forehead to let me know this was no criticism.

Although the evening was quite warm, there was a stiff breeze blowing. I trembled. Margarethe felt it and pulled me closer.

"Yes, hold me tight, my darling." I suddenly had a flash of the tiles of polished granite that Margarethe had brought back from her visit with the mason. "I'm so afraid."

"Not surprising, given all the war talk. But let's enjoy this perfect moment—a balmy summer evening, with the stars winking overhead."

I found Margarethe's embrace comforting and moved closer. I wanted to be as close as possible and to feel her hold me fast, for despite her warm arms around me, I felt so cold. Margarethe gave my shoulders another squeeze, allowing me to feel a hint of her strength. For the moment, I put aside my fears and placed my trust in her unwavering calm, even if the display was only for my benefit, or for the benefit of others, as when she had read to the nuns in the refectory.

The little breeze grew stronger and finally, Margarethe said: "It is getting a bit chilly. Let's go inside." She led me in and then off to bed. Once there, she continued her reassurances in the one way guaranteed to blot out all fears and worries.

Afterward, Margarethe slept soundly beside me, while I lay awake. My mind was still active, worrying about the prospect of war and anxiously imagining what it could bring. I was in Ireland during the Great War. It was something that went on in other countries, not ours. The details, while troubling, were remote.

Perhaps Margarethe could envision what lay ahead. Already a practicing surgeon during the war, she had cut off many a shattered limb. Her doctoral dissertation, which I'd read at my father's instigation while I was a medical student, was a treatise on the care of amputation stumps. Margarethe never spoke of her experiences during the war, saying only that such horrors cannot be described and, if possible, should be forgotten. But we had already experienced so many horrors under the Nazis.

How would one not think that the future could only be worse?

Also by Elena Graf

PASSING RITES SERIES

THE IMPERATIVE OF DESIRE

A coming-of-age story that takes a young woman from La Belle Époque, through a world war, a revolution that outlawed the German nobility, the roaring twenties, to the decadent demimonde of Weimar Berlin. A quirk of inheritance law allows Margarethe von Stahle to inherit her family's titles. Margarethe reluctantly marries, but that doesn't prevent her from finding solace in the arms of women. She trains under the best surgeons in Germany and England and rises to prominence as London's infamous "Lady Doctor." Finally, duty requires her to return to her homeland and take the reins of the family fortunes.

LIES OF OMISSION

In 1938, the Nazis are imposing their doctrine of "racial hygiene" on hospitals and universities, forcing professors to teach false science and doctors to collaborate in a program to eliminate the mentally ill and handicapped. Margarethe von Stahle is desperately trying to find a way to practice ethical medicine. She has always avoided politics, but now she must decide whether to remain on the sidelines or act on her convictions.

ACTS OF CONTRITION

World War II has finally come to an end and Berlin has fallen. Nearly everything Margarethe von Stahle has sworn to protect has been lost. After being brutally abused by occupying Russian soldiers, Margarethe must rely on the kindness of her friends to survive. Fortunately, the American Army has brought her former protégée, Sarah Weber, back to Berlin. Margarethe must confront the painful events that occurred during the war.